Alec Forbes of Howglen

By George MacDonald

A New Edition
Updated and Introduced by
Michael Phillips

The Cullen Collection
of the Fiction of George MacDonald
Volume 5

The Cullen Collection

of the Fiction of George MacDonald

New editions of George MacDonald's classic fiction works
updated and introduced by Michael Phillips

Alec Forbes of Howglen, 1865
Published by Hurst & Blackett (U.K.)

Alec Forbes of Howglen: A New Edition
By George MacDonald, Michael Phillips, editor

October 2018
A new and expanded edition of *The Maiden's Bequest*
published by Bethany House Publishers, 1985.

Grateful appreciation is acknowledged for those who have contributed directly and indirectly to this set of new editions of George MacDonald's fiction, going all the way back to the folks at Bethany House publishers in the early 1980s who launched the most ambitious MacDonald publishing project since MacDonald's own lifetime. More recently, there have been many who have contributed in various ways to the research, counsel, design, and proofreading for *The Cullen Collection,* especially including David Hiatt, Lora Hattendorf, Joseph Dindinger of Wise Path Books, and of course Judy Phillips, a full co-laborer in every facet of this project. A special note of thanks is due our friend and colleague, Wheaton's Dr. Rolland Hein, the preeminent MacDonald scholar of our time, for his gracious permission to quote from his excellent biography, *George MacDonald: Victorian Mythmaker,* in the introductions to these volumes. More complete acknowledgements are found in Volume 38 of the series, *George MacDonald A Writer's Life,* which comprises the complete collection of introductions to the 37 fiction titles.

Interior title design by Joan Grytness.

The Cullen Collection of the Fiction of George MacDonald, Volume 5

Published by SUNRISE BOOKS in cooperation with WISE PATH BOOKS—
Preserving the works of George MacDonald for future generations

ISBN 978-1724091697

Alec Forbes of Howglen

This updated edition of a 19th century literary gem,
first cut, polished, and set by George MacDonald,
is now presented in a fresh setting for a new generation

The Cullen Collection of the Fiction of George MacDonald

1. Phantastes (1858)
2. David Elginbrod (1863)
3. The Portent (1864)
4. Adela Cathcart (1864)
5. Alec Forbes of Howglen (1865)
6. Annals of a Quiet Neighbourhood (1867)
7. Robert Falconer (1868)
8. Guild Court (1868)
9. The Seaboard Parish (1868)
10. At the Back of the North Wind (1871)
11. Ranald Bannerman's Boyhood (1871)
12. The Princess and the Goblin (1872)
13. Wilfrid Cumbermede (1872)
14. The Vicar's Daughter (1872)
15. Gutta Percha Willie (1873)
16. Malcolm (1875)
17. The Wise Woman (1875)
18. St. George and St. Michael (1876)
19. Thomas Wingfold Curate (1876)
20. The Marquis of Lossie (1877)
21. Paul Faber Surgeon (1879)

22. Sir Gibbie (1879)
23. Mary Marston (1881)
24. Castle Warlock (1881)
25. The Princess and Curdie (1882)
26. Weighed and Wanting (1882)
27. Donal Grant (1883)
28. What's Mine's Mine (1886)
29. Home Again (1887)
30. The Elect Lady (1888)
31. A Rough Shaking (1890)
32. There and Back (1891)
33. The Flight of the Shadow (1891)
34. Heather and Snow (1893)
35. Lilith (1895)
36. Salted With Fire (1897)
37. Far Above Rubies (1898)

The introductions to the 37 volumes form a continuous picture of George MacDonald's literary life, viewed through the prism of the development of his written legacy of works. While each book can of course be read on its own, every introduction picks up where that to the previous volume left off, with special attention to the title under consideration. The introductions together, as a biography of MacDonald's life as a writer, are compiled in Volume 38.

38. George MacDonald A Writer's Life

Contents

NOTE: As the introductions to the 37 volumes of *The Cullen Collection* form a continuous portrait of George MacDonald's life, and as many of the introductions contain comprehensive and detailed discussion and analysis of the title in question—its plot, themes, and circumstances of writing—some first-time readers may choose to skip ahead to the story itself, saving the introduction for later, so as not to "spoil the story."

"Papa seems so quietly happy."

—Louisa MacDonald, May 4, 1872, from Deskford (near Cullen)

"Papa does enjoy this place so much."

—Louisa MacDonald, May 6, 1872 from the Seafield Arms Hotel, Cullen

"Papa oh! so jolly & bright & happy...Papa was taken for Lord Seafield yesterday."

—Louisa MacDonald, Sept. 2, 1873, from Cullen

"Papa is very poorly. He ought to go to Cullen for a week I think."

—Louisa MacDonald, October 5, 1873, from London

Foreword

The Cullen Collection
of the Fiction of George MacDonald

The series name for these works of Scotsman George MacDonald (1824-1905) has its origins in the 1830s when the boy MacDonald formed what would be a lifelong affection for the northeast Scottish village of Cullen.

The ocean became young George's delight. At the age of eleven, writing from Portsoy or Cullen, he announced to his father his intention to go to sea as a sailor—in his words, "as soon as possible." The broad white beach of Cullen Bay, the Seatown, the grounds of Cullen House, the temple of Psyche ("Temple of the Winds"), Cullen Burn, the dwellings along Grant Street, Scarnose, and especially Findlater Castle, all seized the youth's imagination with a love that never left him. MacDonald continued to visit Huntly and Cullen throughout his life, using his childhood love for his homeland as the backdrop for his richest novels, including what is arguably his greatest work of fiction, *Malcolm*, published in 1875.

We therefore honor MacDonald's unique relationship to Cullen with these newly updated editions of his novels. In Cullen, in certain respects more than in any other place, one finds the transcendent spirit of George MacDonald's life and the ongoing legacy of his work still magically alive after a century and a half. This release of *The Cullen Collection of the Fiction of George MacDonald* coincides with a memorial bench and plaque established on Cullen's Castle Hill commemorating MacDonald's visits to the region.

To those readers familiar with my previous editions of MacDonald's novels, I should make clear that eighteen of the volumes in this new series (including this one) are updated and expanded titles from the Bethany House series of the 1980s. Limitations of length dictated much about how those previous volumes were produced. To interest a publisher in the project during those years when MacDonald was a virtual unknown in the publishing world, certain sacrifices had to be made. Cuts to length had to be more severe than I would have preferred. Practicality drove the effort.

Added to that was the challenge of working with editors who occasionally changed MacDonald's wording and *removed* more than I intended, then also sometimes took liberties to the opposite extreme by *inserting* words, sentences, even whole paragraphs that originated from neither myself *nor* MacDonald. Those editions were also subject to sanitizing editorial scrutiny, which occasionally removed aspects of MacDonald's more controversial perspectives, and added evangelically correct words and phrases to bring the text more in line with accepted orthodoxy. As MacDonald himself knew, there are times an author has little say in details of final text, design, art, or overall quality. Thus, the covers and titles were not mine. And I was often kept in the dark about internal textual changes and was unable to correct them. Yet, too, many of MacDonald's expansive perspectives *were* preserved (though what was excised and what was left often seemed random and inconsistent) for which I applaud Bethany's openness. Their publications of the 1980s helped inaugurate a worldwide renaissance of interest in MacDonald and we owe them our gratitude. Frustrating as the process occasionally was, I thus remain enormously grateful for those editions. They were wonderful door-openers for many thousands into MacDonald's world.

Hopefully this new and more comprehensive set of MacDonald's fiction will take up where they left off. Not constrained by the limitations that dictated production of the former volumes, these new editions, though identical at many points, have been expanded—sometimes significantly. In that sense they reflect MacDonald's originals somewhat more closely, while still preserving the flavor, pace, and readability of their predecessors. Needless to say, the doctrinal scrubbings have been corrected and the deleted passages reinstated. Nineteen additional titles have been added. The thirteen realistic novels among these have been updated according to the same priorities that guided the earlier Bethany House series. That process will be explained in more detail in the introductions to the books of the series. The final six, which would more accurately be termed "fantasy," have not been edited in any way. They are faithful reproductions of the originals exactly as they were first published. These six titles—*Phantastes, At the Back of the North Wind, The Princess and the Goblin, The Wise Woman, The Princess and Curdie,* and *Lilith*—are so well known and have been published literally in hundreds of editions through the years, that it has seemed best to reproduce them for *The Cullen Collection* with the same texts by which they are generally known. *

---

* A word of clarification at this point will hopefully alleviate minor confusions that may arise about certain usages of punctuation and capitalization. In speaking of the original texts of MacDonald's books, a phrase such as the "texts by which they are generally known," is not really accurate. For most of MacDonald's books there are no *absolutely* authoritative texts. Editions vary widely, even so-called "first editions." This is a theme that will be developed in the introductions to other editions of *The Cullen Collection*, and is a fascinating study in itself. Suffice it at this point to say that punctuation and capitalization varies. Sometimes the differences are between U.S. and U.K. editions—American publishers capitalizing lower case words from the British editions (in addition to changing words such as labour, honour, odour, parlour, neighbourhood, etc. to their American spellings). This is especially the case with the God-pronouns *He* and *Him*. MacDonald usually wrote these in the lower case, as he did nouns of direct address in dialogue—mother, father, aunt, uncle, your majesty, etc.—which are occasionally capitalized in U.S. editions.

The ambiguity is heightened, however, when MacDonald himself is inconsistent in his usage. Sometimes he *does* capitalize *He* and *Him*. Sometimes God is referred to as *father*, at other times as *Father*. But he is inconsistent (whether by intent or blunder I have never been able to ascertain)—with *he* and *Him* (both referring to God or Jesus), and *father* and *Father*, perhaps even occurring in the same sentence.

Punctuation, likewise, varies from edition to edition—colons, dashes, quotation marks, paragraph breaks being the most common differences. Quotation marks ('single') sometimes follow U.K. convention, at other times U.S. convention ("double"). But it is not so simple as whether a particular edition was published in the U.K. or U.S. Some U.K first editions use American quotation marks, and likewise some U.S. editions use British spellings. It is very confusing.

Most readers won't notice and won't care about such tiny details. But the occasional purist may say, "Hey, wait a minute, my original edition has a colon here, and this new edition has a comma!" Granted, there won't be many who will be so persnickety. But for those few of you, I will only say that I have made use of as many original editions as possible—for nearly every title at least two, sometimes more—to compare these minor

Dedicated followers of all great men and women continually seek hints that reveal their inner being—the *true* man, the *true* woman. What were they *really* like? What made him or her tick? Many biographies and studies attempt to answer such questions. In George MacDonald's case, however, a panorama of windows exists that reveals far more about his person than the sum-total of everything that has been written about him over the years. Those are the novels that encompass his life's work. The volumes of this series represent the *true* spiritual biography of the man, a far more important biography than life's details can ever tell.

In 1911, six years after his father's death, George MacDonald's son Ronald wrote of the man with whom he had spent his life:

> *"The ideals of his didactic novels were the motive of his own life...a life of literal, and, which is more, imaginative consistency with his doctrine...There has probably never been a writer whose work was a better expression of his personal character. This I am not engaged to prove; but I very positively assert...that in his novels...and allegories...one encounters...the same rich imagination, the same generous lover of God and man, the same consistent practiser of his own preaching, the same tender charity to the sinner with the same uncompromising hostility to the sin, which were known in daily use and by his own people counted upon more surely than sunshine."* [*]

Thirty years after the publication of my one-volume biography *George MacDonald Scotland's Beloved Storyteller,* it now gives me great pleasure to present this thirty-seven-volume "biography" of the man, the Scotsman, the prophetic spiritual voice who is George MacDonald. [†]

How fitting is the original title in which Ronald MacDonald's sketch of his father quoted above first appeared, *From A Northern Window.* For any attempted portrait of the man George MacDonald becomes at once a window into his homeland as well.

Therefore, I invite you to gaze back in time through the "northern windows" of these volumes. Picture yourself perhaps near the cheerful hearth described in the opening pages of *What's Mine's Mine,* looking out the window to the cold seas and mountains in the distance, where perhaps you get a fleeting glimpse of highlanders Ian and Alister Macruadh.

---

distinctions. Then I have followed what I consider the "best" usage or punctuation under the circumstances (which is obviously my own judgment call) and that which I consider the most likely usage MacDonald himself originally would have employed. But obviously in some cases I may be mistaken.

[*] "George MacDonald: A Personal Note" by Ronald MacDonald, Chapter 3 in *From A Northern Window,* James Nisbet & Co., 1911, reprinted in book form as *From A Northern Window,* Volume One in The Masterline Series, Sunrise Books, Eureka, CA 1989.

† For the texts of the books of the series, and quotes referenced from them, I have preserved most British spellings. In my introductions, when I am speaking for *myself,* I use American spellings. In quoting from other books and authors, I obviously retain the usage of the original source.

Or imagine yourself walking up Duke Street in Huntly from MacDonald's birth home, following in the footsteps of fictional Robert Falconer to the town square.

Or envision yourself on some windswept highland moor with Gibbie or Cosmo Warlock.

Or walk up the circular staircase of Fyvie Castle to Donal Grant's tiny tower hideaway where he began to unravel the mysteries of that ancient and spooky place.

Or walk up from Cullen's Seatown in your mind's eye alongside Malcolm selling the fish in his creel, turning at the Market Cross into Grant Street and continuing past Miss Horn's house and up the hill to the entrance of the Cullen House grounds.

Or perhaps climb Castle Hill to the George MacDonald memorial bench and gaze across the sweep of Cullen Bay as Malcolm's story comes to life before your eyes.

From any of these settings, whether real or imaginary, drift back through the years and gaze through the panoramic windows of these stories, and take in with pleasure the drama, relationships, images, characters, settings, and spiritual truths George MacDonald offers us as we are drawn into his world.

Michael Phillips
Cullen, Morayshire
Scotland, 2017

INTRODUCTION

Alec Forbes of Howglen

A Little Grey Town in Aberdeenshire

While it cannot be said that *Alec Forbes of Howglen* "launched" George MacDonald's writing career when it was released in 1865, it certainly *solidified* his name as among Victorian Britain's leading novelists.

As that year opened, though he had published eight books between 1851 and 1864, the momentum of George MacDonald's career as a writer was still sputtering along somewhat fitfully. His first realistic novel, *David Elginbrod,* had done well two years earlier. But one book does not a career make. Thousands of one-book-wonders come and go through the years, authors who are never heard from again. Three more titles (one, a device for a collection of short stories, the second a reprint of poems, the third scarcely more than a novella) had been released on the heels of *Elginbrod's* success. But they represented nothing significantly *new* from the Scots author. Some critics complained that those recent releases were mere recycled flotsam and jetsam out of MacDonald's past files.

Photograph c. 1863-65.

If MacDonald was going to make it as a novelist, he had to show that he could do it again. He had to prove that the success of *David Elginbrod*—as a major work of fiction—wasn't just a one-off. The critics, it might be said, were getting restless.

As 1865 dawned, therefore, much was on the line. MacDonald had to demonstrate that he hadn't just been lucky, but that he could *keep* writing novels that would sell, that people would read, and that the ambivalent critics would rave about.

And that's exactly what he did. This was the book that proved it.

MacDonald's other miscellaneous writings continued. He was planning new editions of fairy tales and poetry, as well as a collection of sermons. But the idea brewing in his mind for a second Scottish novel, which he spent much of 1864 writing, was the book his future hinged upon. Set in his hometown of Huntly, it was a story he hoped would be a worthy follow-up to *David Elginbrod.*

He delivered the manuscript, to which he gave the lackluster title "The Little Grey Town," to Hurst and Blackett, publishers of *David Elginbrod,* in the early months of 1865. They changed the title to *Alec Forbes of Howglen* and published MacDonald's new effort in June of that year.

Alec Forbes was a resounding success. It was not merely a worthy second realistic novel, it was a masterful and timeless work of fiction—a book with enormous depth of characterization, wide breadth of plot, unexpected humor, tear-jerking pathos, and deft craftsmanship in the sheer "art" of storytelling. Throughout the more than 150 years that have passed since its publication, many have hailed *Alec Forbes* as the most skillfully designed and executed of all George MacDonald's novels.

Like its predecessor *Elginbrod, Alec Forbes of Howglen* sold well and received rave reviews. The *Athenaeum* wrote: "It is something to rejoice the heart that even in these days a novel can be written full of strong human interest without any aid from melo-dramatic scene-painting, social mysteries, and the physical force of incidents." The magazine's review continued by saying that it was the "development of the inner life and spiritual history of the characters" that set *Alec Forbes* apart, even though "it is not a religious novel, and yet the growth of the religious element in each personage is the pervading idea." [1]

MacDonald had indeed demonstrated that he could do it again—even better than before! And he would keep doing so for the next thirty years.

Again, the dialect of MacDonald's boyhood is the vehicle for much of the dialogue in *Alec Forbes.* The author must have assumed that the visually daunting regional Doric speech would not hurt sales. Obviously he was right.

As William Raeper again reminds us, the mystique of Scotland found England's readers well able to handle it, no doubt better than most readers would be able to today:

"The Scottish portion of MacDonald's writing...is an important contribution to Scottish Victorian literature and stands as part of the uneasy tradition linking Scotland and England. For MacDonald can be seen as a traditional 'lad of pairts' hailing from a poor background, passing through university...and then hitting the high road to England to make for fame and fortune. It is an almost legendary path and, arriving in London, MacDonald would have found a swarm of Scottish writers rubbing shoulders with each other and a publishing business that was dominated by Scots...

"The Makars, Dunbar and Henryson, were the flowers of fifteenth century Scottish literature, and later, while Edinburgh had been flourishing as the Athens of the North, Burns had emerged, writing in a Scots which the London public seemed able to read with pleasure. MacDonald had no compunction therefore in putting large stretches of Scots into his novels...

"But if the use of Scots may have put some readers off, it was the pictures of Scotland that drew many people to MacDonald's books...Though his view of Scotland is undoubtedly romantic, his descriptions of Rothieden and Glamerton have a cutting edge." [2]

Writing *Alec Forbes of Howglen*, one can see that MacDonald enjoyed himself. Not only is the setting based on MacDonald's boyhood, so too are many incidents and personalities in the story. The same is true of *Robert Falconer* and *Ranald Bannerman's Boyhood.* Taken together, these books portray the Huntly of the 1820s and 1830s nearly to perfection. The fictional Howglen is the MacDonald farm situated across the River Bogie (the fictional Glamour) from the town. On the other side of town ran the Deveron (fictionalized as the Wan Water). MacDonald's father and uncle operated a mill on the Bogie just down from their farm, whose operations are vividly described both here and in *Robert Falconer.* The flood portrayed in the book actually took place during late August and early September of 1829 when George was four.

When writing *George MacDonald Scotland's Beloved Storyteller,* I wandered over nearly every inch of Huntly and its surroundings, reliving the incidents of the novels as if I were part of them. At the time, the MacDonald mill was still standing. From the bridge across the Bogie I looked down on what I take to have been MacDonald's model for Tibbie Dyster's cottage where it still stood nearly (though not quite!) *in* the river, surviving a century of winters and springs since MacDonald's time. This is a book wonderfully true to place, and rooted in the early life of its author.*

How many of the escapades of Alec and his friends, therefore, had their roots in MacDonald's own childhood, we have no way of knowing. But we sense the pure delight of boyhood which not even the *tawse* † could entirely dim. In *Alec Forbes,* MacDonald offers his readers a picture of the love he had for the young at heart, those who could find a way to enjoy life whatever their surroundings.

As most reviewers have maintained, it is a tightly constructed story. Few long spiritual digressions are found in *Alec Forbes.* It is the smoothest flowing, most cohesive of his novels. Every character is crucial to the development of the plot, every incident follows the next in logical progression. There is less point, more plot...less meaning, more movement...fewer lessons, more laughs. Looking at it purely from a literary standpoint, those familiar with the body of MacDonald's work praise its unity as a piece of literature because of the tight consolidation of its elements. Rolland Hein calls it "the most delightful of all the novels." [3] Richard Reis says, "*Alec Forbes of Howglen* is MacDonald's best novel." [4]

Principles of truth are reflected just as strongly, but it is not as *heavy* a book as some of his others. Here is good old-fashioned theatrical soap opera at its finest, complete with landlord-villain, pending mortgage, doubtful inheritance, along with duplicity, tragedy, foreclosure, and romance.

So much of this book has become part of my life that I find myself thinking about it unconsciously. Whenever I see snow, I immediately picture Alec in my mind standing beside his pile of snowballs. When I see a small boat, I think of Annie and Alec and Curly floating down the Glamour. When I think of rats, I am transported instantly to Annie's garret. Many other images crowd into my brain—the schoolmaster's *tawse,* harvest time in the fields, the flood, Juno, and, of course, the faces of Annie and Alec as I picture them in my imagination.

Along with *David Elginbrod* which preceded it, and *Robert Falconer* which followed three years later, *Alec Forbes of Howglen* contributed to the triad for which MacDonald became best known in the 1860s as a renowned literary figure. Whether they were his "best" alongside the achievements of the following decade—*North Wind, Malcolm, The Marquis of Lossie, Sir Gibbie* and *Thomas Wingfold*—would make an interesting discussion. Nevertheless, these heavily Scottish novels established the three cornerstones of MacDonald's reputation.

---

* See Chapters 2, 3, 4 of *George MacDonald Scotland's Beloved Storyteller* for a more thorough treatment of MacDonald's boyhood in Huntly.

† A leather strap split into thin strips at the end, used as punishment in old Scottish schools.

Richard Reis, author of the well-done analytical study *George MacDonald's Fiction,* writes: "The author of twenty-nine novels may be expected to produce at least one which is better than commonplace; such is MacDonald's *Alec Forbes of Howglen.* In plot especially, this work is intriguing, well-motivated, tightly integrated, and more original than most of MacDonald's realistic tales...There are several aspects of *Alec Forbes of Howglen* which set it apart...especially in plot. Every incident is effectively integrated into the story." [5]

The main characters, Annie and Alec, grow, travel, mature and change while maintaining their roots and earlier relationships. In *Robert Falconer* we observe just the opposite. As Robert leaves Rothieden, so do we as readers, almost never to set eyes on it again. When Donal Grant leaves home for Auchars, we see Janet and Robert and the region of Gormgarnet but once again, very briefly. In *Alec Forbes,* however, we stay in touch with the story's origin and roots.

Robert Wolff notes: "*Alec Forbes* does not fall apart because important characters vanish from the scene; instead they remain and grow and develop. When the hero goes off to the University, the author manages to follow his adventures there while simultaneously keeping his reader in touch with the fortunes of those left behind in Glamerton. *Alec Forbes* is all of a piece." [6]

And Reis adds, "Perhaps the most striking aspect of *Alec Forbes of Howglen* is the fact that its happy ending is as compromised as life itself. The hero does not, as in so many Victorian novels...rise in the world and obtain...worldly 'success'; instead, Alec's reform is rewarded by a good though not brilliant wife, and an honorable but humble career as a farmer. One imagines him laboring and sweating, unknown and anonymous, for the rest of his life, rather than becoming a 'success'...and mingling with nobility as he might have." [7] This is not a "rags-to-riches" fairy tale, but something far better.

Of note in this regard is the interesting illumination of Britain's class distinctions. This is especially incongruous for American readers, who would not readily perceive the social hierarchy existing between Annie, Mrs. Forbes, Margaret Anderson, Robert Bruce, and the other personalities of the story. One still observes traces of that hierarchy in Scotland even today, and it was endemic to the entire cultural milieu of the nineteenth century. All MacDonald's novels are woven upon a social fabric that is virtually unknown in the American consciousness. If Mrs. Forbes's attitude toward Annie strikes us as out of place and snobbish, we need only remind ourselves of George and Louisa MacDonald's chagrin at their son Greville's marriage to a woman "below" them. (She was a nurse.) Louisa even rushed to London (too late) to try to stop the marriage. MacDonald wrote to her later, "What a woman for any gentleman to marry!" [8] It's almost shocking to read such words from MacDonald's pen. Even he and Louisa were not immune to what looks haughty to us, but was simply in the air of British culture 150 years ago. MacDonald, from a farming family, had gradually risen in society to the point where he considered his son a "gentleman" who was *above* marrying a nurse. It would seem that MacDonald had forgotten his own humble origins.

MacDonald scholar and biographer, Wheaton's Rolland Hein, identifies *Alec Forbes* as the first in MacDonald's writing of the particular form of fiction known by the German term "Bildungsroman." He explains as follows:

"His reputation now established as a promising young novelist, MacDonald turned to the *Bildungsroman* type, producing two of his finest works, *Alec Forbes of Howglen* and *Robert Falconer.* The *Bildungsroman*—or novels of apprenticeship—typically depict a child growing up and making various mistakes and false starts in life, until as a young adult he finds his true profession and a productive orientation to reality. Like German folktales, also so influential in MacDonald's thinking, this genre originated with the Germans in the late nineteenth century.

"This form became immensely popular in England throughout the nineteenth century. In the 1860s, Dickens's *David Copperfield* (1849-1850) and George Elliot's *The Mill on the Floss* (1860) were two of the most widely admired…

"The novel…demonstrates MacDonald's ability to re-create a child's way of looking at the world, certainly one of his strengths as a writer. His children are among his most memorable characters. They result in part from his love of children, but they also issue from his insistence that a childlike approach to life is essential to true spirituality—one of his pervading themes." [9]

Somewhat unique to *Alec Forbes* is MacDonald's handling of the religiosity of the community. MacDonald introduces two distinct churches of Glamerton, both Calvinist in their outlook and neither "right" nor "wrong." There are no slashing attacks from MacDonald in any direction. Rather, he encourages us to appreciate both the weaknesses and strengths in the two worshiping bodies, allowing room for humanness and growth. Perhaps setting the story in his hometown enabled him to recall fondly much in his own past, and the people who had contributed to making him the man he was (social incongruities notwithstanding). There are no faultless saints here, just real people with both blind spots and human qualities which endear them to us. George Macwha, the carpenter, says the "muckle kirk" * does well enough for him, but his friend Thomas Crann, a dedicated and staunch member of

---

* "Muckle"—a colorful Scottish word with a host of nuanced meanings, technically "much," but adapted from that foundation to *very, big, large, a great deal*…and hence "the *big* church…the *main* church…the most important church," the Church of Scotland.

the evangelical sect of the Missionars views Macwha's shallowness with scorn. Yet with all his narrowness and inability to see beyond the confines of his own system of belief, we are drawn to Crann, and he becomes one of the book's principal characters. Poor Mr. Cowie hasn't the faith or understanding to help Annie through her troubles about eternal hell-fire. Yet he has the compassion to offer help on a far more homely and personal level (which Crann doesn't), and we love him for it. In the same way, we find ourselves drawn to Malison and Mr. Cupples through all their faults.

There is indeed profound theology here, though it comes in smaller doses than in *Robert Falconer* or *Thomas Wingfold*. It may be Falconer's question to Shargar about repentant devils that is most often quoted, but MacDonald makes the question even more blunt here, coming from the mouth of skeptic Mr. Cupples to Calvinist Thomas Crann (one of MacDonald's delightful fictional friendships): "But just suppose, Thomas, if the devil were to repent?" *

In *Alec Forbes* we are also given more detail about MacDonald's legendary (though debated) sojourn in a "great library in the north." (See footnote, "The Great Library in the North" in the introduction to *The Portent* for a more complete discussion.) About this season in MacDonald's life, many have speculated from *Alec Forbes* and *The Portent* the likelihood that MacDonald himself fell in love with a beautiful young lady of the house whose library he had been engaged to catalog during his university years. Given the impressionable age of the youth, and the possible circumstances surrounding his brief months as librarian, it is not difficult to theorize that the lady of the mansion formed the basis for some of MacDonald's later heroines. Do we not see many common threads in the personalities of Florimel, Euphra, Arctura, and *Alec Forbes's* Kate—beautiful, sly, coy, eyes hinting at subtle design, occasional impishness? In his development of these women, MacDonald conveys duplicity, seduction, and cunning. And Kate's background in the story places her origin, though unnamed, very near Thurso—whose castle MacDonald's son Greville identifies as his father's own "library in the north." Responding to Alec's question, "Where were you born?" Kate answers, "In the north of Sutherlandshire—near the foot of a great mountain, from the top of which, on the longest day, you can see the sun, or a bit of him at least, all night long."

On the other hand, many of MacDonald's women eventually reveal a deeper, true-hearted desire to grow and shake off the masquerade—Arctura and Florimel being the most prominent. Then there are *Wingfold's* Helen and *What's Mine's Mine's* Mercy—two women who are

* As an interesting sidelight that partially explains the reason for the new editions of *The Cullen Collection*—this entire passage was excised by my doctrinally skittish publishers from my earlier version of 1985.

neither designing nor coy nor duplicitous, but are simply *asleep*. MacDonald refashions *The Sleeping Beauty* tale in many of his novels. It is not a mere kiss that awakens them, however, but something far better—spiritual reality, and the truth of the divine Fatherhood.

The Portent's Alice personifies both sides to this almost paradoxical feminine ambiguity that MacDonald explores in book after book. Her sleepwalking (something MacDonald uses repeatedly) is the precise symbol for the state of her personality and spiritual condition—and she thus serves as a "type" for other characters like Helen and Mercy who are walking through life spiritually and intellectually "asleep." Obviously this complexity of feminine characterization cannot but raise the question whether indeed these women somehow represent a composite originating in MacDonald's own experience. He continued portraying complex women throughout his writing life (including the outright evil characters of Sepia, Lady Ann, Lufa, Lady Cairnedge, and Lilith) almost as if he was driven to try to understand them.

How much of Mr. Cupples's stirring story of the library may be autobiographical we can only conjecture. Most intriguing is the fact that the falsehood of the girl's flirtation toward the young Cupples is revealed to the reader without Cupples even himself seeing it. A single laugh at her triumph over helpless Cupples is the only evidence of her venom. But it is enough, and Cupples is undone, just as is Alec by a flash from Kate's eyes.

Is the fascination Kate exercises over Alec straight out of MacDonald's own biography? With Mr. Cupples's story and Kate's Sutherland origins, it hardly seems there can be any doubt of it. It cannot be coincidental that now for three titles in a row (*The Portent, Adela Cathcart, Alec Forbes*), a great northern library enters into the narrative.

In spite of the flood and the trials of school and rats and watered-down milk, *Alec Forbes* rings with a light spirit of gladness. Winter comes to Glamerton just as bitterly as it does to Rothieden. Times are cruel for Annie in her garret. And school is a harsh place indeed. (The real schoolmaster of Huntly during MacDonald's early boyhood was reportedly worse than the portrayal of Malison.) Yet the whole mood remains one of joy and discovery.

Feel the difference between Robert Falconer's winter in Rothieden:

> *How drearily the afternoon had passed. He had opened the door again and looked out. There was nothing alive to be seen, except a sparrow picking up crumbs...At last he had trudged upstairs...remained there till it grew dark...There was even less light than usual in the room...for a thick covering of snow lay over the glass of the small skylight. A partial thaw, followed by a frost, had fixed it there. It was a cold place to sit, but the boy had some faculty for enduring cold when that was the price to be paid for solitude...what was to be seen...could certainly not be called pleasant. A broad street with*

low houses of cold, gray stone, as uninteresting a street as most any to be found in the world...The sole motion was the occasional drift of a film of white powder which the wind would lift like dust from the snowy carpet that covered the street. Wafting it along for a few yards, it would drop again to its repose, foretelling the wind on the rise at sundown—a wind cold and bitter as death—which would rush over the street and raise a denser cloud of the white dust to sting the face of any improbable person who might meet it in its passage.

And the picture MacDonald paints of Alec Forbes's Glamerton:

The winter came. One morning, all the children awoke, and saw a white world around them. Alec jumped out of bed in delight. It was a sunny, frosty morning. The snow had fallen all night, with its own silence, and no wind had interfered with the gracious alighting of the feathery water. Every branch, every twig, was laden with its sparkling burden of down-flickered flakes, and threw long lovely shadows on the smooth featureless dazzle below. Away, away, stretched the outspread glory, the only darkness in it being the line of the winding river. All the snow that fell on it vanished, as death and hell shall one day vanish in the fire of God. It flowed on, black through its banks of white. Away again stretched the shine to the town, where every roof had the sheet that was let down from heaven spread over it, and the streets lay a foot deep in yet unsullied snow, soon, like the story of the ages, to be trampled, soiled, wrought, and driven with human feet, till, at last, God's strong sun would wipe it all away. *

From the door opening into this fairy-land, Alec sprang into the untrodden space, as into a new America. He had discovered a world, without even the print of human foot upon it. The keen air made him happy; and the face of nature, looking as peaceful as the face of a dead man dreaming of heaven, wrought in him jubilation and leaping. He was at the school door before a human being had appeared in the streets of Glamerton. Its dwellers all lay still under those sheets of snow, which seemed to hold them asleep in its cold enchantment.

Then, too, this is simply one of MacDonald's funniest books. I should say rather, a story *imbued* with humor throughout, for in MacDonald's world humor and pathos are so tightly interwoven that you often don't know whether to laugh or cry. His wordplay and turns of phrase, hilarious irony, biting satire, witty understatement, juxtaposition of opposites, and simple wisecrack, all season this story with laugh-out-loud moments that

* This wonderfully descriptive paragraph, with its theologically profound implications, provides another example of the editorial difficulties I encountered with my edited editions of MacDonald's novels in the 1980s. The sentence, "All the snow that fell on it vanished, as death and hell shall one day vanish in the fire of God," appeared in the published version as, "All the snow that fell on it vanished." The wonderfully descriptive final thirteen words were stricken by an editor. Such examples, which were numerous, illustrate the reality that MacDonald was writing for a Christian readership deeply fearful of any threat to doctrinal orthodoxy. And sadly, little has changed in 150 years.

hit when you least expect them, from Annie's botching of the correct Shorter Catechism answer to Bruce's inglorious exit from the church business meeting.

Humor notwithstanding, William Raeper insightfully reminds us,

"As in every picture of Eden—there are snakes...

"The realities of life...are only too vividly portrayed...Children wincing under the lash of Murdoch Malison and the miserable Saturday morning sessions where they are forced to learn their Shorter Catechism...Murdoch Malison strides centre stage of the book like some monstrous figure of Vice...and it is sobering to think that his original in life, Colin Stewart, was, if anything, worse...Malison aims to become a minister of the Church of Scotland and, though his failure in the pulpit brings about a change in his personality, the link between violence and religion has been made. The violence the children suffer to their bodies at school is inflicted on their spirits at church. After listening to the sermon at the Missionar Kirk, Annie Anderson fears that: 'A spiritual terror was seated on the throne of the universe, and was called God...' MacDonald's idyll is a dualistic one, possessing both light and shade, and alongside Alec's and Annie's pleasant pursuits in the building of the boat, throwing snowballs, clapping sods of turf on chimneys as a joke and burying Bruce's shop half in snow, there is both cruelty and darkness." [10]

MacDonald's portrayals of people stand out. The gradual changes he weaves into our sympathies for Malison and Cupples catch us off guard. Who can read of Malison in the pulpit without empathy and pity? And his poignant relationship with sad little Truffey sets us up for such a rush of tears, exactly as MacDonald planned. And Mr. Cupples is far from the usual MacDonald counselor and advisor. No David Elginbrod, Andrew Comin, or Sandy Graham here, only a failed scholar who seems but a wretched drunkard. Yet because of the complex character MacDonald draws, we delight all the more when the reformed and rejuvenated Cupples dances about Glamerton filled with the joy of life.

And of course there is the maiden heroine of the story, Annie herself. Her personality is subdued, slow to show itself, waiting to flower—with hints of the "waking" feminine personhood we saw in *The Portent's* Alice, yet without an ounce of the conflicted half of that persona. In *Alec Forbes*, MacDonald portrays *both* halves of the feminine mystique that obviously fascinated him—the one personified in Annie, the other in Kate.

Annie emerges, in a sense, as MacDonald's perfection of womanhood. She is of a single piece—as a lonely child, as a mature and humble young woman, she is always growing in the same direction. There are no detours—her character of humility, service, spiritual hunger, devotion, and love continue to unfold, revealing ever deeper layers to the intrinsic personhood that has been there all along.

Annie is not a usual leading lady. She is simplicity itself. Even as she grows and matures, Annie's true nature remains dormant. She faces life without airs or sophistication. She cares nothing for what other people think. We will discover that same trait in many of MacDonald's heroes and heroines—a complete lack of self-defense or concern for reputation. Their determination to *do* and *be* according to what is right and true defines their character, not what anyone else thinks of them. As Annie grows and awakens to deeper feelings, she dares not reveal them, hardly dares admit them to herself. She personifies meekness, of those who inherit the earth.

Many of George MacDonald's novels take place in part in the genteel surroundings of aristocratic families, complete with formal drawing rooms, castles, titles, and inheritances. If the hero is poor when the story opens, chances are he will become a nobleman before it is over. In *Alec Forbes,* however, we never see London, we meet no lairds or ladies, we enter no mansions anywhere in Glamerton. The whole of the down-to-earth narrative takes place in humble surroundings and involves simple (though still class-bound) folk.

At the time of its publication, however, not everyone was pleased with the portrayals in *Alec Forbes.* Writing of both *Alec Forbes* and *Robert Falconer,* William Raeper says, "MacDonald's thirst for accuracy sometimes caused trouble when the characters in his novels were too easily recognizable...MacDonald's grandmother...did burn a violin...belonging to her reprobate son Charles, and she did take in four bastard children of Sir Andrew Leith Hay of Leith Hall near Huntly. One of those sons grew into a prosperous if greedy shopkeeper and was pilloried by MacDonald as Robert Bruce in *Alec Forbes of Howglen.* This novel gave the shopkeeper and his family such a blacking that they had to move away from Huntly to Aberdeen. The character of Thomas Crann was based on James Maitland, a well-known local evangelist." [11]

The character of Tibbie, too, was drawn from real life. When MacDonald visited Huntly in the summer of 1848 just prior to entering seminary, some friends requested him to conduct an informal meeting at the home of a ninety-year-old blind woman who was confined to bed and unable to attend church. MacDonald spoke to the ten or twelve who were present on Mark 6:48 and Jesus' calming the waters of the storm. The bedridden hostess for the evening was one Tibbie Christie, and the parallel is obvious. [12]

This new edition of *Alec Forbes*—as with most of the other books in *The Cullen Collection*—has been updated for publication. In the Introduction to *David Elginbrod,* I briefly set out the parameters for the process which establish the foundation for this set of new editions. The factors in MacDonald's writings requiring updating vary from title to title. Some require more, some less, and for different reasons. The dialect is more problematic in some of MacDonald's originals, tangential digressions in others. My intent is always to tightly weave the progress of the story line while preserving the content, spiritual themes, and wonderfully evocative essence of MacDonald's writing style and craft. But the process and specifics are different in every case.

Alec Forbes has in general needed less tightening. The original simply contains fewer extraneous diversions.

The Scottish dialect of such passages as the following, however, have been rendered into more current usage.

> *"Gin it hadna been for the guid wife here, 'at cam' up, efter the clanjamfrie had ta'en themsel's aff, an' fand me lying upo' the hearthstane, I wad hae been deid or noo. Was my heid aneath the grate, guidwife?"*
>
> *"Na, nae freely that, Mr. Cupples; but the blude o't was. Mr. Forbes, ye maun jist come doon wi' me. I'll jist mak' a cup of tay till him."*
>
> *"Tay, guidwife! Deil slocken himsel' wi yer tay! Gie me a sook of the tappit hen."*
>
> *"'Deed, Mr. Cupples, ye's hae neither sook nor sipple of that spring."*
>
> *"Ye rigwiddie carlin!" grinned the patient.*
>
> *"Never a glaiss sall ye hae fra my han', Mr. Cupples. It wad be the deid of ye. And forbye, thae ill-faured gutter-partans toomed the pig afore they gaed."*
>
> *"Gang oot of my chaumer wi' yer havers," cried Mr. Cupples, "and lea' me wi' Alec Forbes. He winna deave me wi' his clash."*

It is not that this dialogue is impossible to decipher. But the story certainly flows more smoothly without having to stop every few words to puzzle out the meaning. (As noted in other volumes of *The Cullen Collection,* some of the dialect has been left, especially in the early portions and elsewhere when appropriate, to flavor the narrative with the atmosphere of Scotland. Then, using the familiar film-making technique, the text gradually morphs into recognizable English.)

Beyond the story and characters themselves, *Alec Forbes* occupies a singular turning point in the publication history of George MacDonald's corpus of works. All three of its fiction predecessors were slow to see new editions published after the initial release. *David Elginbrod* was not released in one volume for eight years or published in the United States for nine. It sold well, but MacDonald was far from a household name. It took *The Portent* and *Adela Cathcart* even longer—they did not find their way to the U.S. for eleven years.

Everything changed with *Alec Forbes,* then positively ignited with the next title which followed it, *Annals of a Quiet Neighbourhood.*

Released in three volumes in June of 1865, it took Hurst and Blackett only two years to come out with a one-volume edition of *Alec Forbes,* some indication of the mounting demand for MacDonald's books. More significant, however, was the international attention MacDonald began to receive. Tauchnitz of Leipzig, Germany published *Alec Forbes* in two small-size volumes (in English, it should be noted) as part of their "Collection of British Authors" series, in 1865, nearly simultaneous with the triple decker—a somewhat remarkable indication that MacDonald was being noticed abroad. It was the first of many Tauchnitz editions that would follow, for which, it is believed Tauchnitz followed the rules and paid for the copyright. The thousands of these Tauchnitz editions still in circulation today, in their unique 4½ x 6¼ inch two-volume format, give ongoing evidence a century-and-a-half later of what soon became the worldwide popularity of this most unusual Scottish author.

The momentum of George MacDonald's career as a novelist was starting to build.

Perhaps a brief quote from Lewis Carroll will focus our thoughts as we begin to read. In the entry for January 16, 1866, from *The Diaries of Lewis Carroll,* the creator of *Alice in Wonderland* wrote, "*Alec Forbes*...is very enjoyable, and the character of Annie Anderson is one of the most delightful I have ever met with in fiction...The Scotch dialect, too, is pleasant enough when one gets a little used to it." [13]

Therefore, sit back and enjoy. This is the stuff of which rainy nights and crackling fires and cozy chairs are made—if you have a cup of tea beside you, so much the better! Here is the sparkle of life—the pains and wonders of childhood, the delights of the seasons, the exuberance and pleasure of youth, the awe of dawning maturity, the uncertainty of spiritual yearnings, and the heart-tugging agony of first loves.

Michael Phillips
Cullen, Morayshire
Scotland, 2017

NOTE ON FOOTNOTES: For the reader's ease in referencing frequently quoted titles, I have dispensed with the scholarly ciphers, more mystifying than helpful for the average fiction reader. These books will therefore be noted in the footnotes below as follows, rather than with the formal notations of op. cit., loc. cit., ibid., etc.

Greville, *Biography*—*George MacDonald and His Wife* by Greville MacDonald, George Allen & Unwin, London, 1924.

Hein, *Mythmaker*—*George MacDonald, Victorian Mythmaker* by Rolland Hein, Star Song Publishing, Nashville, TN, 1993.

Raeper, *MacDonald*—*George MacDonald* by William Raeper, Lion Publishing, Tring, England, 1987.

Reis, *Fiction*—*George MacDonald's Fiction* by Richard Reis, originally published as *George MacDonald* by Twayne Publishers, New York as Volume 119 in *Twayne's English Authors Series,* 1972; revised edition published by Sunrise Books, Eureka, CA, 1988 as Volume 3 in the *Masterline Series.*

1 The *Athenaeum*, June 17, 1865, quoted in Hein, *Mythmaker* p. 183.
2 Raeper, *MacDonald*, pp. 190-91, 193.
3 Rolland Hein, *The Harmony Within: The Spiritual Vision of George MacDonald*, William B. Eerdmans, Grand Rapids, Michigan, 1982; republished as Volume 1 in The Masterline Series by Sunrise Books, Eureka, Ca, 1989, p. 119.
4 Reis, *Fiction*, p. 140.
5 Reis, *Fiction*, pp. 61, 63-64.
6 Robert Lee Wolff, *The Golden Key*, Yale University Press, 1961, pp. 207-08.
7 Reis, *Fiction*, p. 64.
8 MacDonald to Louisa, March 5, 1888, quoted in Raeper, *MacDonald*, p. 358.
9 Hein, *Mythmaker* pp. 181-82.
10 Raeper, *MacDonald*, pp. 188-89.
11 Raeper, *MacDonald*, p. 190.
12 Greville, *Biography*, p. 113.
13 Charles Dodgson, *Diary*, January 16, 1866.

Alec Forbes of Howglen

1865

The Cullen Collection
Volume 5

George MacDonald

. . . . . . a faith sincere
Drawn from the wisdom that begins with fear

WORDSWORTH.— *Second Evening Voluntary.*

– One –

Burying Day

The farmyard was full of the light of a summer noonday. Not a living creature was to be seen in all the square enclosure, though barns and stables formed the greater part of it, while one end was occupied by a house. Through the gate at the other end, far off in fenced fields might be seen the dark forms of cattle. And on a road nearer by, a cart crawled along, drawn by one sleepy horse. An occasional weary low came from some imprisoned cow, or animal of the cow-kind, but not even a cat crossed the yard. The door of the empty barn was open and through the opposite doorway shone the last year's ricks of corn, * standing golden in the sun.

Although a farmyard is not, either in Scotland or elsewhere, the liveliest of places about noon in the summer, there was a peculiar cause rendering this one, at this moment, exceptionally deserted and dreary. There were, however, a great many more people about the place than usual. But they were all gathered in the nicest room of the

---

Drawing taken from frontispiece of Hurst & Blackett first 1-volume edition.

* Covered stacks of straw from previous harvest of grain (corn).

house—a room of tolerable size, with a clean boarded floor, a mahogany table black with age, and chairs with high straight backs. Every one of these chairs was occupied by a silent man whose gaze was either fixed on the floor or lost in the voids of space. Most were clothed in black from head to foot and each wore a black coat. Their hard, thick, brown hands—hands evidently unused to idleness—grasped their knees or, folded in each other, rested upon them. Some bottles and glasses, with a plate of biscuits, on a table in a corner seemed to indicate that the meeting was not entirely for business purposes. Yet there were no signs of any sort of enjoyment. Nor was there a woman to be seen in the company.

Suddenly a man appeared at the open door whose shirtsleeves showed very white against his other clothing, which, like that of the rest, was black.

"If any of ye want to see the corpse, noo's yer time," he said to the assembly.

No one responded to his offer. With a slight air of discomfiture, for he was a busy man and liked bustle, the carpenter turned on his heel and re-ascended the narrow stairs to the upper room where the corpse lay waiting for its final dismissal.

"I reckon they've all seen him afore," he remarked as he rejoined his companion. "Poor fellow! He's sure some worn. There'll be no muckle of *him* to rise again."

"George, man, dinna jeest i' the face o' a corp," returned the other. "Ye kenna whan yer ain turn may come."

"It's no disrespeck to the deid, Thamas. That ye ken weel eneuch. I was only pityin' the worn face of him, leukin up there atween the buirds, as gien he had gotten what he wanted sae lang, and was thankin' heaven for that same. I jist dinna like to pit the lid ower him."

"Hoot! hoot! Lat the Lord luik efter his ain. The lid of the coffin disna hide frae his een." *

---

* "George, man, don't jest in the face of a corpse…you don't know when your own turn may come."

"It's no disrespect to the dead, Thomas. That you know well enough. I was only pitying his poor worn face, looking up there between the boards, as if he had got what he wanted so long, and was thanking heaven for it. I just don't like to put the lid over him."

"Hoot, hoot! Let the Lord look after his own. The lid of the coffin doesn't hide from his eye."

The last speaker was a stout, broad-shouldered man, a stonemason by trade, powerful and somewhat asthmatic. He was regarded in the neighbourhood as a very religious man, but was more respected than liked because his forte was rebuke.

Together they lifted the last covering of the dead, laid it over him, and fastened it down. And now there was darkness about the dead. But he knew it not, because he was full of light. For this man was one who all his life had striven to be better.

Meantime, the clergyman having arrived, the usual religious ceremonial of a Scottish funeral—the reading of the Word and prayer—was going on below.

"The minister's come, Thomas," said the carpenter.

"Come or gang," said Thomas, "it's muckle the same. The word itsel' oot of his mou' fa's as deid as chaff upo' clay. Honest Jeames there'll rise ance mair, but never a word that man says, wi' the croon of 's heid i' the how of 's neck, 'll rise to beir witness of his ministrations."

"Hoot, Thamas! It's no for the likes of me to flee i' your face—but jist say a fair word for the livin' ower the deid, ye ken."

"Na, na. It's fair words maks foul wark, and the wrath of the Almichty maun purge this toon or a' be dune. There's a heap of graceless gaeins on in't, and that puir feckless body, the minister, never gies a pu' at the bridle of salvation, to haud them aff of the scaur of hell." *

The stonemason generally spoke of the Almighty as if he were in a state of restrained indignation at the wrongs he endured from his children. If Thomas was right in this, then certainly he himself was one of his offspring. If he was wrong, then there was much well worth his unlearning.

When the prayer was over, the company again seated themselves, waiting till the coffin, now descending the stairs, should be placed in

---

* "Come or go…it's much the same. The word itself out of his mouth falls as dead as chaff upon clay. Honest James there'll rise once more, but never a word that man says, with the crown of his head bowed to the hollow of his neck, will rise to bear witness of his ministrations."

"Hoot, Thomas! It's not for the likes of me to fly in your face—but just say a kind word for the living over the dead, you know."

"No, no. It's kind words that make foul work, and the wrath of the Almighty must purge this town before all is done. There's a heap of graceless goings on in it, and that poor weak body, the minister, never gives a pull at the bridle of salvation to keep them off the cliff of hell."

the hearse, which stood at the door. One after another slowly rose and withdrew to the door, watched in silence, and at last fell in behind the body and moved in an irregular procession from the yard. They were joined by several more men in gigs and on horseback. And thus they crept, a curious train, away toward the resting place of the dead.

It would be a dreary rest, indeed, if that were their resting place—on the side of a low hill, without tree or shrub to beautify it, or even the presence of an old church to seem to sanctify the spot. There was some long grass in it, though, climbing up as if it sought to bury the gravestones in their turn. And that long grass was a blessing. Better still, there was a sky overhead, in which men cannot set up any gravestones.

– Two –

Auntie and Brownie

When the last man had disappeared, the women began to come out as if emerging from an eastern harem. The first to enter the deserted room was a hard-featured, reproachful-looking woman, the sister of the departed. She instantly began to put the place in order, as if she expected to have her turn on the morrow. In a few moments a servant-girl appeared and began to assist her. She had been crying, and the tears continued to come in spite of her efforts to suppress them. In the vain attempt to dry her eyes with the corner of her apron, she nearly dropped one of the chairs which she was both dusting and restoring to its usual place. Her mistress turned upon her with a kind of cold fierceness.

"Is that how ye show yer regard for the dead, by breaking the chairs he left behind him? Let it sit and go out and look for that poor half-witted Annie. If it had only been the Almighty's will to hae taken her and left him, honest man."

"Dinna say a word against the child, mem. The dead'll hear ye and not lie still."

"Go and do what I tell ye this minute! What business do ye have to go crying about the hoose? He wasna a drop of blood of yers."

To this the girl made no reply but left the room in quest of Annie. When she reached the door, she stood for a moment on the threshold and shouted, *"Annie!"*

But apparently startled at the sound of her own voice where the unhearing dead had so recently passed, she let the end of the call die away and set off to find the missing child by the use of her eyes alone.

First she went into the barn, and then through it into the field, round the ricks one after another, then into the grain loft—but all to no avail. At length she came to the door of one of the cow-houses. She looked round the corner into the stall next to the door. This stall was occupied by a favourite cow—brown with large white spots—called Brownie. Her manger was full of fresh-cut grass. Half buried in the grass at one end, with her back against the wall, sat Annie, holding one of the ears of the hornless Brownie with one hand and stroking the creature's nose with the other.

She was a delicate child, about nine years old, with blue eyes half full of tears, hair somewhere between dark and fair, and a pale face on which a faint smile was glimmering. The old cow continued to hold out her nose to be stroked.

"Isn't Brownie a fine cow, Betty?" said the child as the maid went on staring at her. "Poor Brownie! Nobody minded me and so I came to you, Brownie."

She laid her cheek—white, smooth, and thin—against the broad, flat, hairy forehead of the friendly cow. Then turning again to Betty, she said—

"Don't tell auntie where I am, Betty. Let me be. I'm best here with Brownie."

Betty said not a word but returned to her mistress.

"Where's the bairn, Betty? At some mischief or other?"

"Hoot, mem! The bairn's well enough. Bairns mustn't be followed like calves."

"Where is she?"

"I canna just downright exactly take it upon me to say," answered Betty, "but I have no fear about her. She's a wise child."

"Ye're no the lassie's keeper, Betty. I see I must seek her oot myself. Ye're aiding and abetting as usual."

So saying, auntie Meg went out to look for her niece. It was some time before the natural order of her search brought her at last to the byre. By that time Annie was almost asleep in the grass, which the cow was gradually pulling away from under her. Through the open door the child could see the sunlight lying heavy upon the hot stones that paved the yard. But where she was it was so dark and cool, and the cow was such good, kindly company, and she was so safe hidden from auntie, as she thought—for no one had ever found her there before and she knew Betty would not tell—that, as I say, she was nearly asleep with comfort, half buried in Brownie's dinner.

But she was roused all at once to a sense of exposure and insecurity. She looked up, and at that moment the hawk nose of her aunt came round the door. Auntie's temper was none the better than usual that it had pleased the Almighty to take the brother whom she loved and to leave behind this child whom she regarded as a painful responsibility. And now with her small, fierce eyes, and her big, thin nose—both red with suppressed crying—she did not appear to Annie to embody the maternal love of the universe.

"Ye plaguesome brat!" she cried. "Betty has been looking for ye and I have been looking for ye far and near, in the very rat holes, and here ye are on yer own father's burying day taking up with a cow!"

The causes of Annie's preference for the society of Brownie to that of auntie might have been tolerably clear to an onlooker. For to Annie and her needs there was in Brownie's large, mild eyes and her hairy, featureless face, which was all nose and no nose, more of the divine than in the human form of auntie Meg. And there was something of an indignation quite human in the way the cow tossed her head and neck toward the woman that darkened the door, as if warning her off her premises.

Without a word of reply, Annie rose, flung her arms around Brownie's head, kissed the white star on her forehead, disengaged herself from the grass, and got out of the manger. Auntie seized her hand with a rough but not altogether ungentle action, and led her away to the house.

The stones felt very hot to her little bare feet.

– Three –

Final Thoughts

By this time the funeral was approaching the churchyard. It stopped at the gate of the yard, and from there it was the hands of friends and neighbours, not undertakers or hired helpers, that bore the dead man to his grave. When the body had been settled into its final place of decay, the last rite to be observed was the silent uncovering of the head, as a last token of respect and farewell.

Before the grave was quite filled the company had nearly gone. Thomas Crann, the stonemason, and George Macwha, the carpenter, alone remained behind, for they had some charge over the arrangements and were now taking a share in covering the grave. At length the last sod was laid upon the mound and stamped into its place, where soon the earth's broken surface would heal, as society would flow together again, closing over the place that had known the departed and would know him no more. Then Thomas and George sat down opposite each other, on two neighbouring tombstones, and wiping their brows, each gave a sigh of relief, for the sun was hot.

"Tis a weary world," said George.

"What right hae ye to say it, George?" answered Thomas. "Ye've never fought wi' it, never held the sword o' the Lord. And so, when the bridegroom comes, ye'll be ill-off for a light."

"Hoot, man! Dinna speak such things in the very churchyard."

"Better hear them in the churchyard than at the closed door, George!"

"Well," rejoined Macwha, anxious to turn the current of the conversation, "just tell me honestly, Thomas Crann, do ye believe that the dead man—God be with him—"

"No praying for the dead in my hearing, George! As the tree falleth, so it shall lie."

"Well, I didna mean anything."

"That I verily believe. Ye seldom do!"

"But I just wanted to ask," resumed George, nettled at his companion's persistent discourtesy, "if ye believe that James Anderson here, honest man beneath oor feet, crumbling away—do ye believe that his honest face will one day part the mounds and come up again, jist here, in the face o' the light, the very same as it vanished when we put the lid over him? Do ye believe that, Thomas Crann?"

"No, no, George, man. Ye know little about what ye're saying. It'll be a glorified body he'll rise wi'. Tis sown in dishonour and raised in glory. Hoot! Ye *are* ignorant, man!"

Macwha got more nettled still at his tone of superiority.

"Would it be a glorified wooden leg he'd raise with if he had been buried wi' one?" he asked.

"His own leg would be buried somewhere."

"Ow, ay! No doubt. And it would come hopping over the Pacific or the Atlantic to join its original stump, would it? But supposing the man had been born *without* a leg—eh, Thomas?"

"George! George!" said Thomas with great solemnity, "look after yer own soul and the Lord'll look after yer body—legs and all. Man, ye're not converted, so how can ye understand the things o' the spirit? Aye, jeering and jeering!"

"Well, well, Thomas," rejoined Macwha, mollified in perceiving that he had not altogether gotten the worst in the tilt of words, "I would only take the liberty o' thinking that when he was aboot it, the Almighty might as well make a new body altogether as go patching up the old one. So I'll just be making my way home now."

"Mind yer immortal part, George," said Thomas with a final thrust, as he likewise rose to go home with him on the box of the hearse.

"If the Lord takes such good care o' the body, Thomas," retorted Macwha with less irreverence than appeared in his words, "maybe he wouldna object to give a look to my poor soul as weel. For they say it's worth more. I wish he would, for he kens better than me hoo to set aboot the job."

So saying, he strode briskly over the graves and out of the churchyard, leaving Thomas to follow as fast as suited his unwieldy strength.

— Four —

A Conversation

Meantime, another conversation was going on in one of the gigs as it bore two of the company from the place of the tombs. One of the two was a cousin of the deceased. His name was no less than Robert Bruce. The other was called Andrew Constable and was a worthy elder of the kirk.

"Well, Robert," began the latter, after they had gone on in silence for half a mile or so, "what's to be done with little Annie Anderson and her auntie Meg, now that the good man's gone home and left them here?"

"They can't have much left after the doctor and all's settled for."

"I'm sure you're right there. It's long since he was able to do a day's work."

"James Dow looked well after the farm, though."

"No doubt. He's a good servant. But there can't be much money left."

A pause followed.

"What do you think, Andrew?" recommenced Bruce. "You're well known as an honest and level-headed man. Do you think that folk would expect anything of me if the worst came to the worst?"

"Well, Robert, I don't think there's much good in looking to what folk might or might not expect of you."

"That's just what I was thinking myself. For you see, I have my own family and a hard enough time already."

"No doubt, no doubt. But—"

"Ay, ay, I know what you would say. I mustn't altogether disregard what folk might think because of my shop. If I once got—not to say a bad name—but just the wind of not being so considerate as I might have been, there's no saying but that folk might start walking on past my door and across to Jamie Mitchell's yonder."

"Do what's right, Robert Bruce."

"But a body must take care of his own, otherwise who's to do it?"

"Well," rejoined Andrew with a smile, for he understood Bruce well enough, although he pretended to have mistaken his meaning, "then if the bairnie falls to you, no doubt you must take charge of her."

"I didn't mean James Anderson's bairns—I mean my own."

"Robert, whatever way you decide, I hope it may be such a decision that will allow you to cast your care upon *Him*."

"I know all about that, Andrew. But my opinion on that text is just this—that every vessel has to hold what fills it by itself, and what runs over may be committed to Him, for you can hold it no longer. Them that won't take care of what they have will be destroyed. It's a lazy, thoughtless way to be going to the Almighty with every little thing. You know the story about my namesake and the spider?"

"Ay, well enough," answered Andrew.

But he did not proceed to remark that he could see no connection between that story and the subject in hand. Bruce's question did not take him by surprise. It was well understood that he was in the habit of making all possible references to his great namesake of ancient Scotland. Indeed, he wished everybody to think, though he seldom ventured to assert it plainly, that he was lineally descended from the king. * Nor did Andrew make further remark of any sort with regard to the fate of Annie or the duty of Bruce. He saw that his companion wanted no advice—only some talk and possibly some sympathy as to what the world might think of him.

But with this perplexity Andrew could accord Bruce very little sympathy indeed. He did not care to buttress a reputation quite undermined by widely reported acts of petty meanness and selfishness. Andrew knew well that it would be a bad day for poor Annie if she came under Bruce's roof, and he therefore silently hoped that auntie Meg might find some way of managing without having to part with the child. For he knew too that, though her aunt was fierce and hard, she had yet a warm spot somewhere about her heart.

---

* *Robert Bruce, or "Robert the Bruce"— Robert I King of Scots, 1306-1329.—MP*

Margaret Anderson had known perfectly well for some time that she and Annie must part before long. The lease of the farm would expire at the close of the autumn of next year. And as it had been rather a losing affair for some time, she had no desire to request a renewal. When her brother's debts were paid, there would not remain, even after the sale of the livestock, more than a hundred and fifty pounds. For herself, she planned to take a job as a maid—which would hurt her pride more than it would alter her position in the world, for her hands were used to doing more of the labour than those of the maid who had assisted her on the farm. But what was to become of Annie she could not yet see.

Meantime there remained for the child just a year more of the native farm, with all the varieties of life which had been so dear to her. Auntie Meg made sure she prepared her for the coming change. But it seemed to Annie so long in coming that it never would come. While the year lasted she gave herself up to the childish pleasures of the place without thinking of their approaching loss.

And why should Annie think of the future when the present was full of such delights? If she did not receive much tenderness from auntie, at least she was not afraid of her. The pungency of her temper acted as salt and vinegar to bring out the true flavour of the other numberless pleasures around her. Were her excursions far afield, perched aloft on Dowie's shoulder, any less delightful that auntie was scolding at home? And if she was late for one of her meals and auntie declared she should have to fast, there still remained rosy-faced Betty who connived to bring the child the best of everything that was at hand, and put cream in her milk and butter on her oatcake. And Brownie was always friendly, ever ready for a serious emergency, when auntie's temper was less placid than usual, to yield a corner of her stall as a refuge for the child. And the cocks and hens, and even the peacock and turkey, knew her perfectly and would come when she called them—if not altogether out of affection for her, at least out of hope in her bounty. And she would ride the horses to water, sitting sideways on their broad backs like a barefooted lady.

And when the morning was wet, and the sound of the flails came to her from the barn, she would watch for the moment when her aunt's back was turned, and then scurry across the yard, like a mouse to its hole. For auntie's first impulse was always to oppose whatever

Annie desired. Once in the barn, she would bury herself like a mole in the straw, and listen to the unfailing metronome of the flails, till she fell so fast asleep as to awake only when her uncomfortable aunt dragged the unruly lassie out ignominiously by the heels. But the unruly lassie was one of the gentlest of girls, what adventurousness she had being the result of faith, and not of hardihood.

And then there were the great delights of the harvest field—soon to become great golden splendours to the memory. With the reapers she would remain from morning till night, sharing in their meals and lightening their labour with her gentle frolic. Every day after the noon meal she would go to sleep on the shady side of a stook of straw, on two or three sheaves which Dowie would lay down for her in a choice spot.

Indeed, the little mistress was very fond of sleep and would go to sleep anywhere, this habit being indeed one of her aunt's chief grounds of complaint. Before haytime, for instance, when the grass in the fields was long, if she came upon any place that took her fancy she would tumble down at once and fall asleep on it. On such occasions it was no easy task to find her in the midst of the long grass that closed over her. But in the harvest field, at least, no harm could come of this habit, for *Dooie,* as she always called him, watched over her like a mother.

The only discomfort of the harvest field was that the sharp stubble forced her to wear shoes. When the grain had all been carried home and the potatoes had been dug up and heaped in warm pits for the winter, and the mornings and evenings grew cold, then she had to put on both shoes and stockings, which she did not like at all.

So with gentle gliding through a whole winter of ice and snow, through a whole spring of promises slowly fulfilled, through a summer of glory, and another autumn of harvest joy, the day drew nearer when they must leave the farm.

And still to Annie it seemed as far off as ever.

– Five –

Robert Bruce

One lovely evening in October, the shadows were falling from the western sun and a keen little wind was just getting ready to come out the moment the sun would be out of sight. Annie, who was helping fasten up the cows for the night, drawing iron chains around their soft necks, saw a long shadow coming in at the narrow entrance of the yard. As she watched, she found that the cause of the great shadow was only a little man, none other than her father's cousin, Robert Bruce. Alas! how little a man may cast a great shadow!

He came up to Annie and addressed her in the smoothest voice he could find, fumbling at the same time in his coat pocket.

"How are you tonight, Annie? Are you well? And how's your auntie?"

He waited for no reply to any of these questions, but went on, "See what I have brought you from the shop."

So saying, he put into her hand about a half dozen sweet candies, wrapped up in a bit of paper. With this gift he left her and walked on to the open door of the house, which as a cousin he considered himself privileged to enter, unannounced even by a knock. He found the mistress in the kitchen, looking over the cooking of supper.

"How are you tonight, Margaret?" he said in a tone of conciliatory smoothness. "You're busy as usual, I see. Well, the hand of the diligent maketh rich, you know."

"That portion of the Word must be of limited application," returned Margaret. Withdrawing her hand from her cousin's, she turned again to the pot hanging over the fire. "No man would dare to say that my hand hasna been the hand of the diligent. But God kens I'm none the richer for it."

"We mustn't complain, Margaret. Right or wrong, it's the Lord's will."

"It's easy for you, Robert Bruce, with yer money in the bank, to speak that way to a poor, lonely body like me that has to work for her bread when I'm no so young as I might be. Not that I'm aboot to die o' old age either."

"I haven't so much in the bank as some folk may think, though what there is is safe enough. But I have a good business down yonder, and it might be better yet if I had more money to put into it."

"Take it oot of the bank then, Robert."

"The bank, did you say? I can't do that."

"And why not?"

"Cause I'm like the hens, Margaret. If they don't see one egg in the nest, they have no heart to lay another. I dare not meddle with the bank."

"Well, let it sit then, and lay away at yer leisure. Hoo's the mistress?"

"Not that well, and not that bad. The family's rather hard upon her. But even with all that I can't keep her out of the shop. She's like me—she would always be turning a coin. But what are you going to do yourself, Margaret?"

"I'm going to my uncle and aunt—old John Peterson and his wife. They're old and frail now and they want someone to look after them."

"Then you're well provided for. Praise be thanked, Margaret."

"Ow ay, no doubt," replied Margaret with bitterness, of which Bruce took no notice.

"And what's to come of the bairnie?" he pursued.

"I'll just have to get some decent person in the town to take her in and let her go to the school. It's time. The old folk wouldn't be able to put up with her for a week."

"And what'll that cost you, Margaret?"

"I dinna ken. But the lassie's able to pay for her own upbringing."

"It's no far that a hundred and fifty pounds will go in these times, and it would be a pity to take from the principal. She'll be marrying someday."

"Oh, indeed, maybe. Bairns will be fools."

"Well, couldn't you lend it out at five percent, and then there would be something coming from it? That would be seven pounds ten in the year, and the bairnie might almost—not easily I grant—be brought up on that."

Margaret lifted her head and looked at him.

"And who would give five percent for Annie's inheritance when he can get four and a half from the bank, on good security?"

"Just myself, Margaret. The poor orphan has nobody but you and me to look to. And I would willingly do that much for her. I'll tell you what—I'll give her five percent for her money. And for the little interest I'll take her in with my own bairns and she can live and eat and go to school with them, and then—after a while—we'll see what comes next."

To Margaret this seemed a very fair offer. It was known to all that the Bruce children were well enough dressed and looked well fed. And although Robert had the character of being somewhat mean, she did not regard that as the worst possible fault, or one likely to injure the child. So she told her cousin she would think about it, which was quite as much as he could have expected. He left all but satisfied that he had carried his point and was optimistic about his prospects.

Was it not a point worth carrying—to get both the money and the owner of it into his hands? Not that he meant conscious dishonesty to Annie. He only rejoiced to think that he would thus satisfy any expectations the public might have on him and would enjoy besides a splendid increase of capital for his business. And he was more than certain that he could keep the girl on less than the interest would come to. And then, if anything should happen to her—she had always been rather delicate—the result was worth waiting for. If she did well, he had three sons growing up, one of whom might take a fancy to the young heiress and would have the means to marry her. Grocer Robert was as deep in his foresight and scheming as King Robert of time past.

But James Dow was not pleased when he heard of the arrangement—which was completed in due time.

"I canna abide that Bruce," he said. "He wouldn't fling a bone to a dog afore he'd taken a poke at himself." He agreed, however, with his mistress that it would be better to keep Annie unaware of her destiny as long as possible. This consideration sprang from the fact that her aunt, now that she was on the eve of parting with Annie, felt a delicate growth of tenderness sprouting over the old stone wall of her affection for the child. It arose in part from the doubt as to whether Annie would be entirely comfortable in her new home.

– Six –

The Little Gray Town

A day that is fifty years off comes as certainly as if it had been in the next week, and Annie's feelings of infinite duration did not stop the sandglass of Old Time. The day arrived when everything was to be sold by public auction. A great company of friends, neighbours and acquaintances gathered and much drinking of whisky-punch went on in the kitchen, as well as in the room where, a year earlier, the solemn funeral assembly had met.

Little Annie understood what all the bustle meant. The day of desolation so long foretold by her aunt had at length actually arrived. All the things she knew so well were vanishing from her sight forever.

She was in the barn when the sound of the auctioneer's voice in the grain-yard made her look over the half door and listen. Gradually the truth dawned on her, and she burst into tears over an old rake that had just been sold, which she had been accustomed to call hers because she had always dragged it during the harvest time. Then, wiping her eyes hastily, she fled to Brownie's stall and buried herself in the manger and began crying again. After a while the fountain of tears was for the time exhausted. She sat disconsolately gazing at the old cow feeding away as if food were everything and an auction nothing at all. Soon footsteps approached the stable and, to her dismay, two men she did not know untied Brownie and actually led her away before her eyes. She continued to stare at the empty space where Brownie had stood. But how could she sit there without Brownie! She jumped up, sobbing so that she could hardly breathe, and rushed across the yard into the crowded and desecrated house, and up the stairs to her own little room. There she threw herself on the bed, buried her eyes in the pillow, and, overcome with grief, fell fast asleep.

When she awoke in the morning she remembered nothing of Betty's undressing her and putting her to bed. The day that was gone seemed only a dreadful dream. But when she went outside she found that yesterday would not stay among her dreams. Brownie's stall was empty. The horses were all gone and most of the cattle. Those that remained looked like creatures forgotten. The pigs were gone, too, and most of the poultry. Two or three favourite hens were left, which auntie was going to take with her. But of all the living creatures Annie had loved, not one had been kept for her. Her life grew bitter with the bitterness of death.

In the afternoon her aunt came up to her room where she sat in tearful silence. She told her that she was going to take her into the town and then proceeded, without further explanation, to put all her little personal effects into an old trunk which Annie called her own. Along with some trifles that lay about the room, she threw into the bottom of the box about a dozen old books which had been on the chest of drawers since long before Annie could remember. The poor child let her do as she pleased and asked no questions, for the shadow in which she stood was darkening and she did not care what came next.

For an hour the box stood on the floor like a coffin. Then Betty came, with red eyes and red nose, and carried it downstairs. Auntie came up again, dressed in her Sunday clothes. She dressed Annie in her best frock and bonnet—adorning the victim for sacrifice—and led her down to the door. There stood a horse and cart. In the cart was some straw and a sack stuffed with hay. As Annie was getting into the cart, Betty rushed out from somewhere, grabbed her up, kissed her in a vehement and disorderly manner, and before her mistress could turn round in the cart, gave her into James Dow's arms and vanished with strange sounds of choking.

Dowie thought to put her in with a kiss, for he dared not speak, but Annie's arms went round his neck and she clung to him sobbing—clung till she roused the indignation of auntie, at the first sound of whose voice Dowie was free and Annie was lying in the cart with her face buried in the straw. Dowie then mounted in front. The horse—one Annie did not know—started off gently, and Annie was borne away, helpless, to meet the unknown.

She had often been along this road before, but it had never looked as it did now. The first half mile went through fields whose crops were gone. The stubble was sticking through the grass and the potato stalks, which ought to have been gathered and burned, lay scattered about the brown earth. Then came two miles of moorland country, high, and bleak, and barren, with hillocks of peat in all directions standing beside the black holes out of which they had been dug. These holes were full of dark water, frightful to look at, while along the side of the road went deep black ditches half-full of the same dark water. There was no danger of the cart getting into them, for the ruts were too deep to let the wheels out, but it jolted so dreadfully from side to side, as it crawled along, that Annie was afraid every other moment of being tilted into one of the frightful pools. Across the waste floated now and then the cry of a bird, but other sound there was none in this land of dreariness. Next came some scattered, ragged fields, the outskirts of cultivation which seemed to draw closer and closer together while the soil grew richer and more hopeful, till after two miles more they entered the first straggling precincts of the gray market town.

By this time the stars were shining clear in the cold, frosty sky, and candles or train-oil lamps were burning in most of the houses—for this was long before gas had been heard of in those parts. A few faces were pressed close to the windowpanes as the cart passed and some rather untidy women came to their doors to look.

"That'll be little Annie Anderson," they said. "She's gaein hame to bide wi' her cousin, Robert Bruce, up in the Wast Wynd. Puir wee lassie!"

But Annie was too miserable already because of leaving her old home to care much to what new one she was going. Had it not been for the absorption of this grief, she could not have been indifferent to the prospect of going to live with her cousin, although her dislike to him had never assumed a more active form than that of wishing to get away from him as often as he came near her.

By and by the cart stopped at Bruce's shop door, whose upper half was glass, in small panes. Dowie got down and went into the shop. The house was a low one, although of two stories, built of gray stone with thatched roof. Inside each of the windows on either side of the door burned a single tallow candle, revealing to the gaze of Annie what she could not but regard as a perfect mine of treasures. For besides calico and sugar and all the varied stock in the combined trades of draper and grocer, Robert Bruce sold penny toys and halfpenny picture books and every kind of candy which had as yet been revealed to the young generations of Glamerton.

But Annie did not have long to contemplate these wonders from the outside, for Bruce came to the door and, having greeted his cousin and helped her down, turned to take Annie. Dowie was there before him, however, and now held the pale child silent in his arms. He carried her into the shop and set her down on a sack in front of the counter. Upon it Annie drearily surveyed the circumstances.

Auntie was standing in the middle of the shop. Bruce was holding the counter open and inviting her to enter.

"You'll come in and take a cup of tea after your journey, Margaret?" he said.

"No, I thank ye, Robert Bruce. James and I must jist turn and go back home again. There's much to look after yet, and we mustn't neglect our work. The house furniture's all to be picked up in the morning."

Then she turned to Annie.

"Noo Annie, lass," she said, "ye'll be a good bairn and do as ye're told. And mind ye dinna disturb things in the shop."

A smile of peculiar significance glimmered over Bruce's face at the sound of this injection. Annie made no reply but stared at Mr. Bruce.

"Good-bye to ye, Annie!" said her aunt, rousing the girl a little from her stupor.

She then gave her a kiss—the first, as far as the child knew, that she had ever given her—and went out. Bruce followed her out and Dowie came in. He took her up in his arms.

"Good-bye to ye, my bonnie bairn," he said. "Be a good lass and ye'll be taken care of. Dinna forget that. Mind ye say yer prayers."

Annie kissed him with all her heart but could not reply. He set her down again and went out. She heard the harness rattle and the cart roll off. She was left sitting on the sack.

Presently Mr. Bruce came in and, passing behind his counter, proceeded to make an entry in a book. It was a memorandum of the day and hour when Annie was put down on that very sack—so methodical was he. And yet it was some time before he seemed to awake to remembrance of the presence of the child. Looking up suddenly at the pale, weary thing as she sat with her legs hanging lifelessly down the side of the sack, he said—pretending to have forgotten her—

"Oh, bairn, are you still there?"

Going round to her he set her feet down on the floor and led her by the hand through the mysterious gate of the counter and through a door behind it. Then he called in a sharp, decided tone:

"Mother, you're wanted."

Immediately a tall, thin, anxious-looking woman appeared, wiping her hands in her apron.

"This is little Miss Anderson," said Bruce, "come to stay with us. Give her a biscuit and take her up the stairs to her bed."

As it was the first, so it was the last time he called her Miss Anderson, at least while she was one of the household. Mrs. Bruce took Annie by the hand in silence and led her up two narrow stairs into a small room with a skylight. There by the shine of the far-off stars, she undressed her. But she forgot the biscuit and, for the first time in her life, Annie went supperless to bed.

She lay for a while trying to imagine herself in Brownie's stall among the grass and clover, and so get rid of the vague fear she felt at being in a strange place without light. She did not like not knowing what was next to her in the dark. But the fate of Brownie and everything else she had loved came back upon her. The sorrow drove away the fear, and she cried till she could cry no longer, and then she slept. It is by means of sorrow sometimes that He gives his beloved sleep.

– Seven –

The Robert Bruces

The following morning Annie woke early and dressed herself. But there was no water to wash with and she crept down the stairs to look for some. Nobody, however, was awake. She looked wistfully at the back door of the house, for she longed to get outside into the fresh air. But seeing she could not open it she went back up to her room. She was as lonely as if she had anticipated the hour of the resurrection, and was the only one up of the buried millions. All that she had left of home was her box, and she would have taken herself to a desolate brooding over its contents. But it had not been brought up, and neither could she carry it up herself, nor would she open it in the kitchen where it stood. So she sat down on the side of her bed, and gazed round the cheerless room. At home she had had chequered curtains to her bed. Here there were none of any kind. Her eyes rested on nothing but bare rafters and boards. And there were holes in the roof and round the floor, which she did not like. They were not large, but they were dreadful. For they were black, nor did she know where they might go to. And she grew very cold.

At length she heard some noise in the house, and in her present mood any human noise was a sound of deliverance. It grew and was presently enriched by a mixture of baby screams and the sound of the shop shutters being taken down. At last footsteps approached her door. Mrs. Bruce entered, and finding her sitting dressed on her bed, exclaimed:

"Ow! You can dress yourself, can you?"

"Ay, well enough," answered Annie as cheerily as she could. "But," she added, "I want some water to wash myself with."

"Come down to the pump then," said Mrs. Bruce.

Annie followed her to the pump where she washed in a tub. She then ran dripping into the house for a towel, but was dried by the hands of Mrs. Bruce in her dirty apron.

By this time breakfast was nearly ready, and in a few minutes more Mrs. Bruce called Mr. Bruce from the shop and the children from the yard, and they all sat round the table in the kitchen—Mr. Bruce to his tea and oatcake and butter and Mrs. Bruce and the children to badly made oatmeal porridge and sky-blue milk. This quality of the milk was remarkable seeing that they had cows of their own. But then they sold milk. And if any customer had accused her of watering it, Mrs. Bruce's best answer would have been to show how much better what she sold was than what she retained. She put twice as much water in what she used for her own family—with the exception of the portion destined for her husband's tea.

There were three children, two boys with great jaws—the elder a little older than Annie—and a very little baby. After Mr. Bruce had prayed for the blessing of the Holy Spirit upon their food, they gobbled down their breakfasts with a variety of inarticulate noises. When they finished, the Bible was brought out, a psalm was sung, in a fashion not very extraordinary to the ears of Annie, a chapter was read—it happened to tell the story of Jacob's speculations in the money market of his day and generation. The exercise concluded with a prayer of a quarter of an hour, in which the God of Jacob was especially invoked to bless the Bruces, His servants, in their store, and to prosper the labours of that day in particular. The prayer would have been much longer but for the click of the latch of the shop door which brought it to a speedy close. And almost before the *Amen* was out of his mouth, Robert Bruce was out of the kitchen.

When he had served the early customer, he returned and, sitting down, drew Annie toward him and addressed her with great solemnity.

"Now, Annie," he said, "you'll get today to play by yourself. But you must go to school tomorrow. We can have no idle folk in this house, so we must have no words about it."

Annie was not one to make words about that or anything. She was only too glad to get away from him. Indeed, the prospect of school, after what she had seen of the economy of her home, was rather enticing. So she answered, "Very well, sir."

Seeing her so agreeable, Mr. Bruce added, in the tone of one conferring a great favour and knowing he did so,

"You can come into the shop for the day and see what's going on. When you're more of a woman you may be fit to stand behind the counter yourself—who knows?"

Robert Bruce regarded his shop as his Bannockburn where all his enemies, namely customers, were to be defeated that he might be enriched with their spoils. It was, therefore, a place of such consuming interest in his eyes that he thought it must be interesting to everybody else. Annie followed him into the shop and saw quite a fabulous wealth of good things around her. Lest she should put forth her hand and take, however, the militant eyes of Robert Bruce never ceased watching her with quick recurring glances, even when he was cajoling some customer into a doubtful purchase.

Long before the noon dinner arrived, Annie was heartily sick of the monotony of buying and selling in which she had no share. Not even a picture book was taken down from the window for her to look at. Mr. Bruce looked upon them as far below the notice of his children, although he derived a keen enjoyment from the transfer—by their allurements—of the halfpence of other children from their pockets into his till.

"Nasty trash of lies," he remarked, apparently for Annie's behalf, as he hung the fresh bait up in his window, "only fit for dirty laddies and lassies."

He stood on the watch in his shop like a great spider that ate children, and his windows were his web.

They dined at noon on salt herrings and potatoes—much better fare than bad porridge and watered milk. Robert Bruce the younger, who inherited his father's name and disposition, made faces at Annie across the table as often as he judged it prudent to run the risk of discovery. But Annie was too stupefied with the change to mind it much. Indeed, it required all the attention she could command to stop the herring bones on the way to her throat.

After dinner, business was resumed in the shop, with the resemblance of an increase in vigour, for Mrs. Bruce went behind the counter and gave her husband time to sit down at the desk to write letters and make out bills. Not that there was much of either sort of clerkship necessary, but Bruce was so fond of business that he liked to seem busier than he was. As it happened to be a half holiday, Annie was sent with the rest of the children into the garden to play.

"And mind," said Bruce, "that you keep away from the dog."

Outside, Annie soon found herself at the mercy of those who had none. It is marvellous what an amount of latent torment there is in boys, ready to come out the minute an object presents itself. It is not exactly cruelty. They are unaware, for the most part, of the suffering brought on by their actions. So children, even ordinarily good children, are ready to tease any child who simply looks teasable. Now the Bruces, as was natural, were not good children. And they despised Annie because she was a girl and because she had no self-assertion. If she had shown herself aggressively disagreeable, they would have made some attempt to conciliate her. But as it was, she became at once the object of a succession of spiteful annoyances, varying in intensity with the fluctuating invention of the two boys. At one time they satisfied themselves with making insulting grimaces at her, at another, they rose to rubbing her face with dirt, or tripping her. Their persecution bewildered her and the resulting stupor was a kind of support to her for a while. But at last she could endure it no longer, being really hurt by a fall, and ran crying into the shop, where she sobbed out,

"Please, sir, they won't let me be."

"Don't come into the shop with your stories. Make it up among yourselves."

"But they won't make it up."

Robert Bruce rose indignant at such an interruption of his high calling and strode outside with the assumption of much parental grandeur. He was instantly greeted with a torrent of assurances that Annie had fallen and then laid the blame on them. He turned sternly to her and said—

"Annie, if you tell lies, you'll go to hell."

But paternal partiality did not prevent him from addressing them with a lesson also, though of quite a different tone.

"Mind, boys," he said in a condescending tone, "that poor Annie has neither a father nor a mother, and you must be kind to her."

He then turned and left them for the more important concerns within doors. The persecution began anew, though in a somewhat mitigated form. The little wretches were perfectly able to temporarily abstain from such intense pleasure until a more suitable occasion.

Somehow the day passed, although I must not close my account of this first day without mentioning something which threatened yet more suffering.

After worship the boys crawled away to bed, half-asleep, or, I should say, only half-awake from their prayers. Annie lingered behind.

"Can't you take off your own clothes as well as put them on, Annie?" asked Mrs. Bruce.

"Ay, well enough. Only I would so like a little candle," was Annie's trembling reply, for by now she had a foreboding instinct.

"Candle! No, no child," proclaimed Mrs. Bruce. "You'll get no candle here. You would have the house in a flame around our ears. I can't afford candles. You can just feel your way up the stairs. There's thirteen steps to the first landing, and twelve to the next."

With choking heart, but without reply, Annie went.

Groping her way up the steep ascent, she found her room without difficulty. As it was again a clear, starlit night, she was able to find everything she wanted. The trouble at her heart kept her imagination from being as active as it would otherwise have been, in recalling the terrible stories of ghosts and dead people with which she was far too familiar. She soon got into bed, and, as a precautionary measure, buried her head under the blankets before she began to say her prayers, which, under the circumstances, she had thought she might be excused for leaving till she had lain down. But her prayers were suddenly interrupted by a terrible noise of scrambling and scratching and scampering in the very room beside her.

The child's fear of rats amounted to a frenzied horror. She dared not move a finger. To get out of bed with those creatures running about the room was as impossible as it was for her to cry out. But Annie's heart did what her frozen tongue could not do—it cried out with a great and bitter cry to one who was more ready to hear than Robert or Nancy Bruce. And what her heart cried was this:

"O God, take care o' me frae the rats."

There was no need to send an angel from heaven in answer to this little one's prayer—the cat would do. Annie heard a scratch and a mew at the door. The rats made one frantic scramble and were still.

"It's pussy!" she cried, recovering in joy the voice that had failed her for fear.

Fortified by her arrival and still more by the feeling that it was a divine messenger sent in answer to her prayer, Annie sprang out of bed, darted across the room, and opened the door to let her in. A few minutes more and Annie was fast asleep, guarded by God's angel, the cat. Ever after she took care to leave the door ajar.

There are ways of keeping the door of the mind also, ready as it is to close, ajar for the cat.

– Eight –

School

"Now, Annie, put on your bonnet and go to the school with the rest, and be a good girl."

This was the Bruce's parting address to Annie before he left the kitchen for the shop, after breakfast and worship had been duly observed. Having just risen from his knees, his voice, as he stooped over the child, retained all the sanctity of its last occupation. It was quarter to ten o'clock and the school was some five minutes distant.

With a flutter of fearful hope Annie obeyed. She ran upstairs, made herself as tidy as she could, smoothed her hair, put on her bonnet, and was waiting at the door when her companions joined her. It was very exciting to look forward to something that might not be disagreeable.

As they went, the boys got one on each side of her in a rather sociable manner. They had gone half the distance and not a word had been spoken when Robert Bruce junior opened the conversation abruptly.

"You'll get it!" he said as if he had been brooding upon the fact for some time and now it had broken out.

"What'll I get?" asked Annie timidly, for his tone had already filled her with apprehension.

"Such lickin's," he answered with apparent relish at the thought. "Won't she, Johnnie?"

"Ay, will she," answered Johnnie, following his leader with confidence.

Annie's heart sank within her. The poor little heart was used to sinking now. But she said nothing, resolved—if possible—to avoid all occasions for "getting it."

Not another word was spoken before they reached the school, the door of which was not yet open. A good many boys and girls were assembled, waiting for the master, filling the street with the musical sound of children's voices fluctuating through a very comprehensive scale. None of them took any notice of Annie, so she was left to study the outside of the school. It was a long, low, thatched building, of one story and a garret, with five windows toward the street and some behind. It had been a weaving-shop originally, full of hand-looms, when the trade in linen was more prosperous than it was now. From the thatch some of the night's frost was dripping in slow, clear drops.

Suddenly a small boy cried out: "The master's coming!" and instantly the noise sank to a low murmur.

Looking up the street, Annie saw the figure of the descending dominie. He was dressed in what seemed to be black but was in reality dark gray. He came down the hill of the street swinging his arms and walking at a rapid pace. With the door key in his hand already pointing toward the key hole, he went through the little crowd, which cleared a wide path for him, without word or gesture of greeting on either side. In he strode, followed at the heels by the troop of boys, big and little, and lastly by the girls—and the last of all, a short distance, by Annie, like a motherless lamb that followed the flock because she did not know what else to do. She found she had to go down a step into a sunken passage and then up another step, through a door on the left and into the school. There she saw a double row of desks, with a clear space down the middle between the rows. Each scholar was hurrying to his place at one of the desks, where each then stood.

Murdoch Malison already stood in solemn posture at the front of the class, prepared to commence the extempore prayer, which was printed in a kind of blotted stereotype upon every one of their brains. Annie had barely succeeded in reaching a vacant place among the girls when he began. The boys were silent as death while the master prayed, but a spectator might easily have discovered that the chief good some of them got from the ceremony was a perfect command of the organs of sound. But their restraint was limited to those organs. Projected tongues, deprived of their natural exercise, turned themselves into the means of telegraphic dispatches to all parts of the room throughout the ceremony, along with winking eyes, contorted features, and a wild use of hands. The master, afraid of being himself detected in the attempt to combine prayer and vision, kept his eyelids tight and played the spy with his ears alone. The boys and girls, understanding the source of their security perfectly, believed that the eyelids of the master would keep faith with them, and so sported themselves without fear in the delights of their dumb show.

As soon as the prayer was over, they dropped with noise and bustle into their seats. But presently Annie was rudely pushed out of her seat by a girl who, arriving late, had stood outside the door till the prayer was over and then entered unnoticed during the subsequent confusion. Some little ones on the opposite side, however, liking the look of her, made room beside them. The desks were double, so that the two rows at each desk faced each other.

"Bible class, come up," were the first words of the master ringing through the room and resounding in Annie's ears.

A moment of chaos followed during which all the boys and girls considered capable of reading the Bible arranged themselves in one great crescent across the room in front of the master's desk. Each read a verse—neither more nor less—often leaving half of a sentence to be taken up by another, thus perverting what was intended as a help to find the truth into a means of hiding it—a process constantly repeated, and with far more serious results, when the words of truth fall, not into the hands of the incapable, but under the protection of the ambitious.

Not knowing what to do, Annie had not dared to stand up with the class. A few moments after it was dismissed, she felt herself overshadowed by an awful presence, and looking up she saw the face of the master bending down over her. He proceeded to question her, but for some time she was too frightened to give a rational account of her learning, the best of which was certainly not of a kind to be appreciated by the master even if she had understood it enough to set before him. For, besides her aunt, who had taught her to read, and nothing more, her only instructors had been Nature, with her whole staff, including the sun, moon, and wind, the grass, the corn, Brownie the cow, and her own faithful subject, Dowie.

Thus she was put into the spelling book, which excluded her from the Bible class. She was also condemned to copy with an uncut quill, over and over again, a single straight stroke. Dreadfully dreary she found it, and over it she fell fast asleep. Her head dropped on her outstretched arm and the quill dropped from her sleeping fingers. But she was soon roused by the voice of the master. "Ann Anderson!" it called in a burst of thunder, and she awoke to shame and confusion, amidst the titters of those around her.

Before the morning was over she was called up, along with some children considerably younger than herself, to read and spell. The master stood before them, armed with a long, thick strap of horsehide, prepared by steeping in brine, black and supple with constant use, and cut into fingers at one end, which had been hardened in the fire.

Now there was a little pale-faced, delicate-looking boy in the class who blundered a good deal. Every time he did so the cruel serpent of leather went at him, coiling round his legs with a sudden, hissing swash. This made him cry and his tears blinded him so that he could not even see the words which he had been unable to read before. He still attempted to go on, and still the instrument of torture went at his thin little legs, raising upon them plentiful blue welts, to be revealed when he was undressed for the night to the indignant eyes of pitying mother or aunt, who would yet send him back to the school the next morning without fail.

At length either the heart of the master was touched by the sight of his sufferings and repressed weeping, or he saw that he was demanding the impossible, for he staid execution and passed on to the next, who was Annie.

It was no wonder after such an introduction to the ways of school that the trembling child, who could read tolerably well, should fail utterly in making anything like coherence of the sentence before her. Had she been left to herself, she would have taken the little boy in her arms and cried with him. As it was, she struggled mightily with her tears but did not read to much better purpose than the poor boy who was still busy wiping his eyes with his sleeve. But being a newcomer as well as a girl, and her long dress ill-suited to this kind of incentive to learning, she escaped for the time.

That first day at school was a dreadful experience of life. Well might the children have prayed with David—"Let us fall into the hands of the Lord, for his mercies are great, and not into the hands of men."

At one o'clock they were dismissed and went home to dinner, to return at three.

In the afternoon Annie was made to write figures on a slate. She wrote till her back ached. The monotony was relieved only by the execution of criminal law upon various offending boys, for the master was a hard man with a severe, if not an altogether cruel, temper and a savage sense of duty. The punishment was mostly in the form of blows delivered with varying force, but generally with the full swing of the *tawse*, as it was called, thrown over the master's shoulder and brought down with the whole strength of his powerful right arm on the outstretched hand of the culprit. There were other modes of punishment, of which the restraints of art would forbid the description, even if it were possible for any writer to conquer his disgust so far as to attempt it.

Annie shivered and quaked. Once she burst out crying but managed to choke her sobs, even if she could not hide her tears.

A fine-looking boy, three or four years older than herself, whose open countenance was set off by masses of dark brown hair, was called up to receive chastisement, merited or unmerited, as the case might be. The master was fond of justice, and justice according to him consisted of vengeance. He did not want to punish the innocent, it is true, but I doubt whether the discovery of a boy's innocence was not occasionally a disappointment to him.

Without a word of defence the boy held out his hand with his arm at full length, received four stinging blows upon it, grew very red in the face, and returned to his seat with the suffering hand sent into retirement in his pocket. Annie's admiration of his courage caused her to make up her mind to bear more patiently the persecution of the little Bruces. And if ever her turn should come to be punished—as no doubt it would whether she deserved it or not—she resolved to take the whipping as she had seen Alec Forbes take it.

At five the school was dismissed for the day, but not without another prayer. A succession of jubilant shouts arose as the boys rushed out into the street. Every day to them was a cycle of strife, suffering, and deliverance. Birth and death, with the life struggle between, were shadowed out in it—with this difference, that the God of a corrupt Calvinism in the person of Murdoch Malison ruled that world, and not the God revealed in the man Christ Jesus. Most of them, having felt the day more or less a burden, were now going home to heaven for the night.

Annie, having no home, was among the few exceptions. Dispirited and hopeless—a terrible condition for a child—she wondered how Alec Forbes could be so merry. She had but one comfort left, that no one would prevent her from creeping up to her own desolate garret, which was now the dreary substitute for Brownie's stall. There the persecuting boys were not likely to follow her. And if the rats were in the garret, so was the cat—or at least the cat knew the way to it. There she might think in peace about some things she had never had to think about before.

– Nine –

A New Friend

Thus at home, if home it could be called, and at school, Annie's days passed—as most days pass.

She became interested in what she had to learn, if not from the manner in which it was presented to her, yet from the fact that she had to learn it. Happily or unhappily she began to get used to the sight of the penal suffering of her schoolfellows. Nothing of the kind had yet come upon her, for it would have been hard even for one more savage than Mr. Malison to punish the nervous, delicate, anxious little orphan who was so diligent and quiet as a mouse. She had a scared look, too, that may have moved the heart of Malison if he had ever been inclined to pay the least attention to the looks of children.

The loss of human companionship, the loss of green fields and of country sounds and smells, and a constant sense of oppression, were quickly working sad effects on her. The little colour she had slowly died out of her cheek. Her face grew thin and her blue eyes looked wistful and large. Not often were tears to be seen in them now, and yet they looked well acquainted with tears—like fountains that had been full yesterday. She never smiled, for there was nothing to make her smile.

But she gained one thing by this desolation. The thought of her dead father came to her, as it had never come before, and she began to love him with an intensity she had known nothing of till now. Her mother had died at her birth and she had been her father's treasure. But in the last period of his illness she had seen less of him, and the blank left by his death had, therefore, come upon her gradually. Before she knew what death was, she had begun to forget. In the minds of children the grass grows very quickly over their buried dead. But now she learned what death meant, or rather what love had been. It was not, however, an added grief. It comforted her to remember how her father had loved her. And she said her prayers oftener because they seemed to go somewhere near the place where her father was. She did not think of her father being where God was, but of God being where her father was.

The winter was drawing nearer, too, and the days were now short and cold. A watery time began, and for many days in a row the rain kept falling without interruption. I almost think Annie would have died without her dead father to think about. On one of those rainy days, however, she began to find that it is in the nature of good things to come about in odd ways. It had rained the whole day, not tamely in a drizzle but in real earnest—dancing and rebounding from the pools. Now and then the school became silent, just to listen to the wide noise made by the busy cataract of the heavens, each drop a messenger of good, a sweet returning of earth's aspirations, in the form of Heaven's *Amen!* But the boys thought only of the fun of dabbling in the torrents as they went home or the delights of fishing in the swollen and muddy rivers.

The afternoon was waning. It was nearly time to go, and still the rain was pouring. In the gathering gloom there had been more than the usual amount of wandering from one part of the school to another, and the elder Bruce had stolen toward a group of little boys, next to which Annie sat with her back toward them. If it was not the real object of his expedition, at least he took the opportunity to give Annie a spiteful dig with his elbow which forced from her an involuntary cry.

Now the master occasionally indulged in throwing his *tawse* at the offender, not so much for the sake of hurting—though that happened as well—as of humiliating, for the culprit had to bear the instrument of torture back to the hands of the executioner. He threw the tawse at Annie, half, let us suppose, in thoughtless cruelty, half in evil jest.

It struck her sharply, even before she had recovered her breath after the blow Bruce had given her. In pain and terror she stood, pale as death, and staggered up to the master, carrying the whip with something of the horror she would have felt had it been a snake. With a grim smile he sent her back to her seat. The moment she reached it her self-control gave way and she burst into despairing, silent tears. The desk was still shaking with her sobs, and some of the girls were still laughing at her grief as the master dismissed his pupils.

There could be no better fun for most of the boys and some of the girls than to wade through the dirty water running between the schoolhouse and the street. Many of them dashed through it at once, shoes and all. But as it was too wide to cross in a single bound, some of the boys and almost all the girls took off their shoes and stockings and carried them across the steadily rising rivulet. But the writhing and splashing water looked so ugly that Annie shrank from fording it. She was still standing looking at it in perplexity and dismay, with the forgotten tears still creeping down her cheeks, when she was suddenly caught up from behind by a boy who was carrying his shoes in his other hand.

She glanced timidly around to see who it was, and the brave, brown eyes of Alec Forbes met hers, lighted by a kind, pitying smile. In that smile the cloudy sky of the universe gently opened and the face of God looked out upon Annie. It gave her, for that brief moment, all that she had been dying for lack of for weeks—weeks that seemed as long as years. She could not help it—she threw her arms round Alec Forbes's neck and sobbed as if her heart would break. She did not care about the Bruces or the rats or even the schoolmaster now.

Alec clasped her tighter and vowed in his heart that if ever that brute Malison lifted his hand toward her again, he would fly at his throat. He would have carried her farther, but as soon as they were onto the street, Annie begged him to set her down and he complied. Then bidding her good night, he turned and ran home barefoot through the flooding town.

The two Bruces had gone on ahead with the two umbrellas, one of which Annie had shared in coming to school. She was very wet before she got home. But no notice was taken of the condition she was in, the consequence of which was a severe cold and cough, which, however, were not regarded as obstacles to her going to school the next day.

That night she lay awake for a long time, and when at last she fell asleep, she dreamed she took Alec Forbes home to see her father—out the street and the long road, over the black moor, and through the fields, in at the door of the house, and up the stair to her father's room, where he lay in bed. She told him how kind Alec had been to her and how happy she was going to be now. And her father had put his hand out of the bed and laid it on Alec's head, and said: "Thank ye, Alec, for being kind to my poor Annie." And then she cried, and woke crying—strange tears out of dreamland, half of sorrow and half of joy.

With what changed feelings she seated herself in school the next day. After the prayer, she glanced around to catch a glimpse of her new friend. There he was, radiant as usual. He took no notice of her and she had not expected he would. But now that he had befriended her, it was not long before he found out that her cousins were by no means friendly to her and took every sheltered opportunity of giving her a pinch or a shove, or making grimaces at her.

In the afternoon, while she was busy over an unusually obstinate addition sum, Robert came up stealthily behind her, licked his finger, watched for his opportunity, and then rubbed the answer from her slate. The same moment he received a box on the ear, which no doubt filled his head with more noises than that of the impact. He yelled with rage and pain and, catching sight of the administrator of justice as he was returning to his seat, bawled out in a tone of fierce contempt: "Sanny Forbes!"

"Alexander Forbes! Come up," resounded the voice of the master. Forbes, not being a first-rate scholar, was not a favourite with him, for Mr. Malison had no sense for what was fine in character or disposition. Had the name reaching his ears been that of one of his better Latin scholars, Bruce's cry would most likely have passed unheeded.

"Hold up your hand," he said without requesting or waiting for an explanation.

Alec obeyed. Annie gave a smothered shriek and, tumbling from her seat, rushed up to the master. When she found herself face to face with the tyrant, however, she could not speak a single word. She opened her mouth but throat and tongue refused to comply with their offices and she stood gasping. The master stared, his arm arrested in the act to strike, and his face turned over his left shoulder. All the blackness of his anger at Forbes he was now lowering upon Annie.

He stood thus for one awful moment. Then, motioning her aside with a sweep of his head, he brought down the tawse on Alec's hand.

Annie gave a choking cry, and Alec, so violent was the pain, involuntarily withdrew his hand. But instantly ashamed of his weakness, he presented it again and received the remainder of his punishment without flinching. The master then turned to Annie. Finding her still speechless he gave her a push and said,

"Go to your seat, Ann Anderson. The next time you do that I will punish you severely."

Annie sat down and neither sobbed nor cried. But it was days before she recovered from the shock.

– Ten –

A Visit from Auntie

For some time neither of the young Bruces ventured even to make a wry face at her at school. But their behaviour to her at home was only so much the worse.

Two days after the rainstorm, as Annie was leaving the kitchen after worship to go up to bed, Mr. Bruce called her.

"Annie Anderson," he said, "I want to speak to you."

Annie turned, trembling.

"I see you know what it's about," he went on, staring full in her pale face. "You can't even look me in the eye. Where are the sugar candies? I know well enough where they are, and so do you."

"I know nothing about them," answered Annie with a sudden revival of energy.

"Don't lie, Annie. It's enough to steal, without lying."

"I'm not lying," she answered, starting to cry. "Who said I took the candies?"

"That's not the point. You wouldn't cry that way if you were innocent. I never missed anything before. And you know well enough there's an eye that sees all things, and you can't hide from it."

Bruce could hardly have intended that it was by inspiration from on high that he had discovered the thief of his sweets. But he thought it better to avoid mentioning that the informer was his own son. Johnnie, on his part, had thought it better not to mention that he had been incited to the act by his brother Robert. And Robert had thought it better not to mention that he did so partly to shield himself, and partly out of revenge for the box on the ear which Alec Forbes had given him. The information had been yielded to the inquisition of the parent who said with truth that he had never missed anything before. I suspect, however, that a course of petty and cautious pilfering at length passed the narrow bounds within which it could be concealed from the keen eyes of the boys' father.

"I don't want to hide from it!" cried Annie. "God knows," she went on in desperation, "I wouldn't touch a grain of salt without permission."

"It's a pity, Annie, that some folk don't get their share of Mr. Malison's discipline. I don't want to lick you myself because you're other folk's bairn. But I can hardly hold my hand off you."

It must not be supposed from this statement that Robert Bruce ever ventured to lay hands on his own children. He was too much afraid of their mother, who, perfectly submissive ordinarily, would have flown into the rage of a hen with chicks if even her own husband had dared to chastise one of *her* children. The shop might be more Robert's than hers, but the children were more hers than Robert's.

Overcome with shame and righteous anger, Annie burst out in the midst of fresh tears.

"I wish Auntie would come and take me away! It's an ill house to be in."

These words had a visible effect upon Bruce. He expected a visit from Margaret Anderson within a day or two, and he did not know what the effect of whatever stories Annie might tell would be. The use of Annie's money had not been secured to him for any lengthened period. Dowie, anxious to take all precautions for his little mistress, consulted a friendly lawyer on the subject to make sure Annie should not be left defenceless in the hands of a man of whose moral qualities Dowie had no exalted opinion. The sale at the farm had turned out better than expected and the sum committed to Bruce was two hundred pounds, to lose which now seemed to him nothing short of ruin. Not doubting Annie to be the guilty person, he thought it better to count the few pieces of candy he might lose as additional interest and not quarrel with his creditor for extorting it. So with the weak cunning of his kind he went to the shop, brought back a bit of sugar candy about the size of a pigeon's egg, and said to the still-weeping child,

"Don't cry, Annie. I can't stand to see you crying. If you want a bit of candy any time, just tell me and don't help yourself. That's all. Here."

He thrust the lump into Annie's hand, but she dropped it on the floor and rushed upstairs to her bed as fast as the darkness would let her. In spite of her indignation she was soon sound asleep.

Bruce searched for the rejected candy until he found it. He then restored it to the drawer he had taken it from and resolved to be more careful in the future of offending little Annie Anderson.

When the Saturday arrived upon which he expected Margaret's visit, Bruce was on the watch the whole afternoon. From his shop door he could see all along the street and a good way beyond it. Being very quick sighted, he recognized Margaret when she was yet a great distance away as she sat in an approaching cart.

"Annie!" he called, opening the inner door as he returned behind the counter.

Annie, who was upstairs in her own room, immediately appeared.

"Annie," he said, "run out at the back door and through the yard and over to Laurie Lumley's and tell him to come over to see me directly. Don't come back without him. That's a good child!"

He sent her off with this message, knowing well enough that the man had gone to the country that day and there was no one at his house who was likely to know where he had gone. He hoped that Annie would go and look for him in town and so be gone during her aunt's visit.

"Well, Margaret," he said with his customary greeting, in which the foreign oil sought to overcome the home-bred vinegar, "how are you today?"

"Oh, not that bad," answered Margaret with a sigh.

"And how's Mr. and Mistress Peterson?"

"Brawly. How's Annie coming on?"

"Not that bad. She's still some riotous."

He thought to please her with the remark because she had been in the habit of saying the same thing herself. But distance had made Annie dearer and her aunt's nose took fire with indignation as she replied:

"The lassie's well-mannered enough. *I* saw nothing of the sort aboot her. If ye canna guide her, that's *yer* fault!"

Bruce was abashed, but not confounded. He was ready in a moment.

"I never knew any good to come of being too hard on children," he said. "She's as easy to guide as a cow going home at night, only you must just let her know that you're there, you know."

"Ow, ay," said Margaret, a little bewildered in her turn.

"Would you like to see her?"

"What else did I come for?"

"Well, I'll go and look for her."

He went to the back door and called aloud, "Annie, your auntie's here and wants to see you."

"She'll be here in a minute," he said to Margaret as he re-entered the shop.

After a little more random conversation, he pretended to be surprised that Annie did not make her appearance, and went once more to the door and called her name several times. He then pretended to search for her in the yard and all over the house and returned with the news that she was nowhere to be seen.

"She's afraid that you're come to take her with you and she's run away somewhere. I'll send the laddies to look for her."

"No, no, never mind. If she doesn't want to see me, I'm sure I don't need to see her. I'll be off to the town," said Margaret, her face growing red as she spoke.

She bustled out of the shop, too angry with Annie to say farewell to Bruce. She had not gone far, however, before Annie came running out of a narrow alley, almost into her aunt's arms. But there was no refuge for her there.

"Ye little limmer!" cried Margaret, seizing her by the shoulder, "what made ye run away? I dinna want ye, ye brat!"

"I didn't run away, auntie."

"Robert Bruce called ye to come in himself."

"It was him that sent me to Laurie Lumley's to tell him to come to the shop."

Margaret could not make heads or tails of it. But as Annie had never told her a lie, she could not doubt her. So taking time to think about it, she gave her some rough advice and a smooth penny and went away on her errands. She was not long in coming to the conclusion that Bruce wanted to part her and the child, and this offended her so much that she did not go near the shop for a long time. Thus Annie was forsaken and Bruce had what he wanted.

He needed not have been so full of scheming. Annie never said a word to her aunt about their treatment of her. It is one of the marvels in the constitution of children how much they can bear without complaining. Parents have no right to suppose all is well in the nursery or schoolroom merely from the fact that the children do not complain. Servants and tutors may be cruel, and children will be silent—partly, I presume, because they forget so soon.

But vengeance of a sort soon overtook Robert Bruce the younger. For the evil spirit in him—derived from no such remote ancestor as the king—would not allow him a long respite from evil-doing, even in school. He knew Annie better than his father did, that she was not likely to complain of anything, and that the only danger lay in the chance of being discovered in the deed.

One day when the master had left the room to confer with some visitor at the door, he saw Annie stooped down tying her shoe. Perceiving, he thought, that Alec Forbes was looking the other direction, he gave Annie a strong push from behind. She fell on her face in the middle of the floor. But Alec caught sight of the deed and was down upon him in a moment. Having already proved that a box on the ear was of no lasting effect, Alec gave him a downright good thrashing. He howled vigorously, partly from pain, partly in the hope that the same consequences as before would overtake Forbes. He was still howling when Mr. Malison re-entered.

"Robert Bruce, come up," he bawled the moment he opened the door.

And Robert Bruce went up and, notwithstanding his protests, received a second and more painful punishment from the master. For him there was no fixed principle as to the party on whom the punishment should fall. Punishment, in his eyes, was enough in itself. He was not capable of seeing that punishment falling on the wrong person was not *punishment* at all, but only *suffering*.

If Bruce howled before, he howled ten times worse now and went home howling. Annie was sorry for him and tried to say a word of comfort to him, but he repelled her advances with hatred and blows. As soon as he reached the shop, he told his father that Forbes had beaten him without his having said a word to him, which was as correct as it was untrue, and that the master had taken Forbes's part and had licked him soundly, an assertion of which there was proof enough on his body. Robert the elder was instantly filled with smouldering wrath, and from that moment he hated Alec Forbes. For like many others of low nature, he had yet some animal affection for his children, combined with an endless amount of partisanship on their behalf. Indeed, for nothing in the world but money would he have sacrificed what seemed to him their interests.

A man must learn to love his children, not because they are his, but because they are *children,* otherwise his love will scarcely be a better thing in the end than the party spirit of the faithful politician.

– Eleven –

The Shorter Catechism

In her innermost heart Annie now dedicated herself to the service of Alec Forbes. Nor was it long before she had an opportunity to help him.

One Saturday the master made his appearance in black instead of white stockings, which was regarded by the scholars as a bad omen. And fully were their prognostications justified. The joy of the half-holiday for Scots boys and girls has a terrible weight laid on the opposite scale—I mean the other half of the day. This weight, which brings the day pretty much on a level with all other days, consists in a free use of the Shorter Catechism. This, of course, made them hate the Catechism, though I am not aware that that was of any great consequence, or much to be regretted.

For my part, I wish the spiritual engineers who constructed it had, after laying the grandest foundation-stone that truth could afford them, glorified God by going no further. Certainly many a man would have enjoyed him sooner, if it had not been for their work. But, alas! the Catechism was not enough. The tormentors of youth had gone further, and provided what they called Scripture proofs of the various assertions of the Catechism—a support of which it stood greatly in need. Alas! I say, for the boys and girls who had to learn these proofs, called texts of Scripture, but too frequently only morsels torn bleeding and shapeless from "the lovely form of the Virgin Truth!" For these tasks, combined with the pains and penalties which accompanied failure, taught them to dislike the Bible as well as the Catechism, and that was a matter of altogether different import.

Every Saturday, then, Murdoch Malison's pupils had to learn so many questions of the Shorter Catechism, with proofs from Scripture. Whoever failed in this task was condemned to imprisonment for the remainder of the day, or, at least, till the task should be accomplished. The imprisonment was sometimes commuted for chastisement—or finished off with it, when it did not suit the convenience of the master to enforce the full term of a school day. Upon certain Saturdays, moreover, one in each month, a repetition was required of all the questions and proofs that had been, or ought to have been, learned since the last observance of the same sort.

The day in question was one of those of accumulated labour, and the only proofs Alec Forbes had succeeded in demonstrating was proof of his inability for the task. In consequence he was condemned to be kept in—a trial hard indeed for one whose chief delights were the open air and the active exertion of his growing bodily power.

Seeing his downcast expression filled Annie with such concern that she lost track of the class and did not know when her turn came until suddenly the master was standing before her in silent expectation. As he approached he had made no sound and then stood till the universal silence had at length aroused Annie's consciousness. Then with a smile on his thin lips, but a lowering thundercloud on his brow, he repeated the question:

"What doth every sin deserve?"

Annie, bewildered and burning with shame at finding herself the core of the silence, could not recall a word of the answer given in the Catechism. So in her confusion she fell back on her common sense and experience.

"What doth every sin deserve?" repeated the tyrant.

"A lickin'," whimpered Annie, her eyes filling with tears.

The master seemed much inclined to consider her condemned out of her own mouth and to give her a whipping at once, for it argued more than ignorance to answer as she had instead of *the wrath and curse of God* as plainly set down in the Scotch Targum. But reflecting, perhaps, that she was a girl, and a little one, and that although it would be more gratification to him to whip her, it might be equal suffering to her to be kept in. He therefore instead gave a side wave of his head, indicating the culprit's doom to be kept in for the afternoon. Annie took her place with the condemned with a flutter of joy in her heart that Alec Forbes would not be left without a servant to wait on him. A few more boys made up the unfortunate party, but they were younger ones and so there was no companion for Forbes, who evidently felt the added degradation of being alone. The hour arrived and the school was dismissed. The master strode out, locking the door behind him, and the defaulters were left alone to chew the bitter cud of ill-cooked Theology.

For some time there was a dreary silence in the room. Alec sat with his elbow on his desk, biting his nails. Annie sat dividing her silent attention between her book and Alec. The other boys seemed to be busy with their catechisms, in the hope of getting out as soon as the master returned. At length Alec took out his knife, and out of sheer boredom, began to whittle away at the desk in front of him. When Annie saw that, she crept across the floor and sat down at the opposite desk. Alec looked up at her, smiled, and went on with his whittling. Annie slid a little nearer and then asked him to hear her say her catechism. He consented and she repeated the lesson perfectly.

"Now let me hear you, Alec," she said.

"No, thank you, Annie. I can't say it. And I won't say it for all the teachers in creation."

"But he'll lick you, Alec, and I can't stand it," said Annie, the tears rising to her eyes.

"Well, I'll try—to please you, Annie," said Alec, seeing that the little thing was in earnest.

How her heart bounded with delight! That great boy, so strong and brave, trying to learn a lesson to please her!

But it would not work.

"I can't remember a word of it, Annie. I'm dreadful hungry besides. I was in too big a hurry with my breakfast. If I had known what was coming, I would have laid in a better stock," he added, laughing rather drearily.

As he spoke he looked up and his eyes wandered from one window to another for a few moments.

"No, it's no use," he resumed at last. "I have eaten too much to escape that way anyway."

Annie was as sad over Alec's hunger as any mother over her child's. She felt it pure injustice that he should ever be hungry. But unable to think of any way to help him, she could only say,

"I don't know what you mean, Alec."

"When I was no bigger than you I could squeeze out of a smaller hole than that," he answered, pointing to the open windowpane in an upper corner of the windows. "But I've eaten too much since then."

Annie sprang to her feet.

"If you could get through it once, I can get through it now, Alec. Just hold me up a bit. You *can* lift me, you know."

She looked at him shyly and gratefully.

"But what'll you do when you *are* out, Annie?"

"Run home and get a loaf to bring back with me."

"But Rob Bruce'll see your head between your feet before he'll give you a loaf of bread. And it's too far to run to my mother's. Murdoch would be back long before that."

"Just help me out and leave the rest to me," said Annie confidently. "If I don't fetch a loaf of white bread, never trust me again."

The idea of bread, a rarity and consequently a delicacy to Scots country boys, was too much for Alec's imagination. He jumped up and put his head out of one of the open panes to see if the coast was clear. He saw a woman approaching whom he knew.

"I say, Lizzie," he called.

The woman stopped.

"What do you want, Master Alec?"

"Just stand there and pull this lassie out. We're kept in together and nearly starving."

"The Lord preserve us! I'll go for the key."

"No, no, *we* would have to pay for that. Take her out—that's all we want."

"He's a coarse creature, that master of yours. I would go to see him hanged."

"That'll come in good time," said Alec. "But never mind Murder Malison. Just pull out the little lassie, will you?"

"Where is she?"

Alec jumped down and held Annie up to the open window, less than a foot square. He told her to put her arms through first. Then between them they got her head through, at which point Lizzie caught hold of her—the school was so low—and dragged her out and set her on her feet. But a windowpane was broken in the process.

"Now, Annie," cried Alec, "never mind the window. Run!"

She was off like a live bullet.

She scampered home prepared to encounter whatever dangers were necessary, the worst to her mind being the danger of not succeeding and thus breaking faith with Alec. She had sixpence of her own in coppers in her box. But how was she to get into the house and out again without being seen? With the utmost care she managed to get in the back door unnoticed and up to her room. In a moment more the six pennies were in her hand and she was back in the street. She ran straight for the baker's shop.

"A six-penny loaf," she panted out.

"Who wants it?" asked the baker's wife.

"There's the coins," answered Annie, laying them on the counter.

The baker's wife gave her the loaf with the biscuit, which from time immemorial had always graced a purchase in the amount of sixpence, and Annie sped back to the school like a runaway horse to his stable.

As she approached, out popped the head of Alec Forbes. He had been listening for the sound of her feet. She held up the loaf as high as she could and he stretched down as low as he could and so their hands met on the loaf.

"Thank you, Annie," said Alec. "I won't forget this. How did you get it?"

"Never mind that. I didn't steal it," answered Annie. "But how shall I get in again?" she added, suddenly waking up to that difficult necessity, looking up at the window above her head.

"I'm a predestined idiot!" said Alec with an impious allusion to the Catechism as he scratched his helpless head. "I never thought of that."

It was clearly impossible.

"You'll catch it," said one of the urchins to Annie, with his nose flattened against the window.

The roses of Annie's face turned pale, but she answered stoutly,

"Well, I care as little as the rest of you, I'm thinking."

By this time Alec had made up what was often a bullheaded mind.

"Run home, Annie," he said. "And if Murder tries to lay a finger on you Monday, *I'll* murder *him.* Faith! Run home before he comes and catches you at the window."

"No, Alec," pleaded Annie.

"Hold your tongue," interrupted Alec, "and run, will you?"

Seeing he was quite determined, Annie—though not wanting to leave him, and in terror of what was implied in the threats he uttered—obeyed him and turned to walk leisurely home, avoiding the quarters where there might be a chance of meeting her jailer.

She found that no one had observed her former visit, and the only remarks being made concerned with the disgrace of being kept in.

When Mr. Malison returned to the school about four o'clock, he found all quiet as death. The boys appeared totally absorbed in the Catechism. But to his additional surprise the girl was absent.

"Where is Ann Anderson?" he said in a condescending voice.

"Gone home!" cried two of the little prisoners.

"Gone home!" echoed the master in a tone of savage incredulity. Although not only was it plain enough that she was gone, from former experience he probably knew well enough how her escape had been made.

"Yes," said Forbes. "It was me who made her go. I put her out at the window. And I broke the window," he added, knowing it would be found out sooner or later, "but I'll get it mended on Monday."

Malison turned white as a sheet with rage. Indeed, the hopelessness of the situation had made Alec speak with too much nonchalance.

Anxious to curry favour, the third youngster called out,

"Sandy Forbes made her go and fetch him a loaf of white bread."

Of this bread, the little informer still had some of the crumbs sticking to his jacket. How corrupting is a reign of terror! The bread was eaten, and now the giver was being betrayed by the urchin in the hope of gaining a little favour with the tyrant.

"Alexander Forbes, come up."

Beyond this point I will not here carry the narrative.

Alec bore his punishment with great firmness. After he had spent his wrath, the master allowed them all to part without further reference to the Shorter Catechism.

– Twelve –

The Next Monday

The Sunday following was anything but a day of repose for Annie—she looked with such frightful anticipation to the coming Monday. Nor was the assurance with which Alec Forbes had sent her away, and which she was far from forgetting, any consolation. For in a conflict with such a power of darkness as Mr. Malison, how could Alec, even if sure to be victorious as any knight of old story, come off without injury terrible and not to be contemplated! Yet as she listened to the evening sermon, a sermon quietly and gently enforcing the fate of the ungodly, it was not with exultation at the tardy justice that would overtake such men as Murdoch Malison or Robert Bruce, nor yet with pity for their fate, that she listened, but with heart-aching fear for her friend, the noble, the generous Alec Forbes, who withstood authority, and was therefore in danger of hell-fire. About her own final doom, she was not interested enough to speculate.

The awful morning dawned. When she woke and the thought of what she had to meet came back to her, she turned sick, not metaphorically but physically. Yet breakfast time would come, and worship did not fail to follow, and then to school she must go. There all went on as usual for some time. The Bible class was called up, heard, and dismissed. Annie was beginning to hope that the whole affair was somehow or other going to pass by. She had heard nothing of Alec's fate after she had left him imprisoned, and except for a certain stoniness in his look, his face gave no sign. She dared not lift her eyes from the spelling book in front of her to look in the direction of the master. No murderer could have felt more keenly as if all the universe were one eye and that eye was fixed on him than Annie.

Suddenly the awful voice resounded through the school, and the words it uttered—though even after she heard them it seemed too terrible to be true—were,

"Ann Anderson, come up."

For a moment she lost consciousness, or at least memory. When she recovered herself she was standing before the master. His voice seemed to have left two or three unanswered questions somewhere in her head. What they were she had no idea. But presently he spoke again and, from the tone, what he said was evidently the repetition of a question—probably put more than once before.

"Did you, or did you not, go out at the window on Saturday?"

She did not see that Alec Forbes had left his seat and was slowly lessening the distance between them and him.

"Yes," she answered, trembling from head to foot.

"Did you, or did you not, bring a loaf of bread to those who were kept in?"

"Yes, sir."

"Where did you get it?"

"I bought it, sir."

"Where did you get the money?"

Every eye in the school was fixed upon her, those of her cousins sparkling with delight.

"I got it out of my own chest, sir."

"Hold up your hand."

Annie obeyed, with a most pathetic dumb terror pleading in her face.

"Don't touch her," said Alec Forbes, stepping between the executioner and his victim. "You know well enough it was all my fault. I told you so on Saturday."

Murder Malison, as the boys called him, turned with the tawse on his shoulder and answered him with a hissing blow over his head, followed by a succession of furious blows upon every part of his body as the boy twisted and writhed and doubled. At length, making no attempt to resist, he was knocked down by the storm. He lay prostrate under fierce lashes, the master holding him down with one foot.

Finally Malison stopped, exhausted, and white with rage turned toward Annie, who was almost in a fit of agony, and repeated the order:

"Hold up your hand."

But as he turned, Alec bounded to his feet, his face glowing and his eyes flashing. He scrambled round in front and sprang at the master's throat just as the tawse was descending. Malison threw him off, lifted his weapon once more and swept it with a stinging lash round his head and face. Alec, feeling that this was no occasion to regard the rules of a fair fight, lowered his head like a ram and rushed full tilt against the pit of Malison's stomach. The tall man doubled up and crashed backward into the peat fire which was glowing on the hearth. In the attempt to save himself, he thrust his right hand into it.

Alec rushed forward to drag him off the fire, but he was up before he reached him, his face concealing the pain.

"Go home!" he shouted to the scholars throughout the room, and sat down at his desk to hide his suffering.

For one brief moment there was silence. Then a tumult arose, a shouting and screeching, and the whole school rushed to the door, as if the devil had been after them to catch whoever was last through it. Strange was the uproar that invaded the ears of Glamerton—strange, that is, at eleven o'clock in the morning on Monday, the uproar of jubilant freedom.

But the culprits, Annie and Alec, stood and stared at the master, whose face was covered with one hand, while the other hung helpless at his side. Annie stopped, partly out of pity for the despot and partly because Alec stopped. Alec stopped because he was the author of the situation—at least he never could give any better reason.

At length Mr. Malison lifted his head and made a movement toward his hat. He started when he saw the two standing there. But the moment he looked at them their courage failed them.

"Run, Annie!" said Alec.

Away she bolted, and he was after her as well as he could, which was not with his usual fleetness by any means. When Annie had rounded a corner, she stopped and looked back for Alec. He was a good many paces behind her, and now she first discovered the condition of her champion.

Now that the excitement was over, he could scarcely walk. He was a mass of wales and bruises from head to foot. He put his hand on her shoulder to help steady himself and made no opposition to her accompanying him as far as the gate of his mother's garden, which was nearly a mile from the town on the farther bank of one of the rivers which watered the valley plain in which Glamerton had stood for hundreds of years. Then she went slowly home, bearing with her the memory of the smile which, in spite of pain, had illuminated his welted red cheeks as she left him.

When she got home she saw at once, from the black looks of the Bruces, that the story—whether in its true form or not—had arrived before her.

Nothing was said, however, till after worship that evening. Then Bruce gave her a long lecture on the wickedness and certain punishment of "takin' up with loons like Sanny Forbes." But he came to the conclusion, as he confided to his wife that night, that the lassie was already growing hardened. She had not shed even a single tear of remorse as a result of his lecture.

The moment Annie lay down on her bed she fell to weeping over the sufferings of Alec. She was asleep a moment after, however. If it had not been for the power of sleep in the child, she would undoubtedly have given way long before now to the hostile influences around her and died.

There was considerable excitement about the hearths of Glamerton that night from the news carried home by the children of the master's defeat. Various were the judgments elicited by the story. The religious portion of the community seemed to their children to side with the master. The worldly—namely, those who did not profess to be particularly religious—all sided with Alec Forbes, with the exception of a fish-cadger who had one son, the plague of his life.

Among the religious there was, at least, one exception too. He had no children of his own, but he had a fancy for Alec Forbes. That exception was Thomas Crann, the stonemason.

– Thirteen –

A Visit to Howglen

Thomas Crann was building a house, for he was both a contractor and a day labourer. He had arrived at the point in the process where the assistance of a carpenter was necessary. Therefore, he went to George Macwha, whom he found planing at his workbench. This bench was in a workshop with two or three more benches in it, some pine boards set up against the wall, a couple of cartwheels sent in for repairs, and the tools and materials of his trade all about. The floor was covered with shavings, or *spales* as they are called by northern consent.

After a short and gruff greeting on the part of Crann, and a more cordial reply from Macwha, who stopped his labour to attend to his visitor, they began to discuss the business at hand. Once that had been satisfactorily completed, the conversation took a more general scope, accompanied by the sounds of Macwha's busy instrument.

"A terrible laddie, that Sanny Forbes!" said the carpenter. "They say he licked the dominie and almost killed him."

"I've known worse laddies than Sanny Forbes," was Thomas's curt reply.

"Ow, indeed! I know nothing against the laddie. Him and our Willie's always together."

Thomas's sole answer was a grunt, and a silence of a few seconds followed before he spoke.

"I'm not sure that thrashing the schoolmaster is such a bad sin. He's a dour creature that Murdoch Malison wi' his fair face and smooth words. I dinna doobt that the children hae the worst of it in general. And for Alec I hae great hopes. He comes o' good stock. His father, honest man, was one o' the Lord's own. And if his mother's been some too soft on him and has given the lad too long a tether, he'll come right afore long, for he's worth looking after."

"I don't rightly understand ye, Thomas."

"I don't think the Lord'll lose the grip o' his father's son. He's not converted yet, but he's well worth converting, for there's good stuff in him."

Thomas did not consider how his common sense was running away with his theology. But Macwha was not the man to bring him to task on that score. His only reply lay in the *whishk, whashk* of his plane. Thomas resumed.

"He jist needs what ye need yerself, George Macwha."

"What's that, Thomas?" asked George, with a grim attempt at a smile, as if to say, "I know what's coming but I'm not going to mind it."

"He jist needs to be well shaken over the mouth o' the pit. He must smell the brimstone o' the everlasting burning. He's none o' yer soft boards that ye can smooth with a sweep of yer arm. He's a blue hardstone that's difficult to dress, but once dressed, it stands up against the weather. I like to work on such stone myself. None o' yer soft sandstone that ye could cut with a knife for me!"

"Well, I dare say ye're right, Thomas."

"And besides, they say he took his own licks without saying a word, and flew at the master only when he was going to lick the poor orphan lassie—James Anderson's lassie, ye ken."

"Ow, ay! Tis the same tale they all tell. I have no doubt it's correct."

"Well, let him take it then, and be thankful! For it's no more than was well spent on him."

With these conclusive words Thomas departed. He was no sooner out of the shop than out from behind the stack of deal boards standing against the wall, came Willie, the eldest hope of the house of Macwha—a dusky-skinned, black-eyed, curly-headed, roguish-looking boy, Alec Forbes's companion and occasional accomplice. He was more mischievous than Alec and sometimes led him into unseen scrapes. But whenever anything extensive had to be executed, Alec was always the leader.

"What are ye hiding for, ye rascal?" said his father. "What mischief are ye up to now?"

"Nothing," was Willie's cool reply.

"What made ye hide then?"

"Tom Crann never sets eye on me but he accuses me o' something."

"Ye get no more than ye deserve, I dinna doobt," returned George. "Here, take the chisel and cut that beading into lengths."

"I'm going over the river to ask after Alec."

"Ay, ay! there's always something!—What ails Alec now?"

"Mr. Malison's nearly killed him. He hasna been to school for two days."

With these words Willie bolted from the shop and set off at full speed. The latter part of his statement was perfectly true.

The day after the fight, Mr. Malison came to the school as usual, but with his arm in a sling. To Annie's dismay, Alec did not make his appearance.

It had of course been impossible to conceal his corporal condition from his mother. The heart of the widow so yearned over the suffering of her son, though no confession of suffering escaped Alec's lips, that she vowed in anger that he should never cross the door of that school again. For three days she held immovably to her resolution, much to Alec's annoyance and to the consternation of Mr. Malison, who feared that he had not only lost a pupil but made an enemy. For Mr. Malison had every reason for being as smooth-faced with the parents as possible—he had ulterior hopes in Glamerton. The clergyman was getting old, and Mr. Malison was a licentiate of the Church. Although the people had no direct voice in the filling of the pulpit, it was very desirable that a candidate should have none but friends in the parish.

Mr. Malison made no allusion whatever to the events of Monday, and things went on as usual in the school, with just one exception. For a whole week the tawse did not make an appearance. This was owing in part at least to the state of his hand. But if he had ever wished to be freed from the necessity of using the lash, he might have derived hope from the fact that somehow or other the boys were no worse than usual during this week.

As soon as school was over on that first day of Alec's absence, Annie darted off on the road to Howglen where he lived and never slowed to a walk until she reached the garden gate. Fully conscious of the inferiority of her position, she went to the kitchen door. The door was opened to her knock before she had recovered breath enough to speak. The servant saw a girl with shabby dress and a dirty bonnet, from underneath which hung a disorderly mass of hair—for Annie was not kept so tidy on the interest of her money as she had been at the farm. The girl, I say, seeing this, and finding besides that Annie had nothing to say, took her for a beggar, returned to the kitchen and brought her a piece of oatcake, the common dole to the young beggars of the time. Annie's face flushed crimson, but she said gently, having by this time got her runaway breath a little more under control,

"No, I thank you. I'm no beggar. I only wanted to know how Alec was today."

"Come in," said the girl, "and I'll tell the mistress."

Annie followed the maid into the kitchen and sat down on the edge of a wooden chair, like a perching bird, until she should return.

"Please, mem, here's a lassie wanting to know how Master Alec is," said Mary, with her hand on the handle of the parlour door.

"That must be little Annie Anderson, mamma," said Alec, who was lying on the sofa.

Alec had told his mother all about the affair. Some of her friends from Glamerton, who likewise had sons at the school, had called and given their versions of the story, in which the prowess of Alec was made more of than in his own account. Indeed, all his fellow scholars except the young Bruces sang his praises aloud. For whatever the degree of their affection for Alec, every one of them hated the master. So the mother was proud of her boy—far prouder than she was willing for him to see.

Therefore, she could not help feeling some interest in Annie and some curiosity to see her. She had known James Anderson, her father, and he had been her guest more than once when he had called on business. Everybody had liked him. This general approbation owed itself to his genuine kindness of heart. So Mrs. Forbes was prejudiced in Annie's favour—but far more by her own recollections of the father than by her son's representations of the daughter.

"Tell her to come up, Mary," she said.

So Annie, with all the disorganization of school about her, was shown, considerably to her discomfort, into Mrs. Forbes's dining room.

There was nothing remarkable in the room, but to Annie's eyes it seemed magnificent, for carpet and curtains, sideboard and sofa, were luxuries altogether strange to her eyes. She entered timidly and stood close to the door. But Alec scrambled from the sofa, and taking hold of her by both hands, pulled her up to his mother.

"There she is, mamma!" he said.

And Mrs. Forbes, although her sense of the fitness of things was not gratified at seeing her son treat with familiarity a girl so neglectedly attired, yet received her kindly and shook hands with her.

"How do you do, Annie?" she said.

"Quite well, I thank you, mem," answered Annie, showing in her voice that she was awed by the grand lady, yet mistress enough of her manners not to forget a pretty modest courtesy as she spoke.

"What's going on at school today, Annie?" asked Alec.

"Not much out of the ordinary," answered Annie. "The master's a bit quieter than usual. I fancy he's the better behaved for his burnt fingers. But, oh, Alec!"

And here the little maiden burst into a passionate fit of crying.

"What's the matter, Annie?" said Mrs. Forbes, as she drew nearer, genuinely concerned at the child's tears.

"Oh, mem! You didn't see how the master licked him."

Tears from some mysterious source sprang to Mrs. Forbes's eyes. But at that moment Mary opened the door and said—

"Master Bruce is here, mem, wanting to see ye."

"Tell him to walk up, Mary."

"Oh no, no, mem! Don't let him come till I'm gone. He'll take me with him," cried Annie.

Mary stood waiting the result.

"But you must go home, you know, Annie," said Mrs. Forbes kindly.

"Ay, but not with *him,*" pleaded Annie.

From what Mrs. Forbes knew of the manners and character of Bruce, she was not altogether surprised at Annie's reluctance. So turning to the maid, she said—

"Have you told Mr. Bruce that Miss Anderson is here?"

"Me tell him! No, mem."

"Then take the child into my room till he is gone.—But perhaps he knows you are here, Annie?"

"He can't know that, mem. He jumps at things sometimes, though. He's sharp enough."

"Well, we shall see."

So Mary led Annie away to the sanctuary of Mrs. Forbes's bedroom.

The Bruce was not upon Annie's track at all. But his visit will need a few words of explanation.

Bruce's father had been a faithful servant to Mr. Forbes's father, who had held the same farm before his son, both having been what are called gentlemen farmers. The younger Bruce, being anxious to set up a shop, had—for his father's sake—been loaned the money by the elder Forbes. This money he had repaid before the death of the old man, who had never asked any interest on it. Before many more years had passed, Bruce, who had a wonderful capacity for petty business, was known to have accumulated some savings in the bank. Now the younger Forbes, being considerably more enterprising than his father, had spent all his capital upon improvements about the farm—draining, fencing, and the like—when his younger brother, to whom he was greatly attached, applied to him in an emergency. As he had no cash of his own he thought of Bruce. To borrow from him for his brother would not involve exposing the fact that he was in a temporarily embarrassing financial position—an exposure very undesirable in a country town like Glamerton.

After a thorough investigation of the solvency of Mr. Forbes, Bruce supplied him with a hundred pounds upon personal bond, at the usual rate of interest, for a certain term of years. Mr. Forbes died soon thereafter, leaving his affairs somewhat strained because of his outlay. Mrs. Forbes had paid the interest of the debt now for two years. But as the rent of the farm was heavy, she found this additional sum a burden. She had good reason to hope for better times, thinking that the farm must soon increase its yield. Mr. Bruce, on his part, regarded the widow with somewhat jealous eyes, because he very much doubted whether, when the day arrived when the note came due, she would be able to pay him the money she owed him. That day, however, was not yet at hand. It was this diversion of his resources, and the moral necessity for a nest egg for Annie, as he had represented the case to Margaret Anderson, which had urged him to show hospitality to Annie Anderson and her little fortune.

So neither was it anxiety for the welfare of Alec that induced him to call on Mrs. Forbes. Indeed, if Malison had killed him outright, he would have been rather pleased than otherwise. But he was in the habit of reminding the widow of his existence by an occasional call, especially when the time approached for the half yearly payment of the interest. And now the report of Alec's condition gave him a suitable pretext for looking in upon his debtor without appearing too greedy after his money.

"Well, mem, how are you today?" he said as he entered, rubbing his hands.

"Quite well, thank you, Mr. Bruce. Take a seat."

"And how's Mr. Alec?"

"There he is to answer for himself," said Mrs. Forbes, looking toward the sofa.

"How are you, Mr. Alec, after all this?" said Bruce.

"Quite well, thank you," answered Alec, in a tone that did not altogether please either of his listeners.

"I thought you had been rather sore," returned Bruce in an acid tone.

"I've got a bruise or two, that's all," said Alec.

"Well, I hope it'll be a lesson to you."

"To Mr. Malison, you should say, Mr. Bruce. I am perfectly satisfied, for my part."

His mother was surprised to hear him speak like a grown man, as well as annoyed by his behaviour to Bruce, in whose power she feared they might one day find themselves. But she said nothing. Bruce, likewise, was rather nonplussed. He grinned and was silent.

"I hear you have taken James Anderson's daughter into your family now, Mr. Bruce."

"Oh, ay, mem. There was nobody to look after the wee lassie. So, though I could but ill-afford it, with my own small family growing up, I was in a manner obliged to take her, James Anderson being a cousin of my own, you know, mem."

"Well, I'm sure it was very kind of you and Mrs. Bruce. How does the child get on?"

"Middling, mem—middling. She's just some the worse for taking up with loons."

Here he glanced at Alec with an expression of successful spite. He certainly had the best of it now.

Alec restrained the reply that rushed to his lips. A little small talk followed, and the visitor departed with a laugh from between his teeth as he took leave of Alec, a laugh which I can only describe as embodying an *I told you so* sort of satisfaction.

Almost as soon as he was out of the house, the parlour door opened and Mary brought in Annie. Mrs. Forbes's eyes were instantly fixed on her with mild astonishment, and something of a mother's tenderness awoke in her heart toward the little child. What she would not have given for such a daughter! During Bruce's call Mary had been busy with the child. She had combed and brushed her thick brown hair, venturing with it a stroke of originality no one would have expected of her. She had then washed her face and hands and neck, made the best she could of her poor, dingy dress, and put one of her own Sunday collars upon her.

Annie had submitted to it all without question, and thus adorned, Mary had introduced her again into the dining room. Mrs. Forbes was captivated by the pale, patient face, and the longing blue eyes that looked at her as if the child felt that she ought to have been her mother but somehow they had missed each other. They gazed out of the shadows of the mass of dark brown wavy hair that fell to her waist. But Mrs. Forbes was speedily recalled to a sense of propriety by observing that Alec too was staring at Annie with a mingling of amusement, admiration, and respect.

"What have you been about, Mary," she said in a tone of attempted reproof. "You have made a fright of the child. Take her away."

When Annie was once more brought back with her hair restored to its net, silent tears of mortification were still flowing down her cheeks. When Annie cried the tears always rose and flowed without any sound or convulsion. Rarely did she sob. This completed the conquest of Mrs. Forbes's heart. She drew the little one to her and kissed her, and Annie's tears instantly ceased, while Mrs. Forbes wiped away those still lingering on her face. Mary then went to get the tea, and Mrs. Forbes having left the room for a moment to recover that self-possession, the loss of which is peculiarly objectionable to a Scotswoman, Annie was left seated on a footstool before the bright fire while Alec lay on the sofa looking at her.

"I wouldn't want to be grand folk," mused Annie aloud, forgetting that she was not alone.

"We're not grand folk, Annie," said Alec.

"Ay, you are," returned Annie persistently.

"Well, why wouldn't you like it?"

"You must always be afraid of spoiling things."

"Mamma would tell you a different story," rejoined Alec, laughing. "There's nothing here to spoil."

Mrs. Forbes returned. Tea was brought in. Annie behaved herself like a lady, and after tea ran home with mingled feelings of pleasure and pain. For notwithstanding her assertion to Alec, the kitchen fire, small and dull, the smelling shop, and her own dreary attic room, did not seem more desirable after her peep into the warmth and comfort of the house at Howglen.

Questioned as to what had delayed her return from school, she told the truth, she had gone to ask after Alec Forbes and they had kept her to tea.

"I told them that you ran after the loons!" said Bruce triumphantly. Then stung with the reflection that *he* had not been asked to stay to tea, he added, "It's not for the likes of you, Annie, to go to gentlefolk's houses where you're not wanted. So don't let me hear of it again."

But it is wonderful how Bruce's influence over Annie, an influence of distress, was growing gradually weaker. He could make her uncomfortable enough. But as to his opinion of her, she had almost reached the point of not caring a straw for that. And she had faith enough in Alec to hope that he would defend her from whatever Bruce might have said against her.

Whether Mary had been talking in the town, as is not improbable, about little Annie Anderson's visit to her mistress, and so the story of the hair came to be known, or not, I cannot tell. But it was a notable coincidence that a few days later Mrs. Bruce came to the back door with a great pair of shears in her hand, and calling Annie, said:

"Come here, Annie! Your hair's too long. I must just cut it. It's giving you sore eyes."

"There's nothing the matter with my eyes," said Annie gently.

"Don't talk back. Sit down," returned Mrs. Bruce, leading her into the kitchen.

Annie cared very little for her hair, and well enough remembered that Mrs. Forbes had said it made a fright of her. So it was with no great reluctance that she submitted to the operation. Mrs. Bruce chopped it short all the way around. This permitted what there was of it to fall about her face, there being too little to confine in the usual prison of the net. Thus, her appearance did not bear such marks of deprivation, or in other Scottish words, "she didna luik sae dockit," as might have been expected.

Her wavy locks of rich brown were borne that night by the careful hands of Mrs. Bruce to Rob Guddle, the barber. Nor was the hand less careful that brought back their equivalent in money—for such long and beautiful hair commanded a good sum. With a smile to her husband, half loving and half cunning, Mrs. Bruce dropped the amount in the till.

– Fourteen –

Alec and Thomas

Although Alec Forbes was not a boy of quick receptivity as far as books were concerned, and therefore was no favourite with Mr. Malison, he was not by any means a common or stupid boy. His own eyes could teach him more than books could, for he had a quick observation of things about him, both in nature and in humanity. He knew all the birds, all their habits, and all their eggs. Not a boy in Glamerton could find a nest quicker than he, nor when found treated it with such respect. For he never took young birds and seldom more than half the eggs. Indeed, he was rather an uncommon boy, having, along with more than the usual amount of activity even for a boy, a tenderness of heart altogether rare in boys. He was as familiar with the domestic animals and their ways of feeling and acting as Annie herself. He detested cruelty in any form, and yet, as the occasion required, he could execute stern justice.

He was equally at home in the world of men around him. He knew the simple people of the town wonderfully well and took to Thomas Crann more than to anyone else, even though Thomas often read him long lectures. To these lectures Alec would listen seriously enough, believing Thomas to be right, though he could never make up his mind to give any attention to what was required of him as a result.

The first time Alec met Thomas after the affair with the dominie was on the day before he was to go back to school, for his mother had yielded at last to his desire to return. Thomas was building an addition to a water mill on the banks of the Glamour not far from where Alec lived, and Alec walked there to see how the structure was progressing. He expected a sharp rebuke for his behaviour to Mr. Malison, but somehow he was not afraid of Thomas despite his occasional gruffness. The first words Thomas said, however, were:

"Weel, Alec, can ye tell me the name of King David's mither?"

"I *cannot*, Thomas," answered Alec. "What was it?"

"Find out. Look in yer Bible. Hae ye been back to the school yet?"

"No. I'm going tomorrow."

"Ye're not going to fight wi' the master before the day's over, are ye?"

"I don't know," answered Alec. "Maybe he'll pick a fight with me. But you know, Thomas," he continued, defending himself from what he supposed Thomas was thinking, "King David himself killed the giant."

"Ow, ay! I'm not thinking of that. Maybe ye did right. But take care, Alec—"

Here Thomas paused from his work. Turning toward the boy with a trowel full of mortar in his hand, he spoke very slowly and solemnly.

"—Take care that ye bear no malice against the master. Justice done for the sake of a private grudge will bounce back on the doer. I hae little doobt the master'll be the better for it. But if ye be the worse, it'll be an ill job, Alec, my man."

"I have no ill will at him, Thomas."

"Weel, jist watch yer own heart and beware of it. I would counsel ye to try and please him a grain more than usual. It's not that easy to the carnal man, but ye ken we ought to crucify the old man, with his affections and lusts."

"Well, I'll try," said Alec, to whom it was not nearly so difficult as Thomas imagined.

And he did try. And the master seemed to appreciate his efforts and to accept them as a peace offering, thus showing that he really was the better for the punishment he had received.

It would be a great injustice to judge Mr. Malison too harshly by the customs of his day. It was the feeling of the time and the country that the tawse should be used unsparingly. *Law* was, and in great measure still is, the highest idea of the divine generated by the ordinary mind. It had to be supported at all risks, even by means of the leather strap.

In the hands of a wise and even-tempered man, no harm could result from the use of this instrument of justice. But in the hands of a fierce-tempered and changeable man of small moral stature, and liable to prejudices and offense, it became the means of unspeakable injury to those under his care.

Mr. Malison had nothing of the childlike in him, and consequently he never saw the mind of the child whose body he was assailing with a battery of excruciating blows. A *man* ought to be able to endure wrongful suffering and be none the worse. But who dares demand that of a child? It is indeed well for such cruel masters that even they are ultimately judged by the heart of a father, and not by the law of a king—worst of all the fictions of an ignorant and low theology. And if they must receive punishment in the end, at least it will not be like the heartless punishment which they inflicted on the boys and girls under their law.

Annie began to be regarded as a protégé of Alec Forbes, and as Alec was a favourite with most of his classmates, and was feared where he was not loved, even her cousins began to look upon her with something like respect and to lessen their persecutions. But she did not therefore become much more reconciled to her position, for the habits and customs of her home were distasteful to her, and its whole atmosphere uncongenial. Nor could it have been otherwise in any house where the entire aim was, first, to make money, and next, not to spend it.

The heads did not in the least know that they were unkind to her. On the contrary, Bruce thought himself the very pattern of generosity if he gave her a scrap of string. And Mrs. Bruce, when she said to inquiring neighbours, "The bairn's just like other children—she's good enough," thought herself a pattern of justice and even forbearance. But both were jealous of her in relation to their own children.

When Mrs. Forbes sent for her one Saturday, soon after her first visit, they hardly concealed their annoyance at the preference shown her by one who was under such great obligation to them, the parents of children every way superior to her.

– Fifteen –

The Plot

The winter drew on—a season as different from the summer in those northern latitudes, as if it belonged to another solar system. Cold and stormy, it is yet full of delight for all beings that can either romp, sleep, or think it through. But alas for the old and sickly, in poor homes, with scanty food and heat! Little children suffer too, though the gift of forgetfulness does for them what the gift of faith does for their parents—helps them over many troubles, besides tingling fingers and stony feet. There would be many tracks of those small feet in the morning snow, leading away across the fresh-fallen clouds from the house and cottage doors, for the barbarity of *morning-school*, that is, an hour and a half of dreary lessons before breakfast, was in full operation at Glamerton.

The winter came. One morning, all the children awoke, and saw a white world around them. Alec jumped out of bed in delight. It was a sunny, frosty morning. The snow had fallen all night, with its own silence, and no wind had interfered with the gracious alighting of the feathery water.

Every branch, every twig, was laden with its sparkling burden of down-flickered flakes, and threw long lovely shadows on the smooth featureless dazzle below. Away, away, stretched the outspread glory, the only darkness in it being the line of the winding river. All the snow that fell on it vanished, as death and hell shall one day vanish in the fire of God.

It flowed on, black through its banks of white. Away again stretched the shine to the town, where every roof had the sheet that was let down from heaven spread over it, and the streets lay a foot deep in yet unsullied snow, soon, like the story of the ages, to be trampled, soiled, wrought, and driven with human feet, till, at last, God's strong sun would wipe it all away.

From the door opening into this fairy-land, Alec sprang into the untrodden space, as into a new America. He had discovered a world, without even the print of human foot upon it. The keen air made him happy, and the face of nature, looking as peaceful as the face of a dead man dreaming of heaven, wrought in him jubilation and leaping. He was at the school door before a human being had appeared in the streets of Glamerton. Its dwellers all lay still under those sheets of snow, which seemed to hold them asleep in its cold enchantment.

Before any of his fellows made their appearance, he had kneaded and piled a great heap of snowballs, and stood by his pyramid, prepared for the offensive. He attacked the first that came, and soon there was a troop of boys pelting away at him. But with his store of balls at his foot, he was able to pay pretty fairly for what he received, till, that being exhausted, he was forced to yield the unequal combat.

By-and-by the little ones gathered, with Annie amongst them. But they kept aloof, for fear of the flying balls, for the boys had divided into two equal parties, and were pelting away at each other. At length the woman who had charge of the school-room, having finished lighting the fire, opened the door, and Annie, who was very cold, made a run for it, during a lull in the fury of the battle.

"Stop!" cried Alec, and the flurry ceased. One boy, however, just as Annie was entering the room, threw a snowball at her. He missed, but Alec did not miss him. For scarcely was the ball out of his hand when he received another, right between his eyes. Over he went amidst a shout of satisfaction.

When the master appeared at the top of the lane, the fight came to an end. As he entered the school, the group round the fire broke up and dispersed. Alec had entered close behind the master and overtook Annie as she went to her seat, for he had observed as she ran into the school that she was limping.

"What's the matter with you, Annie?" he said.

"Juno bit me," she answered.

"Ay! Very well!" returned Alec in a tone that had more meaning than the words themselves.

Soon after the Bible class was over and they had all taken their seats, a strange quiet stir and excitement gradually arose, like the first motions of a whirlpool at the turn of the tide. The master became aware of more than the usual flitting to and fro among the boys, just like the coming and going which precludes the swarming of bees. But as he had little or no constructive power, he never saw beyond symptoms. These were to him mere isolated facts, signifying disorder.

"John Morison, go to your seat!" he cried.

John went.

"Robert Rennie, go to your seat."

Robert went. And this continued till, six having been thus passed by, the master could stand it no longer. The *tawse* was thrown and a *licking* followed, making matters a little better from the master's point of view.

Now I will try to give, from the scholar's side, a peep of what passed.

As soon as he was fairly seated, Alec said in a low voice across the double desk to one of the boys on the opposite side, calling him by his nickname,

"I say, Divot, do ye ken Juno?"

"Maybe not!" answered Divot. "But if I dinna, my left leg does."

"I thought ye kenned the shape of her teeth, man. Just give Scrumpie there a dig in the ribs."

"What are ye after, Divot? I'll give ye a clout on yer ear!" growled Scrumpie.

"Hoot, man! The General wants ye."

The General was Alec's nickname.

"What is it, General?"

"Do ye ken Juno?"

"Hang the beast! I ken her too weel. She took her dinner off one of my hips last year."

"Just creep over to Cadger there and ask if he kens Juno. Maybe he's forgotten her."

Cadger's reply was interrupted by the interference of the master, but a pantomimed gesture conveyed to the General sufficient assurance of Cadger's memory in regard to Juno and her favours. Such messages and replies, notwithstanding more than one licking, kept passing the whole of the morning.

Juno was Robert Bruce's dog. She had the nose and legs of a bulldog but was not by any means purebred, and her behaviour was worse than her breed. She was a great favourite with her master who ostensibly kept her chained in his backyard for the protection of the house and store. But she was not by any means popular with the rising generation, for she was given to biting, with or without provocation, and every now and then she got loose.

Complaint had been made to her owner but without avail. Various vows of vengeance had been made by certain of the boys. But now Alec Forbes had taken up the cause of humanity and justice. For the brute had bitten Annie, and *she* could have given no provocation.

It was soon understood throughout the school that war was to be made upon Juno, and that every able-bodied boy must be ready when called out by the General. The minute they were dismissed the boys gathered in a knot at the door.

"What are ye going to do, General?" asked one.

"Kill her," answered Alec.

"How?"

"Stone her to death, like the man who broke the Sabbath."

"Broken bones for broken skins, eh? Ay!"

"But there's no stones to be gotten in the snow, General," said Cadger.

"You gomeril! We'll get more stones than we can carry frae the side of the road up yonder."

A confused chorus of suggestions and exclamations now arose, in the midst of which Willie Macwha, whose obvious nickname was Curly, came up. He was usually at the heart of every conspiracy.

"Here's Curly!"

"Well, is it all settled?" he asked.

"She's condemned but not executed yet," said Grumpie.

"How will we get at her?" asked Cadger.

"That's jist the problem," said Divot.

"We can't kill her in her own yard," said Houghie.

"No. We must just bide our time and take her when she's oot and aboot," said the General.

"But who's to ken that? And hoo are we to gather?" asked Cadger, who seemed both of a practical and a despondent turn of mind.

"Jist hold yer tongues and listen to me," said Alec.

The excited assembly was instantly silent.

"The first thing is to store plenty of ammunition."

"Ay, ay, General."

"Where had we best stow the stones, Curly?"

"In our yard. They'll never be noticed there."

"That'll do. Some time tonight, ye'll all carry what stones ye can—and make sure they're of a serviceable nature—to Curly's yard. He'll be watching for ye. And, I say, Curly, yer rigging-stone overlooks most of the town?"

"Ay, General."

"Well, buy two or three blue lights—hae ye coins?"

"Not one, General."

"Here ye be, then," said Alec, "for expenses of the war. And ye hae an old gun, dinna ye?"

"Ay, I have, but she's an old one."

"Load her to the mouth. But stand well back from her when ye fire if ye can."

"I'll take care, General."

"Scrumpie, ye dinna live that far from the dragon's den. Ye just keep yer eye on her comings and goings. As soon as ye see her loose in the yard, ye be off to Willie Macwha. Then, Curly, ye burn the blue lights from the top of yer house and fire yer gun, and when I see or hear the signal I'll be over in seven minutes and a half. Every one of ye that hears must look after the next, and we'll gather at Curly's. Bring yer bags for the stones, them that has bags."

"But what if ye dinna hear, for it's a long road, General?" interposed Cadger.

"If I'm not at yer yard in seven and a half minutes, Curly, send Linkum after me. He's the only one that can run. It's all that he can do, but he does it well. Once Juno's oot, she's not in a hurry to get back in again."

The boys separated and went home in a state of excitement to their dinners. The sun now set between two and three o'clock and there were no long evenings to favour the plot. Perhaps their hatred of the dog would not have driven them to such extreme measures—even though she had bitten Annie Anderson—had her master been a favourite or even generally respected. But Alec knew well enough that the townspeople were not likely to sympathize with Bruce on the ill treatment of his cur.

When the dinner and the blazing fire had filled him so full of comfort that he was once more ready to encounter the cold, Alec rose to leave the house again.

"Where are you going, Alec?" said his mother.

"Into the yard, mamma."

"What can you want in the yard—it's full of snow?"

"It's just the snow I want, mamma."

And in another moment he was under the clear blue night-heaven, with the keen, frosty air blowing on his warm cheek, busy with a wheelbarrow and shovel, slicing and shovelling in the snow. He was building a hut with it, after the fashion of the Eskimo hut, with a very thick circular wall, which began to lean toward its own centre as soon as it began to rise. He had pitched his hut at the foot of a flag-staff he had erected earlier.

Often he paused in his work and turned toward the town, but no signal came. When called in to tea, he gave a long wistful look townwards, but saw no sign. Out he went again afterward but there came no news that Juno was ranging the streets, and he was forced to go to bed at last and take refuge from his disappointment in sleep.

The next day he strictly questioned all his officers as to the manner in which they had fulfilled their duty and found no just cause of complaint.

"What are you in such a state about, Alec?" asked his mother that night.

"Nothing very particular, mamma," answered Alec, ashamed at his lack of self-command.

"You've looked out at the window twenty times in the last half hour," she persisted.

"Curly promised to burn a blue gaslight, and I wanted to see if I could see it."

Suspecting more, his mother was forced to be content with his answer.

But that night also passed without sight of the light, which Curly had said he would ignite before firing the gun. Juno kept safe in her barrel, little thinking of the machinations against her in the wide snow-covered country all around.

Alec finished his Eskimo hut and with the snow falling again that night, it looked as if it had been there all winter. As it seemed likely that a long spell of white weather had set in, Alec resolved to enlarge his original ice-dwelling and was hard at work in the execution of this project on the third night, or rather late afternoon or *forenight* as they call it there.

– Sixteen –

Juno

"What can that be, over at the town there?" said Mary to her mistress late the following afternoon, as in passing she peeped out of the window.

"What is it, Mary?" asked Mrs. Forbes.

"That's just what I don't know, mem. It's a curious kind of blue light.—It's not canny.—And, preserve us all! It's cracking as well," cried Mary, as the subdued sound of a far-off explosion reached her.

This was of course no other than the roar of Curly's gun. But at the moment Alec was too busy in the depths of his snow-vault to hear or see the signals.

By and by a knock came to the kitchen door. Mary went and opened it.

"Where's Alec? Is he at home?" said a rosy boy, almost breathless from past speed and present excitement.

"He's in the yard."

The boy turned immediately and Mary shut the door.

Linkum sought Alec's snow house, and as he approached he heard Alec whistling a favourite tune as he shovelled away at the snow.

"General!" cried Linkum in ecstasy.

"Here!" answered Alec, flinging his spade down and bolting in the direction of the call. "Is it you, Linkum?"

"She's out, General."

"The devil have her if she ever gets in again, the brute! Did ye go to Curly?"

"Ay, did I. He fired the gun and burned his light, and waited seven minutes and a half. Then he sent me for ye, General!"

"Confound it!" cried Alec and tore through the shrubbery and hedge, the nearest way to the road, followed by Linkum, who even at full speed was not a match for Alec. Away they flew like the wind, along the well-beaten path to the town, over the footbridge that crossed the Glamour, and full speed up the hill to Willie Macwha, who was anxiously awaiting the commander with a dozen or fifteen more. They all had their book bags, pockets, and arms filled with stones. One bag was filled and ready for Alec.

"Now," said the General, in the tone of Gideon of old, "if any of ye are feart of the brute, just go home now."

"Ay, ay, General."

But nobody stirred.

"Who's watching her?"

"Doddles, Gapey, and Goat."

"Where was she last seen?"

"Taking up with another tyke on the square."

"Doodles'll be at the pump to tell where they've gone."

"Come along then. This is how ye're to go. We mustn't all go together. Some of ye—ye three—down the Back Wynd. You six up Lucky Hunter's Close. And the rest by Gowan Street. The first at the pump waits for the rest."

"How are we to make the attack, General?"

"I'll give my orders as the case may demand," replied Alec.

And away they shot.

The muffled sounds of the feet of the various companies, as they thundered past upon the snow, roused the old wives dozing over their knitting by their fires, causing various remarks:—

"Some mischief of the loons!"

"Some ploy of the laddies!"

"Some devilry of the rascals from Malison's school!"

They reached the square almost together and found Doddles at the pump, who reported that Juno had gone down into the inn-yard, and Gapey and Goat were watching her. Now she would have to come out to get home again, for there was no back way. So by Alec's orders they dispersed a little to avoid observation and drew gradually between the entrance of the inn-yard and the way Juno would take to go home.

The town was ordinarily lighted at night with oil lamps, but moonlight and snow had rendered them for some time unnecessary.

"There she is! There she is!" cried several at once in a hissing whisper of excitement.

"Hold still!" cried Alec. "Wait till I tell ye. Dinna ye see that there's Long Tom's dog with her, and he's done nothing. We mustn't punish the innocent with the guilty."

A moment later the dogs took their leave of each other and Juno went off at a slow slouching trot in the direction of her own street.

"Close in!" cried Alec.

Juno found her way barred in a threatening manner, and sought to pass meekly by.

"Let at her, boys!" cried the General.

A storm of stones was their answer to the order, and a howl of rage and pain burst from the animal. She turned, but found that she was the centre of a circle of enemies.

"Let at her! Hold at her!" yelled Alec.

Thick as hail the well-aimed stones flew from the practiced hands, though of course in the frantic rushes of the dog to escape, not half of them took effect. She darted first at one and then at another, snapping wildly, and meeting with many a kick and blow in return.

The neighbours began to look out at their shop doors and windows, for the boys, rapt in the excitement of the sport, no longer laid any restraint upon their cries. Andrew Constable, the clothier, from his shop-door, Rob Guddle, the barber, from his window, with his face shadowed by Annie's curls, Redford, the bookseller, from the top of the stairs that led to his shop, in short, the whole of the shopkeepers on the square of Glamerton were regarding this battle of odds. The half-frozen place looked half-alive. But none of the good folks cared so much to interfere, for flying stones are not pleasant to encounter. And indeed they could not clearly make out what was the matter. In a minute more a sudden lull came over the hubbub. They saw all the group gather together in a murmuring knot.

The fact was this. Although cowardly enough now, the brute, infuriated with pain, had made a determined rush at one of her antagonists, and a short hand-to-teeth struggle was now taking place, during which the stoning ceased.

"She has a grip of my leg," said Alec, "and I have a grip of her throat. Curly, put your hand in my jacket pocket and take out a bit of twine you'll find there."

Curly did as he was bid and drew out a yard and a half of garden line.

"Put it in a single turn round her neck, and two or three of ye take a hold at each end, and pull for yer lives!"

They hauled with hearty vigour, and Juno's teeth relaxed their hold of Alec's calf. In another minute her tongue was hanging out of her mouth, and when they ceased the strain she lay limp on the snow. With a shout of triumph they started off at full speed, dragging the brute by the neck through the street. Alec tried to follow them, but found his leg too painful and was forced to go limping home.

When the victors had run till they were out of breath, they stopped to confer. The result of their conference was that in solemn silence they drew her home to the back gate, and finding all still in the yard, deputed two of their company to lay the dead body in its kennel.

Curly and Linkum drew her into the yard, tumbled her into her barrel, which they set up on end, undid the string, and left Juno lying neck and tail together in ignominious peace.

Before Alec reached home his leg had swollen very large and was so painful that he could hardly limp along. For Juno had taken no passing snap but a great, strong mouthful. He concealed his condition from his mother for that night. But next morning his leg was so bad that there was no longer a possibility of hiding it. To tell a lie would have been so hard for Alec there was nothing for it but confession. His mother scolded him to a degree considerably beyond her own estimation of his wrongdoing, telling him he would get her into disgrace in the town as the mother of a lawless son who meddled with other people's property in a way little better than stealing.

"I fancy, mamma, a fellow's legs are aboot as muckle his ain property as the tyke was Rob Bruce's. It's no the first time she's bitten half a dizzen legs that were neither her ain nor her maister's."

Mrs. Forbes could not well answer this argument. So she took advantage of the fact that Alec had, in the excitement of self-defence, lapsed into Scots.

"Don't talk so vulgarly to me, Alec," she said. "Keep that for your ill-behaved companions in the town."

"They are no worse than I am, mamma. I was at the bottom of it."

"I never said they were," she answered.

But in her heart she thought if they were not, there was little amiss with them.

– Seventeen –

Revenge

Alec was once more condemned to the sofa, and Annie had to miss him and wonder what had become of him. She always felt safe when Alec was at school and grew timid when he was not, even though whole days would sometimes pass without either speaking to the other.

About noon, when all was tolerably harmonious in the school, the door opened and the face of Robert Bruce appeared, with gleaming eyes of wrath.

"God preserve us!" said Scrumpie to his neighbour. "Such a lickin' as we're gonna get! Here's Rob Bruce! Who's gone and telled him?"

Some of the gang of conspirators, standing in a group near the door, stared in horror. Among them was Curly. His companions declared afterward that had it not been for the strength of the curl, his hair would have stood upright. For, following Bruce and led by the string, came an awful apparition—Juno hobbling on three of her own feet, a pitiable mass of caninity—looking like the resuscitated corpse of a dog that had been nine days buried.

"She's not dead after all! Devil take her, for he's in her," said Doddles.

"We didna kill her enough," said Curly.

And now the storm began to break. The master had gone to the door and shaken hands with his visitor, glancing with a puzzled look at the miserable animal which had just enough shape left to show that it was a dog.

"I'm very sorry, Mr. Malison, to come to you with my complaints," said Bruce. "But just look at the poor dumb animal! She couldn't come herself, so I had to bring her. Stand still, you brute!"

For Juno, having caught sight of some boy's legs, began to tug at the string with feeble earnestness—no longer, however, regarding the said legs as made for dogs to bite but as fearful instruments of vengeance, in league with stones and cords. So the straining and pulling was all homeward. But her master had brought her as chief witness against the boys and she must remain.

"Eh, lass!" he said, hauling her back by the string. "If you had but the tongue of the prophet's ass, you would soon point out the rascals that mistreated you. But here's the just judge that'll give you your rights, and that without fee or reward.—Mr. Malison, she was one of the bonniest bicks you could ever set your eyes upon—"

A smothered laugh gurgled through the room.

"—till some of your loons—no offense, sir—I know well enough they're not yours, nor a bit like you—some of your pupils, sir, have just driven the soul out of her with stones."

"Where does the soul of a bitch live?" asked Goat, in a whisper, of the boy next to him.

"The devil kens," answered Gapey. "If it doesn't live in the bottom of Rob Bruce's belly."

The master's wrath, ready enough to rise against boys and all their works, now showed itself in the growing redness of his face. This was not one of his worst passions—in those times he grew white—for this injury had not been done to himself.

"Can you tell me which of them did it?"

"No, sir. There must have been more than two or three at it, or she would have frightened them away. The best-natured beast in all the town!"

"William Macwha!" cried Malison.

"Here, sir."

"Come up."

Willie ascended to the august presence. He had made up his mind that, seeing so many had known all about it and some of them had already turned cowardly, it would be of no use to deny the deed.

"Do you know anything about this cruelty to the poor dog, William?" said the master.

Willie gave a Scotsman's answer, which, while evasive, was yet answer and more. "She bit me, sir."

"When? While you were stoning her?"

"No, sir. A month ago."

"You're a lying wretch, Willie Macwha, as you well know in your own conscience!" cried Bruce. "She's the quietest, kindliest beast that ever was born. See, sir—just look here. She'll let me put my hand in her mouth and take no more notice than if it were her own tongue."

Now, whether it was that the said tongue was still swollen and painful, or that Juno disapproved of the whole proceeding, I cannot tell. But the result of this proof of her temper was that she made her teeth meet through Bruce's hand.

"Damn the bitch!" he roared, snatching the hand away with the blood beginning to flow.

A laugh, not smothered this time, billowed and broke through the whole school. The fact that Bruce should be caught swearing, added to the yet more delightful fact that Juno had bitten her master, was altogether too much.

"Eh! Isna it good we didna kill her after all?" said Curly.

"Good doggie," said another, patting his own knee as if to entice her to come and be petted.

"At him again, Juno!" said a third.

Bruce, writhing with pain and mortified at the result of his would-be proof of Juno's incapability of biting, still more mortified at having so far forgotten himself as to utter an oath, and altogether unnerved by the laughter, turned away in confusion.

"It's their fault, the bad boys! She never did the like before. They have ruined her temper," he said as he left the school, following Juno who was tugging away at the string as if she had been a blind man's dog.

"Well, what have you to say for yourself, William?" said Malison.

"She began it, sir."

This best of excuses could not, however, satisfy the master. The punishing mania had possibly taken fresh hold upon him. But he would ask more questions first.

"Who besides you tortured the animal?"

Curly was silent. He had neither a very high sense of honour, nor many principles to come and go upon, but he had a considerable amount of devotion to his party, which is the highest form of conscience to be found in many.

"Tell me their names!"

Curly was still silent.

But a white-headed urchin, whom innumerable whippings, not bribe, had corrupted, cried out in a wavering voice:

"Sanny Forbes was one of them, and he's not here, cause Juno bit him."

The poor creature gained little by his treachery, for the smallest of the conspirators fell on him when school was over and gave him a thrashing, which he deserved more than even one of Malison's.

But the effect of Alec's name on the master was amazing. He changed his manner at once, sent Curly to his seat, and nothing more was heard of Juno or her master.

The following morning, the neighbours across the street stared in bewildered astonishment at the place where the shop of Robert Bruce had been. Had it been possible for an avalanche to fall like a thunderbolt from the heavens, they would have supposed that one had fallen in the night and overwhelmed the house. Door and window were invisible, buried in a mass of snow. Spades and shovels in boys' hands had been busy for hours, during the night, throwing it up against the house, the door having first been blocked up with a huge snowball, which they had rolled in silence the whole length of the long street.

Bruce and his wife slept in a little room immediately behind the shop, that they might watch over their treasures. Bruce's first movement in the morning was always into the shop to unbolt the door and take down the shutters. His astonishment when he looked upon a blank wall of snow may well be imagined. He did not question that the whole town was similarly overwhelmed. Such a snowstorm had never been heard of before, and he thought with uneasy recollection of the oath he had uttered in the schoolroom. He imagined for a brief moment that the whole of Glamerton lay overwhelmed by divine wrath, because he, under the agony of a bite from his own dog, had consigned her to a quarter where dogs and children are not admitted. In his bewilderment, he called aloud:

"Nancy! Robbie! Johnnie! We're buried alive!"

"Preserve us all, Robert! What's happened?" cried his wife, rushing from the kitchen.

"I'm not buried that I know of," cried Robert the younger, entering from the yard.

His father rushed out to the back door and, to his astonishment and relief, saw the whole world about him. It was a private judgment, then, upon him and his shop. And so it was—a very private judgment. It was probably the result of his thoughts upon it that he never again carried complaints to Murdoch Malison.

Alec Forbes had nothing to do with this revenge. But Bruce always thought he was at the bottom of it and hated him all the more. He disliked all *loons* but his own, but Alec Forbes he hated above the rest. For in every way he was the very opposite to Bruce himself. Mrs. Bruce always followed her husband's lead, being capable only of two devotions—the one to her husband and children, and the other to the shop. Of Annie they highly and righteously disapproved, partly because they had to feed her and partly because she was friendly with Alec. This disapproval rose into dislike after their sons had told them that it was because Juno had bitten her that the boys of the school, with Alec for a leader, had served her as they had.

For the rest of Juno's existence, the moment she caught sight of a boy she fled as fast as her four bowlegs would carry her, not daring even to let her tail stick out behind her, lest it should afford a handle against her.

– Eighteen –

A Snow Fairy

When Annie heard that Alec had been bitten she was miserable. She knew that his bite must be worse than hers, or he would not be kept at home. The modesty of the maidenly child made her fear to intrude, but she could not keep herself from following the path to his house to see how he was. But when she arrived she could not quite make up her mind to knock at the door, for despite her kindness she was a little afraid of Mrs. Forbes.

So she wandered around the side of the house until she came upon the curious heap of snow with the small round tunnel opening into it. She examined Alec's Eskimo hut all around, and then, seeing that the tunnel into it was hollow, she entered. The passage was dark but she groped her way till she came to the cell at the end. Here a faint ghostly light from the evening glimmered through the roof, reflecting from the white surface of the cave with a faint bluish light. It was not so cold here as in the outer air where a light, frosty wind was blowing. Annie seated herself and before long, as was her custom, fell fast asleep.

In the meantime, Alec was sitting alone by the light of the fire, finishing the last of a story. His mother had gone into town. When he was through reading he got a candle and went out into the descending darkness to see how his little snow room looked in candlelight. As he entered he could hardly believe his eyes.

A figure was there—motionless—dead perhaps. A frost-queen, a snow fairy—the spirit that made the snow and built the hut and dwelt in it! If he had not come then, Annie might indeed have slept on till her sleep was too deep for any voice of the world to rouse her.

Her face was pale and deathly cold, and it was with difficulty that he woke her. He took hold of her hands, but she did not move. He sat down, took her in his arms, spoke to her—became frightened when she did not answer, and began shaking her. Still she would not open her eyes. But he knew she was not dead yet, for he could feel her heart beating. At length she lifted her eyelids, looked up in his face, gave a low happy laugh, like the laugh of a dreaming child, and was fast asleep again the next moment.

Alec hesitated no longer. He got her out of the chamber, then rose with her in his arms and carried her into the parlour and laid her down on the rug before the fire with a pillow under her head. When Mrs. Forbes came home, she found Alec reading and Annie sleeping beside the fireside. Before his mother had recovered from her surprise, Alec had the first word.

"Mamma!" he said, "I found her sleeping in my snow hut outside, and if I hadn't brought her in, she would have been dead by this time."

"Poor little darling," thought Mrs. Forbes. She stooped and drew the child back from the fire. After making the tea, she proceeded to take off Annie's bonnet and shawl. By the time she had got rid of them, Annie was beginning to move and Alec rose to go to her.

"Let her alone," said his mother. "Let her come to herself slowly. Come to the table."

Alec obeyed. They could see that Annie had opened her eyes and lay staring at the fire. What was she thinking about? She had fallen asleep in the snow hut and here she now was by a bright fire!

"Annie, dear, come to your tea," were the first words she heard. She rose and went, and sat down at the table with a smile, taking it all as the gift of God, or a good dream, and never asking how she had come to be so happy.

– Nineteen –

Alec's Boat

The spirit of mischief had never been so thoroughly aroused in the youth of Glamerton as it was this winter. The snow lay very deep, while almost every day a fresh fall added to its depth and the cold strengthened their impulses to muscular exertion.

"The loons are jist growing perfect deevils," said Charlie Chapman, the wool carder, as he bolted into his own shop, the remains of a snowball melting down the back of his neck. "We must hae another constable to hold them in order," he muttered.

The existing force of law was composed of one long-legged, short-bodied, middle-aged man who was so slow in his motions that the boys called him "Stumpin' Steenie" and stood in no more awe of him than they did of his old cow—which, her owner being a widower, they called *Mrs. Stephen*—when she went up the street, hardly able to waddle along for the weight of her udder. So there was some ground for the wool carder's remark. How much a second constable would have helped, however, is doubtful.

"I never saw such gallows birds," chimed in a farmer's wife who was standing in the shop. "They had a rope across the Wast Wynd in the snow and down I came on my knees as sure's yer name's Charles Chapman—wi' more of my legs oot of my coats than was altogether to my credit."

"I'm sure ye can hae no reason to take shame of yer legs," was the gallant rejoinder, to which their owner replied with a laugh, "They werena made for public inspection, anyway."

"Hoot! Nobody saw them. I'll warrant ye didna lie there long! But the loons—they're jist past all! Did ye hear what they did to Rob Bruce?"

"Fegs! They tell me they all but buried him alive."

"Ow! Ay! But there's a later story."

Here Andrew Constable, the clothier, dropped in and Chapman turned to him with the question:

"Did *ye* hear what the loons did to Robert Bruce the night afore last?"

"No. What was that? They hae a spite at puir Rob, I believe."

"Weel, it didna look altogether like respect, I must allow. I was standing at the counter of his shop and Robert was serving a little bairn wi' a pennyworth of candy, when all at once there came such a blast and a reek fit to smother ye oot of the fire and the shop was full of the reek and smoke afore ye knew it. 'Preserve us all!' cried Rob. But before he could say another word, from inside the house, scushlin in her old shoes, comes Nancy running and opens the door wi' a screech. 'Preserve's all!' she yelled, 'Robert, the chimney's plugged!' And fegs! The house was as full as it could be, from cellar to attic, of the blackest smoke that ever burned frae coal. Oot we ran, and it was a sight to see the creature Bruce wi' his long neck looking up at the chimneys. But not a spark came out of them—or smoke either, for that matter. It was easy to see what was amiss. The loons had been up the rigging and flung a handful of blasting powder down each smoking chimney and then covered them wi' a big divot of turf upon the mouth of them. Not one of them was in sight, but I doubt if any of them was far away. There was nothing for it but to get a ladder and jist go up and take off the pot lids. But eh! Poor Robert was jist rampin' wi' rage! Not that he said much, for he dared not open his mouth for fear of swearing. And Robert wouldna swear, ye ken."

"What laddies were they, Charles, do ye ken?" asked Andrew.

"There's a heap of them up to tricks. If I didna hae the rheumateese hounding away between my shoulders tonight, it winna be because of them. For as I came over from the ironmonger's there, I jist got a ball in the back of my neck that almost sent me a falling wi' my snoot in the snow. And there it stuck, and at this present moment it's running down the small of my back as if it were a stream down a hillside. We must hae another constable!"

"Hoot, hoot, Charles! Ye dinna need a constable to dry yer back. Go to yer wife wi' it," said Andrew. "She'll give ye a dry shirt. Let the laddies work it off. As long as they keep their hand frae what doesna belong to them, I dinna mind a little mischief now and then. They'll not turn out the worse for a prank or two."

The fact was, none of the boys would have dreamed of interfering with Andrew Constable. Everybody respected him, not because he was an elder in the church but because he was a good-tempered, kindly, honest man.

While Alec was confined to the house, he had been busy inventing all kinds of gainful employment for the period of the snow. His lessons never occupied much of his thoughts. The first day of his return, when school was over, he set off rejoicing in his freedom, still revolving what he was to do next, for he wanted some steady employment with an end in view.

In the course of his solitary walk he came to the Wan Water, the other river that flowed through the wide valley—and wan enough it was now with its snow-sheet over it. As he stood looking at its still, dead face, all at once a summer vision of live water arose in his mind. He thought of how delightful it would be to go sailing down the rippling river with the green fields all about him and the hot afternoon sun over his head. His next thought was both an idea and a resolve. Why shouldn't he build a boat, for he had always a fancy for the sea, and boats, and rigging of all sorts.

He *would* build a boat. He would set about it at once. Here was work for the rest of the winter!

His first step must be to go home and have his dinner, his next—to consult George Macwha, who had been a ship carpenter in his youth. He would run over in the evening before George had finished his work and commit the plan to his judgment.

It was a still lovely night, clear and frosty, with millions of stars overhead. Away in the north, the streamers were shooting hither and thither, with marvellous evanescence and re-generation, a lawless dance of the northern lights in their ethereal beauty, shining, with a wild ghostly changefulness and feebleness, all colours at once, now here, now there, like a row of slender organ-pipes, rolling out and in and along the sky. Up and down they darted, and away and back—and always in the direction he did not expect them to take. He thought he heard them crackle, and he stood still to listen, but he could not be sure that it was not the snow sinking and crisping beneath his feet. All around him was still as a world too long frozen. In the heavens alone was there motion. There this entrancing dance of colour and shape went on, wide beneath, and tapering up to the zenith! Truly there was revelry in heaven!

Alec walked on till the windows of the town began to throw shadows across the snow. The street was empty. From end to end nothing moved but an occasional shadow. As he came near to Macwha's shop he had to pass a row of cottages which stood with their backs to a steep slope. Here too all was silent as a frozen city.

But when he was about opposite the middle of the row, he heard a stifled laugh and then a kind of muffled sound as of hurrying steps. In a moment more, every door in the row was torn open and out bolted the inhabitants—here an old woman, there a shoemaker with an awl in his hands, here a tailor with his shears, and there a whole family of several trades and ages. Everyone rushed into the middle of the road, turned around, and looked up. Then arose such a clamour of tongues that it broke on the still air like a storm.

"What's up, Betty?" asked Alec of a decrepit old creature, bent almost double with rheumatism, who was trying hard to see something or other in the air or on the roof of her cottage.

But before she could speak, the answer came to him in another form, addressing itself to his nose instead of his ears. For out of the cottages floated clouds of smoke, pervading the air with a variety of scents—burning oak bark, burning leather cuttings, damp firewood and peat, the cooking of red herrings, the boiling of porridge, the baking of oatcake, etc. Happily for all the inhabitants, "the deevil loons" had used no powder here.

But the old woman, looking round when Alec spoke and seeing that he was one of the obnoxious schoolboys, broke out upon him.

"Go and take the divot off my chimney, Alec, like a good lad! Ye shouldna play such tricks on poor old folks like me. I'm jist in tears from the smoke in my old eyes."

As she spoke she wiped her eyes with an apron.

Alec did not wait to clear himself of an accusation so gently put, but was on the roof of Lucky Lapp's cottage before she had finished her appeal to his generosity. He pitched the divot halfway down the hillside at the back of the cottage. Then he scrambled from one chimney to the other and went on pitching the sods down the hill. At length two of the inhabitants, who had climbed up at the other end of the row, met him, and taking him for a repentant sinner at best, made him their prisoner, much to his amusement, and brought him down, saying that it was too bad of gentlefolks' sons to persecute the poor in that way.

"I didna do it," said Alec.

"Dinna lie," was the curt rejoinder.

"I'm not lying."

"Who did it then?"

"I can guess. And it shan't happen again if I can help it."

"Tell us who did it."

"I winna say names."

"He's one o' them!"

"The fowl thief, take him! I'll give him a hiding," said a burly shoemaker coming up. "The loons are not to be borne with any longer."

He caught Alec by the arm.

"I didna do it!" persisted Alec.

"Who killed Rob Bruce's dog?" asked the shoemaker, squeezing Alec's arm to point the question.

"I did," answered Alec, "and I will do yers the same good turn if he bites children."

"And quite right too!" said the shoemaker's wife. "Let him go. I'll be bound he's not one of them."

"Tell us about it, then. How did ye come to be here?"

"I went up to take the divot off Lucky Lapp's chimney. Ask her. Once up I thought I might give the rest of ye a good turn, and this is what I get for it."

"Well, well! Come in and warm ye, then," said the shoemaker, convinced at last.

So Alec went in, had a chat with them, and then went on to George Macwha's.

The carpenter took to his scheme at once. Alec was a fair hand at all sorts of work, and being on the friendliest terms with Macwha, it was soon arranged that the vessel should be laid in the end of the workshop and that, under George's directions and what help Willie chose to render, Alec should build his boat himself. Just as they concluded their discussion, in came Willie, wiping some traces of blood from his nose. He pantomimed a gesture of vengeance at Alec.

"What have ye been after now, laddie?" asked his father.

"Alec's jist given me a bloody nose," said Willie.

"What do ye mean, Curly?" asked Alec in amazement.

"That divot that ye flung off Lucky Lapp's chimney," said Curly, "came right onto the back of my head as I lay on the hillside. Ye pretend ye didn't see me, no doubt."

"I say, Curly," said Alec, putting his arm around his shoulders and leading him aside, "we must have no more of this kind of work. It's shameful. Dinna ye see the difference between choking an ill-fared tyke of a dog and choking a poor widow's chimney?"

"Twas only for fun."

"It's no fun that both sides can't laugh at, Curly."

"Rob Bruce wasn't laughing when he brought the bick to the school, nor yet when he went home again."

"That wasna for fun, Curly. That was downright earnest."

"Well, well, Alec, say no more aboot it."

"No more will I. But if I was you, Curly, I would take Lucky a sack of kindling in the morning."

"I'll take them tonight, Alec. Father, hae ye an old sack?"

"There's one up in the loft. What do ye want with a sack?"

But Curly was in the loft almost before the question had left his father's lips. He was down again in a moment and on his knees filling the sack with shavings and all the chips he could find. In a few moments more Curly was off to Widow Lapp with his bag of shavings.

"He's a fine boy, that Willie of yours, George," said Alec to Willie's father. "He only needs to have a thing well put before him and he acts upon it directly."

"It's good for him he makes a cronie of you, Alec. There's a heap of mischief in him.—Where's he off wi' that bag?"

Alec told the whole story, much to the satisfaction of George, who could appreciate the repentance of his son. From that day on he thought even more of young Alec, and of Willie as well.

"Now, Curly," said Alec as soon as he reappeared with the empty sack, "your father's going to let me build a boat, and you must help me."

"What's the use of a boat in this weather?" said Curly.

"Ye gomeril!" returned his father. "Ye never look an inch past the point of yer nose. Ye wouldna think of a boat afore the spring. Haith!

The summer would be over and the water frozen again afore ye had it built. Look at Alec there. He's worth ten of ye!"

"I know that every bit as well as ye do, father. Jist start us off with it, father."

"I can't attend to it jist now, but I'll get ye started tomorrow morning."

So here was an end to the troubles of the townsfolk from the loons, and without any increase of the constabulary force. For Curly being withdrawn there was no one else of sufficiently inventive energy to take the lead. Curly soon had both his hands quite occupied with boat building.

– Twenty –

Dowie

Every afternoon now, the moment dinner was over, Alec set off for the workshop and did not return till eight o'clock or sometime later. Mrs. Forbes did not at all relish this change in his habits, but had the good sense not to interfere.

One day he persuaded her to go with him and see how the boat was getting on. This caused in her some sympathy with his work. For there was the boat—a skeleton it is true, and not nearly ready for the clothing of its planks or its final skin of paint—yet an undeniable boat to the motherly eye of hope. And there were Alec and Willie working away before her eyes, doing their best to fulfil the promise of its looks. A little quiet chat she had with George Macwha in which he lauded the praise of her boy also went a long way to reconcile her to his nightly desertion of her.

But Mrs. Forbes never saw a little figure lying in a corner half-buried in wood shavings and fast asleep. It was, of course, Annie Anderson. Having heard of the new occupation of her hero, she had one afternoon three weeks before found herself at George's shop door. It seemed that she had followed her feet and they had taken her there before she knew where they were going. Peeking in, she watched Alec and Willie for some time at their work without showing herself. But George, who came up behind her as she stood, took her by the hand and led her in, saying kindly:

"Here's a new apprentice, Alec. She wants to learn boat building."

"Annie, is that you?" said Alec. "Come on in. There's a fine heap of spales you can sit on and see what we're about."

And so saying he seated her on the shavings and half-buried her with an armful more to keep her warm.

"Close the door, Willie," he added. "She'll be cold. She's not working, you see."

Whereupon Willie shut the door, and Annie found herself very comfortable indeed. There she sat, in perfect contentment, watching the progress of the boat—a progress not very perceptible to her inexperienced eyes. But after she had sat for a good while in silence, she looked up at Alec and said:

"Is there nothing I can do to help you, Alec?"

"Nothing, Annie. Lassies can't saw or plane, you know."

Again she was silent for a long time, and then with a sigh she looked up.

"Alec, I'm so cold!" she said.

"I'll bring my plaid to wrap you in tomorrow."

Annie's heart bounded with delight, for here was what amounted to an express invitation to return.

"But come with me," Alec went on, "and we'll soon get you warm again. Give me your hand."

Annie gave Alec her hand, and he lifted her out of the heap of spales and led her away. She never thought of asking where he was leading her. They had not gone far down the street when a roaring sound fell upon her ear, growing louder and louder as they went on till they turned a sharp corner, and there saw the smithy fire. The door of the smithy's shop was open, and they could see the smith at work some distance off. The fire glowed with gathered rage at the impudence of the bellows blowing in its face. The huge smith, with one arm flung over the shoulder of the insulting party, urged it to the contest, while he stirred up the other to increased ferocity by poking a piece of iron into the very middle of it.

Annie was delighted to look at it, but there was a certain fierceness about the whole affair that made her shrink from going nearer. She could not help feeling a little afraid of the giant smith with his brawny arms that twisted and tortured iron bars all day long—and his black, fierce-looking face. Again he stooped, caught up a great iron spoon, dipped it into a tub of water, and poured the spoonful on the fire—a fresh insult, at which it hissed and sputtered, like one of the fiery flying serpents of which she had read in her Bible—gigantic, dragon-like creatures to her imagination. But not the slightest motion of her hand lying in Alec's indicated reluctance as he led her into the shop and right up to the wrathful man.

"Peter Whaup, here's a lassie that's most frozen to death with cold. Will you take her in and let her stand by your fire and warm herself?"

"I'll do that, Alec. Come in, my bairn. What do they call ye?"

"Annie Anderson."

"Ow, ay! I know all about ye well enough. Ye can leave her with me, Alec. I'll look after her."

"I must go back to my boat, Annie," said Alec apologetically, "but I'll come back for you again."

So Annie was left with the smith, of whom she was not the least afraid now that she had heard him speak. With his leather apron he swept a space on the front of the elevated hearth of the forge, clear of dust and cinders. Then, having wiped his hands on the same apron, he lifted the girl as tenderly as if she had been a baby and set her down on this spot, about a yard from the fire and on a level with it. And there she sat in front of the smith, looking back and forth between the smith and the fire. He asked her a great many questions about herself and the Bruces, and her former life at home. And every question he asked he put in a yet kindlier voice. Sometimes he would stop in the middle of blowing, lean forward with his arm on the handle of the bellows, and look full in the child's face till she was through answering him.

"Ay, ay!" he would say, resuming his blowing slowly, with eyes that shone in the light of the fire. For this terrible smith's heart was just like his fire. He was a dreadful fellow for quarrelling when he got a drop too much of the drink. But to this little woman-child his ways were as soft and tender as a mother's.

"And ye say ye liked it at the farm best?" he said.

"Ay. But, you see, my father died—"

"I ken that, my bairn. The Lord hold tight to ye!"

It was not often that Peter Whaup indulged in a pious remark. But this was a genuine one, and may be worth recording for the sake of Annie's answer.

"I'm thinking he holds tight to us all, Mr. Whaup."

Then she told him about the rats and the cat. For hardly a day passed at this time without her not merely retelling it but reflecting on it. And when she was done the smith drew the back of his hand across both his eyes and then pressed both hard with the thumb and forefinger of his right hand. But he hardly needed to do so, for Annie would never have noticed his tears and the heat from the fire would have quickly dried them. Then he pulled out the red-hot iron bar which he seemed to have forgotten ever since Annie came in, and standing with his back to her to protect her from the sparks, he put it on his anvil and began to lay on it as if in a fury while the sparks flew from his blows. Then, as if anxious to hear the child speak again, he put the iron once more in the fire, proceeded to rouse the wrath of the coals, and said:

"Ye kent James Dow, then?"

"Ay, well that. I knew Dowie as well as Brownie."

"Who was Brownie?"

"Ow, nobody but my own cow."

"An' James was kind to ye?"

To this question no reply followed. But Peter, who stood looking at her, saw her lips and the muscles of her face quivering an answer, which if uttered at all could come only in sobs and tears.

But the sound of approaching steps and voices restored her composure. Over the half door of the shop appeared two men, each bearing on his shoulder the shares of two ploughs to be sharpened. The instant she saw them she tumbled off her perch, and before they had got the door opened she was halfway to it, crying, "Dowie! Dowie!" In another instant she was lifted high in Dowie's arms.

"My little mistress!" he exclaimed kissing her. "How do ye come to be here?"

"I'm safe enough here, Dowie. Don't be afraid. I'll tell you all about it. Alec's in George Macwha's shop yonder."

"And who's Alec?" asked Dowie.

Leaving them to their private communications, James Dow's young companion and the smith set to work sharpening the blades of the ploughs. In about fifteen minutes Alec returned to the shop.

Addressing herself to Dowie, who still held her in his arms, Annie said, "This is Alec, that I told you about. He's right good to me. Alec, here's Dowie, that I like better than anybody in the world."

She turned and kissed the bronzed face, which was a clean face notwithstanding the contrary appearance given it by a beard of three days' growth, which Annie's kiss was too full of love to mind.

Later, Dowie carried Annie home in his arms, and on the way she told him all about the kindness of Alec and his mother. He asked her many questions about the Bruces. But her patient nature, and the instinctive feeling that it would make Dowie unhappy, caused her to withhold representing the hardships of her position in too strong colours. Dowie, however, had his own thoughts on the matter.

"How are ye tonight, Mr. Dow?" said Robert, who treated him with oily respect because he was not only acquainted with all Annie's affairs but was a kind of natural if not legal guardian of her and her property. "And where did you fall in with this stray lammie of ours?"

"She's been with me all this time," answered Dow, declining with Scotch instinct to give an answer before he understood the drift of the question. A Scotsman would always like the last question first.

"She's some ill for running out," said Bruce, with soft words addressed to Dow, and a cutting look flung at Annie, "without asking permission, and we don't know where she goes. That's not right for such small girls."

"Never ye mind, Mr. Bruce," replied Dow. "I know her better than you, not meaning any offense, seeing she was in my arms afore she was a week old. Let her go where she likes, and if she does what she shouldn't do, I'll bear all the blame for it."

Now there was no great anxiety about Annie's welfare in the minds of Mr. and Mrs. Bruce. The shop and their own children—chiefly the former—occupied their thoughts. The less trouble they had from the presence of Annie the better pleased they were—provided they could always escape the judgment of neglect. Hence it was that Annie's absences were but little inquired into.

But Bruce did not like the influence that James Dow had with her, and before they retired for the night, he had another lecture ready for Annie.

"Annie," he said, "it's not becoming for one in your station to be so familiar. You'll be a young lady someday, and it's not right to take up with servants. There's James Dow, just a labouring man, and beneath your station altogether, and he takes you up in his arms as if you were a child of his own. It's not proper."

"I like James Dow better than anybody in the whole world," said Annie, "except—"

Here she stopped short. She would not expose her heart to the gaze of this man.

"Except who?" urged Bruce.

"I'm not going to say," returned Annie firmly.

"You're a perverse lassie," said Bruce, pushing her away with forceful acidity in the combination of tone and push.

She walked off to bed, caring nothing for his rebuke. Since Alec's kindness had opened to her a well of the water of life, she had almost ceased to suffer from the ungeniality of her guardians. She forgot them as soon as she was out of their sight. And certainly they were better to forget than to remember.

— Twenty-One —

Ballads

As soon as she was alone in her room, Annie drew from her pocket a parcel which Dowie had bought for her on their way home. When undone it revealed two or three tallow candles! But how would she get a light? For this was long before matches had risen upon the horizon of Glamerton. There was but one way.

She waited, sitting on the edge of her bed in the cold and darkness, until every sound in the house had ceased. Then she stepped cautiously down the old stairs, which would crack now and then however gentle she attempted to be.

It was the custom in all the houses of Glamerton to *rest* the fire, that is, to keep it gently alive all night by the help of a *truff,* sod cut from the top of a peat moss—a coarse peat in fact, more loose and porous than the proper peat—which they laid close down upon the fire, destroying most of the draught for its live coals. To this sealed fountain of light the little maiden was creeping through the dark house with one of her candles in her hand.

A pretty study she would have made for an artist, her face close to the grate, mouth puckered up to do its duty as a bellows, one hand holding a twisted piece of paper between the bars, while she blew at the live but reluctant fire, a glow spreading over her face at each breath and then fading as the breath ceased till at last the paper caught.

Thus she lit her candle and again with careful steps made her way back up to her own room. Setting the candle in a hole in the floor left by the departure of a knot, she opened her box in which lay the few books her aunt had thrown into it when she left her old home. One of these contained poems of a little-known Scottish poet her father had been fond of reading. She searched in it for something to learn before the following night, and soon found a ballad that struck her fancy. It was very cold work at midnight in winter, and in a garret too, but she feared that the open enjoyment of such a book in the sight of any of the Bruces would only lead to its being confiscated as "altogether unsuitable for one so young."

When she entered George Macwha's workshop the next evening, she found the two boys already busy at their work. Without interrupting them she took her place on the heap of shavings which had remained undisturbed since the previous night. As she sat, unconsciously from her mouth began to come fragments of one of the ballads she had read several times from her father's book. The boys did not know what to make of it at first, hearing something come all at once from Annie's lips which broke upon the silence like an alien sound.

O lat me in, my bonny lass!
It's a lang road ower the hill;
And the flauchterin' snaw began to fa',
As I cam' by the mill.

She continued for two or three more stanzas until her memory failed her.

George Macwha, who was at work in the other end of the shop when she began, had drawn near, chisel in hand, and joined the listeners.

"Well done, Annie!" he exclaimed as soon as she had finished, feeling very shy and awkward at what she had done.

"Say it over again, Annie," said Alec.

This was music to her ears! Could she have wished for more?

She repeated it again, this time adding still another verse that came back to her.

"Eh, Annie! That's real bonnie. Where did you get it?" he asked.

"In an old book of my father's."

"Is there any more like it."

"Ay, lots."

"Just learn another, will you, before tomorrow?"

"I'll do that, Alec."

"Didn't ye like it, Curly?" asked Alec, for Curly had said nothing.

"Ay, fegs!" was Curly's emphatic and uncritical reply.

Such a reception to her verses motivated Annie wonderfully, and she continued her midnight reading with heightened enthusiasm, now carrying the precious volume, which she hoped would bind her yet more closely to the boat and its builders, to and from school, practicing verses the whole way as she went and taking a roundabout road that her cousins might not interrupt her or discover her pursuit.

A rapid thaw set in, and up through the vanishing whiteness dawned the dark colours of mire and dirt on the wintry landscape. But once the snow had vanished a hard black frost set in. The surface of the slow-flowing Glamour and of the swifter Wan Water were chilled and stiffened to ice, which grew thicker and stronger every day. And now, there being no coverlet of snow upon it, the boys came out in troops. In their ironclad shoes and their clumsy skates, they skimmed along those floors of delight that the winter had laid for them. Alec and Willie left their boat—almost forgot it for a time—repaired their skates, joined their schoolfellows, and shot along the solid water with the banks flying past them.

For many afternoons and into the early night, Alec and Curly held on to the joyful sport, and Annie was for a time left lonely. But she was neither disconsolate nor idle. To the boat and her they must return. She went to the shop now and then to see George Macwha, who, of an age beyond the seduction of ice and skates, kept on steadily at his work. To him she would repeat a ballad or two at his request, and then go home to learn another. This was becoming, however, a work of some difficulty, for her provision of candles was exhausted and she had no money with which to buy more. The last candle had come to a tragic end. Hearing footsteps approaching her room one morning, before she had put it away in its usual safety in her box, she hastily poked it into one of the holes of the floor and forgot it. When she sought it at night it was gone. Her first dread was that she had been found out. But hearing nothing of it, she concluded that her enemies the rats had carried it off and devoured it.

"Devil choke them on the wick of it!" exclaimed Curly when she told him the next day, seeking a partner in her grief.

But a greater difficulty had to be encountered. It was not long before she had exhausted the contents of the little book of her father's. There being no more of that type among the contents of her chest, she thought where she might find another, and at last came to the resolution of applying to Mr. Cowie, the clergyman. Without consulting anyone, she knocked at Mr. Cowie's door the very next afternoon.

"Could I see the minister?" she said to the maid.

"I don't know. What do you want?" was the maid's reply.

But Annie was Scottish too and perhaps perceived that she would have but a small chance of being admitted if she revealed the object of her request to the servant. So she only replied, "I want to see himself, if you please."

"Well, come in and I will tell him. What's your name?"

"Annie Anderson."

"Where do you live?"

"At the Bruces', in the Wast Wynd."

The maid went and presently returned with the message that she was to go up the stairs. She conducted her up to the study where the minister sat—a room, to Annie's amazement, filled with books from the top to the bottom of every wall. Mr. Cowie held out his hand to her and said, "Well, my little maiden, what do you want?"

"Please, sir, would you lend me a songbook?"

"A psalm book?" said the minister, supposing he had not heard correctly.

"No, sir, I have a psalm book at home. It's a songbook I want, a book of poems and ballads."

Now the minister was one of the old school—a very worthy, kindhearted man. He knew what some of his Lord's words meant, and among them certain words about little children. He likewise had a feeling of more instinctive origin, that to be kind to little children was an important branch of his office. So he drew Annie close to him as he sat in his easy chair, and said in the gentlest way:

"And what do you want a songbook for, dawtie?"

"To learn bonnie ballads out of it, sir. Don't you think they're the bonniest things in the world?"

For Annie had by this time learned to love ballad verse above everything but Alec and Dowie.

"And what kind of poems do you like?" the clergyman asked, instead of replying.

"I like them best that make you cry, sir."

At every answer she looked up in his face with her open, clear-blue eyes. And the minister began to love her, not merely because she was a child, but because she was this child.

"Do you sing them?" he asked, after a little pause spent gazing into the face of the child.

"No. I only say them. I don't know the tunes."

"And do you say them to Mr. Bruce?"

"Mr. Bruce, sir! Mr. Bruce would say I was daft. I wouldn't say them to him, sir, for all the sweeties in his shop."

"Well, who do you say them to?"

"To Alec Forbes and Willie Macwha. They're building a boat, sir, and they like to have me by them to say songs to them while they work. And I like it right well."

"It'll be a lucky boat, surely," said the minister, "to rise to the sound of rhyme, like some old Norse warship."

"I don't know, sir," said Annie, who certainly did not know what he meant.

"Well, let's see what we can find for you, Annie," said the minister, rising from his chair and taking her by the hand.

He led her into the dining room to ask his daughters' assistance in finding a suitable book. There tea was all laid out. He led her to the table and Annie went without a thought of question or a feeling of doubt. It was a profound pleasure to her not to know what was coming next, provided someone whom she loved did. So she sat down to the tea with the perfect composure of submission to a superior will. It never occurred to her that she had no right to be there, for had not the minister himself led her there? And his daughters were very kind and friendly. In the course of the meal, Mr. Cowie told them the difficulty, and one of his daughters said that she might be able to find what the girl wanted.

After tea she left the room and returned presently with two volumes of ballads of all sorts—some old, some new, some Scottish, some English. She put the books in Annie's hands. The child eagerly opened one of the volumes and glanced at a page. It sparkled with just the right ore of ballad words. The colour of delight grew in her face. She closed the book as if she could not trust herself to look at it while the others were looking at her, and said with a sigh:

"Eh, mem! You won't trust me with *both* of them?"

"Yes, I will," said Miss Cowie. "I am sure you will take care of them."

"That—I—will," returned Annie with an honesty and determination of purpose that made a great impression on Mr. Cowie. She ran home some time later with a feeling of richness of possession such as she had never before experienced.

Her first business was to scamper up to her room and hide the precious treasures in her chest, there to wait all night like the buried dead for the coming morning.

When she confessed to Mr. Bruce that she had had tea with the minister, he held up his hands in the manner which commonly expresses amazement. But what the peculiar character or ground of the amazement was would have to remain entirely unrevealed, for he said not a single word to elucidate the gesture.

The next time Annie went to see the minister, it was on a very different quest from the loan of a songbook.

– Twenty-Two –

Murdoch Malison

One afternoon as Alec went home to dinner, he was considerably surprised to find Mr. Malison leaning on one of the rails of the footbridge over the Glamour, looking down on its frozen surface. There was nothing so unusual in this, but what was surprising was that the scholars seldom encountered the master anywhere except in school. Alec thought to pass, but the moment his foot was on the bridge the master lifted himself up from the railing and turned toward him.

"Well, Alec," he said, "and where have you been?"

"To get a new strap for my skates," answered Alec.

"You're fond of skating, are you, Alec?"

"Yes, sir."

"I used to be when I was a boy. Have you had your dinner?"

"No, sir."

"Then I suppose neither has your mother?"

"She never does until I get home, sir."

"Then I won't intrude on her. I did mean to call this afternoon."

"She will be very glad to see you, sir. Come and take a share of what there is."

"I think I had better not, Alec."

"Do, sir. I'm sure she will make you welcome."

Mr. Malison hesitated. Alec pressed him. He yielded, and they went along the road together.

The school half of Mr. Malison's life was, both inwardly and outwardly, very different from the rest. The moment he was out of school, the whole character—certainly the whole deportment—of the man changed. He was now as meek and gentle in speech and behaviour as any mother could have desired.

Nor was the change a hypocritical one. The master never interfered, or only upon the rarest occasions when pressure from without was brought to bear upon him, as in the case of Juno, with what the boys did out of school. He was glad enough to accept utter irresponsibility for that portion of his time. Between the two parts of the day, as they passed through the life of the master, there was almost as little connection as between the waking and sleeping hours of a sleepwalker.

But as he leaned over the rail of the bridge where a rare impulse to movement had driven him, his thoughts had turned upon Alec Forbes and his antagonism. Out of school he could not help feeling that the boy had not been very far wrong, however subversive of authority his behaviour had been. But it was not therefore the less mortifying to recall how he had been treated by him. He was compelled to acknowledge to himself that it was a mercy Alec was not a boy to follow up his advantage by turning the rest of the school against him, which would have been ready enough to follow such a victorious leader. So there was but one way of setting matters right, as Mr. Malison had generosity enough left within him to perceive, and that was to make a friend of his adversary. Indeed, there is that in the depths of every human breast which makes reconciliation the only victory that can give true satisfaction. Nor was the master the only one to gain by the resolve which thus arose in his mind the very moment before he felt Alec's footsteps upon the bridge.

They walked together to Howglen, talking kindly the whole way, to which talk, and most likely to which kindness between them, a little incident had contributed as well. Alec had that day rendered a passage of Virgil with remarkable accuracy, greatly pleasing to the master, who, however, had no idea what had caused this isolated success. The passage had reference to the setting of sails, and Alec could not rest till he had satisfied himself about its meaning. So he had with some difficulty cleared away the mists that clung about the words, till at length he beheld and understood the facts embodied in them.

Alec had never had praise from Mr. Malison before—at least none that had made any impression on him—and he found it very sweet. And through the pleasure dawned the notion that perhaps he might be a scholar after all if he put his mind to it. Mrs. Forbes, seeing the pleasure on Alec's face, received Mr. Malison with more than the usual cordiality, forgetting once he was present before her eyes the former bitterness she had felt toward him.

As soon as dinner was over, Alec rushed off to the river, leaving his mother and the master together. Mrs. Forbes brought out the whisky-bottle, and Mr. Malison, mixing a tumbler of toddy, filled a wine-glass for his hostess.

"We'll make a man of Alec someday yet," he said.

"Indeed!" returned Mrs. Forbes, somewhat irritated at the suggestion of any difficulty in the way of Alec's ultimate manhood. Perhaps she was glad for the opportunity of speaking her mind at last. "Indeed, Mr. Malison, you ridiculed him a month ago! It would do you well to try your hand at making a man of him now."

For a moment the dominie was taken aback and sat over his toddy growing red. The despotism exercised in the school, even though exercised with a certain sense of justice and right, made the autocrat, out of school, cower before the parents of his helpless subjects. With this quailing in his heart he suddenly perceived that his only chance was to throw himself on the generosity of a woman. He said:

"Well, ma'am, if you had to keep seventy boys and girls quiet, and hear their lessons at the same time, perhaps you would feel yourself in danger of doing in haste what you might repent at leisure."

"Well, well, Mr. Malison, we'll talk no more about it. My laddie's none the worse for it. And I hope you will make a man of him someday, as you say."

"He translated a passage of Virgil today in a manner that surprised me."

"Did he though? He's not a dunce, I know. If it weren't for that stupid boat he and William Macwha are building, he might be made a scholar of. George should have more sense than to encourage such a waste of time and money. He's always wanting something or other for the boat, and I confess I can't find it in my heart to refuse him, for whatever he may be at school, he's a good boy at home, Mr. Malison."

But the schoolmaster did not reply at once, for a light had dawned on him. This was the secret of Alec's translation—a secret worth his finding out. One can hardly believe that this was his first revelation that a practical interest is the strongest incitement to learning. But such was the case. He answered after a moment's pause—

"I suspect, ma'am, on the contrary, that the boat, of which I had heard nothing till now, was Alec's private tutor in the passage of Virgil."

"I don't understand you, Mr. Malison."

"I mean, ma'am, that his interest in his boat made him take an interest in those lines about ships and their rigging. So the boat taught him to translate them."

"I see.

"And that makes me doubt whether we shall be able to make him learn anything to good purpose that he does not take an interest in."

"Well, what *do* you think he is fit for, Mr. Malison? I should like him to be able to be something other than a farmer, whatever he may settle down to at last."

Mrs. Forbes thought, whether wisely or not, that as long as she was able to manage the farm, Alec might as well be otherwise employed. And she had ambition for her son as well. But the master was able to make no definite suggestion. Alec seemed to have no special qualification for any profession, for the mechanical and constructive faculties alone had reached a high point of development in him as yet. So after a long talk, his mother and the schoolmaster had come no nearer than before to a determination of what he was fit for. The interview, however, restored a good understanding between them.

– Twenty-Three –

Religious Talk

It was upon a Friday night that the frost finally broke up. A day of wintry rain followed, dreary and depressing. But the two boys, Alec and Willie, had a refuge from the weather in their boat building. In the early evening of the following Saturday, they were in close conversation about a doubtful point in their labour. George Macwha entered his shop in conversation with Thomas Crann, the mason, who, his bodily labours being quite interrupted by the rain, had the more leisure to bring his mental powers to bear upon the condition of his neighbours.

"Tis a sad pity, George," he was saying as he entered, "that a man like yerself wouldna once take a thought and consider the end of everything the sun shines upon."

"How do ye know, Thomas, that I dinna take such thought?"

"Do ye say that ye *do*, George?"

"I'm a bit of a Protestant, though I'm no missionar."

"Well, well. I can only say that I hae seen no signs of a saving seriousness about ye, George. Ye're too taken up wi' the world."

"How do ye come to think that? Ye build houses, and I make doors for them. And they'll both be standing after both ye and me's laid in the ground. It's well kent that ye have a bit of money in the bank, and I hae none."

"Not a penny hae I, George. I can pray for my daily bread with an honest heart. For if the Lord doesna send it, I hae no bank to fall back on."

"I'm sorry to hear it, Thomas," said George—"But God guide us!" he exclaimed, "there's the two laddies listening to every word we say!"

He hoped thus to turn the current of the conversation, but hoped in vain.

"All the better," persisted Thomas. "They need to be reminded as well as yerself and me that the ways of this world passeth away.—Alec, my man, Willie, my lad, can ye build a boat to take ye over the river of Death? No, ye canna do that. But there's an Ark of the Covenant that'll carry ye safe over, and that's a worse flood to boot.—'Upon the wicked he shall rain fire and brimstone—a furious tempest.'—We had a grand sermon on the Ark of the Covenant from young Mr. Mirky last Sabbath night. Why won't ye come and hear the Gospel for once at least, George Macwha? Ye can sit in my seat."

"I'm obliged to ye," answered George, "but the muckle kirk does well enough for me."

"The muckle kirk!" repeated Thomas in a tone of contempt. "What do ye get there but the dry bones of morality upon which the wind of the Word has never blown to put life into the poor skeleton. Come to our kirk and ye'll get a rousing, I can tell ye, man. Eh! man, if ye were once converted, ye would know how to sing."

Before the conversation had reached this point another listener had arrived. The blue eyes of Annie Anderson were fixed upon the speaker from over the half door of the workshop. The drip from the thatch eaves was soaking her shabby little shawl as she stood, but she was utterly heedless of it in listening to Thomas Crann, who talked with authority and a kind of hard eloquence of persuasion.

I ought to explain here that the *muckle kirk* meant the parish Presbyterian church. The religious community to which Thomas Crann belonged was an independent body which commonly went by the name of *Missionars* in that district, a name arising apparently from the fact that they were among the first in that neighbourhood to advocate sending missionaries out to the heathen.

"Are ye not going to get a minister of yer own, Thomas?" resumed George after a pause, still wishing to turn the cartwheels of the conversation out of the deep ruts in which the stiff-necked Thomas seemed determined to keep them moving.

"We'll wait a while and try the spirits. We're not like you—forced to swallow any jabble of lukewarm water that's been standing in the sun from year's end to year's end just because the patron pleases to stick a pump in it and call it the well of salvation. We'll know where the water comes from. We'll taste them all, and choose accordingly."

"Well, I wouldna like the trouble nor the responsibility of that."

"I dare say not."

"No. Nor the shame of pretending to judge my betters," added George, now a little nettled, as was generally the end result of Thomas's sarcastic tone.

"George," said Thomas solemnly, "none but them that has the Spirit can know the Spirit."

With these words he turned and strode slowly and gloomily out of the shop—no doubt from dissatisfaction with the result of his attempt.

The child-heart of Annie was perfectly convinced that Thomas was possessed of some divine secret, the tone of his voice having a greater share in producing this conviction than anything he had said. As he passed out she looked up reverently at him, as one to whom deep things lay open. Thomas had a kind of gruff gentleness toward children which they found very attractive. And this meek maiden he could not threaten with the vials of wrath. He laid his hard, heavy hand kindly on her head, saying:

"Ye'll be one of the Lord's lambs, won't ye, now? Ye'll go into the fold after him, won't ye?"

"Ay, will I," answered Annie, "if he'll let in Alec and Curly too."

"Ye must make no bargains wi' him. But if they'll go in, he'll not hold them oot."

Somewhat comforted, the honest stonemason strode away through the darkness and rain to his own rather cheerless home where he had neither wife nor child to welcome him. An elderly woman took care of his house, whose habitual attitude toward him was half of awe and half of resistance. The moment he entered, she left the room where she had been sitting, without a word of welcome, and betook herself to the kitchen, where she prepared his plate of porridge or bowl of brose. With this in one hand, and a jug of milk in the other, she soon returned, placing them like a peace-offering on the table before him. Having completed the arrangement by the addition of a horn spoon from a cupboard in the wall, she again retired in silence. The moment she vanished Thomas's blue cap was thrown into a corner, and with folded hands and bent head he prayed a silent prayer over his homely meal.

By this time, having received sufficient instruction from George Macwha, Alec and Curly were in full swing with their boat building. But the moment Thomas went, Alec took Annie to the forge to get her well dried out before he would allow her to occupy her place on the heap of shavings.

"Who's preaching at the missionar kirk in the morn, Willie?" asked the boy's father. For Willie knew everything that took place in Glamerton.

"Mr. Brown," answered Curly.

"He's a good man anyway," returned his father. "There's not many like him. I think I'll turn missionar myself for once, and go hear him tomorrow night."

At the same instant Annie entered the shop, her face glowing with the heat of the forge and the pleasure of rejoining her friends. Her appearance turned the current and no more was said about the missionar kirk. Only a few minutes had passed before she had begun to repeat to the eager listeners one of the two new poems she had got ready for them from the book Miss Cowie had loaned her.

– Twenty-Four –

Hellfire

Whatever effect the arguments of Thomas might or might not have had upon the rest, Annie had heard enough to make her want to go to the missionar kirk. Was it not plain that Thomas Crann knew something that she did not know? And where could he have learned it but at the said kirk? For she was one of those simple creatures who perceive at once that if they are to set anything right for themselves or other people, they must begin with their own selves, their inward being and life. So without knowing that George Macwha intended to be there, and with no expectation of seeing Alec or Curly, and without having consulted any of the Bruce family, she found herself, a few minutes after the service had commenced, timidly peering through the inner door of the chapel.

She started back, with mingled shyness and awe, from the huge solemnity of the place. Every eye seemed to dart toward her the moment she made a chink of light between the door and its post. And what added to the effect on Annie was, that the reputation of Mr. Brown having drawn a great congregation to hear him preach that evening, she, peeping through the door, saw nothing but live faces, whereas Mr. Cowie's church, though much larger, was only so much emptier.

She withdrew in dismay to go up into the gallery upstairs, where, entering from behind, she would see fewer faces than she had when opening the door below from right behind the preacher. She stole to a seat as a dog might steal across the room to creep under the master's table. When she ventured to lift her head, she found herself in the middle of a sea of heads. The minister was reading, in a solemn voice, a terrible chapter of denunciation out of the prophet Isaiah, and

Annie was soon seized with a deep listening awe. The severity of the chapter was, however, considerably softened by the gentleness of an old lady sitting next to her who put into her hand a Bible, smelling sweetly of dried leaves, in which Annie followed the reading word for word.

For his sermon, Mr. Brown chose for his text these words of the Psalmist: "The wicked shall be turned into hell, and all the nations that forget God." His sermon was less ponderous in construction and multitudinous in division than usual, for it consisted simply of answers to the two questions: "Who are the wicked?" and "What is their fate?" The answer to the first question was, "The wicked are those that forget God." The answer to the latter was, "The torments of everlasting fire." Upon Annie the sermon produced the immediate conviction that she was one of the wicked and that she was in danger of hellfire. The distress generated by the sermon, however, like that occasioned by the chapter of prophecy, was considerably lessened by the kindness of the unknown hand, which kept up a counteractive ministration of peppermint lozenges. But the preacher's representations grew so much in horror as the sermon approached its end, that when at last it was over and Annie drew one long breath of exhaustion, she became aware that the peppermint lozenge which had been given her a quarter of an hour before was still lying undissolved in her mouth.

When all had ceased—when the prayer, the singing, and the final benediction were over—Annie crept out into the dark street as if into the outer darkness. She felt the rain falling upon something hot, but she hardly knew that it was her own cheeks being wet by the heavy drops. Her first impulse was to run to Alec and Curly, put her arms around their necks and entreat them to flee from the wrath to come. But she could not find them tonight. She must go home. For herself she was not too much afraid. For there was a place where her prayers were heard as certainly as at the mercy seat of old—a little garret room, namely, with holes in the floors out of which came rats, but with a door as well, in through which came the prayed-for cat.

But alas for Annie and her chapel going! For as she was creeping up from step to step in the dark, the feeling came over her that it was no longer against the rats that she had to pray. A spiritual terror was seated on the throne of the universe, and was called God—and to whom should she pray against it? Amidst the darkness, a deeper darkness fell.

She knelt by her bedside but she could not lift up her heart, for was she not one of them that forgot God, and was she not therefore very wicked? And was not God angry with her every day?

But there was Jesus Christ. She would cry to him. But did she believe in him? She tried hard to convince herself that she did. At last she laid her weary head on the bed and groaned in despair. At that moment a rustling in the darkness broke the sad silence with a throb of terror. She jumped to her feet. She was exposed to all the rats in the universe now, for God was angry with her, and she could not pray. The cat would not help now!

With a stifled scream she darted to the door and half tumbled down the stairs in an agony of fear.

"What makes you make such a din in the house on the Sabbath night?" shouted Mrs. Bruce.

But little did Annie feel the reproof. And as little did she know that the dreaded rats had this time been messengers of God to drive her from a path in which lies madness. She was forced at length to go to bed, where God made her sleep and forget him, and the rats did not come near her again that night.

Curly and Alec had been in the chapel too, but they were not of a temperament to be disturbed by Mr. Brown's discourse.

– Twenty-Five –

Truffey

Little as Murdoch Malison knew of the worlds of thoughts and feelings which lay within those young faces assembled as usual the next day, he knew almost as little of the mysteries that lay within himself.

Annie was haunted all day with the thought of the wrath of God. When she forgot it for a moment it would return again with a sting of actual physical pain, which seemed to pierce her heart. Before school was over she had made up her mind what to do.

And before school was over, Malison's own deed had opened his own eyes, had broken through the crust that lay between him and the vision of his own character.

There is not be found a more thorough impersonation of his own theology than a Scots schoolmaster of the rough, old-fashioned type. His pleasure was law, irrespective of right or wrong, and the reward of submission to law was immunity from punishment. He had his favourites in various degrees, whom he chose according to inexplicable directions of feeling. These found it easy to please him, while those with whom he was not primarily pleased found it impossible to please him.

Now there had come to the school about two weeks before, two unhappy-looking little twin orphans, with thin white faces and bones in their clothes instead of legs and arms, committed to the mercies of Mr. Malison by their grandfather. Bent into all the angles of a grasshopper, and lean with ancient poverty, the old man tottered away with his stick in one hand and saying in a quavering, croaking voice, "Now ye jist give them their whips well, Master Malison, for ye know that he that spareth the rod spoileth the bairn."

Thus authorized, Malison certainly did "give them their whips well." Before that day was over, they had both lain shrieking on the floor under the torture of the lash. And such poor half-clothed, half-fed creatures they were, and looked so pitiful and cowed, that one cannot help thinking it must have been for his own glory rather than their good that he treated them thus.

But in justice to Malison, another fact must be mentioned which, although inconsistent with the one just recorded, was in perfect consistency with the theological subsoil from whence both sprang. After about a week, during which they had been whipped almost every day, the orphans came to school with a cold and a terrible cough. Then his observant pupils saw the man who was both cruel judge and cruel executioner feeding his victims with licorice till their faces were stained with its exuberance.

The old habits of severity, which had in some measure been interrupted, had returned upon him with gathered strength, and this day Annie was to be one of the victims. Although he would not dare to whip her, he was about to incur the shame of making this day, pervaded as it was with the fumes of the sermon she had heard the night before, the most wretched day that Annie's sad life had yet seen. The spirits of the pit seemed to have broken loose and filled Murdoch Malison's schoolroom with the stench of their fire and brimstone.

She sat longing for school to be over that she might follow a plan which had a glimmer of hope in it. Stupefied with her labouring thoughts, she fell fast asleep. She was roused by a stinging blow from the tawse, flung with unerring aim at the back of her bare neck. She sprang up with a cry and, tottering between sleep and terror, proceeded at once to take the leather snake back to the master. She would have fallen halfway had not Alec caught her in his arms. He reseated her and, taking the tawse from her trembling hand, carried it himself to the tyrant. Upon him Malison's fury broke loose, expelling itself in a dozen blows on the right hand which Alec held up without flinching. As he walked to his seat, burning with pain, the voice of the master sounded behind him.

"Ann Anderson," he bawled, "stand up on the seat."

With trembling limbs Annie obeyed. She could scarcely stand at first and her knees shook beneath her. For some time her colour kept alternating between crimson and white, but at last settled into a deadly pallor. Indeed, it was to her a terrible punishment to be exposed to the looks of all the boys and girls in the school. The elder of the two Bruces tried hard to make her see one of his vile grimaces, but feeling as if every nerve in her body were being stung with eyes, she never dared to look away from the book which she held upside down before her. This was the punishment for falling asleep, as hell was the punishment for forgetting God, and there she had to stand for a whole hour.

"What a shame! Damn that Malison!" and various other subdued exclamations were murmured about the room, for Annie was a favourite with most of the boys, and yet more because she was "the General's sweetheart," as they said. But these expressions of popular feeling were too faint to reach her ears and comfort her isolation and exposure. Worst of all, she soon had to witness all the more clearly an outbreak of the master's temper far more painful than she had yet seen, both from its cruelty and its consequences.

A small class of mere children, among whom were the Truffey orphans, had been committed to the care of one of the bigger boys while the master was engaged with another class. Every boy in the latter had already had his share of punishments, when a noise in the children's class attracted the master's attention. He turned and saw one of the Truffeys hit another boy in the face. He strode upon him at once. Asking not a single question as to the reason for the provocation, he took him by the neck, fixed it between his knees, and began to lash him with stinging blows. In his agony the little fellow managed to twist his head about and get a mouthful of the master's leg, employing his teeth in a most canine and praiseworthy manner. The master caught him up and threw him on the floor. There the child lay, motionless. Alarmed and cooled off as a result, Malison proceeded to lift him. He was apparently lifeless, but he had only fainted with pain. When he came to himself a little, it was found that his leg was hurt. It appeared afterward that the kneecap was greatly injured. Moaning with pain, he was sent home on the back of a big parish scholar.

Annie stared at all this with horror. The feeling that God was angry with her grew upon her, and Murdoch Malison became for a time inseparably associated with her idea of God.

The master still looked uneasy, threw the tawse into his desk, and beat no one more that day. Indeed, only half an hour of school time was left. As soon as it was over, he set off at a rapid pace for the old grandfather's cottage.

What passed there was never known. The other Truffey came to school the next day as usual and told the boys that his brother was in bed. In that bed he lay for many weeks, and many were the visits the master paid him. This did much with the townsfolk to wipe away his reproach. They spoke of the affair as an unfortunate accident, and pitied the schoolmaster even more than the victim.

When at length the poor boy was able to leave his bed, it became apparent that he would be a cripple for life.

The master's general behaviour was certainly modified by this consequence of his fury, but it was some time before the full reaction arrived.

– Twenty-Six –

Mr. Cowie Again

When Annie descended from her hateful position just before the final prayer, it was with a deeper sense of degradation than any violence of the tawse on her poor little hands could have produced. Nor could the attentions of Alec, anxiously offered as soon as they were out of school, console her as they once might have, for such was her sense of condemnation that she dared not take pleasure in anything. The thought of having God against her took the heart out of everything. Nothing else was worth minding till something was done about that. As soon as Alec left her, she walked straight to Mr. Cowie's door.

She was admitted at once and shown into the library where the clergyman sat in the red, dusky glow of the fireplace.

"Well, Annie, my dear," he said, "I am glad to see you. How does the boat get on?"

Deeply touched by his kindness which fell like dew upon the parching misery of the day, Annie burst into tears. Mr. Cowie was greatly distressed. He drew her between his knees, laid his cheek against hers, and said with soothing tenderness:

"What's the matter with my dawtie?"

After some vain attempts at speech, Annie succeeded in giving the following account of the matter, much interrupted with sobs and fresh outbursts of weeping.

"You see, sir, I went last night to the missionar kirk to hear Mr. Brown. And he preached a grand sermon. But I haven't been able to bide myself since then. For I'm one of the wicked that God hates, and I'll never get to heaven, for I can't help forgetting him sometimes.

And the wicked'll be turned into hell and all the nations that forget God. And I can't stand it."

In the heart of the good man rose a gentle indignation against the schismatics who had thus terrified and bewildered that sacred being, a small child. He thought for a moment and then gave in to his common sense.

"You haven't forgotten your father, have you, Annie?" he said.

"I think about him most every day," she answered.

"But there comes a day now and then when you don't think much about him, doesn't there?"

"Yes, sir."

"Do you think he would be angry with his child because she was so much taken up with her books or her play—"

"I never play with anything, sir."

"Well, with learning poems and songs to say to Alec Forbes and Willie Macwha? Do you think he would be angry that you didn't think about him that day, especially when you can't see him?"

"Indeed no, sir. He wouldn't be so hard upon me as that."

"What do you think he would say?"

"If Mr. Bruce were to get after me for it, my father would say: 'Let the lassie alone. She'll think about me another day—there's time enough!'"

"Well, don't you think your Father in heaven would say the same?"

"Maybe he might, sir. But, you see, my father was my own father, and would make the best of me."

"And is not God kinder than your father?"

"He couldn't be that, sir. And there's the Scripture besides."

"He sent his own Son to die for us."

"Ay—for the elect, sir," returned the little theologian.

Now this was more than Mr. Cowie was well prepared to meet, for certainly this terrible doctrine was perfectly developed in the creed of his own Scottish church as well—the assembly of divines having sat upon the Scripture egg till they had hatched it in their own likeness. Poor Mr. Cowie! There were the girl's eyes, blue and hazy with tearful questions, looking up at him hungrily—O starving little brothers and sisters! God does love you, and all shall be, and therefore is, well.—But the minister could not say this, gladly as he would have said it if he could, and the only result of his efforts to find a suitable reply was that he lost his temper—not with Annie, but with the doctrine of election.

"Go home, Annie, my bairn," he said, "and don't trouble your head about election and all that. It's not a good doctrine. No mortal man can ever get to the bottom of it. I'm thinking we maybe shouldn't have much to do with it. Go home, dawtie, and say your prayers to be preserved from the wiles of Satan. There's a sixpence to you."

His kind heart was sorely grieved that he had no more to give her. She had asked for bread, and he had but a stone, as he thought, to give her. But for my part I think the sixpence had more of bread in it than any theology he might have been expected to have at hand. For, so given, it was the symbol and the sign of love, which is the heart of divine theology.

Annie, however, drew back from the offer

"No, thank you, sir," she said. "I couldn't take it."

"Will you not take it, child, to please an old man?"

"Indeed I will, sir. I would do a lot more than that to please you."

And again the tears filled her blue eyes as she held out her hand—receiving in it a shilling which Mr. Cowie, for more relief to his own burdened heart, had substituted for the sixpence.

"It's a shilling, sir!" she said, looking up at him with the coin lying on her open palm.

"Well, why not? Isn't a shilling a sixpence?"

"Ay, sir. It's two of them."

"Well, Annie," said the old man, suddenly elevated into prophecy for the child's need, "when God offers us a sixpence, it may turn out to be two. Good night, my bairn."

But Mr. Cowie was sorely dissatisfied with himself. For not only did he perceive that the heart of the child could not thus be satisfied, but he began to feel something new stirring in his own heart. The fact was that Annie was further along than Mr. Cowie. She was a child looking to find the face of her Father in heaven, he was but one of God's babies, who had been receiving contentedly and happily the good things he gave him but never looking up to find the eyes of him from whom the good gifts came. And now the heart of the old man, touched by the motion of the child's heart—yearning after the truth about her Father in heaven, and yet scarcely believing that he could be so good as her father on earth—began to stir uneasily within him. He went down on his knees and hid his face in his hands.

Annie, though not satisfied, went away comforted. After such a day of agony and humiliation, Mr. Cowie's kiss came with gracious restoration and blessing. It had something in it which was not in Mr. Brown's sermon. And yet if she had gone to Mr. Brown, she would have found him kind too—very kind. But solemnly kind, severely kind. His long, saintly face beamed with religious tenderness—not human cordiality, not sympathy with the unhappiness which his own teaching had produced, nay, inclined rather to gloat over this unhappiness as the sign of grace bestowed and an awakening conscience.

But notwithstanding the comfort Mr. Cowie had given her—the best he had, poor man!—Annie's distress soon awoke again. To know that she could not be near God in peace and love without fulfilling certain mental conditions, that he would not have her just as she was now, filled her with an undefined but terribly real misery, only the more distressing that it was vague.

It was not, however, the strength of her love to God that made her unhappy in being thus barred out from him. It was rather the check thus given to the whole upward tendency of her being, with its multitude of undefined hopes and longings now drawing nigh to the birth. It was in her ideal self rather than her conscious self that her misery arose. And now, dearly as she loved Mr. Cowie, she began to doubt whether he knew much about the matter. He had put her off without answering her questions, either because he thought she had no business with such things, or because he had no answer to give. This latter possibility added greatly to her unhappiness, for it gave birth to a fearful doubt as to the final safety of kind Mr. Cowie himself.

But there was one man who knew more about such secret things, she fully believed, than any other man alive, and that man was Thomas Crann. Thomas was a rather dreadful man, with his cold eyes, high shoulders, and wheezing breath, and Annie was afraid of him. But she would have encountered the terrors of the Valley of the Shadow of Death to get rid of the demon nightmare that lay upon her heart, crushing the life out of it. So she plucked up courage, and resolved to set out for the house of the Interpreter. Judging, however, that he could not yet be home from his work, she thought it better to go home first herself.

After eating a bit of oatcake with a mug of blue milk, she went up to her garret and waited drearily, but did not try to pray.

– Twenty-Seven –

Thomas Crann

It was very dark by the time she left the house, for the night was drizzly. But she knew the windings of Glamerton almost as well as the way up her garret stair. Thomas's door was half open and a light was shining from the kitchen. She knocked timidly. Her knock was too gentle and was not heard inside. But as she was passing the door a moment later, Jean saw Annie standing alone on the threshold. She stopped with a start.

"The Lord preserve us, lassie!" she cried.

"Jean, what are ye swearing at?" cried Thomas angrily.

"At Annie Anderson," answered Jean simply.

"Why are ye swearin' at *her*? I'm sure she's a respectable lassie. What does the bairn want?"

"What do ye want, Annie?"

"I want to see Thomas, if you please," answered Annie.

"She wants to see ye, Thomas," shouted Jean, remarking in a low voice, "He's as deaf as a doornail, Annie Anderson."

"Let her come in," bawled Thomas.

"He's telling ye to come in, Annie," said Jean, as if she had been interpreting his words. "Go in there, Annie," she said, throwing open the door of the room adjoining the kitchen where Thomas was sitting in the dark, which was often his custom.

The child entered and stood just inside, not knowing even where Thomas sat. But a voice came to her out of the gloom. "Ye're not feart at the dark, are ye, Annie? Come in."

"I don't know where I'm going."

"Never mind that. Come straight ahead. I'm watching ye."

Thomas had been sitting in the dark till he could see in it—which, however, is not an invariable result. But she obeyed the voice and went straight forward into the dark, evidently much to the satisfaction of Thomas. Seizing her arm with one hand, he laid the other, calloused and heavy, on her head, saying:

"Now, my lass, ye'll know what faith means. When God tells ye to go into the dark, go!"

"But I don't like the dark," said Annie.

"No human soul can," responded Thomas. "Jean, bring a candle directly."

This was not the answer that might have been expected of him. But he had begun with the symbolic and mystical in his reception of Annie, and perhaps there was something in the lovely childishness of her unconscious faith, while she all the time thought herself a dreadful unbeliever, that kept Thomas to the simplicities of the mystical part of his nature. Thomas's mind was a rendezvous for all extremes. In him they met, and showed that they met by fighting all day long. If you knocked at his inner door, you never could tell what would open it to you—all depending on what happened to be uppermost in the wrestle.

A candle was brought and set on the table, showing two or three geranium plants in the window. Why her eyes should have fixed upon these, Annie tried to discover afterward, when she was more used to thinking. But she could not tell, except it were that they were so scraggy and wretched, half-drowned in the darkness and half-blanched by the miserable light, and therefore must have been very like her own feelings as she stood before the ungentle but not unkind stonemason.

"Well, lassie," he said when Jean had retired, "what do you want with me?"

Annie burst into tears.

"Jean, go into the kitchen directly!" cried Thomas, on the mere chance of his attendant having lingered at the door. And the sound of her retreating footsteps, though managed with all possible care, immediately justified his suspicion. This interruption turned Annie's tears aside, and when Thomas spoke next, she was able to reply.

"Now, my bairn," he said, "what's the matter?"

"I was at the missionar kirk last night," faltered Annie.

"Ay! And the sermon took a grip of ye?—No doubt, no doubt. Ay?"

"But I can't help forgetting *him,* Thomas."

"But ye must try and not forget him, lassie."

"So I do. But it's dour work, and almost impossible."

"So it must ever be, to the old Adam impossible, to the young Christian a weary watch."

Hope began to dawn upon Annie.

"A body might have a chance then," she asked, "even if she did forget him sometimes?"

"No doubt, lassie. The nations that forget God are them that don't care, that never bother their heads or their hearts about him—them that were never called, never chosen."

Annie's troubles returned like a sea wave that had only retired to gather strength.

"But how's a body to know whether she *be* one of the elect?" she said trembling.

"That's a hard matter. It's not necessary to know beforehand. Just let that alone in the meantime."

"But I can't let it alone. It's not altogether for myself either. Could *you* let it alone, Thomas?"

This home-thrust prevented any questioning about the second clause of her answer. And Thomas dearly loved plain dealing.

"Ye hae me there, lassie. No, I couldn't let it alone. And I never did let it alone. I plagued the Lord night and day till he let me know."

"I tried hard last night," said Annie, "but the rats were too many for me."

"Satan has many wiles," said the mason reflectively.

"Do you think they weren't rats?" asked Annie.

"Ow! No doubt. I dare say."

"Cause if I thought they were only devils, I wouldn't care a hoot for them."

"It's much the same whatever ye call them if they keep ye from the throne of grace, lassie."

"What am I to do then, Thomas?"

"Ye must keep at it lassie, like the poor widow did with the unjust judge. And if the Lord hears ye, ye'll know ye're one of the elect, for it's only his own elect that the Lord does hear."

Alas for the parable if Thomas's theories were to be carried out in its exposition! For they would lead to the conclusion that the Lord and the unjust judge were one and the same person. To Thomas's words Annie's only reply was a fixed gaze which he answered thus:

"Ay, lassie, little ye know about watching and praying. Say what they like, tis my firm belief that there is, and can be, but one way of coming to the knowledge of the secret whether ye be one of the chosen."

"And what's that?" entreated Annie, whose life seemed to hang upon his lips.

"Jist this. Get a sight of the face of God. It's my own belief that no man can get a glimpse of the face of God but one of the chosen. I'm not saying that a man's not one of the elect that hasna had that favour vouchsafed to him, but this I do say, that he canna *know* his election without that. Try ye to get a sight of the face of God, lassie, then ye'll know and be at peace. Even Moses himself couldna be satisfied without that."

"What is it like, Thomas?" said Annie, with an eagerness which awe made very still.

"No words can tell that. It's all in the spirit. When ye see it, ye'll ken it. There's no fear of mistaking *that*."

Teacher and scholar were silent. Annie was the first to speak. She had gained her quest. "Am I to go home now, Thomas?"

"Ay, go home, lassie, to yer prayers. But I don't doubt it's dark. I'll go wi' ye.—Jean, my shoes!"

"No, no. I could go home blindfolded."

"Hold yer tongue. I'm going home wi' ye, bairn.—Jean, my shoes!"

"Hoot, Thomas! I've just cleaned them!" cried old Jean from the kitchen at the second call.

"Fetch them here directly."

Jean brought them and sulkily put them down before him. In another minute the great shoes, full of nails half an inch long, were replaced on the tired feet. With her soft little hand clasped in the great calloused hand of the stonemason, Annie trotted home by his side. With Scottish caution, as soon as they had entered the shop, instead of turning to leave, Thomas went up to the counter and asked for an ounce of tobacco, as if his appearance along with Annie was merely accidental. Annie, with perfect appreciation of the reticence, ran through the gap in the counter.

She was so far comforted and so much tired that she fell asleep at her prayers by the bedside. Presently she awoke in terror. It was Pussy, however, that had waked her, as she knew by the green eyes. She then closed her prayers rather abruptly, clambered into bed, and was soon fast asleep.

And in her sleep she dreamed that she stood in the darkness in the midst of a great field full of peat bogs. She thought she was kept in there, unable to move for fear of falling into one of the hundred quagmires about her on every hand, until she should pray enough to get herself out of it. And she tried hard to pray, but she could not. And she fell down in despair, overcome with the terrors of those frightful holes full of black water which she had seen on her way to Glamerton. But a hand came out of the darkness, laid hold of hers, and lifting her up, led her through the bog. And she dimly saw the form that led her, and it was that of a man who walked looking down on the ground. She tried to see his face but she could not, for he walked always a little in front of her. And he led her to the old farm, where her father came to the door to meet them. And he looked just the same as in the old happy days, only, his face was strangely bright. And with the joy of seeing her father, she awoke to a gentle sorrow that she had not seen also the face of her deliverer.

The next evening she wandered down to George Macwha's and found the two boys at work. She had no poetry to give them, no stories to tell, no answer to their questions as to where she had been the night before. She could only stand in silence and watch them. The skeleton of the boat grew beneath their hands, but it was on the workers and not on their work that her gaze was fixed. For her heart was burning within her and she could hardly restrain herself from throwing her arms about their necks and imploring them to seek the face of God!

Oh! If only she knew that Alec and Curly were of the elect! But they alone could find that out. There was no way for her to peer into that mystery. All she could do was watch their wants, have the tool they needed next ready to their hand, clear away their shavings from before the busy plane, and lie in wait for any chance of putting her little strength to help. Perhaps they were not of the elect! She would minister to them, therefore, all the more tenderly.

“What’s come over Annie?” said the one to the other when she had gone.

But there was no answer to the question to be found. Could they have understood her if she had told them what had come over her?

– Twenty-Eight –

The Schoolmaster's New Friend

And so the time went on, slow-paced, with its silent destinies. Annie said her prayers, read her Bible, and tried not to forget God. Ah, could she have only known that God never forgot her. Whether she forgot him or not, he gave her sleep in her dreary garret, gladness even in Murdoch Malison's schoolroom, and the light of life everywhere! He was now leading on the blessed season of spring, when the earth would be almost heaven to those who had passed through the fierceness of the winter. Even now, the winter, old and weary, was halting away before the sweet approaches of the spring—a symbol of that eternal spring before whose slow footsteps death itself, "the winter of our discontent," shall vanish. Death alone can die everlastingly.

I have been lengthy in my account of Annie's first winter at school because what impressed her should impress those who read her history. But by degrees the school became less difficult for her. She grew more interested in her work. A taste for reading began to wake in her. If ever she came to school with her lesson unprepared, it was because some book of travel or history had had attractions too strong for her. And all that day she would go about with a guilty sense of neglected duty.

With Alec it was very different. He would often find himself in a similar situation. But the neglect would make no impression on his conscience. Or if it did, he would struggle hard to keep down the sense of dissatisfaction which strove to rise within him and enjoy himself in spite of it.

Still Annie haunted George Macwha's workshop where the boat soon began to reveal the full grace of its lovely outlines. As I have said, reading became a delight to her, and Mr. Cowie threw open his library, with very few restrictions, to her. She carried every new book home with a sense of richness and a feeling of *upliftedness* which I cannot describe. Now that the days were growing longer she had plenty of time to read. Although her so-called guardians made cutting remarks upon her idleness, they had not yet compelled her to needlework. With the fear of James Dow before their eyes, they let her alone. As to her doing anything in the shop, she was far too much an alien to be allowed to minister in the lowest office in that sacred temple of Mammon. So she read anything she could lay her hands on, and as often as she found anything particularly interesting she would take the book to the boat, where the boys were always ready to listen to whatever she brought them. And this habit made her more discerning.

Before I leave the school, however, I must give one more scene out of its history.

One midday in spring, just as the last of a hail shower was passing away and one sickly sunbeam was struggling out, the schoolroom door opened and in came Andrew Truffey with a smile on his worn face, which shone in touching harmony with the watery gleam of the sun between the two hailstorms, for another was close at hand. He swung himself on the new pivot of his humanity, namely his crutch. He looked very long and deathly, for he had grown several inches while lying in bed.

The master rose hurriedly from his desk and advanced to meet him. A deep stillness fell upon all the scholars. They dropped all their work and gazed at the meeting between the two. The master held out his hand. With awkwardness and difficulty Andrew presented the hand which had been holding the crutch. Not yet thoroughly used to the management of it, he staggered and would have fallen. But the master caught him in his arms and carried him to his old seat beside his brother.

"Thank ye, sir," said the boy with another gleamy smile, through which his thin features and pale eyes told plainly of his sad suffering—all the master's fault, as the master knew.

"Look at the dominie," said Curly to Alec. "He's crying."

For Mr. Malison had returned to his seat and had laid his head down on the desk, evidently to hide his emotion.

"Hold your tongue, Curly," returned Alec. "Don't look at him. He's sorry for poor Truffey."

Everyone behaved to the master that day with marked respect. And from that day forward Truffey was in universal favour.

Let me once more assert that Mr. Malison was not a bad man. The misfortune was that his notion of right fell in with his natural fierceness. Along with that, theology had come in and wrongly taught him that his pupils were in their own nature bad—with the badness for which the only remedy he knew or could introduce was blows. Independent of any remedial quality that might be in them, these blows were an embodiment of justice. "Every sin," as the catechism teaches, "deserveth God's wrath and curse both in this life and that which is to come." The master therefore was only a co-worker with God in every blow he inflicted on his pupils.

I do not mean that he reasoned thus but that such were the principles he had to act upon. And I must add, that with all his brutality, he was never guilty of such cruelty as one reads about occasionally as perpetuated by certain English schoolmasters. Nor were the boys ever guilty of such cruelty to their fellows as is not only permitted but excused in the public schools of England.

And now the moderation which had at once followed upon the accident was confirmed. Punishment became less frequent still, and when it was inflicted its administration was considerably less severe. Nor did the discipline of the school suffer in consequence. If one wants to make a hard-mouthed horse more responsive to the rein, he must relax the pressure and friction of the bit and make the horse feel that he has to hold up his own head. If the rider supports himself by the reins, the horse will pull.

But the marvel was to see how Andrew Truffey haunted and dogged the master. There was no hour of a day off from school in which Truffey could not tell where the master was about town. If one caught sight of Andrew hobbling down a street or leaning against a building, he could be sure the master would pass within a few minutes. And the haunting of little Truffey worked so on the master's conscience that if the better nature of him had not asserted itself in love to the child, he would have been compelled to leave the place. For think of having a visible sin of your own, in the shape of a lame-legged little boy, peeping at you round every corner!

But he did learn to love the boy, and therein appeared the divine vengeance—ah, how different from human vengeance!—that the outbreak of unrighteous wrath reacted on the wrongdoer in shame, repentance, and love.

– Twenty-Nine –

The Bonnie Annie

At length the boat was calked, tarred and painted.

One evening as Annie entered the workshop, she heard Curly cry, "Here she is, Alec!" and Alec answer,

"Let her come. I'm just done."

Alec stood at the stern of the boat with a pot in one hand and a paintbrush in the other. When Annie came near, she discovered to her surprise, and not a little to her delight, that he was finishing off the last E of "THE BONNIE ANNIE."

"There," he said, "that's her name. How do you like it, Annie?"

Annie was much too pleased to reply. She looked at it for a while with a flush on her face. Then turning away, she sought her usual seat on the heap of shavings.

How much that one winter, with its dragons and heroes, its boat-building and its poetry, its discomforts at home and its consolations abroad, its threats of future loss and comforts of present hope, had done to make the wild country child into a thoughtful little woman!

Now, who should come into the shop at that moment but Thomas Crann—the very man of all men not to be desired on the occasion. The boys had contemplated a certain ceremony of christening, which they dared not carry out in the presence of the stonemason—without which, however, George Macwha was very doubtful whether the little craft would prove a lucky one. By common understanding they made no allusion to the matter, thus postponing it for the present.

"Ay! ay! Alec," said Thomas, "so yer boat's built at last!"

He stood contemplating it for a moment, not without some hardly perceptible signs of admiration, and then said:

"If ye had her out on a lake of water, do ye think ye would jump out over the side if the Saviour told ye, Alec Forbes?"

"Ay, would I, if I were right sure he wanted me."

"Ye would stand and parley with him, no doubt?"

"I'd be behooved to be right sure it was his own self, ye ken, and that he did call me."

"Ow, ay, laddie! That's all right. Well, I hope ye would. Ay, I always had good hopes of ye, Alec, my man. But there may be such a thing as leaping into the sea, out of the ark of salvation. And if ye leap in when he doesn't call ye, or if ye don't get a grip of his hand when he does, ye're sure to drown, as sure as one of the swine that ran headlong in and perished in the water."

Alec had only a dim sense of his meaning, but he had faith that it was good, and so listened in respectful silence. Surely enough of sacred as well as lovely sound had been uttered over the boat to make her faithful and fortunate.

At length the day arrived when *The Bonnie Annie* was to be launched. It was a bright Saturday afternoon in the month of May, full of a kind of tearful light which seemed to say: "Here I am, but I go tomorrow." Though there might be plenty of cold weather and hail and snow still to come, yet there would be no more frozen waters and the boughs would be bare and desolate no more. A few early primroses were peeping from the hollows damp with moss and shadow along the banks, and the trees by the stream were in small, young leaf. There was a light wind full of memories of past summers and promises for the new one at hand, one of those gentle winds that blow the eyes of the flowers open that the earth may look at the heaven. In the midst of this baby-waking of the world, the boat was to glide into her new life.

Alec got one of the men on the farm to yoke a horse to bring the boat to the river. With George's help she was soon placed in the cart, and Alec and Curly climbed in beside her. The little creature looked very much like a dead fish as she lay jolting in the hot sun, with a motion irksome to her delicate sides, her prow sticking awkwardly over the horse's back, and her stern projecting as far beyond the cart behind.

When they had got about halfway, Alec said to Curly:

"I wonder what's come of Annie, Curly? It would be a shame to launch the boat without her."

"Indeed it would. I'll just run and look for her, and ye can look after the boat."

So saying, Curly was out of the cart with a bound. Away he ran over a field of potatoes as straight as the crow flies, while the cart went slowly on toward the Glamour.

"Where's Annie Anderson?" he cried as he burst into Robert Bruce's shop.

"What's *your* business with her?" asked the Bruce—a question which, judging from his tone, wanted no answer.

"Alec wants her."

"Well, he can keep wanting her," retorted Robert, shutting his jaws with a snap and grinning a smileless grin from ear to ear, like the steel clasp of a purse.

Curly left the shop at once and went around the house into the yard, where he found Annie loitering up and down with the Bruces' baby in her arms and looking very tired. This was in fact the first time she had had to carry the baby, and it fatigued her dreadfully. Till now Mrs. Bruce had the assistance of a ragged child whose father owed them money for groceries. He could not pay it and they had taken his daughter instead. Long ago, however, she had slaved it out and had gone back to school.

The sun was hot, the baby was heavy, and Annie felt all arms and back—they were aching so with the unaccustomed drudgery. She was all but crying when Curly darted to the gate, his face glowing from his run and his eyes sparkling with excitement.

"Come, Annie," he cried, "we're going to launch the boat!"

"I can't, Curly. I have the bairn to mind."

"Take the bairn into its mither."

"I don't dare."

"Lay it down on the table and run."

"No, no, Curly. I couldn't do that. Poor little creature!"

"Is the beastie heavy?" asked Curly with deceitful interest.

"Dreadful."

"Let me try."

"You'll drop her."

"I'm not so weak as that. Give me a hold of her."

Annie yielded her charge, but no sooner had Curly possession of the baby than he bounded away with her toward a huge sugar cask that stood in the yard just opposite the kitchen window. The cask, having been converted into a reservoir, stood under a spout and was at this moment half full of rainwater. Curly, having first satisfied himself that Mrs. Bruce was at work in the kitchen and would therefore be sure to see him, climbed a big stone that lay beside the barrel and pretended to lower the baby into the water, as if trying to see how much she would endure without crying.

In a moment he received such a box on the ear that, had he not been prepared for it, he would have in reality dropped the child into the barrel. The same moment the baby was in its mother's arms, and Curly was sitting at the foot of the barrel, nursing his head and pretending to suppress a violent attack of weeping. The angry mother sped into the house with her rescued child.

No sooner had she disappeared than Curly was on his feet scudding back to Annie, who had been staring over the garden gate in utter bewilderment at his behaviour. She could no longer resist his pleading. Off she ran with him to the banks of the Glamour, where they soon came upon Alec and the man in the act of putting the boat on the slip, which in this case was a groove hollowed out of a low part of the bank, so that she might glide in more gradually.

"Hurrah! There's Annie!" cried Alec. "Come on, Annie. Here's a glass of whisky I got from my mother to christen the boat. Fling it at her name."

Annie did as she was told, to the perfect satisfaction of all present, particularly of the long, spare, sinewy farm servant who had contrived, when Alec's back was turned, to swallow the whisky and substitute Glamour water, which no doubt did equally well for the purposes of the ceremony. Then with a gentle push from all, *The Bonnie Annie* slid into the Glamour, where she lay afloat in contented grace, as unlike herself in the cart as a swan waddling wearily to the water is unlike the true swan-self when sitting gracefully in the water.

"Isn't she bonnie?" cried Annie in delight.

And indeed she was, in her green and white paint, lying like a great water beetle ready to scamper over the smooth surface. Alec sprang on board, nearly upsetting the tiny craft. Then he held it by a bush on the bank while Curly handed in Annie, who sat down in the stern. Curly then got in himself and he and Alec each seized an oar.

But what with their inexperience and the nature of the channel, they found it hard to get along. The river was so full of great stones that in some parts it was not possible to row. They knew nothing about the management of a boat and were no more at ease than if they had been afloat in a tub. Alec being stronger in the arms than Curly, they went round and round for some time, as if in a whirlpool. At last they gave it up in weariness, and allowed *The Bonnie Annie* to float along the stream, taking care only to keep her off the rocks. Past them went the banks—here steep and stony but green with moss where little trickling streams found their way into the channel, there spreading into low shores covered with lovely grass full of daisies and buttercups, from which there rose a willow whose low boughs swept the water. A little while ago they had skated down its frozen surface and had seen a snowy land shooting past them. Now with an unfelt gliding they floated down, and the green meadows dreamed away as if they would dream past them forever. Suddenly, as they rounded the corner of a rock, a great roar of falling water burst on their ears and they started in dismay.

"The sluice is up!" cried Alec. "Take to your oar, Curly."

Along this part of the bank, some twenty feet above them, ran a millstream, which a few yards lower down poured by means of a sluice into the river. This sluice was now open, for, from the late rains, there was too much water and the surplus rushed from the stream into the Glamour in a foaming cataract. Seeing that the boys were uneasy, Annie got very frightened and, closing her eyes, sat motionless.

Louder and louder grew the tumult of the waters till their sound seemed to fall in a solid thunder on her brain. The boys tried hard to row against the river but without success. Slowly and surely it carried them down into the very heart of the boiling fall, for on this side alone was the channel deep enough for the boat, and the banks were too steep and bare to afford any hold on branches or shrubs. At last the boat, drifting stern foremost, entered the fall. A torrent of water struck Annie and tumbled into the boat as if it would beat the bottom out of it. Annie was tossed about in fierce waters and ceased to know anything.

When she came to herself she was in an unknown bed, with the face of Mrs. Forbes bending anxiously over her. She would have risen, but Mrs. Forbes told her to lie still, which indeed Annie found much more pleasant.

As soon as they had got under the fall, the boat had filled and floundered. Alec and Curly could swim like otters and were out of the pool at once. As they went down, Alec had made a plunge to lay hold of Annie, but had missed her. The moment he got his breath he swam again into the boiling pool, dived, and got hold of her. But he was so stupefied by the force of the water falling upon him and beating him down that he could not get out of the raging depth—for here the water was many feet deep—and as he would not let go of his hold on Annie, was in danger of being drowned.

Meantime Curly had scrambled on shore and climbed up to the millstream where he managed to shut the sluice down hard. In a moment the tumult had ceased and Alec and Annie were in still water. In a moment more he had her on the bank, apparently lifeless, and he then carried her home to his mother in terror. She immediately resorted to one or two of the usual restoratives and was presently successful.

As soon as she had opened her eyes, Alec and Curly hurried off to get out their boat. They met the miller in an awful rage. The sudden onset of twice the quantity of water on his overshot wheel had set his machinery off as if it had been bewitched, and one old stone, which had lost its iron girdle, had flown into pieces, to the frightful danger of the miller and his men.

"Ye ill-designed villains!" he cried at them, "what made ye close the sluice? I'll teach ye to mind what ye're about. Devil take ye rascals!"

He seized one in each brawny hand.

"Annie Anderson was drowning in the waste water," answered Curly promptly.

"The Lord preserve us!" cried the miller, relaxing his hold. "How was that? Did she fall in?"

The boys told him the whole story. In a few minutes more the backfall was again turned off, and the miller was helping them get their boat out. *The Bonnie Annie* was found uninjured. Only the oars and cushions had floated down the stream and were never seen again.

Alec had a terrible scolding from his mother for getting Annie into such mischief. Indeed, Mrs. Forbes did not like the girl's being so much with her son. But she comforted herself with the probability that by and by Alec would go to college and forget her.

Meantime, she was very kind to Annie and took her home herself, in order to excuse her absence, the blame of which she laid entirely on Alec, not knowing that thereby she greatly aggravated any offense of which Annie might have been found guilty. Mrs. Bruce solemnly declared her conviction that a judgment had fallen upon her for Willie Macwha's treatment of her baby.

"If I hadn't just gotten a glimpse of him in time, he would have drowned the bonny infant before my very eyes!"

This first voyage of *The Bonnie Annie* may seem a bad beginning, but I am not sure that most good ends have not had such a bad beginning. Perhaps the world itself may be received as a case in point. Alec and Curly went about for a few days with a rather subdued expression. But as soon as the boat was refitted, they got George Macwha to go with them for cockswain, and under his instructions they made rapid progress in rowing and sculling.

Then Annie was again their companion. The boat being by this time fitted with a rudder, she had several lessons in steering in which she soon became proficient. Many a moonlight row they now had on the Glamour, and many a night after Curly and Annie had gone home would Alec again unmoor the boat and float down the water alone—not always sure that he was not dreaming himself.

I think it was in these seasons that he began first to become aware of a certain stillness pervading the universe like a law, a stillness ever closing and returning with gentleness not to be repelled, seeking to infold and penetrate with its own healing the minds of the noisy children of the earth.

– Thirty –

Changes

My story must have shown already that, although several years younger than Alec, Annie had more character in the way of thought than he. Alec had not yet begun to look realities in the face. The very nobility and fearlessness of his nature had preserved him from many such actions which give occasion for looking within oneself and asking where things are leading. Full of life and restless impulses to activity, all that could be properly required of him as yet was that the action into which he rushed should be innocent, and if mischievous then usually harmless.

Comfortless at home and gazing all about her to see if there was a rest anywhere for her, Annie had been driven by the outward desolation away from the window of the world to that other window which opens on the regions of silent being where God is, and into which his creatures enter. Alec, whose home was happy, knew nothing of that sense of discomfort which is sometimes the herald of a greater need. But he was soon to take a new start in his intellectual relations, nor in those alone, seeing that the changes which were about to come upon him also bore a dim sense of duty. The fact of his not being a scholar in the mind of Murdoch Malison arose from no deficiency of intellectual *power,* but only of intellectual *capacity*—the enlargement of which requires only a fitting motivation from without.

The season went on, and the world, like a great flower afloat in space, kept opening its thousandfold blossoms. Hail and sleet were things lost in the distance of the year—storming away in some far-off region of the north, unknown to the summer generation. The butterflies, with wings looking as if all the flower painters of fairyland had wiped their brushes upon them in random yet artistic sport, came forth in the freedom of their wills and the faithful ignorance of their minds. The birds, the poets of the animal creation, awoke to utter their own joy and awake a similar joy in others of God's children. Then the birds grew silent, because their history had laid hold upon them, compelling them to turn their words into deeds, keep eggs warm and hunt for worms. The butterflies died of old age and delight. The green life of the earth rushed up in grain to be ready for the time of need. The corn grew ripe and therefore weary, hung its head, died, and was laid aside for a life beyond its own. The keen, sharp old mornings and nights of autumn came back as they had come so many thousand times before, and made human limbs strong and human hearts sad and longing. Winter would soon be near enough to stretch out a long forefinger once more, and touch with the first frosty shiver some little child that loved summer and shrank from the cold.

There had been growing in Alec, though it was still a vague sense in his mind, that he was not doing as well as he might, that the mischief of boyhood had already begun to extend further than it ought toward manhood. The plot with his less-noble companions to kidnap Stumpin' Steenie's cow, cadger James Joss's gaunt horse, and tie them all together in a train with several more cows and calves, a sheep, wool-carder Charles Chapman's goat, a string of disreputable dogs, and bringing up the rear Andrew Truffey's white rabbit, who were then paraded ingloriously through the middle of town, had proved the final straw.

The resulting death of poor Truffey's rabbit stung Alec with remorse, which replacing it could not entirely remove. A rebuke from Thomas Crann brought the sobering realization toward the light of Alec's own consciousness. Once the harvest was past and school begun afresh, Alec began to work better. Mr. Malison saw the change and acknowledged it. This in turn reacted on Alec's feelings for the master. During the following winter, he made three times the progress he had made in any winter preceding it.

For the sea of summer ebbed away and the rocky channels of the winter appeared, with its cold winds, its ghostlike mists, and the damps and shiverings that clung about the sepulchre in which Nature lies sleeping. The boat was carefully laid up across the rafters of the barn, well wrapped in a shroud of tarpaulin. It was buried up in the air, and the Glamour on which it had floated so gaily would soon be buried under the ice. Summer alone could bring them together again—the one from the dry gloom of the barn, the other from the cold seclusion of its wintry sleep.

Meanwhile, Mrs. Forbes was somewhat troubled in her mind as to what should be done with Alec, and she often talked to the schoolmaster about him. Of higher birth socially than her late husband, she had the ambition that her son should be educated. She was less concerned about his exercise of some profession as that he obtain an education, for she was not at all willing that the farm which had been in her husband's family for hundreds of years should pass into the hands of strangers, especially as Alec himself had the strongest attachment to the ancestral soil.

At length his increased diligence, which had not escaped her observation and was testified to by Mr. Malison, confirmed her determination that he should at least go to college. Whether the university beyond that would remain to be seen. He would be no worse a farmer for having an A.M. after his name, and the curriculum was common to all the professions. So it was resolved that in the following winter he should compete for a bursary.

The communication that his fate lay in that direction roused Alec still more. Now that a future object made them more attractive, he turned his attention to his studies with genuine earnestness, and on a cloudy day toward the end of October—several months before his sixteenth birthday—Alec found himself on the box seat of the Royal Mail coach, with his trunk on the roof behind him, bound for a certain city where his future—at least for the present—lay.

– Thirty-One –

First Days in the City

After driving through long streets, brilliant with shops of endless marvel, the coachman pulled up for the last time. It was a dull drizzly evening, with sudden windy gusts, and, in itself, dark as pitch. But Alec descended, cold and wet, in a brilliant light which flowed from the door of the hotel. A porter took charge of his box, hoisted it on his back, and led the way to the address he gave him.

Notwithstanding the drizzle, and the angry rushes of the wind round the street-corners, the foot-pavements were filled with men and women, moving in different directions, like a double row of busy ants. Through queer short cuts that terribly bewildered the way, the porter led him to the house, and pushing the door open, went up two flights of stone stairs and knocked at a door on the landing. Alec was shown into a room where a good fire was blazing away with a continuous welcome. When seated by it drinking his tea, he saw the whole world golden through the stained windows of his imagination.

He rose in the morning with the feeling that something intense was going on all around. But the door into life generally opens behind us, and a hand is put forth which draws us in backwards. The sole wisdom for man or boy who is haunted with the hovering of unseen wings, with the scent of unseen roses, and the subtle enticements of melodies unheard, is work. If he follow any of those, they will vanish. But if he work, they will come unsought, and, while they come, he will believe that there is a fairy land, where poets find their dreams, and prophets are laid hold of by their visions.

Alec stood at the window, and peered down into the narrow street, through which, as in a channel between rocks burrowed into dwellings, ran the ceaseless torrent of traffic. He felt at first as if life at least had opened its gates, and he had been transported into the midst of its drama. But to no mere onlooker will Life any more than Fairyland open its secret. A man must become an actor before he can be a true spectator.

He went and wandered about the streets. To his country-bred eyes they were full of marvels—which would soon be as common to those eyes as one of the furrowed fields on his father's farm.

As no one but Alec had come to the college from Glamerton that year, he did not know one of his fellow students. There were very few in the first class indeed who had had any previous acquaintance with each other. But before many days had passed, like had begun to draw to like and opposites to their natural opposites.

Some of the youths were of the lowliest origin—the sons of ploughmen and small country shopkeepers—shock-headed lads, with much of the looks and manners of year-old bullocks, mostly with freckled faces and a certain general irresponsiveness of feature, soon to vanish as the mental and nervous motions became more frequent and rapid. Some, on the other hand, showed themselves at once the aristocracy of the class by their carriage, dress, and social qualifications.

Alec belonged to the middle class. Well dressed, he yet knew that his clothes had a country air and that beside some of the others he cut a poor figure. A certain superiority of manner distinguished these others, indicating that they had been accustomed to more of the outward refinements of life than he.

The competition was held within the first week. Alec gained a small scholarship, and then the lectures commenced.

On the second day after the commencement of lectures, it was made known to the new arrivals that the Magistrand Debating Society would meet that evening. Curious, Alec walked through the dark from his lodgings in the new town, for the gateway beneath the tower with that crown of stone which is the glory of the ancient borough gathered beneath it. Through narrow crooked streets, with many dark courts on each side, he came to the open road which connected the two towns.

As the meeting progressed, a certain second year classman—popularly known by his nickname as *sheep*—stood up to give his opinion on some subject in dispute. Now for whatever reason, his speech was inarticulate as he hemmed and stammered, resulting in a torrent of hisses, the loudest of which came from the newly arrived first year students. His resulting indignation broke out in sarcastic contempt heaped on the newly arrived young clodhoppers, who, having just come from herding their fathers' cows, could express their feelings in no more suitable language than that of the bovine animals which had been their principal and fit associates. He concluded his address with his eyes resting with withering scorn upon Alec Forbes. Alec instantly started to his feet amidst a confusion of plaudits and hisses, but, finding it absolutely impossible to speak so as to be heard, contented himself with uttering a sonorous *ba-a-a-a,* and instantly dropped into his seat, all the other outcries dissolving in shouts of laughter at the other's expense.

After this he was popular, but without immediately knowing it he had made an adversary of the young man whose ridicule he had turned back on him. Beauchamp was no great favourite even in his own set. For there is one kind of religion in which the more devoted a man is, the fewer proselytes he makes—the worship of himself.

One morning about two months after the beginning of the session, the professor of the Greek class looked up at the ceiling with sudden discomposure. There had been a heavy fall of snow in the night and one of the students had tightly packed a large snowball and, before the arrival of the professor, had thrown it against the ceiling with such forceful precision that it stuck right over the centre of his chair. This was perhaps the first time that such a trick had been dared in the first class, belonging more properly to the advanced depravity of the second or third. When the room had warmed, the snow began to drip on the head of the old professor.

The moment he looked up, seeing what was the matter, Alec sprang from his seat, rushed out of the classroom and returned with a long broom which the groundskeeper had been using to clear footpaths across the quadrangle. The professor left his chair, Alec jumped up on the desk and swept the snow from the ceiling. He then wiped the seat with his handkerchief and returned to his place. The gratitude of the old man shone in his eyes.

"Thank you, Mr. Forbes," he stammered. "I am ek-ek-ek-exceedingly obliged to you."

The professor was a curious, kindly little man—lame, with a brown wig, a wrinkled face, and a long mouth, of which he made use of the half on the right side to stammer out humorous and often witty sayings. Somehow Professor Fraser's stutter never interfered with the point of the joke. He seemed, while hesitating on some unimportant syllable, to be arranging what was to follow and strike the blow with a sudden rush.

"Gentlemen," he continued upon this occasion, "the Scripture says you're to heap c-c-coals of fire on your enemy's head. When you are to heap drops of water on your friend's w-w-wig, the Scripture doesn't say."

The same evening Alec received a note asking him to breakfast with him the following morning, which was Saturday and consequently a holiday. It was usual with the professors to invite a dozen or so of the students to breakfast on Saturdays, but on this occasion Alec was the sole guest.

As soon as Alec entered the room, Mr. Fraser hobbled to meet him with outstretched hand of welcome and a kindly smile on his face.

"I hope you've brought an appetite with you. Sit down. Always respect old age, Mr. Forbes. You'll be old yourself some day—and you won't like it any more than I do. I've had my young days, though, and I mustn't grumble."

While Mr. Fraser began to fill the teacups, Alec said, "My mother told me in a letter I had from her yesterday that your brother, sir, had married a cousin of hers."

"What! Are you a son of Mr. Forbes of Howglen?"

"Yes, sir."

"You young rascal! Why didn't your mother send you straight to me when you arrived?"

"She didn't want to trouble you, I suppose, sir."

"People like me that haven't any relatives must make the most of the relatives they have. I am in no danger of being troubled that way. You've heard of my poor brother's death?"

"No, sir."

"He died last year. He was a clergyman, you know. When you come next session, I hope to show you his daughter—your cousin, you know. She is coming to live with me. People that don't marry don't deserve to have children. But I'm going to have one after all. She's in school now. What are you thinking of going into, Mr. Forbes?"

"I haven't thought much about it yet, sir."

"Ah, I dare say not. If I were you, I would be a doctor. If you're honest you're sure to do some good. I think you're just the man to be a doctor—you respect your fellowmen. And you don't laugh at old age, Mr. Forbes."

And so the kind, garrulous old man went on, talking about everything except Greek. This was the first time Alec's thoughts had been turned toward a profession. The more he thought about it the better he liked the idea of being a doctor. At length, after one or two talks about it with Mr. Fraser, he resolved to pursue it and to get into the anatomy course for the rest of the session. The Greek and Latin were relatively easy for him, and it would be that much time gained if he entered the first medical class at once. His mother was more than satisfied with the proposal. Mr. Fraser smoothed the way with the medical professor, and he, with a hard study of the books for the course, was soon busy making up the two months he had lost.

The first day of his attendance in the anatomy room was a memorable one. He had considerable misgivings about the new experience and tried to prepare himself with calmness. When he entered the room he found the group already gathered. He drew timidly toward the table on the other side, not daring to glance at something which lay on the table—something very pale and white. He felt as if all the others were looking at him as he kept staring, or trying to stare, at other things in the room. But all at once, from an irresistible impulse, he faced round and looked at the table.

There lay the dead body of a woman with a young, sad face. Alec's lip quivered and his throat swelled with a sensation of choking. He turned away and bit his lip hard to keep down his emotion.

One of the students, sneering at his discomposure, made a brutal jest. He heard quiet words of sarcasm against "the young clodhopper" who was not yet fit for a *man's* occupation. Now first he recognized the fellow as his antagonist from the meeting his first week in the city.

After this, as often as Patrick Beauchamp and he passed each other walking up and down the arcade, Beauchamp's high, curved upper lip would curve yet higher.

– Thirty-Two –

Mr. Cupples

Alec remained in his room during the week-end to read and study his medical and anatomical books. One day his landlady said:

"Have ye been up the stairs to visit Mr. Cupples yet?"

"I didn't know you had anybody up the stairs. Who's Mr. Cupples?"

"Weel, he knows that best himsel'! But he's a queer one, he is. He's some scholar though, folk say—grand at the Greek and mathematics. Only ye mustn't be frightened at him."

"I'm easily frightened," said Alec with a laugh. "But I would like to see him."

"Go up then, and clap at the garret door."

"But what reason am I to give for disturbing him?" asked Alec.

"Ow, none at all. Jist take a mouthful of Greek with ye to ask the right meaning of."

"That will do first rate," said Alec, "for I have just been puzzling over a sentence for the last half hour."

He caught up his book and bounded away up the garret stairs. At the top he found himself under the bare roof with only boards and slates between him and the clouds. The landing was lighted by a skylight, across which diligent and undisturbed spiders had woven their webs for years. He stood outside for a moment or two, puzzled as to which door he ought to try, for all the doors about looked like closed doors. At last, with the aid of his nose, he made up his mind, and knocked.

"Come in!" cried a voice.

He opened the door and entered.

"What do you want?" said the voice, its source almost invisible in the thick fumes of genuine pigtail tobacco from his pipe through which it sent cross odours as of genuine Glenlivat.

"I would like you to help me with a bit of Homer, if you please, Mr. Cupples—I'm not up to Homer yet."

"Do you think I have nothing else to do than to grind the grandeur of an old heathen into little pieces for a young sinner like you?"

"You don't know what I'm like, Mr. Cupples," returned Alec, remembering his landlady's injunction not to be afraid of this man.

"You young dog! There's stuff in you!" Then composing himself a little, he said, "Come through the smoke and let's look at you."

Alec obeyed and found the speaker seated by the side of a little fire in an old easy chair. Mr. Cupples was a man who might have been almost any age between twenty-five and fifty—at least Alec's experience was insufficient for the task of determining to what decade of human years he belonged. He was a little man, in a long, black coat much too large for him, and dirty gray trowsers. He had no shirt collar visible, although a loose rusty stock revealed the whole of his brown neck. His hair was long, thin, and light, mingled with gray, and his ears stood far out from his large head. His eyes were rather large, well-formed, bright and blue. His hand, small and dirty, grasped a tumbler of toddy, while his feet, in slippers of different colours, balanced themselves on a small table.

"Well, you look like one of the right sort," he said at length. "I'll do what I can for you. Where's your Homer?"

So saying, he rose with care and went toward a cupboard in the corner. Glancing around the little garret room, Alec saw a bed and a small chest of drawers, a painted table covered with papers, and a chair or two. An old broadsword leaned against a wall in a corner. A half-open cupboard revealed bottles, glasses, and a dry-looking cheese. To the corresponding cupboard on the other side of the fire, which had lost a corner by the descent of the roof, Mr. Cupples now dragged his slippers, feeling in his waistcoat pocket as he went for the key. There was another door, partly sunk in the slope of the ceiling.

When he opened the cupboard, a dusky glimmer of splendid bindings filling the whole recess shone out upon the dingy room. From a shelf he took a volume of Homer, bound in leather with red edges and, having closed the door again, resumed his seat in the easy chair. Having found the passage he read it through aloud. Then pouncing at once upon the shadowy word which was the key to the whole, he laid open the construction and meaning in one sentence of explanation.

"Thank you! thank you!" exclaimed Alec. "I see it all now as plain as English."

"Stop, stop, my young bantam!" said Mr. Cupples. "Don't think you're going to break into my privacy and get off with the booty so cheaply. You must now construe the whole sentence to me."

Alec did so reasonably well. Mr. Cupples put several questions to him, which gave him more insight into Greek than a week's work in the class would have done, and ended with a small lecture suggested by the passage, drinking away at his toddy all the time, after which followed some small talk. The lecture and the toddy ended together. Laying his head back against the chair, he said sleepily:

"Go away—I don't know your name.—Come and see me tomorrow night. I'm drunk now."

Alec rose, making some attempts at thanks. Receiving no syllable of reply, he went out, closing the door behind him and leaving Mr. Cupples to his dreams.

– Thirty-Three –

A New Friend

Meantime, at Glamerton the winter passed very much like former winters to all but three—Mrs. Forbes, Annie Anderson, and Willie Macwha. To these the loss of Alec was dreary. So they were in a manner compelled to draw closer together. At school, Curly assumed the protectorship of Annie which had naturally fallen upon him, although there was now comparatively little occasion for its use. And Mrs. Forbes, finding herself lonely in her parlour during the long *forenights*, got into the habit of sending Mary at least three times a week to fetch her. This was not agreeable to the Bruce, but the kingly inheritor awaited his hour, and Mrs. Forbes had no notion of the amount of offense she gave with her invitations.

That parlour at Howglen was to Annie a little heaven hollowed out of the winter. The warm curtains drawn, the fire blazing defiantly—the angel with the flaming sword to protect their Paradise from the frost—it was indeed a contrast to the sordid shop and the rat-haunted garret.

After tea they took turns to work and to read. There were more books in the house than usual even in that of a *gentleman farmer*. Several of Sir Walter's novels, besides some travels and a little Scottish history, were read between them that winter. In poetry, Annie had to forage for herself. Mrs. Forbes could lend her no guiding hand in that direction.

The bond between them grew stronger every day. Annie was to Mrs. Forbes an outlet for her maternity, which could never have outlet enough without a girl as well as a boy to love. Annie, as a result, was surrounded by many holy influences, which, operating at a time when she was growing fast, had their full effect upon both her mind and body. In a condition of rapid change, mass is more yielding and responsive.

One result in her was that she began to manifest a certain sober grace in her carriage and habits. Mrs. Forbes came to Annie's aid with dresses of her own, which they altered and remade together. It will easily be believed that no avoidable expense remained unavoided by the Bruces. Indeed, but for the feeling that she must be decent on Sundays, they would have let her go yet shabbier than she was when Mrs. Forbes thus partially adopted her. Now that she was warmly and neatly dressed, she began to feel and look more like the lady-child she really was. No doubt the contrast was very painful when she returned from Mrs. Forbes's warm parlour to sleep in her own garret with the snow on the roof, scanty covers on the bed, and rats in the floor. It is wonderful how one gets through what one cannot avoid.

Robert Bruce was making money, but not so fast as he wished, which led to a certain change in the Bruces' habits with important results for Annie. The returns of the shop came only in small sums, although the profits were great, for customers were chiefly of the poorer classes of the town and neighbourhood who preferred his shop to the more showy establishments of some of his rivals. A sort of confidentially flattering way that he had with them pleased them and contributed greatly to keeping them true to his counter. And as he knew how to buy as well as how to sell, the poor people, if they had not the worth of their money, had at least good merchandise. But, as I have said, although he was making haste to be rich, he was not succeeding fast enough. So he began thinking about the Missionar Kirk and how it was getting rather large and successful.

A month or two before this time the Missionars had made choice of a very able man for their pastor—a man of genuine and strong religious feeling who did not allow his theology to interfere with the teaching given him by God's Spirit more than he could help, and who, if he had been capable of making a party at all, would have made it with the poor against the rich. This man had gathered about him a large congregation of the lower classes of Glamerton, and Bruce had learned with some uneasiness that a considerable portion of his customers was to be found in the Missionar Kirk on Sundays, especially in the evenings.

There was a grocer among the Missionars who, Bruce feared, might draw some of his subjects away from their allegiance to him. Should he join the congregation, he would not only retain the old but also have a chance to gain new customers as well.

So he took a week to think about it, a Sunday to hear Mr. Turnbull alone in order that the change might not seem too abrupt, and the next Sunday, five minutes before the hour, he and his family were seated in a pew under the gallery, adding greatly to the prestige both of the place and himself in the eyes of his Missionar customers.

Although Annie found the service more wearisome than good Mr. Cowie's, lasting as it did three quarters of an hour longer. Yet occasionally when Mr. Turnbull testified of that which he himself had seen and known, the honest heart of the maiden recognized the truth, and listened absorbed.

The young Bruces, for their part, would gladly have gone to sleep, which would perhaps have been the most profitable use to which they could put the time. But they were kept upright and in a measure awake by the constant application of the paternal elbow and the judicious administration, on the part of the mother, of the unfailing peppermint lozenges, to which in the process of ages a certain sabbatical character has attached itself. To Annie, however, no such ministration extended, for it would have been a downright waste, seeing she could keep awake without it.

One bright frosty morning, the sermon happened to have no relation to the light around or within them, but only to the covenant made with Abraham. Annie, neither able to enter into the subject nor to keep from shivering with the cold, tried to amuse herself by gazing at one brilliant sun streak on the wall. She discovered it to be gradually shortening itself and retreating toward the window by which it had entered the room. Wondering how far it would move before the sermon was over, and whether it would have shone so bright if God had made no covenant with Abraham, she was earnestly watching it pass from spot to spot, and from cobweb to cobweb, when she caught sight of a very peculiar face turned in the same direction—that is, not toward the minister, but toward the traveling light. She thought the woman was watching it as well as she, and wondered whether she too was hoping for a bowl of hot broth as soon as the sunbeam had gone a certain distance—broth being the Sunday fare with the Bruces. The face was very plain, seamed and scarred as if the woman had fallen into a fire when a child, and Annie had not looked at her two seconds before she realized that the woman was perfectly blind. But she saw too that there was a light on the face, a light which neither came from the sun in the sky nor the sunbeam on the wall. It was the ugliest face. But over it, as over the rugged channel of a sea, flowed the transparent waves of a heavenly light.

When the service was over, almost before the words of the benediction had left the minister's lips, the people hurried out of the chapel as if they could not possibly endure one word more. But Annie stood staring at the blind woman. When at length she followed her out into the open air, Annie found her standing by the door, turning her sightless face on all sides as if looking for someone and trying hard to open her eyes that she might see better. Annie watched her till, seeing her lips move, she knew half by instinct that she was murmuring, "The bairn's forgotten me!" Thereupon she walked up to her and said gently:

"If you'll tell me where you live, I'll take you home."

"What do they call *you,* bairn?" returned the blind woman in a gruff, almost manlike voice, hardly less unpleasant to hear than her face was to look at.

"Annie Anderson," answered Annie.

"Ow, ay! I thought as much. I know aboot ye. Give me a hold of yer hand. I live in that wee house down at the bridge, between the dam and the Glamour, ye ken. Ye'll keep me away from the stones?"

"Ay, I will," answered Annie confidently.

"I could go alone, but I'm growing some old noo, and I'm jist rather feared for falling."

"Well, what made you think it was me? I never spoke to you before," said Annie as they walked on together.

"Well, tis jist half guessing, and half a kind of judgment—putting things together, ye ken, my bairn. Ye see, I know all the bairns that come to our kirk already. And I heard tell that Master Bruce was come. So when a lassie spoke to me that I never heard afore, I jist kind of knew it must be yersel'."

All this was spoken in the same harsh voice, but the woman held Annie's hand kindly and yielded like a child to her guidance, which was as careful as that of the angel that led Peter.

It was a new delight to Annie to have someone to whom she, a child, could be a kind of mother, to whom she could fulfill a woman's highest calling—that of *ministering unto*. And it was with something of a sacred pride that she led her safely home through the snowy streets and down the steep path that led from the level of the bridge, with its three high stone arches, to the little meadow where her cottage stood. Before they reached it, the blind woman, whose name was Tibbie (Isobel) Dyster, had put many questions to her and had come to a tolerably correct knowledge of her character, circumstances, and history.

As soon as they entered the cottage, Tibbie was entirely at her ease. The first thing she did was to lift the kettle from the fire and feel the fire with her hands in order to find out in what condition it was. She would not allow Annie to touch it—she could not trust the creature that had nothing but eyes to guide her with such a delicate affair. The very hands looked like blind eyes trying to see, as they went wandering over the tops of the live peats. She rearranged them, put on some fresh pieces, blew a little at them all astray and to no purpose, was satisfied, coughed, and then sank in a chair to take her bonnet off. Most women of her station wore only a mutch or close cap, but Tibbie wore a bonnet with a brilliantly gay ribbon, so fond was she of bright colours, although she had nothing but the testimony of others, vague enough before it succeeded in crossing the dark distances of her brain, as to the effect of those even with which she adorned her own person.

Her room was very bare, but was as clean as it was possible for a room to be. Her bed was in the wall which divided it from the rest of the house, and this one room was her whole habitation. The other half of the cottage was occupied by an old cripple, nearly bedridden, to whose many necessities Tibbie ministered. The eyes of the one and the legs of the other worked in tolerable harmony. And if they had a quarrel now and then, it was no greater than gave a zest to their relations. These particulars, however, Annie did not learn till afterwards.

Annie looked all about the room, and seeing no signs of any dinner for Tibbie was reminded thereby that her own chances had considerably diminished.

"I must go home," she said with a sigh.

"Ay, lassie, they'll be waiting their dinner for ye."

"No fear of that," answered Annie, adding with another sigh, "I doubt there'll be much of the broth left when I get home."

"Well, jist stay, bairn, and take a cup of tea with me. It's all I hae to offer ye. Will ye stay?"

"Maybe I would be in your way," objected Annie feebly.

"Na, na, no fear of that. Ye'll read a bit to me afterward."

"Ay, will I."

And Annie stayed all the afternoon with Tibbie and went home with the Bruces after the evening service.

It soon grew into a custom for Annie to take Tibbie home from the chapel—a custom to which the Bruces could hardly have objected had they been so inclined. But they were not so inclined, for it saved the broth—that is, each of them got a little more in consequence, and Annie's absence was therefore a Sabbath blessing.

Much as she was neglected at home, however, Annie was steadily gaining a good reputation in the town. Old men said she was a *gude bairn* and old women said she was a *douce lassie*. Those who enjoyed finding fault more than giving praise turned their silent approbation of Annie into expressions of disapproval of the Bruces—"letting her go like a beggar, as if she was no kin of theirs, when tis weel kent whose heifer Rob Bruce is ploughing with."

But Robert nevertheless grew and prospered all day, and dreamed at night that he was the king, digging the pits for the English cavalry and covering them again with the treacherous turf. Somehow the dream never went further. The field and the kingship would vanish and he would remain Robert Bruce, the general dealer, plotting still, but in his own shop.

– Thirty-Four –

Alec and Mr. Cupples

The next evening Alec knocked at Mr. Cupples's door and entered. The strange creature was sitting in the same position as before, looking as if he had not risen since the previous night. But there was a certain Sunday look about the room which Alec could not account for. The same pictures were on the wall, the same tumbler of toddy was steaming on the table amidst the same little array of books and papers covered with the same dust and marked with the same circles from the bottoms of wet glasses. The same black pipe reposed between the teeth of Mr. Cupples.

After he had been seated for a few moments, however, Alec all at once discovered the source of the reformation of the place—Mr. Cupples had on a white shirt and collar. Although this was no doubt the chief cause of the change of expression in the room, in the course of the evening Alec discovered further signs of improvement, one, that the hearth had been cleared of a great heap of ashes and now looked as if belonging to an old maid's cottage instead of a bachelor's garret.

"More Greek, laddie?" asked Mr. Cupples.

"No, thank you," answered Alec. "I only came to see you. You told me to come again tonight."

"Did I? Well, I protest against being made accountable for anything that fellow Cupples may choose to say when I'm not at home."

Here he emptied his glass of toddy and filled it again from the tumbler.

"Shall I go away?" asked Alec, half bewildered.

"No, no, sit still. You're a good sort of innocent, I think. I won't give you any toddy though. You needn't look so greedy at it."

"I don't want any toddy, sir. I never drank a tumbler in my life."

"For God's sake!" exclaimed Mr. Cupples with sudden eager energy, leaning forward in his chair, his blue eyes flashing—"for God's sake, never drank a drop!"

He sank back in his chair and said nothing for some time. Alec thought he was drunk again and rose to go.

"Don't go yet," said Mr. Cupples authoritatively. "You come at your will, you must go at mine.—If I could but get a kick at that fellow Cupples! But I declare I can't help it. If I were God, I would cure him of drink. It's the very first thing I would do."

Alec could not help being shocked at the irreverence of the words. But the solemnity of Mr. Cupples's face speedily dissipated the feeling. Suddenly changing his tone, he went on:

"What's your name?"

"Alec Forbes."

"Alec Forbes. I'll try to remember it. I seldom remember anybody's name, though. I sometimes forget my own.—So how goes the war on the older classmen?"

Alec laughed. "No so bad, though there's a fellow in my anatomy class who is determined not to give me a moment's respite. But if I cannot survive the taunts of Patrick Beauchamp, I'll never be a doctor in the end."

"Patrick Beauchamp!" exclaimed Cupples. "The devil take him!"

"You know him?"

"Indeed I do. He comes of a bad lot! I know all about them. They're from Strathspey, where my father came from—at least his father was. If the young fellow turns out well, it'll be a wonder. I'll tell you all about them."

Mr. Cupples then launched into a somewhat rambling account of Patrick Beauchamp's antecedents, indicating by his detail that there must have been personal relations of some kind between them or their families. Perhaps he hinted at something of the sort when he said that old Beauchamp was a hard man even for a lawyer.

Beauchamp's mother, he said, was the daughter of a Highland chief, whose pedigree went back to an Irish king of remote date. Mrs. Beauchamp had all the fierceness without much of the grace belonging to the Celtic nature. She grew to despise, then hate, her husband while giving her son every advantage her position could afford, moulding and modelling him after her own heart.

"So you see, Mr.—I forget yer name," he concluded, "—Forbes? yes, Forbes, if the rascal takes after his mother, you have made a dangerous enemy."

Alec laughed.

"I see something like poetry lying about the table, Mr. Cupples," Alec said. "Would you let me look at it?"

Mr. Cupples glanced at him sharply, then replied:

"Broken bits of them! But the rainbows lose their colour once you take the keystone out of them. Let them sit there—bridges over nothing, with no road over the top of them, like the stone bridge of Drumdochart after the flood. Ay, ay, you can look at them if you like. You can make a kirk and a mill of them if you like, they have laid there long enough. Only don't say a word to me about any of them. I'm going to fill my pipe again. But I won't drink more tonight cause it's the Sabbath, and I'm going to read my book. So hold your tongue."

So saying, he proceeded to get the tobacco out of his pipe by knocking it on the hob while Alec took up the paper that lay nearest. He found it contained a fragment of a poem in the Scots tongue, and searching amongst the rest of the scattered sheets, he soon got the whole of it together.

Now, although Alec had but little acquaintance with verse, he was able, thanks to Annie Anderson, to enjoy a ballad very heartily. There was something in this one which, associating itself in his mind with the strange being before him, moved him more than he could account for.

When he had finished reading it, he found himself gazing at the man who had penned it. He could not quite get the verses and Mr. Cupples into harmony. Not daring to make any observation, however, he sat with the last sheaf still in his hand and a reverential stare on his face. Suddenly lifting his eyes, Mr. Cupples exclaimed—

"What are you glaring at me for? I'm neither ghost nor warlock! Damn you! Get out, if you're going to stick me through with your eyes that way!"

"I beg your pardon, Mr. Cupples. I didn't mean to be rude," said Alec humbly.

"Well, I've had enough of you for one night. I can't stand glaring eyes, especially in the heads of idiots and innocents like you."

I am sorry to have to record what Alec learned from the landlady afterward, that Mr. Cupples went to bed that night, notwithstanding it was the Sabbath, more drunk than she had ever known him. Indeed, he could not properly be said to have gone to bed at all, for he had tumbled on the floor in his clothes and clean shirt, where she had found him fast asleep the next morning, with his book terribly crumpled under him.

"But," asked Alec, "what *is* Mr. Cupples?"

"That's a question he couldna weel answer himself," was the reply. "He does a heap o' things—writes for the lawyers sometimes, buys an' sells queer books, gives lessons in Greek an' Hebrew—but he doesna like that—he canna stand to be contradicted, an' laddies is always that way, helps anybody that wants help in the way o' numbers when their books go wrong. He's a kind of librarian at yer own college, Mr. Forbes. The old man's dead and Mr. Cupples is jist doing the work. They won't give him the run o' the place 'cause he has a reputation for drinking. But they'll get as much work oot o' him as if they did, and for half the money. He can do most anything all day, but the minute he comes home, oot comes the drink an' he jist sits doon an' drinks till he turns the world over on top o' him."

The next day about noon, Alec went into the library where he found Mr. Cupples busy rearranging the books and the catalogue, both of which had been neglected for years. This was the first of many visits to the library, or rather to the librarian.

There was a certain mazy sobriety of demeanour about Mr. Cupples all day long, as if in the presence of such serious things as books he was bound to be upon his good behaviour and confine his debauchery to taking snuff in prodigious quantities. He was full of information about books and opinions besides. For instance, one afternoon when Alec picked up a book of which he disapproved, the librarian snatched it from his hand and put it back on the shelf.

"A palace of dirt and impudence and spiritual stink," he said. "Let it sit there and rot. You don't need to be reading the likes of that!"

He never would remain in the library after the day began to ebb. The moment he became aware that the first filmy shadow had fallen from the coming twilight, he grabbed his hat, locked the door, gave the key to the sacrist, and hurried away.

The friendly relations between the two struck its roots deeper and deeper during the session, and when it drew to a close when winter was past, it was with regret that Alec bade him good-bye.

– Thirty-Five –

Homecoming

Winter had begun to withdraw its ghostly troops and Glamerton began to grow warmer. Annie, who had been very happy all the time, began to be aware of something more at hand. A flutter scarcely recognizable, as of the wings of awaking delight, now stirred her heart occasionally with a sensation of physical presence and motion. She would find herself giving an involuntary skip as she walked along, and now and then humming a bit of a psalm tune. A hidden well was throbbing in the child's soul. Its waters had been frozen by the winter. The spring, which sets all things springing, had made it flow and swell anew, soon to break forth bubbling. But her joy was gentle, for even when she was merriest, it was in a sober and maidenly fashion, testifying that she had already walked with Sorrow and was not afraid.

Robert Bruce's last strategical move against the community had been tolerably successful, even in his own eyes, and he was so far satisfied with himself that he could afford to be in good humour with other people. Annie, too, came in for a share of this humour. Although she knew him too well to have any regard for him, it was yet a comfort to her to be on such terms with him as not to have to dread a bitter word every time she chanced to meet him. This comfort, however, stood on a sandy foundation.

At length, one bright day in the end of March, Alec came home, not the worse to friendly eyes for having been at college. He seemed the same cheery, active youth as before. The chief differences were that he had grown considerably and that he wore a coat. There was a certain indescribable alteration in tone and manner, a certain crystallization and polish, which the same friends regarded as an indubitable improvement.

The day after his arrival, crossing the square of Glamerton, he saw a group of men talking together, among them his old friend Thomas Crann. He went up and shook hands with him and with Andrew Constable, the clothier.

"Hasn't he grown into a long child?" said Andrew to Thomas, regarding Alec kindly.

"Humph!" returned Thomas, "he'll jist need the longer a coffin."

Alec laughed, but Andrew said, "Hoot!"

Thomas and Alec walked away together. But scarcely a sentence had been exchanged before the stonemason, with a delicacy of perception of which his rough manner and calloused hands gave no indication, felt that a film of separation had come between the youth and himself. Anxious to break through it, he said abruptly:

"How's yer immortal part, Alec? Mind ye, there's a knowledge that worketh death."

Alec laughed—not scornfully—but he laughed.

"Ye may laugh, Alec, but tis the truth," said the mason.

Alec held out his hand, for here their way diverged. Thomas shook it kindly, but walked away gloomily. When he arrived at home, Thomas shut his bedroom door and went down on his knees by his bedside.

In order to prepare for the mathematical studies of the following year, Alec went to the school again in the morning on most days, Mr. Malison being well able to give him the assistance he required. The first time he made his appearance at the door, a silence as of death was the sign of his welcome. But a tumult presently arose and discipline was for a time suspended.

Annie sat still, staring at her book, and turning red and pale alternately. But he took no notice of her, and she tried to be glad of it. When school was over, however, he came up to her in the lane and addressed her kindly.

But the delicate little maiden felt as the rough stonemason had felt, that a change had passed over the old companion and friend. True, the change was only a breath—a mere shadow. Yet it was a measureless gulf between them. Annie went to her garret that night with a sense of sad privation.

But her pain sprang from a source hardly so deep as that of the stonemason. For the change she found in Alec was chiefly of an external kind, and if she had a vague feeling of a deeper change, it had scarcely yet come into her consciousness. When she saw the *young gentleman,* her heart sank within her. Her friend was lost. A shape was going about, looking like the old Alec who had carried her in his arms through the invading torrent. But to complete her confusion of feelings, there was also a certain added reverence for the apparition.

Mrs. Forbes never asked her to the house now, and it was well for her that her friendship with Tibbie Dyster had begun. But as she saw Alec day after day at school, the old colours began to revive out of the faded picture. And when the spring had advanced a little, the boat was got out. Alec could not go rowing in *The Bonnie Annie* without thinking of its godmother and inviting her to join them. Indeed, Curly would not have let him forget her, for he felt that she was a bond between him and Alec, and he loved Alec the more devotedly since the rift between their social positions had begun to show itself. The devotion of the schoolboy to his superior in schoolboy arts had begun to change into something like the devotion of clansman to his chief. And not infrequently would an odd laugh of consciousness between Annie and Curly reveal the fact that they were both watching for a peep or word from Alec.

In due time harvest came, and Annie could no more keep from haunting the harvest than the crane could keep from flying south when the summer was over. She watched all the fields around Glamerton, she knew what response each made to the sun and which would first be ripe for reaping. And the very day that the sickle was put in, there was Annie to see and share in the joy. Unquestioned as uninvited, she became one of the company of reapers, gatherers, binders, and stookers, assembled to collect the living gold of the earth from the early fields of the farm of Howglen.

Sadly her thoughts went back to the old days when Dowie was master of the field and she was Dowie's little mistress. Not that she met with anything but kindness—only it was not the same kindness she had had from Dowie. But the pleasure of being once more near Alec almost made up for every loss. And he was quite friendly, although, she must confess, not quite so familiar as of old. But that did not matter, she assured herself.

The labourers all knew her well and themselves took care that she should have the portion of their food which her assistance had well earned. She never refused anything that was offered her except money. That she had taken only once in her life—from Mr. Cowie, whom she continued to love the more dearly, although she no longer attended his church.

But again the harvest was safely lodged and the sad old age of the year sank through the rains and frosts to his grave.

The winter came and Alec went.

He had not been gone a week when Mrs. Forbes's invitations began again. And, as if to make up for the neglect of the summer, they were more frequent than before. No time was so happy for Annie as the time she spent with her. And this winter she began to make some return in the way of household assistance.

– Thirty-Six –

A New Term

"Hello, bantam!" exclaimed Mr. Cupples to Alec, as he entered the garret within an hour of his arrival in his old quarters. He found the soul of the librarian still hovering in the steam of his tumbler, like one of Swedenborg's damned over the odour of his peculiar hell. As he spoke he emptied the glass, the custom of drinking from which, instead of from the tumbler itself—rendering it impossible to get drunk all at once—is one of the atonements offered by the Scotch to their tutelar god—Propriety. "How are you getting on with the mathematics?"

"Middling only," answered Alec.

"I don't doubt that. Small preparations do well enough for Professor Fraser's Greek, but you'll find it's another story with the mathematics. You must just come to me with it as you did with the Greek."

"Thank you, Mr. Cupples," said Alec heartily. "I don't know how to repay you."

"Repay me! I want no repayment. Only ask me no questions and leave me when I'm drunk."

After all his summer preparation, Alec was still behind in mathematics, but his medical studies interested him more and more all the time.

Not many days after his arrival, Alec resolved to pay a visit to Mr. Fraser. He was sure of a welcome from the old man, for although Alec gave less attention to his Greek now, Mr. Fraser was delighted that he was doing his best to make himself a good doctor. His friendliness toward him had, in fact, increased, for the professor thought he saw in him noble qualities and enjoyed having such a youth near him.

Alec was shown into the professor's drawing room, which was unusual. The professor was seated in an easy chair with one leg outstretched before him.

"Excuse me, Mr. Forbes," he said, holding out his left hand without rising. "I am laid up with the gout—I don't know why. The port wine my grandfather drank, I suppose. *I* never drink it. I'm afraid it's old age. And yon's my nurse.—Mr. Forbes, your cousin, Kate, my dear."

There at the other side of the fire sat a girl, half smiling and half blushing as she looked up from her work. Alec advanced and she rose and held out her hand. She might have been a year older than he, perhaps seventeen or eighteen.

"So you are a cousin of mine, Mr. Forbes," she said when they were all seated by the blazing fire—she with a piece of plain needlework in her hands, he with a very awkward nothing in his, and the professor contemplating his swathed leg on the chair before him.

"So your uncle says," he answered, "and I am happy to believe him. I hope we shall be good friends."

Alec was recovering himself after his initial modesty.

"I hope we shall," she responded with a quick, shy, asking glance from her fine eyes.

Those eyes were worth looking into, if only as a study of colour. They were of many hues marvellously blended. Their glance rather discomposed Alec. He had not yet learned that ladies' eyes are sometimes very disquieting. Yet he could not keep his from wandering toward them. The consequence was that he soon lost the greater part of his senses. After sitting speechless for some moments, he was suddenly seized by a horrible conviction that if he remained silent an instant longer, he would be driven to do or say something absurd. So he did the latter at once by bursting out with the stupid question,

"What are you working at?"

"A duster," she answered instantly—this time without looking up.

Now the said "duster" was of the finest cambric material, so that Alec could see that she was making game of him. This banished his shyness and plucked up his vigour.

"I see," he said, "when I ask you questions, you—"

"Tell lies," she interposed, without giving him time even to hesitate, adding, "Is your mother nice, Mr. Forbes?"

"She's the best woman in the world," he answered with feeling, almost shocked at having to answer such a question.

"Oh, I beg your pardon," returned Kate, laughing, and the laugh revealed very pretty teeth, with a semi-transparent pearly-blue shadow in them.

"I am glad she is nice," she went on. "I should like to know her. Mothers are not *always* nice."

She did not laugh after this childish speech, but let her face settle into perfect stillness—sadness indeed, for a shadow came over the stillness. Mr. Fraser sat watching the two with his amused old face, one side of it twitching in the effort to suppress the smile which sought to break from the useful half of his mouth. The gout could not have been very bad just then.

"I see, Katie, what that long chin of yours is thinking," he said.

"What is my chin thinking, uncle?" she asked.

"That uncles are not always nice either. They snub little girls, sometimes, don't they?"

"I know one who *is* nice, all except for one naughty leg."

She rose as she said this and, going round to the back of the chair, leaned over it and kissed his forehead. The old man looked up to her gratefully.

"Ah, Katie!" he said, "you may make game of an old man like me. But don't try your tricks on Mr. Forbes. He won't stand them."

Alec blushed. Kate went back to her seat, and took up her "duster" again.

Not until she had drawn nearer in approaching her uncle had Alec realized how pretty Kate was. He found too that her great mass of hair was full of glints and golden hints, as if she had twisted up a handful of sunbeams with it in the morning. Before she got back to her seat, he was very nearly in love with her. And if he had talked stupidly before, he talked worse now. At length he went home with the conviction that he had made a great donkey of himself.

When he arrived home he found he could neither read nor think. At last he threw his book to the other side of the room and went to bed, where he found it not half so difficult to go to sleep as it had been to study.

The next day things went better, for he was not yet so lost that a night's rest could do him no good. But it was fortunate that there was no Greek class and that he was not called up to read Latin.

As he left his final class of the day, he said to himself that he would just look in and see how Mr. Fraser was. He was shown into the professor's study.

Mr. Fraser smiled as he entered with a certain grim comicality.

"I hope your gout is better today, sir," he said, sending his glance wide astray of his words.

"Yes, thank you, Mr. Forbes," answered Mr. Fraser, "it is better. Won't you sit down?"

Warned by his earlier smile, Alec was astute enough to decline and presently took his leave. As he shut the study door, he thought he would just peep into the dining room, the door of which stood open opposite the study. There she was, sitting at the table writing.

"Who can that be a letter to?" thought Alec. But it was early days to be jealous.

"How do you do, Mr. Forbes?" said Kate, holding out her hand.

Could it be that he had seen her only yesterday? Or had he simply forgotten what she was like? She was so different from how he had been imagining her.

The fact was merely that she had been writing to an old friend, and her manner for the time, as well as her expression, was affected by her mental proximity to that friend. Indeed, Alec was not long in finding out that one of her witcheries was that she was never the same.

"I am glad to find your uncle much better," he said.

"You have seen him then?"

"Yes."

"Won't you sit down?"

"No, thank you. I must go home," answered Alec, feeling that she did not want him. "Good night," he added, advancing a step.

"Good night, Mr. Forbes," she returned without extending her hand.

Alec bowed and went with the resolution not to repeat his visit too soon. She interfered with his studies throughout the following week, notwithstanding, and sent him wandering out in the streets many times when he ought to have been reading at home.

One bright moonlight night he found himself on the quay, and spying a boat at the foot of one of the stairs, asked the man in it if he was ready for a row. The man agreed. Alec got in, and they rowed out of the river, and along the coast to a fishing village where the man lived, and whence Alec walked home. This was the beginning of many such boating excursions made by Alec in the close of this session. They greatly improved his boatmanship, and strengthened his growing muscles. The end of the winter was mild, and there were not many days unfit for the exercise.

– Thirty-Seven –

Kate

The Saturday after the next Alec received a note from Mr. Fraser, hoping that his new cousin had not driven him away, and inviting him to dine that same afternoon.

He went. After dinner the old man fell asleep in his chair.

"Where were you born?" Alec asked Kate.

She was more like his first impression of her.

"Don't you know?" she replied. "In the north of Sutherlandshire—near the foot of a great mountain, from the top of which, on the longest day, you can see the sun, or a bit of him at least, all night long."

"How glorious!" said Alec.

"I don't know. I never saw him. And the winters are so long and terrible. Nothing but snowy hills about you, and great clouds always coming down with fresh loads of snow to scatter over them."

"Then you don't want to go back?"

"No. There is nothing to make me wish to go back. There is no one there to love me now."

She looked very sad for a few moments.

"Yes," said Alec thoughtfully, "a winter without love must be dreadful. But I like the winter, and we have plenty of it where I come from too."

"Where is your home?"

"Not many miles northwest of here."

"Is it a nice place?"

"Yes, of course—I think so."

"Ah! You have a mother. I wish I knew her."

"I wish you did. True, the whole place is like her to me. But I don't think everybody would admire it. There are plenty of bare, snowy hills there too in winter. But I think the summers and the harvests are as delightful as anything can be, except—"

"Except what?"

"Don't make me say what will make you angry with me."

"Now you must, else I shall think something that will make me *more* angry."

"Except your face," Alec said, frightened at his own boldness, but glancing at her shyly.

She flushed a little, but did not look angry.

"I don't like that," she said. "It makes one feel awkward."

"At least," rejoined Alec boldly, "you must admit it is your own fault."

"I can't help my face," she said, laughing.

"Oh! You know what I mean. You made me say it."

"Yes, after you had half said it already. Don't do it again."

And there followed more of such foolish talk, uninteresting to my readers.

"Where were you at school?" asked Alec after a pause. "Your uncle told me you were at school."

"Near London," she answered.

"Ah, that accounts for your beautiful speech."

"There again. I declare I will wake my uncle if you go on in that way."

"I beg your pardon," protested Alec. "I forgot."

"But," she went on, "in Sutherlandshire we don't talk so horribly as they do around here."

"I dare say not," returned Alec.

"I don't mean you. I wonder how it is that you speak so much better than all the people here."

"I suppose because mother speaks well."

"She does not speak with the accent?"

"She never lets me speak broad Scotch around her."

"Your mother again!"

Alec did not reply.

"I *should* like to see her," pursued Kate.

"You must come and see her then!"

"See whom?" asked Mr. Fraser, rousing himself from his nap.

"My mother, sir," answered Alec.

"Oh, I thought you had been speaking of Katie's friend," said the professor, and fell asleep again.

"Uncle means Bessie Warner who is coming by the steamer from London on Monday. Isn't it kind of him to ask her to come and see me?"

"He is always kind. Was Miss Warner a schoolfellow of yours?"

"Yes—no—not exactly. She was one of the governesses. I must go and meet her at the steamer. Will you go with me?"

"I shall be delighted. When does she arrive?"

"They say about six."

"I will come and fetch you before that."

"Thank you. I suppose I may, uncle?"

"What, my dear?" said the professor, rousing himself again.

"Have my cousin to take care of me when I go to meet Bessie."

"Yes, certainly. I shall be much obliged to you, Mr. Forbes. I am not quite so agile as I was at your age, though my gouty leg is better."

This conversation would hardly have been worth recording had it not led to the walk and the waiting on Monday. They found when they reached the region of steamers that she had not yet arrived. So Alec and Kate walked out along the pier, to pass the time. The pier runs down the side of the river, and a long way into the sea. It had begun to grow dark and Alec had to take great care of Kate among the tramways, coils of rope and cables that crossed their way. At length they got clear of these and found themselves upon the pier, built of great rough stones tapering away into the dark.

"It is a rough season of the year for a lady to come by sea," said Alec.

"Bessie is very fond of the sea," answered Kate. "I hope you will like her, Mr. Forbes."

"Do you want me to like her better than you?" rejoined Alec. "Because if you do—"

"Look how beautiful that red light is on the other side of the river," interrupted Kate. "And there is another farther out."

"When the man at the helm gets those two lights in a line," said Alec, "he may steer straight in, in the darkest night."

"Look how much more glorious the red shine is on the water below!" said Kate.

"It looks so wet," returned Alec—"just like blood."

He almost cursed himself as he said so, for he felt Kate's hand stir as if she would withdraw it from his arm. But after fluttering like a bird for a moment, it settled again upon its perch and there rested.

The day had been quite calm, but now a sudden gust of wind from the northeast swept across the pier and made Kate shiver. Alec drew her shawl closer about her, and her arm farther within his. They were now close to the sea. On the other side of the wall which rose on their left, they could hear the first of the sea-waves. It was a dreary place—no sound even indicating the neighbourhood of life. On one side, the river below them went flowing out to the sea in the dark, giving a cold sluggish gleam now and then, as if it were a huge snake heaving up a bend of its wet back, as it hurried away to join its fellows. On the other side rose a great wall of stone, beyond which was the sound of long waves following in troops out of the dark, and falling upon a low moaning coast. Clouds hung above the sea, and above the clouds two or three disconsolate stars.

"Here is a stair!" said Alec. "Let's go up on the top of the sea wall, and then we shall catch the first glimpse of the light from the steamer."

They climbed the steep, rugged steps and stood on the broad wall, hearing the sea pulses lazily fall at its foot. Feeling Kate draw a deep breath like the sigh of the sea, Alec looked round in her face. There was still light enough to show it frowning and dark and sorrowful and hopeless. It was in fact a spiritual mirror, which reflected in human forms the look of that weary waste of waters. She gave a little start, gathered herself together, and murmured something about the cold.

"Let us go down again," said Alec. "The wind has risen considerably, and the wall will shelter us down below."

"No, no" she answered. "I like it. We can walk here just as well. I don't mind the wind."

"I thought you were afraid of falling off."

"No, not in the dark. I should be, I dare say, if I could see how far we are from the bottom."

So they walked on. The waves no longer fell at the foot of the wall, but now leaned against it as the level of the water steadily rose and fell. The wind kept coming in gusts, tearing a white gleam now and then on the dark surface of the sea. Behind them shone the dim lights of the city, before them all was dark as eternity, except for the one light at the end of the pier. At length Alec spied another out at sea.

"I believe that is the steamer," he said. "But she is a good way off. We shall have plenty of time to walk to the end—that is, if you would like to."

"Certainly, let us go on. I want to stand on the very point," answered Kate.

They soon came to the lighthouse on the wall and there descended to the lower part of the pier, the end of which now plunged with a steep descent into the sea. It was constructed of great stones clamped with iron, and built into a natural foundation of rock. Up the slope the waves rushed, and down the slope they sank again, with that seemingly aimless and resultless rise and fall, which makes the sea so dreary and sad to those men and women who are not satisfied without some goal in view, some outcome of their labours. For it goes on and on, answering ever to the call of sun and moon, and the fierce trumpet of the winds, yet working nothing but the hopeless wear of the bosom in which it lies bound for ever.

They stood looking out into the great dark before them, dark air, dark sea, dark sky, watching the one light which grew brighter as they gazed. Neither of them saw the dusky figure watching them from behind a great cylindrical stone standing on the end of the pier, close to the wall.

A wave rushed up, almost to their feet.

"Let us go," said Kate, with a shiver. "I can't bear it longer. The water is calling me and threatening me. There! See how that wave rushed up as if it wanted me at once!"

Alec again drew her closer to him, and, turning, they walked slowly back. He was silent with the delight of having that lovely creature all to himself, leaning on his arm in the enfolding and protecting darkness, and Kate was likewise silent.

By the time they reached the quay at the other end of the pier, the steamer had crossed the bar, and they could hear the *thud* of her paddles treading the water beneath them eagerly because she was now near her rest. After a few struggles she lay quiet in her place, and they went on board.

Alec saw Kate embrace a girl perhaps a little older than herself, helped her find her luggage, put them into a carriage, and took his leave of them, and went home.

He did not know that all the way back along the pier he and Kate had been followed by Patrick Beauchamp.

– Thirty-Eight –

Mr. Cupples's Warning

Excited, and unable to settle to his work, Alec ran upstairs to Mr. Cupples, whom he had not seen for some days. He found him not more than half-way towards his diurnal goal.

"What's come of you, bantam, these many days?" said Mr. Cupples.

"I saw you last Saturday," said Alec.

"Last Saturday week, you mean," rejoined the librarian. "Hoo's the mathematics coming on?"

"To tell the truth, I'm rather behind," answered Alec.

"I was thinking as muckle. And the anatomy?"

"Middling better."

"That's well. And your friend Beauchamp?"

"No friend of mine! But he's not bothered me again."

"Don't be too sure, bantam."

"What do you mean?"

"He's been dogging your steps—I've seen him more than once taking his bearing of you. And now you've taken to other studies as well—a bonnie young one. The Lord have mercy upon you. The goddess of the rainbow herself has got a hold of you, and you'll be seeing nothing but rainbows."

"What are you prophesying at, Mr. Cupples?" said Alec, wondering how Mr. Cupples could be so well-informed about his personal life.

"I'm not drunk yet," rejoined Mr. Cupples. "I tell you, watch yourself. Beauchamp'll do you a mischief yet. He's been watching you like a hungry devil.

Although Alec had not suspected it, Beauchamp had in fact been haunting him from the very commencement of the session, and Mr. Cupples had caught him in only one of many acts of the kind. Beauchamp's whole consciousness was poisoned by the memory of the evening when Alec had made him look foolish in front of half the school. Beauchamp's pride prevented him from engaging in any contest in which he was not sure of success, the thought of failure being to him unendurable.

Now hate keeps its object present even more than the opposite passion. Love makes everything lovely, hate concentrates itself on the one thing hated. The very sound of Alec's voice became to the ears of Beauchamp what a filthy potion would have been to his palate. Every line of his countenance became disgusting. The fascination of his hate, and his desire of revenge, kept Beauchamp's ears, eyes, and thoughts hovering about Alec Forbes.

No way of gratifying his hatred, however, although he had been brooding over it all the previous summer, had presented itself till now. At last he saw the possibility of working a dear revenge. But even now, to work surely, he must delay long.

Nor is it surprising that his pride should not protect him from the deeper disgrace of walking in underhanded ways. For there is nothing in the worship of self to teach a man to be noble. Even honour will one day fail him who has learned no higher principle.

Notwithstanding the humiliation he had experienced, he retained as yet an unlimited confidence in some gifts which he supposed himself to possess by nature, and to be capable of using with unequalled art.

And true hate, as well as true love, knows how to wait.

– Thirty-Nine –

Tibbie's Cottage

Annie's visits to Tibbie Dyster increased, and she began to read regularly to the blind woman. One Saturday evening, after she had been reading for some time, interrupted frequently by the harsh old woman, the latch of Tibbie's door was lifted and in walked Robert Bruce. He stared when he saw Annie, for he thought her at Howglen and said in a tone of asperity,

"You're everywhere at once, Annie Anderson. A downright runabout!"

"Let the bairn be, Master Bruce," said Tibbie. "She's doing the Lord's will, whether ye may think so or not. She's visiting them that's in the prisonhouse of the dark. She's ministering to them that hae many preevileges na doubt, but hae room for more."

"I'm not saying anything," said Bruce.

"Ye're offending one of his little ones. Take ye hold of the millstone."

"Hoot, toot, Tibbie. I was only wishing that she would keep a small part of her ministrations for her own home and her own folk that have charge to ministering to her. There's the mistress and me just martyrs to that shop! And there's the baby in need of some ministration now and then, if that be what you call it."

A grim compression of the mouth was all Tibbie's reply. She did not choose to tell Robert Bruce that although she was blind—and possibly because she was blind—she heard rather more gossip than anybody else in Glamerton, and that consequently his appeal to her sympathy had no effect upon her. Finding she made no answer, Bruce turned to Annie.

"Now, Annie," he said, "you're not wanted here any longer. I have a word or two to say to Tibbie. Go home and learn your lessons for tomorrow."

"It's Saturday night," answered Annie.

"But you have your lessons to learn for the Monday."

"Ow, ay. But I have a book or two to take home to Mistress Forbes. I think I'll stay with her and come to church with her in the morning."

Now, although all that Bruce wanted was to get rid of her, he went on to oppose her. Common-minded people always feel they give the enemy an advantage if they show themselves content.

"It's not safe for you to run about in the dark."

"I know the road to Mrs. Forbes like the back of my hand."

"No doubt!" he answered with a sneer peculiar to him. "And there's dogs about," he added, remembering Annie's fear of dogs.

But by this time Annie, gentle as she was, had got a little angry.

"The Lord'll take care of me from the dark and the dogs and the rest of you, Mr. Bruce," she said.

And bidding Tibbie good night, she took up her books and departed to wade through the dark and the snow, trembling lest some unseen dog should lay hold of her as she went.

As soon as she was gone, Bruce proceeded to make himself agreeable to Tibbie by retelling all the bits of gossip he could think of. While thus engaged he kept peering earnestly about the room from door to chimney, turning his head on every side, and surveying everything as he turned it. Tibbie perceived from the changes in his voice that he was thus occupied.

"So your old landlord's dead, Tibbie?" he said at last.

"Ay, honest man. He always had a kind word for a poor body."

"Ay, ay, no doubt. But what would you say if I told you I had bought the little house and was your new landlord, Tibbie?"

"I would say that the doorsill wants mending to keep the snow oot, and the poor place is in sore need of new thatch."

"Well, that's very reasonable, no doubt, if all is as you say."

"Be as I say, Robert Bruce?"

"Ay, ay. You see, you're not altogether like other folk. I don't mean you any offense, you know, Tibbie. But you don't have the sight of your eyes."

"Maybe I don't hae the feeling of my old bones either, Master Bruce? Maybe I'm too blind to hae rheumatizm, or to smell the old wet thatch when there's been a scattering of snow or a drop of rain on the roof!"

"I didn't want to anger you, Tibbie. All that deserves attention. It would be a shame to let an old person like you—"

"Not that old, Mr. Bruce, if you knew the truth."

"Well, you're not too young not to need to be well taken care of—are you, Tibbie?"

Tibbie grunted.

"Well, to come to the point. There's no doubt that the house needs a lot of doctoring."

"Indeed it does," interposed Tibbie. "It needs a new door."

"No doubt you're right, Tibbie. But seeing that I have to lay out so much, I'll be compelled to add another threepence onto the rent."

"Another threepence, Robert Bruce! That's three threepence in the place of two. That's a big rise! Ye can't mean what ye say! Tis all I'm able to do to pay my sixpence! An old, blind body like me doesn't fall in with sixpence when she goes looking about with her long fingers when she's dropped something."

"But you do a heap of spinning, Tibbie, with those long fingers. No one in Glamerton spins like you."

"Maybe ay and maybe no. It's no muckle that comes to. I wouldna spin so well if it weren't that the Almighty put some sight into the points o' my fingers cause there was none left in my eyes. And if ye make another threepence a week oot o' that, ye'll be turning the weather that he sent to run my mill into your dam, and I wouldna doobt that it will play ill water wi' yer wheels."

"Hoot, hoot! Tibbie. It hurts my heart to appear so hard-hearted."

"I hae nae doobt ye dinna want to *appear* so. But do ye ken that I make so little by the spinning that the kirk gives me a shilling a week to make up with? And if it werena for kind friends, tis an ill living I would have in dour weather like this. Dinna ye imagine, Mr. Bruce, that I hae anything put away except sevenpence in a stocking. And it would hae to come off my tea or something else I would ill miss."

"Well, that may be very true," rejoined Bruce, "but a body must have their own for all that. Wouldn't the church give you the other threepence?"

"Do ye think I would take it from the kirk to put into yer till?"

"Well, say sevenpence then, and we'll be quits."

"I tell ye what, Robert Bruce—rather than pay ye one penny more than the sixpence, I'll go out in the snow and let the Lord look after me."

Robert Bruce went away and did not purchase the cottage, which was on the market at a low price. He had intended Tibbie to believe, as she did, that he had already bought it. If she had agreed to pay even the sevenpence, he would have left her to go and buy it.

There was no day yet in which Annie did not think of Alec with the same feeling of devotion she had always had, although all her necessities, hopes, and fears were now beyond any assistance he could render. She was far on in a new path toward light and truth, he was loitering behind, out of hearing.

Alec would not have dared to call her concern for him nonsense, but he would have set down all such religious matters as belonging to women and not to youths such as himself just beginning in the ways of the world. He never thought now about the lessons of Thomas Crann. He began to look down upon all his past, and even upon his old companions. Since knowing Kate, who had more delicate habits and ways than he had ever seen, he had begun to refine his own behaviour. While he became more polished in his anxiety to be like her, he became less genial and wide-hearted.

But none of his old friends forgot him. I believe not a day passed in which Thomas did not pray for him in secret, naming him by his name and lingering over it mournfully: "Alexander Forbes—the young man that I thought would hae been plucked frae the burning afore noo. But thy time's the best, O Lord. It's all thy work, and there's no good thing in us. And thou canst turn the heart of man as the rivers of water. And maybe thou hast given him grace to repent already, though I know nothing aboot it."

– Forty –

Annie and Thomas

This had been a sore winter for Thomas, and he had had plenty of time for prayer. He had gone up on a scaffold one day to see that the wall he was building was properly protected from the rain, and his foot slipped on a wet pole. He fell to the ground and one of his legs was broken. Not a moan escaped him—a complaint was out of the question. They carried him home, and the surgeon did his best for him.

Although few people liked him much, he was not left unvisited in his sickness. The members of his own religious community recognized their obligation to minister to him. They would have done more, had they guessed how poor he was. Nobody knew how much he gave away in other directions, but they judged of his means by the amount he was in the habit of putting into the plate at the chapel-door every Sunday. There was never much of the silvery shine to be seen in the heap of copper, but one of the gleaming sixpences was almost sure to have dropped from the hand of Thomas Crann.

Annie went every day to ask about him and every day had a kind reception from Jean. At length one day Jean asked her if she would not like to see him.

"Ay, would I, right well," answered Annie.

Jean led her into Thomas's room where he lay in bed. He held out his hand. Annie put hers into his, saying timidly, "Is your leg very sore, Thomas?"

"Ow no, dawtie. The Lord's been very merciful—jist like himself. It was hard to bide for a while when I couldna sleep. But I jist sleep now like one of the beloved."

"I was right sorry for you, Thomas."

"Ay. Ye've a kind heart, lassie. Ye're surely one of the Lord's bairns—"

"Eh! I don't know," cried Annie, half-terrified at such an assurance from Thomas, and yet delighted at the same time.

"Ay, ye are," continued Thomas confidently. "Now sit ye doon aside me and open the Bible there and read that hunner and seventh psalm. Eh, lassie! but the Lord is good. What right hae I to praise him?"

"You have the best right, Thomas, for hasn't he been good to you?"

"Ye're right, lassie, ye're right. It's wonnerful the common sense of bairns. No doubt they're born in sin and brought forth in iniquity, but if they repent early, they get far ahead of the auld folk."

Thomas's sufferings had made him more gentle—and more sure of Annie's election. Annie saw him often after this, and he never let her go without reading a chapter to him, his remarks upon which were always of some use to her, notwithstanding the limited capacity and formal shape of the doctrinal moulds in which they were cast. For wherever there is genuine religious feeling and *experience*, it will now and then crack the prisoning pitcher, and let some brilliant ray of the indwelling glory out.

Although the framework of Thomas was roughly hewn, he had always been subject to fluctuations of feelings as are more commonly found amongst women. Sometimes he would be lifted to the very "mercy seat of God," as he would say, at others he would fall into fits of doubting whether he was indeed one of the elect. At such latter times he was subject to a great temper, alternately the cause and effect of his misery.

If Jean, who had no idea what he happened to be thinking, dared interrupt his devotions at such a time by calling through the bolted door, the saint who had been kneeling before God in utter abasement and self-contempt would suddenly throw it open wrathful and indignant and boiling over with angry words. Having driven the enemy away in confusion, he would bolt his door again and return to his prayers in twofold misery, the guilt from his anger raising yet another wall of separation between him and God.

This weakness all but disappeared during the worst of his illness, but returned with increased force when his recovery had advanced far enough to allow him out of bed. A deacon of the church, a worthy little weaver, had been half-officially appointed to visit Thomas and find out—which was not an easy task—if he was in want of anything. When James Johnstone arrived, Jean was out. He lifted the latch, entered, and tapped gently at Thomas's door—too gently, for he received no answer. With hasty yet hesitating imprudence, he opened the door and peeped in. Thomas was on his knees by the fireside with his plaid blanket over his head. Startled by the weaver's entrance, he raised his head, and his rugged face, red with wrath, glared out of the thicket of his plaid upon the intruder.

"James, ye're taking the part of Satan, driving a man from his prayers!" he cried fiercely.

"Hoot, Thomas! I beg yer pardon," answered the weaver, rather flurried. "I thought ye might hae been asleep."

"Ye had no business to think for yerself in such a manner. What do ye want?"

"I jist came to see whether ye was in need of anything, Thomas."

"I'm in want of nothing. Good night to ye."

"But really, Thomas," expostulated the weaver, "ye shouldna be doon on yer knees like that, with yer leg in such a weak condition."

"What do ye ken aboot my leg? And what's the use o' knees, but to go doon upon them? Go home, and go doon upon yer own, James, and dinna disturb other folk who ken what theirs was made for."

Thus admonished, the weaver dared not linger. As he turned to shut the door, he wished the mason good night but received no answer. Thomas had sunk forward on the chair in front of him and had already drawn his blanket back over his head.

But the sacred place of the Most High will not be entered in this fashion. It is not by driving away our brother that we can be alone with God. Thomas's plaid could not isolate him with his Maker, for communion with God is never isolation. The chamber with the shut door shuts out God too and one is left alone with himself. The love of brethren opens the door into God's chamber, which is within ours. So Thomas—who was far from hating his brother, and who would have, in fact, struggled to his feet and limped out to do him a service, though he would not have held out his hand to receive one—Thomas, I say, felt worse than ever.

At length another knock came, which although very gentle, he heard and knew well enough.

"Who's there?" he asked, notwithstanding with a fresh access of anger.

"Annie Anderson," was the answer through the door, in a tone which at once soothed the ruffled waters of Thomas's spirit.

"Come in," he said.

She entered, quiet as a ghost.

"Come in, Annie. I'm glad to see ye. Jist come and kneel doon aside me and we'll pray together, for I'm sore troubled wi' an ill temper."

Without a word of reply, Annie knelt down by the side of his chair. Thomas drew the blanket over her head and took her hand, which was swallowed up in his. After a solemn pause, he began to pray in an outbursting agony of his heart:

"O Lord, who dwellest in the licht inaccessible, whom mortal eye hath not seen nor can see, but who dwellest with him that is humble and contrite of heart, and liftest the licht of thy coontenance upon them that seek it. O Lord, dinna let us cry to ye in vain, this thy lammie, and me, thy old sinner. Forgive my sins and my vile temper, and help me to love my neighbour as myself. Let Christ dwell in me, and then I shall do right—not frae myself, for I hae no good thing in me, but frae thy Spirit that dwelleth in us."

After this prayer, Thomas felt refreshed and hopeful. He rose slowly from his knees, sank into his chair, and drew Annie toward him and kissed her. Then he said, "Will ye go on a small errand for me, Annie?"

"That I will, Thomas."

"I would be obliged to ye if ye would jist run doon to James Johnstone and tell him that I'm sorry I spoke to him as I did. And I would take it right kind o' him if he would come an' take a cup of tea wi' me in the morning, and then we could hae worship together. And tell him to think no more o' the way I spoke to him, for I was troubled in my mind, an' I'm an ill-natured man."

"I'll tell him all that you say," answered Annie, "as well as I can remember it. Would you like me to come back and tell you what he says?"

"No, no, lassie. It'll be time for ye to go home to yer bed. And it's a cold night. I ken that by my leg. And ye see, James Johnstone's not an ill-natured man like me. He's a good man, and he's sure to be well-pleased and come to tea. No, no, ye needna come back. Good night to ye, my dawtie. The Lord bless ye for coming to pray with an ill-natured man."

– Forty-One –

Arrival of the Coach

Now that Kate had a companion, Alec never saw her alone. Miss Warner was a nice, open-eyed, fair-faced English girl, with pleasant manners, and though more shy than Kate was yet ready to take her share in conversation. Alec soon perceived that the two girls were both interested in poetry. By making use of the library of the college, he studied with great earnestness those poets they talked about, especially certain volumes of Lord Byron's, so he would be able to keep up with them.

I will not weary my readers with the talk of the three young people enamoured of Byron. Of course the feelings the girls had about him differed materially from those of Alec, so that a great many of the replies and utterances passed wide of the mark. In neither was the admiration much more than an uneasy delight in the vivid though indistinct images of pleasure raised by the magic of that "physical force of words" in which Byron excels all other English poets, and in virtue of which, I presume, the French persist in regarding Byron as our greatest poet, and in supposing that we agree with them.

In Kate's eyes Alec gained considerably from being able to talk about her favourite author, while she appeared to him more beautiful than ever. He began to discover now what I have already alluded to, that is the *fluidity* of her expression, for he was almost startled every time he saw her, by finding her different from what he had expected to find her. She behaved the same to him, but always looked slightly different, so that Alec felt as if he could never quite know her fully.

Had it not been for the help Mr. Cupples gave him toward the end of the session, he would have done poorly in both Greek and mathematics from all the time taken away from them for his new pursuit of poetry. But Alec was so filled with the phantasm of Kate Fraser that, although not totally insensitive to his obligation to Mr. Cupples, he regarded it lightly. Ready to give his life for a smile from Kate, he took all the man's kindness and drunken wisdom as a matter of course.

And when he next saw Annie and Curly, he did not speak to them quite so heartily as on his former return.

In one or two of his letters, which were never very long, Alec had merely mentioned Kate, and now Mrs. Forbes had many inquiries to make about her. Old feelings and thoughts awoke in her mind and made her wish to see the daughter of her old cousin. She wrote to Mr. Fraser asking him to allow his niece to pay her a visit of a few weeks, but she said nothing about it to Alec. The arrangement happened to be convenient to Mr. Fraser, who wished to accept an invitation himself. It was now the end of April, and he proposed that the time should be set for the beginning of June.

When this favourable response arrived, Mrs. Forbes gave Alec the letter to read and saw the flush of delight rise in his face. The observation was gratifying to her, for that Alec should at length marry one of his own people was a pleasing idea.

Alec ran off into the fields. To think that all these old familiar places would one day soon be glorified by *her* presence! That the daisies would bend beneath the foot of the goddess! It was more than he could do to contain his joy and harness his expectation into the carrying out of day-to-day affairs for the month of waiting that followed.

When the day at last arrived, Alec could not rest. He wandered about all day, haunting his mother as she prepared his room for Kate, hurrying away with a sudden sense of the propriety of indifference, and hurrying back on some cunning pretext, while his mother smiled to herself at his eagerness and the transparency of his wiles. At length, as the hour drew near, he could restrain himself no longer. He rushed to the stable, saddled his pony, and galloped off to meet the mail coach. The sun was nearing the west, a slight shower had just fallen, the thanks of the thirsty earth were ascending in odour, and the wind was too gentle to shake the drops from the leaves.

At last as he turned a corner of the road, there was the coach coming toward him. He had just time to wheel his pony around before it was up with him. A little gloved hand greeted him with a wave out the window, and the face he had been longing for shone out lovelier than ever. There were no passengers inside other than Kate. He rode alongside till they drew near the place where the gig was waiting for them. He gave his pony to the man, helped Kate down from the coach and into the small carriage, and then drove her home in triumph to his mother.

On the opposite side of the road from where the coach stopped, a grassy field sloped up to the shoulder of a hill which was crowned with firs. The rays of the sun, now red with rich age, flowed in a wide stream over the grass and shone on an old Scotch fir making its red bark glow. At the foot of the tree sat Tibbie Dyster. From her the luminous red steamed up the trunk and along the branches of the glowing fir, and over the radiant grass of the upsloping field away toward the western sun.

Alec would have found it difficult to say whether or not he had seen the red cloak of the sunset. But from the shadowy side of it there were eyes shining upon him with a deeper and truer, though calmer, devotion than that with which he regarded Kate. Annie sat by Tibbie's side, the side away from the sun. There they were seated side by side—old, scarred, blind Tibbie and cold, gentle Annie with her dark hair, blue eyes, and the sad wisdom of her pale face. Toward the sun-deserted east, between whose gray clouds, faintly smiling back the rosiness of the sun's triumphal death, two or three cold stars were waiting to glimmer.

Tibbie had come out to bask a little, and, in the dark warmth of the material sun, to worship that Sun whose light she saw in the hidden world of her heart, and who is the Sun of all the worlds, to breathe the air, which, through her prison-bars, spoke of freedom, to give herself room to long for the hour when the loving Father would take her out of the husk which infolded her, and say to her: *"See, my child."* With the rest of the travailing creation, she was groaning in hopeful pain—not in the pain of the mother, but in the pain of the child, soon to be forgotten in the following rest.

If some readers want to follow Kate and Alec home, I say, "We will go home with Tibbie and Annie, and hear what they say. I like better to tell about ugly blind old Tibbie than about beautiful young Kate."

"What did the coach stop for, Annie, lass?" asked Tibbie as soon as it had driven on.

"It's a lady going to Mistress Forbes's at Howglen."

"How do ye ken that?"

"Cause Alec Forbes rode out to meet her and then took her home in the gig."

"Ay! ay! I thought I heard more than the ordinary nummer of horse feet as the coach came up. He's a fine lad, that Alec Forbes, isn't he?"

"Ay, he is," answered Annie sadly—not from jealousy, for she still admired Alec from afar, but as looking up from her purgatorial exclusion to the paradise of Howglen where the beautiful lady would have Mrs. Forbes, and Alec too, all to herself.

The old woman caught the tone, but misinterpreted it.

"I doubt," she said, "he winna get any good at that college."

"Why not?" returned Annie. "I was at the school with him and never saw anything to find fault with."

"Ow, no, lassie. Ye had nothing to do finding fault wi' him. His father was a douce man, and maybe a God-fearing man, though he made but few words aboot it. I think we're sometimes too hard on them that promises little, but maybe does more. Ye remember what ye read to me afore we came oot together, aboot the lad that said to his father, *I go not*, but afterward he repented and went."

"Ay."

"Weel, I think we'll go home noo."

They rose and went, hand in hand, over the bridge and round to the end of the parapet, and down the steep descent to the cottage at its foot.

"Now," said Tibbie after they had arrived, "ye'll jist read a chapter to me, lassie, afore ye go home, and then I'll go to my bed. Blindness is a painful way to save candles."

She forgot that it was summer when, in those northern regions, the night has no time to gather before the sun is flashing again in the east.

The chapter happened to be the ninth of John's Gospel, about Jesus curing a man blind from his birth. When she had finished, Annie said:

"Might not he cure you, Tibbie, if you asked him?"

"Ay, he might, an' ay he will," answered Tibbie. "I'm only jist biding his time. But I'm thinking he'll cure me better than he cured the blind man. He'll jist take the body off of me altogether and then I'll see, not with eyes like yers, but wi' my whole speeritual body. I wish Mr. Turnbull would take it into his head to preach aboot that sometime afore my time comes, which winna be that long, I'm thinking. The wheels'll be stopping at my door afore long."

"What makes you think that, Tibbie? There's no sign of death about you, I'm sure," said Annie.

"Well, ye see, I canna well say. Blind folk somehow ken more than other folk aboot things that the sight o' the eye has little to do wi'. But never mind. I'm willing to bide in the dark as long as he likes. It's enough for any bairn to ken that its father's standing in the light, and seeing all aboot him, and sae weel able to guide him. And I ken he's in the light. Ye mind that bit aboot the Lord putting Moses into a clift o' the rock, and then covering him wi' his hand till he was by him? Weel, I canna help thinking sometimes, that the dark aboot me's jist the palm o' the Lord's hand, and I'm like Moses, only wi' this difference, that when the Lord takes his hand off me, it'll be to let me luik in the face o' him, and not to let me see only his back."

When their talk was over, Annie went home to her garret. It was a singular experience the child had in the changes that came to her with the seasons. The winter with its frost and bitter winds brought her a home at Howglen. The summer, whose airs were molten kisses, took it away and gave her the face of nature instead of the face of a human mother. In place of the snug little room in Howglen—in which she heard with quiet exultation the fierce rush of the hail-scattering tempest against the window of the fluffy fall of the snowflakes—she now had the garret room with its curtainless bed and through whose roof the winds easily found their way. But the winds were warmer now, and through the skylight the sunbeams illuminated the floor, showing all the rat holes and wretchedness of decay.

There was comfort out of doors in the daytime—in the sky and the fields and all the goings-on of life. And this night, after her talk with Tibbie, Annie did not much mind going back to the garret. Nor did she lie awake to think about the beautiful lady Alec had taken home with him.

She dreamed instead that she saw the Son of Man. There was a veil over his face like the veil that Moses wore in the scripture she had recently read to Tibbie. But the face was so bright that it almost melted the veil away, and what she saw made her love that face more than the presence of Alec, more than the kindness of Mrs. Forbes or Dowie, and even more than the memory of her father.

– Forty-Two –

Kate at Howglen

Alec did not fall asleep so soon. The thought that Kate was in the house—asleep in the next room—kept him awake. Yet he woke the next morning earlier than usual. There were bands of golden light upon the wall, though Kate would not be awake for hours yet.

He sprang out of bed and ran to the banks of the Glamour. He plunged in and washed the dreams from his eyes with a dive and a swim under the water. Then he rose to the surface and swam slowly about under the overhanging willows. He dressed himself and lay down on the meadow grass, each blade shadowing its neighbour in the slant sunlight. Cool as it still was with the coldness of the vanished twilight, it yet felt warm to his bare feet, fresh from the waters that had crept down through the night from the high mountains. He fell fast asleep, and the sheep came and fed about him as if he had been one of themselves. When he woke, the sun was high, and when he reached the house he found his mother and Kate already seated at breakfast—Kate in the prettiest of cotton dresses, looking as fresh and country-like as the morning itself. The window was open, and through the encircling ivy, as through a filter of shadows, the air came fresh and cool. Beyond the shadow of the house lay the sunshine, a warm sea of brooding glory, of still power, not the power of flashing into storms of splendour beneath strange winds, but of waking up and cherishing to beauty the shy life that lay hidden in all remotest corners of the teeming earth.

"What are you going to do with Kate today, Alec?" said his mother.

"Whatever Kate likes," answered Alec.

"I have no choice," returned Kate. "I don't know yet what I have to choose between. I am in your hands, Alec."

It was the first time she had called him by his name, and a spear of sunshine seemed to quiver in his heart. He was restless as a hyena till she was ready. He then led her to the banks of the river, here low and grassy, with plenty of wild flowers, and a low babblement everywhere.

"This is delightful," said Kate. "I will come here as often as you like, and you shall read to me."

"What shall I read? Would you like one of Sir Walter's novels?"

"Just the thing."

Alec started for the house at full speed.

"Stop!" cried Kate. "You're not going to leave me alone beside this—talking water?"

"I thought you liked the water," said Alec.

"Yes. But I don't want to be left alone beside it. I will go with you and get some handwork."

She turned away from the stream with a strange backward look, and they walked home.

But after getting the book, Kate showed some disinclination to return to the riverside, so Alec made a seat for her near the house, in the shadow of a silver birch, and threw himself on the grass at her feet to begin reading the *Antiquary*, only half understanding it in the enchantment of knowing that he was lying at her feet and only had to look up to see her eyes. At noon Mrs. Forbes sent them a dish of curds and a great jug of cream, with oatcakes and butter soft from the churn. The rippling shadow of the birch played over the white curds and the golden butter as they ate.

Those who have had the happiness to lead innocent boy-lives will know what a marvellous delight it was to Alec to have this girl near him in his own home and his own haunts. He never speculated on her character or nature, for his own principles existed within him only in a latent condition.

The question came up, whether a certain lady in fiction had done right in running away with her lover. Mrs. Forbes made a rather decided remark on the subject. Kate said nothing, but her face glowed.

"Tell us what you think about it, Katie," said Mrs. Forbes.

Kate was silent for a moment. Then with the air of a martyr, from whom the rack can only extort a fuller confession of his faith—

though I fear she had no deeper gospel at the root of it than Byron had brought her—she answered:

"I think a woman must give up everything for love."

"That is very true, I daresay," said Mrs. Forbes. "But I fear you mean only one kind of love. Does a woman owe no love to her father or mother because she has a lover?"

To this plain question Kate made no reply, but her look changed to one of obstinacy.

Her mother died when she was a child, and her father had kept himself shut up in his study, leaving her chiefly to the care of a Shetland nurse, who told her Scandinavian stories from morning to night, with invention ever ready to supply any blank in the tablets of her memory.

Alec thought his mother's opinion the more to be approved, and Kate's the more to be admired, showing the lack of unity in his nature, by thus dissociating the good and the admirable. That which is best cannot be less admirable than that which is not best.

The next day saw Alec walking by the side of Kate mounted on his pony, up a steep path to the top of one of the highest hills surrounding the valley. It was a wild hill, with hardly anything growing on it but heather, which would make it regal with purple in the autumn. No tree could stand the blasts that blew over that hill in winter. Having climbed to the topmost point, they stood and gazed. The country lay outstretched beneath in the glow of a June day, while around them flitted the cool airs of heaven. Above them rose the soaring blue of the June sky, with a white cloud or two floating in it, and a blue peak or two leaning its colour against it. Through the green grass and the green corn below crept two silvery threads, meeting far away and floating as one—the two rivers which watered the valley of Strathglamour. Between the rivers lay the gray stone town, with its roofs of thatch and slate. One of its main streets stopped suddenly at the bridge with the three arches above Tibbie's cottage, and at the other end of the bridge lay the green fields.

The landscape was not one of the most beautiful, but it had a beauty of its own, which is all a country or a woman needs. Kate sat gazing about her in evident delight. She had taken off her hat to feel the wind, letting her hair fall in golden heaps upon her shoulders, in which the wind and the sunbeams played hide-and-seek.

In a moment the pleasure vanished from her face. It clouded over, while the country lay full in the sun. Her eyes no longer looked wide about her, but expressed defeat and retirement. Listlessly she began to gather her hair together.

"Do you ever feel as if you could not get room enough, Alec?" she said wearily.

"No, I don't," he answered, honestly and stupidly. "I always have as much as I want. I should have thought you would too—up here."

"I did feel satisfied for a moment, but it was only a moment. It is gone now."

Alec had nothing to say in reply. He never had anything to give Kate but love, and now he gave her more love. It was all he was rich in. But she did not care for his riches. And so, after gazing a while, she turned toward the descent. Alec picked up her hat and took his place at the pony's head. He was not so happy as he thought he should be. Somehow she was of another order, and he could not understand her—he could only worship her.

The whole of the hot afternoon they spent on the grass. After tea Kate sang, and Alec drank every tone as if his soul lived by hearing. In this region the sun works long after hours in the summer, and they went out to see him go down weary. They leaned together over the gate and looked at the level glory, which now burned red and dim.

"What a long shadow everything throws," said Kate. "Look how the light creeps about the roots of the grass on the ridge, as if it were looking for something between the shadows."

The sun diminished to a star, a spark of crimson fire, and vanished. As if he had sunk into a pool of air and made it overflow, a gentle ripple of wind blew from the sunset over the grass. They could see the grass bending and swaying and bathing in the wind's coolness before it came to them. It blew on their faces at length, and whispered something they could not understand, making Kate think of her mother, and Alec of Kate.

That same breeze blew upon Tibbie and Annie as they sat in the patch of meadow by the cottage. It made Tibbie think of death, the opener of sleeping eyes. For Tibbie's darkness was the shadow of her grave, on the further border of which the light was breaking in music. Death and resurrection were the same thing to blind old Tibbie.

When the gentle, washing wind blew upon Annie, she thought of the wind that bloweth where it listeth, and that if ever the Spirit of God blew upon her, she would feel it just like that wind of summer sunset—so cool, so blessed, so gentle, so living! And was it not God who breathed that wind upon her? Was he not even then breathing his Spirit into the soul of that woman-child?

It blew upon Andrew Constable, as he stood in his shop door, the easy labour of his day all but over. And he said to his little weasel-faced, old-fashioned child who stood leaning against the other door-jamb:

"That's a fine little blast, Isie! Dinna ye like to feel it blowing on yer hot cheeks, dawtie?"

"Ay, I like it weel, daddie," she answered, "but it minds me some of the winter."

It blew upon Robert Bruce, who had just run out into the yard to see how his potatoes and cabbages were coming on. "It's some cold," he said, and ran in again to put on his hat.

Alec and Kate stood looking into the darkening field. A great flock of rooks, which filled the air with their rooky gossip, was flying straight home to an old, gray ruin just visible amongst some ancient trees. Hearing them rejoicing far overhead, Kate searched for them in the darkening sky, found them, and watched their flight till the black specks were dissolved in the distance. They are not the most poetic of birds, but in a darkening country twilight, over silent fields, they blend into the general tone till even their noisy caw suggests repose. But it was room Kate wanted, not rest. She would know one day, however, that room and rest are the same, and that the longings for both spring from the same need.

"What place is that in the trees?" she asked.

"The old castle of Glamerton," answered Alec. "Would you like to go and see it?"

"Yes, very much."

"We'll go tomorrow, then."

"The dew is beginning to fall, Kate," said Mrs. Forbes who now joined them. "You had better come in."

Alec lingered behind. An unknown emotion drew his heart toward the earth. He would see her go to sleep in the twilight, which was now beginning to brood over her, as with the brown wings of a hen. The daisies were all asleep, spotting the green grass with stars of colour, for their closed red tips, like the finger points of two fairy hands, tenderly joined together, pointed up in little cones to keep the yellow stars warm within, that they might shine bright when the great star of day came to look for them again. The trees stood still and shadowy as clouds, but breathing out mysterious odours. The stars overhead, half-molten away in the ghostly light that would not go, were yet busy at their night-work, ministering to the dark sides of the other worlds. There was no moon. A wide stillness and peace, as of a heart at rest, filled space, and lying upon the human souls with a persistent quietness that might be felt, made them know what might be theirs. Now and then a bird sprang out with a sudden tremor of leaves. All was marvel.

In the morning, great sun-crested clouds with dark sides hung overhead. While they sat at breakfast, one of those glorious showers, each of whose great drops carries a sun-spark in its heart, fell on the earth with a tumult of gentle noises. The leaves of the ivy, hanging over the windows, quivered and shook. And between the drops, one of which would have beaten him to the earth, wound and darted in safety a great humble bee.

Kate and Alec went to the open window and looked out on the rainy world, breathing the odours released from the grass and the ground. Alec turned from the window to Kate's face and saw upon it a keen yet solemn delight. But as he gazed he saw a cloud come over it. Instinctively he glanced out again for the cause. The rain had become thick and small, and a light opposing wind had disordered its descent with broken and crossing lines.

This change from a summer to a winter rain had altered Kate's mood, and her face was now, as always, a reflex of the face of nature.

"Shut the window, please, Alec," she said with a shiver.

"We'll have a fire directly," said Alec.

"No," returned Kate, trying to smile. "Just fetch me a shawl from the closet in my room."

Alec had not been in his own room since Kate came. He entered it with a kind of gentle awe, and stood just within the door, gazing as if rebuked. From a pair of tiny shoes under the dressing table radiated a whole roomful of femininity. He was almost afraid to go farther, and would not have dared to look in the mirror. In less than three days her mere presence had made the room marvellous.

Recovering himself, he hastened to the closet, got the shawl, and went down the stairs three steps at a time.

"Couldn't you find it, Alec?" said Kate.

"Oh, yes, I found it at once," answered Alec, blushing.

I wonder whether Kate guessed what made the boy blush. But it does not matter much now, though she did look curiously at him for a moment.

"Just help me with my shawl," she said.

– Forty-Three –

Annie's Kitten

During all this time, Annie had scarcely seen a thing of her aunt, Margaret Anderson. Ever since Bruce had offended her on her first visit, she had taken her business elsewhere and had never even called to see her niece. Annie had met her several times in the street and that was all. Hence, on one of the fine afternoons of that unusually fine summer, and partly perhaps from missing the kindness of Mrs. Forbes, Annie took a longing to see her old aunt and set out for Clippenstrae to visit her. It was a walk of two miles, chiefly along the high road, bordered in part by vegetation. Through this she loitered along, enjoying the few wild flowers and the many lights and shadows, so that it was almost evening before she reached her destination.

"Preserve us all! Annie Anderson, what brings ye here this time of night?" exclaimed her aunt.

"It's a long time since I saw you, auntie, and I wanted to see you."

"Weel, come in the house. Ye're growing into a great muckle queen," said her aunt, inclined to a favourable consideration of her by her growth.

Margaret "didna like bairns—thoughtless craturs—aye wanting ither folk to do for them!" But growth was a kind of regenerating process in her eyes, and when a girl began to look like a woman, she regarded it as an outward sign of conversion, or something equally valuable. So she conducted Annie into the presence of her uncle, a little old man, worn and bent, with gray locks peeping out from under a Highland bonnet.

"This is my brother James's bairn," she said.

The old man received Annie kindly, called her his dawtie, and made her sit down by him on a three-legged creepie stool, talking to her as if she had been quite a child, while she, capable of high conversation as she was, replied in corresponding terms. Her great-aunt was confined to her bed with rheumatism. Supper was preparing and Annie was not sorry to have a share, for indeed, during the summer her meals were often scanty enough. While they ate, the old man kept helping her to the best, talking to her all the time.

"Will ye no come and bide with me, dawtie?" he said, meaning little by the question.

"Na, na," answered Margaret for her. "She's at the school, ye ken, uncle, and we mustna interfere with her schooling.—How does that lying Robert Bruce carry himself to ye, child?"

"Ow, I just never mind him," answered Annie.

"Weel it's all he deserves from ye. But if I were you, I would let him ken that if he plants yer corn, ye have a right to more than his gleanings."

"I don't know what you mean," answered Annie.

"Ow, na, I dare say not. But ye may jist as well know. Robert Bruce has two hunner pound odd of yer own, lassie. And if he doesna treat ye well, ye can jist tell him that I told ye so."

This piece of news did not have the overpowering effect on Annie which her aunt had expected. No doubt the money seemed in her eyes a limitless fortune, but, then, Bruce had it. She might as well think of robbing a bear of her cubs as getting her money from Bruce. Besides, what could she do with it if she had it? And she had not yet acquired the faculty of loving money for its own sake. When she rose to go home, she felt little richer than when she entered, except for the kind words of John Peterson.

"It's too late for ye to go home alone, dawtie," said the old man.

"I'm not that scared," answered Annie.

"Weel, if ye walk with him, the dark'll be light about ye," he said. "Be a good lass, and run home as fast as ye can. Good night to ye, dawtie."

Rejoicing as if she had found her long-lost home, Annie went out into the deep gloaming feeling it impossible that she should be frightened at anything. But when she came to the part of the road bordered with trees, she could not help thinking she saw a figure flitting along from tree to tree just within the deeper dusk of the wood, and as she hurried on, her fancy turned to fear.

Presently she heard awful sounds, like the subdued growling of wild beasts. She would have taken to her heels in terror, but she reflected that thereby she would only ensure pursuit, whereas if she continued to walk slowly she might slip away unnoticed. As she reached a gate leading into the wood, however, a dusky figure came bounding over it and came straight toward her. To her relief it went on two legs, and when it came nearer she recognized some traits of old acquaintance about it. When it was within a couple yards of her, she stopped and cried out joyfully:

"Curly!"—for it was her old vice-champion.

"Annie!" was the equally joyful response.

"I thought you were a wild beast!" said Annie.

"I was only growling for fun to mysel'," answered Curly, who would have done it all the more if he had known there was anyone on the road. "I didn't know I was scaring anybody. How are ye, Annie? And how's Blister Bruce?"

Curly was dreadfully prolific in nicknames.

Annie had not seen him for six months. He had continued to show himself so full of mischief, though of a comparatively innocent sort, that his father thought it better at last to send him to a town at some distance to learn the trade of a saddler, for which he had shown a preference.

This was his first visit to his home. Up to now his father had received no complaints of his behaviour, and had now asked for a holiday for him.

"Ye're some grown, Annie," he said.

"So are you, Curly," answered Annie.

"And how's Alec?"

"He's very well."

Whereupon much talk followed. At length Curly said:

"And how's the rats?"

"Over well and thriving."

"Jist put yer hand in my coat pocket and see what I hae brought ye."

Knowing Curly's propensity, Annie refused.

"It's a wild beast," said Curly.

So saying, he pulled out of his pocket the most delicately coloured kitten, not half the beauty of which could be seen in the gloaming.

"Did you bring this all the way from Spinnie for me, Curly?"

"Ay, did I. Ye see, I dinna like rats either. But ye must keep it out of their way for a few weeks, or they'll tear it all to bits. It'll soon be a match for them though, I'll warrant. She comes of a killing breed."

Annie took the kitten home, and it shared her bed that night.

"What's that meowing?" asked Bruce the next morning, the moment he rose from the genuflexion of morning prayers.

"It's my kitten," answered Annie. "I'll let you see it."

"We have too many mouths in the house already," said Bruce as she returned with the little thing in her arms. "We have no room for more. Here, Rob, take the creature and put a bag around its neck and a stone in the bag and fling it into the Glamour."

Annie, not waiting to parley, darted from the house with the kitten.

Rob bolted after her, delighted with his commission. But instead of finding her at the door, as he had expected, he saw her already a long way up the street, flying like the wind. He started out in keen pursuit. He was now a great lumbering boy, and although Annie's wind was not equal to his, she was faster. She took the direct road to Howglen and Rob kept floundering after her. Before she reached the footbridge, she was nearly breathless and he was gaining quickly upon her. Just as she turned the corner of the road, leading up on the other side of the water, she met Alec and Kate. Unable to speak, she passed without a word. But there was no need to ask the cause of her pale, agonized face, for there was young Bruce at her heels. Alec collared him instantly.

"What are you up to?" he asked.

"Nothing," answered the panting pursuer.

"If you be after nothing, you'll find that nearer home," retorted Alec, twisting him round in that direction and giving him a kick to expedite his return. "Let me hear of you troubling Annie Anderson, and I'll take a piece out of your skin the next time I lay my hands on you. Now go home."

Rob obeyed like a frightened dog, while Annie pursued her course to Howglen as if her enemy had still been on her track. Rushing into the parlour, she fell on the floor before Mrs. Forbes, unable to speak. The kitten sprang out of her arms and took refuge under the sofa.

"Ma'am," she gasped at length, "take care of my kitten. They want to drown it! It's my own. Curly gave it to me."

Mrs. Forbes comforted her and readily undertook the assignment. Annie was very late for school, for Mrs. Forbes made her have another good breakfast before she went. But Mr. Malison was in a good humour that day and said nothing. Rob Bruce looked devils at her. What he had told his father I do not know. But whatever it was, it was all written down in Bruce's mental books to the debit of Alexander Forbes of Howglen.

Mrs. Forbes's heart grieved her when she found to what persecution her little friend was exposed during those times when she did not have her over for daily visits. But she did not see how she could well remedy the situation. She was herself in the power of Bruce, so expostulation from her would be worth little, while to have Annie in the house as before would involve consequences unpleasant to all concerned. She resolved to make up for it by being kinder to her than ever as soon as Alec had followed Kate back to the university. For the present she comforted both herself and Annie by telling her to be sure to come when she found herself in any trouble.

But Annie was not one to apply to her friends except she was in great need of their help. The present case had been one of life and death. She found no further occasion to visit Mrs. Forbes before Kate and Alec were both gone.

– Forty-Four –

Tibbie and Thomas

On a sleepy summer afternoon, just when the sunshine had begun to turn yellow, Annie was sitting with Tibbie on the grass in front of her little cottage, whose door looked up the river. The cottage stood on a small rocky eminence at the foot of the bridge. Underneath the approach to it from the bridge, the dyer's mill-race ran by a passage cut in the rock, leading to the third arch of the bridge built over the Glamour. Towards the river, the rock went down steep to the little meadow. It was a triangular piece of smooth grass growing on the old bed of the river, which for many years had been leaving this side, and wearing away the opposite bank. It lay between the river, the dyer's race, and the bridge, one of the stone piers of which rose from it. The grass which grew upon it was short, thick, and delicate. On the opposite side of the river lay a field for bleaching the linen, which was the chief manufacture of that country. Hence it enjoyed the privilege of immunity from the ploughshare. None of its daisies ever met the fate of Burns's.

Tibbie's blind face was turned toward the sun and her hands were busy as ants with her knitting needles, for she was making a pair of heavy stockings for Annie for the winter.

"Who's that coming, lassie?" she asked.

Annie, who had heard no one, glanced round and said, "It's Thomas Crann."

"That's no Thomas Crann," rejoined Tibbie. "I dinna hear his cough."

Thomas came up pale and limping a little.

"That's not Thomas Crann!" repeated Tibbie before he had time to address her.

"Why not, Tibbie?" returned Thomas.

"I canna hear you breathing."

"That's a sign that I hae all the more breath, Tibbie. I'm so muckle better o' that asthma that I think the Lord must hae blown into my nostrils another breath o' that life he breathed into Adam and Eve."

"I'm right glad to hear it, Thomas. Breath must come from him one way or the other."

"Nae doobt, Tibbie."

"Will ye sit down beside us, Thomas? It's long since I've seen ye."

Tibbie always spoke of *seeing* people.

"Ay, will I, Tibbie. I haena muckle work on my hands these days."

"Annie and me's just been talking about this thing and that thing, Thomas," said Tibbie, dropping her knitting on her knees and folding her palms together. "Maybe *ye* can tell me whether there be any likeness between the light that I can't see and the sound of the water running that I like so well to hear."

For it did not need the gentle warm wind, floating rather than blowing down the river that afternoon, to bring to their ears the sound of the dam built across the river to send the water to the dyer's wheel. For that sound was in Tibbie's cottage day and night, mingled with the nearer, gentler, and stronger gurgling of the swift, deep water in the race that hurried, aware of its work, with small noise and much soft-sliding force towards the wheel.

"Weel, ye see, Tibbie," answered Thomas, "tis almost as hard for the likes of us to understand yer blindness as it may be for ye to understand oor sight."

"Indeed maybe neither of us ken muckle aboot oor own gift. Say anything ye like, as long as ye dinna tell me, as the bairn here once did, that I couldna tell what the light was. I dinna ken what yer sight may be, and I'm thinking I care as little. But I well ken what light is."

"Tibbie, dinna be ill-natured like me. Ye have no call to be that way. I'm trying to answer yer question. And if ye interrupt me again, I'll rise and go home."

"Say away, then, Thomas. Dinna heed me. I'm just cantankerous sometimes. I ken that well enough."

"Ye hae no business to be, Tibbie."

"No more or less than other folk."

"Less, Tibbie."

"How do ye make that oot?" asked Tibbie defensively.

"Ye dinna see the things to anger ye that other folk sees. As I came down the street just now, I came upon the two laddies—ye know them—they're twins, one of them a cripple—"

"Ay, that was Murdoch Malison's work!" interposed Tibbie with indignant reminiscence.

"The man's been sorry for it ever since," said Thomas, "so we mustna go over it again, Tibbie."

"Very well, Thomas. I'll hold my tongue. What aboot the laddies?"

"They were fighting in the street, hitting one another's heads and punching at one another's noses, and doing their best to destroy the very image of the Almighty. So I thrashed them both."

"And what became of the image of the Almighty then?" asked Tibbie with a grotesque contortion of her mouth and a roll of her veiled eyeballs. "I dinna doubt, Thomas, that ye angered yerself more than ye quieted them wi' the thrashing. The wrath of man, ye ken, Thomas, worketh not the righteousness of God."

There was not a person in Glamerton who would have dared to speak thus to Thomas Crann but Tibbie Dyster, perhaps because there was not one who had such a respect for him. Possibly the darkness about her made her bolder. But I think it was her truth, which is another word for *love*, however unlike love the outcome may look, that made her able to speak in this fashion.

There was silence for a long minute. Then he said:

"Maybe ye're in the right, Tibbie. Ye anger me, but I would rather have a body anger me by telling me the truth than I would hae all the fair words in the dictionary. Tis a strange thing, woman, but aye when a body's trying hardest to go upright, he's sure to catch a dreadful fall. Here I hae been wrestling with my bad temper harder than in all my life, and yet I never in all my days licked two laddies for licking one another till jist this very day. I canna seem to get to the bottom o' it."

"There's worse things than an ill temper, Thomas. Not that it's a good thing. And it's none like him that was meek and lowly of heart. But, as I say, there's worse faults than a bad temper. It would be no gain to ye, Thomas, and no glory to him if ye were to overcome yer temper and then think a heap of yerself that ye had done it. Maybe that's why ye're no allowed to be victorious in yer endeavours."

"Indeed, maybe, Tibbie," said Thomas solemnly. "I doobt the fault's not so much in my temper as in my heart. It's more love I need, Tibbie. If I loved my neighbour as myself, I couldna be so ill-natured."

"Resist the devil, Thomas. He's sure to run in the end. But I'm afraid ye're going to go away wi'oot telling me aboot the light and the water. When I'm sitting here listening to the water as it comes murmuring and gurgling doon the river, it puts me in the mind of the text that says, 'His voice was as the sound of many waters.' Now his face is light—ye ken that, dinna ye—and if his voice be like the water, there must be something alike between light and water. That's what made me ask ye, Thomas?"

"Weel, I don't rightly know how to answer ye, Tibbie. But at this moment the light's playing bonnie upon the little dam down there by the mill—shimmering on the water. Eh! it's bonnie, woman, an' I wish ye had the sight of yer eyes to see wi', though ye do pretend to think little of it."

"Well, well, my time's coming, Thomas. I must jist wait till it comes. Ye canna help me, I can see that. If only I could open my eyes for a minute, I would ken all aboot it and be able to answer myself."

All the time they were talking Annie was watching Alec's boat, which had come down the river and was floating in the sunshine above the dam. Thomas must have seen it too, for it was in the very heart of the radiance reflected to them from the watery mirror. But Alec was a painful subject with Thomas, for when they chanced to meet now, nothing more than the passing nod of ordinary acquaintance was exchanged. And certain facts in his nature, as well as certain articles in his creed, made him unable to be indulgent to young people.

So, being one of those who never speak of what is painful to them if they can avoid it, he talked about the light and said nothing about the boat that was in the middle of it. Had Alec been rowing, Tibbie would have heard the oars, but he only paddled enough to keep the boat from drifting onto the dam by the dyer's mill. Kate sat in the stern looking at the water with half-closed eyes, and Alec sat looking at Kate, as if his eyes were made only for her.

And Annie sat in the meadow, and she too looked at Kate. She thought how pretty Kate was, and how she must like being rowed about in the old boat. It seemed quite an old boat now. An age had passed since her name was painted on it. She wondered if *The Bonnie Annie* was worn off the stern yet, or if Alec had painted it out and put the name of the pretty lady instead. When Tibbie and Thomas rose and walked away into the house, Annie lingered behind on the grass.

The sun sank slanting and slow, lower and lower, till at length Alec leaned back with a stronger pull on the oars and the boat crept away up the stream, growing smaller as it crept, and turning a curve in the river, was lost to sight.

Still Annie sat, one hand lying listlessly in her lap and the other plucking blades of grass and making a little heap of them beside her till she had pulled a spot quite bare and the brown earth peeped through between the roots. Then she rose, went to the door of the cottage, called a good night to Tibbie and took her way home.

– Forty-Five –

The Castle Ruin

Though my story has primarily to do with the slow-paced life of a country region where growth and change occur slowly, like the ripening of a harvest and the growth of all good things, there will yet come clouds and rainbows, adventures and coincidences, even in the quietest village.

As Kate and Alec walked along the street on the way to the castle, one of the coaches from the county town drove up with its four thoroughbreds.

"What a handsome fellow the driver is!" said Kate.

Alec looked up at the box. There sat Beauchamp with the reins in his grasp, handling the horses with composure and skill. Beside him sat the owner of the coach, a laird of the neighbourhood. Beauchamp had at last judged the time ripe and this was the first evidence of his closer approach.

A sting went through Alec's heart. Certainly Beauchamp was a handsome fellow, but it was the first time Alec had thought of his own person in comparison with another. That she should admire Beauchamp! The memory of that moment made him writhe on his bed years afterward, for a mental and bodily wound are alike in this, that after there is but the scar of either left, bad weather will revive the torture.

Alec's face fell. They walked on in silence in the shadow of a high wall. Kate looked up at the top of the wall and stopped. Alec looked at her. Her face was as full of light as a diamond in the sun. He forgot all his jealousy. The fresh tide of his love swept it away, or at least covered it.

They walked up to the ruined walls of the castle. Long grass grew about them, close to the very door, which was locked. If old Time could not be kept out, younger destroyers might. Alec had borrowed a key from the caretaker, and they entered by a door in the great tower, under the spiky remnants of the spiral stair projecting from the huge circular wall. To the right, a steep descent led down to the cellars and the dungeon—a terrible place, which needed no popular legends such as Alec had been telling Kate of a walled-up door and lost room, to add to their influence. It was no wonder that when he held out his hand to lead her down into the darkness, she shrank and drew back. A few rays came through the decayed planks of the door which Alec had tried to push closed behind them. One larger ray from the keyhole fell upon Kate's face and showed it blanched with fear.

At that moment a sweet, low voice came from somewhere out of the darkness, saying:

"Don't be frightened, mem, to go where Alec wants you to go. You can trust him."

Staring in the direction of the sound, Kate saw the pale face of a slender half child, half maiden glimmering across the gulf that led to the dungeon. She stood in the midst of a faint light, a dusky and yet radiant creature, seeming to throw off from her a faint brown light—a lovely, earth-stained ghost.

"Oh, Annie! is that you?" said Alec.

"Ay, it is," answered Annie.

"This is an old schoolfellow of mine," he said, turning to Kate who was looking at the girl.

"Oh! Is it?" said Kate with a hint of condescension in her tone.

Between the two maidens, each looking ghostly to the other, lay a dark cavern mouth that seemed to go down to Hades.

"Won't you go down, mem?" said Annie.

"No, thank you," answered Kate decisively.

"Alec'll take good care of you, mem."

"Oh, yes! I dare say, but I would rather not."

Alec said nothing. So Kate would not trust him. Would she have gone with Beauchamp if he had asked her? Ah! If he had asked Annie, she too would have turned pale, but she would have laid her hand in his and gone with him.

"If you want to go up, then," she said, "I'll show you the easiest path. It's round this way."

She pointed to a narrow ledge between the descent and the circular wall, by which they could cross to where she stood. But Alec, who had no desire for Annie's company, declined her guidance and took Kate up a nearer, though more difficult ascent, to the higher level. Here all the floors of the castle lay in dust beneath their feet. The whole central space lay open to the sky.

Annie remained standing on the edge of the dungeon slope. She had been on her way to see Tibbie when she caught a glimpse of Kate and Alec as they passed. Since watching them in the boat the evening before, she had been longing to speak to Alec, longing to see Kate nearer. She guessed where they were going, and across the fields she bounded like a fawn straight as the crows flew. She did not need the key for she knew a hole on the level of the grass, wide enough to let her creep through the two-yard-thick wall. So she crept in and took her place near the door.

After they had rambled over the lower part of the building, Alec took Kate up a small winding stair, past a succession of empty doorways, each leading nowhere because the floors had fallen. Kate was so frightened by coming suddenly upon one after another of these defenceless openings that by the time she reached the broad platform which ran around the top of the tower, she felt quite faint. And when Alec scampered off like a goat to reach the bartizan at the other side, she sank in an agony of fear upon the landing of the stair.

Looking down upon her from the top of the little turret, Alec saw that she was ill, and returning instantly in great dismay, comforted her as well as he could, and got her by degrees to the bottom. There was a spot of grass inside the walls where he had her lie down to rest, and she fell into a doze. And as the sun shone on her through one of the ruined windows, Alec stood so that his shadow fell across her eyes.

After standing thus for some time gazing upon the sleeping beauty on the grass beneath him, he turned his eyes up to the tower from which they had just descended. Looking down upon them from one of the isolated doorways, he saw the pale face of Patrick Beauchamp.

Alec bounded to the stair, rushed to the top and round the platform, but found nobody. Beginning to doubt his eyes, he glanced down from whence he had come, and saw Beauchamp standing over the sleeping girl. He darted down the screw of the stair, but when he reached the bottom Beauchamp had again disappeared.

The same moment Kate began to wake. Alec returned to her side, and they left the place, locked the door behind them, took the key back to the caretaker at the lodge, and went home. After tea, believing he had locked Beauchamp into the castle, Alec returned and searched the building from top to bottom, even got a candle and a ladder and went down into the dungeon, but found no one and went home bewildered.

While Alec was searching the vacant ruin, Beauchamp was seated, a little sore in spots, on the box of a coach halfway back to the house of its owner. The laird whom he was visiting was a relative of his mother. Beauchamp had seen Kate and Alec take the way to the castle, had followed them, and found the door unlocked. Watching them about the place he ascended the stair from another approach. The moment Alec looked up at him he ran down again and had just dropped into a sort of well-like place, which the stair had used to fill on its way to a lower level, when he heard Alec's feet thundering over his head. Determined then to see what the lady was like, for he had never seen her close, he scrambled out and approached her cautiously. He had only a few moments to contemplate her before he saw that Alec had again caught sight of him, and he immediately fled to his former refuge.

The sound of the rusty bolt rather alarmed him, for he had not expected their immediate departure. His first impulse was to see whether he could not get the bolt loose from the inside. This he soon found to be impossible. He next turned to the windows in the front, but there the ground fell away so suddenly that he was many feet from it—an altogether dangerous leap. He was beginning to feel seriously concerned when he heard a voice:

"Do you want to get out, sir? They locked the door."

He turned and could see no one. Approaching the door again, he saw Annie in the dark twilight, standing on the edge of the descent to the vaults. He had passed the spot not a minute before and she was not there then. But instead of taking her for a ghost, he accosted her with easy insolence.

"Tell me how to get out, my pretty girl, and I'll give you a kiss."

Seized with a terror she did not understand, Annie darted into the cavern between them and sped down its steep descent into the darkness. A few yards down she turned aside through a low doorway, into a small room. Beauchamp rushed after her, passed her, and fell over a great stone lying in the middle of his way. Annie heard him fall, sprang forth again, and flew to the upper light. She found her way out and left the discourteous knight a safe captive, fallen upon that horrible stair.

Annie told the keeper that there was a gentleman shut up in the castle, and then ran a mile and a half to Tibbie's cottage without stopping. But she did not say a word to Tibbie about her adventure.

– Forty-Six –

The Spirit of Prophecy

A spirit of prophecy, whether from the Lord or not, was abroad this summer among the clergy of Glamerton, of all persuasions. Nor was its influence confined to Glamerton or the clergy. The neighbourhood and the laity had their share. Those who read their Bibles, of whom there were many in that region, took to reading the prophecies, all the prophecies, and nothing but the prophecies. Upon these every man, either for himself or following in the track of his spiritual instructor, exercised his individual powers of interpretation, whose accuracy did not altogether depend upon the amount of historical knowledge possessed. Whatever was known, whether about ancient Assyria or modern Tahiti, found its theoretical place. Of course the Church of Rome came in for her due share of the application from all parties. And neither the Church of England, the Church of Scotland, nor either of the dissenting sects went without its portion freely dealt, each of the last finding something that applied to all the rest. There were some, however, who cared less for such modes, and, themselves given to a daily fight with antichrist in their own hearts, sought—for they too read the prophecies—to fix their reference on certain sins, and certain persons classed according to these their sins. With a burning desire for the safety of their neighbours, they took upon them the strongest words of rebuke and condemnation, so that one might have thought they were revelling in the idea of the vengeance at hand, instead of striving for the rescue of their neighbours from the wrath to come.

Among these were Thomas Crann and his minister, Mr. Turnbull. To them Glamerton was the centre of creation, providence, and revelation. Every warning finger in the Book pointed to it, and every burst of indignation from the labouring heart of the holy prophets was addressed to its sinners. Thomas was ready to fly at the meekest or the greatest man in Glamerton with terrible denunciations of the wrath of the Almighty for their sins. All the evildoers of the place feared him—the whisky merchant and rich manufacturer and the strong horse doctor included. They called him a wheezing, canting hypocrite, and would go streets out of their way to avoid him.

In the midst of this commotion, the good Mr. Cowie died. He had taken no particular interest in what was going on. Ever since Annie's petition for counsel, he had been thinking, as he had never thought before, about his own relation to God. Now he had carried his thoughts into another world.

He was gently regarded by all—even by Thomas.

"Ay, ay," Thomas said with slow emphasis, "he's gone is he, honest man? Weel, maybe he had the root of the matter in him, although it made little enough show about the yard. There was small flower and less fruit. But judgment dinna belong to us, ye see, Jean."

Thomas would judge the living from morning to night. But the dead—he would leave them alone in better hands.

"I'm thinkin'," he added, "he's been taken away frae the evil to come—frae seeing the terrible consequences of such a soft way of dealing with eternal truth and wi' perishing men—taken away like Eli, when he broke his neck at the ill news. For the fire and brimstane that overthrew Sodom and Gomorrha, is hanging ower this toon, ready to fall and smother us all."

"Hoot! hoot! dinna speak such awful words, Thamas. Ye're nae the prophet Jonah, ye ken."

"Are ye the whale then, to swallow me and my words togither, Jean? I tell ye the wrath of God must be roused against this toon, for it's been growing worse and worse for many a year, till the verra lassies aren't to be trusted out alone."

"What do ye ken aboot the lasses, Thamas? You keep to the men. The lassies are no worse than anywhere else. I can come and gang when and where I like. Never a body says a word to me."

This was true but hardly significant, seeing Jean had one shoulder and one eye twice the size of the others, to say nothing of her other peculiarities. But, rude as Thomas was, he was gentleman enough to confine his reply to a snort and a silence. For had he not chosen his housekeeper upon the strength of those personal recommendations of the defensive importance of which she was herself unaware?

Except for his own daughters there was no one who mourned so deeply the loss of Mr. Cowie as Annie Anderson. She had left his church and gone to the Missionars, but she could never forget his kisses, or his gentle words, or his shilling, for by them Mr. Cowie had given her a more confident notion of God and his tenderness than she could have found in a hundred sermons put together. What greater gift could a man give? Was that not worth ten books full of sound doctrine?

Yet the good man, not knowing this, had often looked back to that interview, and reproached himself bitterly that he, so long a clergyman of that parish, had no help to give the only child who ever came to him to ask such help. So, when he lay on his death-bed, he sent for Annie, the only soul, out of all his parish, over which he felt that he had any pastoral cure.

When she entered his room and found him supported with pillows in his bed, he stretched out his arms to her feebly, held her close to him, and wept.

"I'm going to die, Annie," he said.

"And go to heaven, sir, to the face of God," said Annie, not sobbing but with tears streaming silently down her face.

"I don't know, Annie."

"If God loves you half as much as I do, sir, you'll be well off in heaven. And I'm thinking he must love you more than me. For, you see, sir, God is love itself."

"I sometimes don't know what God thinks of me anymore, Annie. But if ever I do get there, which'll be more than I deserve, I'll tell him about you and ask him to give you the help I couldn't give you."

Love and death make us all children. Can Old Age be an evil thing when it does the same?

Annie had no answer but what lay in her tears. He called his daughter, who stood weeping in the room. She came near.

"Bring my study Bible," he said to her feebly.

She went and brought it.

"Here, Annie," said the dying man, "here's my Bible that I've made too little use of myself. Promise me that if ever you have a house of your own, you'll read out of that book every day at worship. I want you not to forget me, as, if all's well, I shall never forget you."

"I will, sir," responded Annie earnestly.

"And you'll find a new five-pound note between the pages. Take it for my sake."

"Yes, sir," answered Annie, feeling this was no time for objecting to anything.

"And good-bye, Annie. I can't speak anymore."

He drew her to him again and kissed her for the last time. Then he turned his face to the wall, and Annie went home weeping, with the great Bible in her arms.

In the inadvertence of grief, she ran into the shop.

"What have you got there, lassie?" said Bruce, as sharply as if she might have stolen it.

"Mr. Cowie gave me this Bible, cause he's dying himself and doesn't want it any longer," answered Annie.

"Let me look at it."

Annie gave it up with reluctance.

"It's a fine book, and pretty boards. We'll just lay it upon the room table, and we'll have worship out of it when anybody wants."

"I want it myself," objected Annie in dismay, for although she did not think of the money at the moment, she had better reasons for not liking the thought of parting with the book.

"You can have it when you want it. That's enough, surely."

Annie could hardly think his saying so to be much comfort. The door to *the room* was kept locked, and Mrs. Bruce would have boxed anyone's ears whom she met coming from within the sacred precincts.

– Forty-Seven –

The Bible

Before the next Sunday Mr. Cowie was dead, and through some mistake or mismanagement there was no one to preach. So the congregation did each as seemed right in his own eyes. Mrs. Forbes went to the Missionar church in the evening to hear Mr. Turnbull. Kate and Alec accompanied her.

By this time Robert Bruce had become a great man in the community—in his own judgment at least. He had managed to secure one of the most fashionable pews in the chapel. And now when Mrs. Forbes's party entered, and a little commotion rose in consequence—they being more of gentlefolk than the place was accustomed to—Bruce was the first to rise and walk from his seat and request them to occupy his pew. Alec would have passed on, for he disliked the man, but Mrs. Forbes had reasons for being agreeable and accepted his offer. Colds had kept the rest of the Bruces at home, and Annie was the only other occupant of the pew. She crept to the end of it, like a shy mouse, to be as far out of the way as possible.

"Come out, Annie," said Bruce in a loud whisper.

Annie came out, a warm flush over her pale face, and Mrs. Forbes entered, then Kate, and last of all Alec, much against his will. Then Annie reentered, and Bruce resumed his place as guardian of the pew door. So Annie was seated next to Alec, as she had never been before, either in church or in school. But Annie had no feeling of delight and awe like that which Alec felt as he sat close to his beautiful cousin. She had a feeling of pleasure, no doubt, but the essence of that pleasure was faith. She trusted him and believed in him as much as she ever had. In the end, those who trust most will find they are nearest the truth.

Mr. Turnbull was a good man who ventured to think for himself—as far as that may be possible for one upon whose spirit had converged, even before he was born, the influences of a thousand theological ancestors.

He preached an eloquent sermon, showing his hearers that they had all been seeking satisfaction in their own pursuits, in the pride of their own way, that they had been disappointed, even to weariness, and that yet, such was their perversity, they would not acknowledge the hopelessness of the pursuit, and turn to that God who was ready to pardon, and in whose courts a day would give them more delight than a thousand in the tents of wickedness. Moving to his conclusion by presumptuously appropriating the words of the Saviour, "Verily, verily, I say unto you, it shall be more tolerable for Sodom and Gomorrha, in that day, than for you," he ended with a terrible denunciation of wrath upon the sinners who had been called and would not come. "Woe unto you, for ye would not be warned! Woe unto you, for ye knew your Lord's will, and yet committed things worthy of stripes! Therefore your whip shall be one of scorpions! Woe unto you! I say, for, when the bridegroom cometh, ye shall knock in vain at the closed door till the angels of vengeance sweep upon you, and bearing you afar through waste regions, cast you into outer darkness, where shall be weeping and wailing and gnashing of teeth, to the endless ages of a divine eternity."

With these words the preacher burst into impassioned prayer for the souls which he saw exposed to a hell of which he himself knew not the horrors, otherwise he would not have dared preach it, a hell the smoke of whose torments would arise and choke the elect themselves about the throne of God—the hell of Exhausted Mercy.

Soon after the sermon was over, venturing a look around, Alec saw the eyes of Thomas Crann fixed on him. His conscience told him, stung by that glance, that he had behaved ill to his old friend. Nor did this lessen the vague feeling which the sermon had awakened in his mind that something ought to be done, that something was wrong in him somewhere, that it ought to be set right somehow.

A special prayer meeting had been set to be held after the sermon, and Robert Bruce remained to join in intercession for the wicked town and its wicked neighbourhood. He even "engaged in prayer" for the first time in public, astonishing some of the older members by his gift of devotion. He had been officially received into the church only a week or two before, upon profession of faith in the merits of Christ, not in Christ himself—that would not have been definite enough for them. But it would have been all the same to Robert Bruce, for he was ready to believe that he believed anything advantageous.

There had been one or two murmurs against his reception, and he had been visited and talked with several times before the church was satisfied as to his conversion. But nothing was known specifically against him. Having learned many of their idioms, he had succeeded in persuading his examiners, and had possibly persuaded himself at the same time, that he had passed through all the phases of conversion, including conviction, repentance, and final acceptance of offered mercy on the terms proposed, and was now undergoing the slow and troublesome process of sanctification, in corroboration of which he went on to produce talk, and coppers at the chapel-door. Good people as many of those were who thus admitted him to their communion, in the full belief that none but conscious Christians should enjoy that privilege, his reputation for wealth had yet something to do with it. Probably they thought that if the gospel proved mighty in this new disciple, more of his money might be accessible by and by for good purposes, amongst the rest, for sending missionaries to the heathen, teaching them to divorce their wives and wear trowsers. And now he had been asked to pray, and had prayed with much propriety and considerable unction. To be sure, Tibbie Dyster did sniff a good deal during the performance, but then that was a way she had of relieving her feelings, next best to that of speaking her mind.

When the meeting was over, Robert Bruce, Thomas Crann, and James Johnstone, who was one of the deacons, walked away together. Little conversation took place between them, for no subject but a religious one was admissible, and the religious feelings of those who had any were pretty nearly exhausted.

Bruce's, however, were not in the least exhausted. On the contrary, he was so pleased to find that he could pray as well as any of them, and the excitement of doing so before judges had been so new and pleasant to him that he thought he should like to try it again. He thought too of the grand Bible lying up there on the room table.

"Come in, sirs," he said as they approached his door, "and take a part in our family worship."

Neither of his companions felt much inclined to accede to his request, but they both yielded nevertheless. He conducted them upstairs, unlocked the musty room, pulled up the blinds, and admitted enough of lingering light for the concluding devotions of the day. He then proceeded to gather his family together, calling them one by one.

"Mother," he cried from the top of the stair.

"Yes, father," answered Mrs. Bruce.

"Come to worship.—Robert!"

"Ay, father."

"Come to worship.—Johnnie!"

And so he went through the family roll call. When all had entered and seated themselves, the head of the house went slowly to the side table, took from it reverently the late minister's study Bible, sat down by the window, laid the book on his knees, and solemnly opened it.

Now a five-pound note is not thick enough to make a big Bible open between the pages where it is laid. But the note might very well have been laid in a place where the Bible was in the habit of opening.

Without an instant's hesitation, Robert slipped it away, and, crumpling it up in his hand, gave out the twenty-third psalm, over which it had lain, and read it through. Finding it too short, however, for the respectability of worship, he went on with the twenty-fourth, turning the leaf with thumb and forefinger, while the rest of the fingers clasped the note tight in his palm, and reading as he turned:

"He that hath clean hands and a pure heart—"

As soon as he had finished this psalm, he closed the book with a snap, immediately feeling it to have been improper. He put an additional compensating solemnity into the tone in which he said:

"Thomas Crann, will you engage in prayer?"

"Pray yersel'," answered Thomas gruffly.

Whereupon Robert rose, and, kneeling down, did pray himself.

But Thomas, instead of leaning forward on his chair when he kneeled, glanced sharply round at Bruce. He had seen him take something from the Bible and crumple it up in his hand. He would not have felt any inclination to speculate about it had it not been for the peculiarly keen expression of eager surprise and happy greed which came over his face in the act. Having seen that, and being always more or less suspicious of Bruce, he wanted to know more.

He saw Bruce take advantage of the posture of devotion which he had assumed to put something into his pocket unseen of his guests, as he believed.

When worship was over, Bruce did not ask them to stay to supper. Prayers did not involve expense. Supper did.

Thomas went home pondering. The devotions of the day were not to be concluded for him with any social act of worship. He had many anxious prayers yet to offer before his heart would be quiet in sleep. Especially there was Alec to be prayed for, and his dawtie Annie, and in truth the whole town of Glamerton, and the surrounding parishes—and Scotland, and the whole world. Indeed, sometimes Thomas went further, and although it is not reported of him that he ever prayed for the devil, he yet did something very like it once or twice when he prayed for "the haill universe of God, and all the being's in it, up and doon, that we ken unco little aboot."

– Forty-Eight –

The Stickit Minister

The next morning Kate and Alec rose early to walk before breakfast to the top of one of the hills, through a young larch-wood which covered it from head to foot. The morning was cool, and the sun exultant. The dew-diamonds were flashing everywhere, none the less lovely that they were fresh-made that morning. The lark's song was a cantata with the sun and the wind and the larch-odours. How the larks did sing that morning! The only clouds were long pale delicate streaks of lovely gradations in gray—here mottled, there swept into curves. It was just the morning to rouse a wild longing for motion, for the sea and its shore, for endless travel through an endless region of grace and favour, the sun rising no higher, the dew lingering on every blade, and the lark never wearying.

"Are the people of Glamerton very wicked, Alec?" asked Kate.

"I'm sure I don't know," answered Alec. "I suppose they're no worse than other people."

"I thought from Mr. Turnbull's sermon that they must be a great deal worse."

"Oh! they all preach like that—except good Mr. Cowie, and he's dead."

"Do you think he knew better than the rest of them?"

"I don't know that. But that Mr. Turnbull always speaks as if he were in earnest. But there's that fellow Bruce," added Alec dubiously.

"Do you mean the man that put us into his seat?"

"Yes. I can't think what makes my mother so civil to him."

"Why shouldn't she be?"

"I can't bear him. And I can't understand my mother. It's not like her."

In a moment more they were in a gentle twilight of green, flashed with streaks of gold. A forest of delicate young larches crowded them in, their rich brown cones hanging like the knobs that looped up their dark garments fringed with paler green.

And the scent! What a thing to *invent*—the smell of a larch wood! It is the essence of the earth odour, distilled in the thousand-fold leaves of those feathery trees. And the light winds that awoke blew murmurous music, so sharply and sweetly did that keen foliage divide the air.

Having gazed their fill on the morning around them, they returned to breakfast and afterward went down to the river. They stood on the bank over one of the deepest pools, in the bottom of which the pebbles glimmered brown. Kate, abstracted, gazed into it, swinging her neckerchief in her hand. Something fell into the water.

"Oh!" she cried, "what shall I do? It was my mother's!"

The words were scarcely out of her mouth when Alec was in the water. Bubbles rose and broke as he vanished. Kate stood pale, with parted lips, staring into the pool. With a boiling and heaving of the water, after a few moments he rose triumphant, holding the brooch.

"Oh, Alec!" she cried. "You shouldn't have frightened me so."

"I didn't mean to frighten you. It was your mother's brooch."

"Yes, but we could have got it out somehow."

"No other way I know of. Besides, I am almost a water rat."

"But what will your mother say? Now you'll get your death of cold. Come along."

Alec laughed. He was in no hurry to go home. But she seized his hand and half dragged him all the way. He had never been so happy in his life.

That night they had a walk in the moonlight. It was all moon—the trees confused into each other by the sleep of her light, the bits of water, so many moons over again, the pale phantoms of flowers. The whole earth, transfused with reflex light, was changed into a moon-ghost of its former self. They were walking in the moon-world.

The silence and the dimness sank into Alec's soul, and it became silent and dim too. The only sound was the noise of the river, quenched in that light to the sleepy hush of moon-haunted streams. Kate sat down at the foot of an old tree which stood alone in one of the fields. Alec threw himself on the grass, and looked up in her face.

Kate sat as silent as the moon in heaven, which rained down silence. And Alec lay gazing at Kate, till silence gave birth to speech.

"Oh, Kate, how I love you!" he said at length.

Kate started. She was frightened. Her mind had been full of gentle thoughts. Yet she laid her hand on his arm and accepted the love.

"You dear boy!" she said.

Perhaps Kate's answer was the best she could have given. But it stung Alec to the heart, and they went home in a changed silence.

The resolution Kate came to along the way was not so good as her answer. She did not love Alec as he did her. But he was only a boy, and therefore he would not suffer much, she thought. He would forget her as soon as she was out of his sight. Therefore, as he was a very dear boy, she would be as kind to him as she could, for she was going away soon.

She did not realize that Alec would take the kindness she gave as meaning more than she intended by it.

When they reached the house, Alec recovered himself a little and requested her to sing. She complied at once, and was foolish enough to sing a ballad from one lover to another.

Alec sat listening, as if Kate were meaning the song for him and the rosy glow within his heart grew all the brighter. But despite the scent of sweet peas stealing like love through the open window, and despite the throbbing in Alec's chest, and despite the radiance of her own beauty, Kate was only singing a song.

The following Sunday Murdoch Malison, the schoolmaster, was appointed to preach in the parish church. He had never preached there, for he had been no favourite with Mr. Cowie. Now, however, that the good man was out of the way, they gave him a chance, and he caught at it, though not without some misgivings. He came to two resolutions—the first, that he would not read his sermon but would commit it to memory and deliver it as extemporaneous, the second, to follow in the current fashion of preaching so much in favour, and wield the forked lightning of the law against the sins of Glamerton.

So on the appointed day, having put on a new suit of black, he ascended the pulpit stairs, and, conscious of a strange timidity, read the psalm. He cast one furtive glance around as he took his seat for the singing and saw a number of former as well as present pupils gathered to hear him, among whom were the two Truffeys, with their grandfather seated between them. He got through the prayer very well, for he was accustomed to that kind of thing in the school. But when he came to the sermon, he found that to hear boys repeat their lessons and punish them for failure did not necessarily stimulate the master's own memory.

He gave out his text from the prophet Joel and then began. Now if he could have read his sermon, it would have shown itself a most creditable invention. It had a general introduction upon the present punishment of sin, with two heads, each of which had a number of horns called *particulars*. Then there was a tail called an *application* in which the sins of his hearers were duly chastised, with vague and awful threats of some vengeance not confined to the life to come.

But he had resolved not to read his sermon. So he began to repeat it, with sweeps of the hands, pointings of the fingers, and other such tricks of second-rate actors, to aid the self-delusion of his hearers that it was a genuine present outburst from the soul of Murdoch Malison. For they all knew as well as he did, that his sermon was only "cold kail heated again." But some family dishes—Irish stew, for example, or Scotch broth—may be better the second day than the first, and where was the harm? All concerned would have been perfectly content if he had only gone on as he began. But, as he approached the second head, the fear suddenly flashed through his own that he would not be able to recall it. And that moment all the future of his sermon was a blank. He stammered, stared, did nothing, thought nothing—only felt himself in hell.

At length, roused by the sight of the faces of his hearers growing more expectant at the very moment when he had nothing more to give them, he gathered what remained of his wits, and as a last resort, resolved to read the remainder. He had a vague recollection of putting his manuscript in his pocket, but in order to give the change of mode an appearance of the natural, he managed with a struggle to bring out the words:

"But, my brethren, let us betake ourselves to the written testimony."

Everyone concluded he was going to quote from Scripture. But instead of turning over the leaves of the Bible, he plunged his hand into the folds of his coat. Horror of horrors!—the pocket was as empty as his own memory.

The cold dew of agony broke over him. He turned deadly pale. His knees knocked one another. A man of strong will, he made yet a frantic effort to bring his discourse down the inclined plane of a conclusion.

"In summary," he stammered, "my beloved brethren, if you do not repent and be converted and return to the Lord, you will—you will—you will have a very bad harvest."

Having uttered this solemn prediction, Murdoch Malison sat down, a *sticket minister*.* His brain was a vacuum, and the thought of standing up again to pray was intolerable. But he couldn't just sit there, for if he sat, the people would sit too. Something must be done, and there was nobody to do anything. He must get out and then the people would go home. But how could he escape? He cared no more for his vanished reputation. His only thought was how to get out.

Meanwhile, the congregation was variously affected. Some held down their heads and laughed immoderately. These were mostly of Mr. Malison's scholars, the fine edge of whose nature, if it ever had any, had vanished under the rasp of his tortures. Even Alec, who, with others of the assembly, held down his head from sympathetic shame, could not help remembering how the master had made Annie Anderson stand on the bench, and believing for the time in a general retribution in kind.

Andrew Truffey was crying bitterly. His sobs were heard through the church, and some took them for the sobs of Murdoch Malison, who had shrunk into the pulpit like a snail into its shell so that not an atom of his form was to be seen except from the side galleries.

At length the song leader, George Macwha, who had for some time been turning over the leaves of his psalm book, came to the rescue. He rose in the lectern and announced *The hundred and fifty-first psalm.* The congregation could find only a hundred and fifty, and took the last of the psalms for the one meant. But George, either from old spite against the tormentor of boys and girls, or from mere coincidence—he never revealed which—had in reality chosen a part of the *fifty-first* psalm.

---

* *"Sticket"—failed.—MP*

“The hunner and fifty-first psalm,” repeated George, “from the fifteenth verse. And then we’ll all go home. ‘My closed lips, O Lord, by thee, let them be opened.’”

As soon as the singing was over, George left the lectern, and the congregation following his example went straggling out of the church and home.

As soon as the sounds of retiring footsteps were heard no more in the great echoing church, the form of Murdoch Malison slowly rose up above the edge of the pulpit. With his face drained as that of a corpse, he gave a haunted look around and, not seeing little Truffey concealed behind one of the pillars, concluded the place empty. He half crawled, half tumbled down the stair to the vestry, where the sexton was awaiting him. It did not restore his lost composure to discover, in searching for his handkerchief, that the encumbrance of the pulpit gown over his suit had made him put his hand into the wrong pocket, and that in the other his manuscript lay as safe as it had been useless.

He took the gown off quietly, bade the old sexton a gentle good day, and stole away home through the streets. He had wanted to get out, and now he wanted to get in, for he felt very much as Lady Godiva would have felt if her hair or her heroism had proved unworthy of confidence.

Poor Murdoch had no mother and no wife—he could not go home and be comforted. Nor was he a youth to whom a first failure might be of small consequence. He was forty-five, and his head was sprinkled with gray. He was a schoolmaster and everybody knew him. As he walked along the deserted streets, he felt that he was running the gauntlet of scorn. But everyone who saw him coming along with his head sunk on his chest drew back from the window till he had gone by. Returning to the window to watch him go, they saw a solitary little figure about twenty yards behind him, with tears running down its face, stumping slowly step by step, and keeping the same distance from the dejected master.

But however silently Truffey might use his third leg, the master heard the *stump-stump* behind him, and felt that he was followed home every foot of the way by the boy whom he had crippled. He felt, too, in some dim degree which yet had practical results, that the boy was taking divine vengeance upon him, heaping on his head the coals of that consuming fire which is love, which is our God. And when the first shame was over, the thought of Truffey came back with healing on his lonely heart.

When he reached his own door, he darted in and closed it behind him as if to shut out the whole world through which he had passed with that burden of contempt upon his degraded shoulders. He was more ashamed of his failure than he had been sorry for the lamenting Truffey. But the shame would pass. The sorrow would endure.

Meantime, two of his congregation, elderly sisters, were going home together. They were distantly related to the schoolmaster, whom they regarded as the honour of the family and as their bond with the world above them in general and with the priesthood in particular. So when Elspeth addressed Meg with reference to the sermon in a manner which showed her determination to acknowledge no failure, Meg took her cue directly.

"Eh! it's a sore outlook for poor folk like us if things be going that way!"

"Indeed it's that. If the harvest be going to the moles and the bats, it's time we were away home, for it'll be a cold winter."

"Ay, that it will! The minister was so overcome at the prospect, honest man, that it was all he could do to get to the end o' his discoorse."

"He sees into the will of the Almighty. He's been far wi' him—that's very clear."

"Ay."

And hence, by slow degrees, in the middle of the vague prophecies of vengeance there gathered a more definite kernel of prediction—believed by some, disbelieved yet feared by others—that the upcoming harvest would be eaten by the worm that dieth not, that bread would be up to famine prices, and the poor would die of starvation.

But still the flowers came out and looked men in the face and went in again. And still the sun shone on the evil and on the good, and still the rain fell on the just and on the unjust.

And still the denunciations from the pulpits went on. But the human souls thus exposed to the fires seemed only to harden under their influences.

– Forty-Nine –

The Hypocrite

Before the time of Kate's departure, a letter from Professor Fraser arrived, to the purport that if Mrs. Forbes did not mind keeping Kate a little longer he would be greatly indebted to her. It came to Alec like a reprieve from execution. And the *little longer* lengthened into the late harvest of that country.

The summer shone on, and the corn grew, green and bonnie. And Alec's love grew with the corn, and Kate liked him better and better, but was not a whit more inclined to fall in love with him.

One night, after the house was quiet, Alec, finding he could not sleep, rose and went out to play the ghost a while. It was a sultry night. Great piles of cloud were heaped up in the heavens. The moon gleamed and vanished by fits, looking old and troubled when she sighed herself out of a cloud.

"There's a storm coming," said Alec to himself, and watched and waited. There was no wind below. The leaves of the black poplar, so ready to tremble, hung motionless. Not a bat came startling on its unheard skinny wing. But before long a writhing began in the clouds overhead, and they were twisted and torn about the moon. Then came a blinding flash, and a roar of thunder, followed by a bellowing. Then the rain poured down, and the scent of the earth rose into the air. Alec ran to look up at Kate's window. His heart bounded when he saw a white figure looking out into the stormy dark.

"Kate! Kate!" he cried, in a loud whisper, "come out—do come out. It's so splendid!"

She hesitated. But in a few minutes she glided silently out. The same moment another flash flung the darkness aside. She could have counted the houses of Glamerton. The hills rose up within her very soul. The Glamour shone in silver. The harvest gleamed in green. The larch-forest hung like a cloud on the horizon. Then the blank dark folded again its scared wings over the world, and the trees rustled their leaves with one wavy sweep, and were still. And again the rain came down in a tumult—warm, genial summer rain, full of the life of lightning. Alec stood staring through the dull dark, as if he would see Kate by the force of his will alone. The tempest in the heavens had awaked a like tempest in his heart. His hand took hers beseechingly. Another flash came, and he saw her face alive with the storm.

He could not mistake her passion. He knew that it was not for him, that she was a harp played upon by the elements, yet, passioned still more with her passion, he cried aloud,

"Oh, Kate! if you do not love me I shall die."

Kate started, and sought to take her hand from his, but she could not.

"Let me go, Alec," she pleaded.

His fingers relaxed, and she sped into the house like a bird, leaving him standing in the night.

There was no more lightning. The rain fell heavy and persistent though Alec, remaining out in it too long, hardly knew it. The wind rose. And when the dawn came, the clouds were drifting over the sky, and the day was a wet gray fringy mass of wind and rain and cloud and tossing trees.

When Kate made her appearance at breakfast she looked bright and cold. It was a dreary day. Alec crept about the house like a child in disgrace, and the darkness seemed an age in coming. When the candles were brought, he went to bed, feverish with a cold.

For a week there was nothing but wet and windy weather. Alec was in bed. Kate was unhappy. Mrs. Forbes was anxious.

The corn was badly lodged. Patches lay prone, tangled, spiky, and rough. It was evident that if sunshine, strong, healthy sunshine, did not soon break out, the mooncalf-prediction of Murdoch Malison would come true, for the corn, instead of ripening, would start a fresh growth, and the harvest would be a very bad one indeed, whether the people of Glamerton repented or not.

But after a grievous week, that blessed sunshine did come. The corn rose up from its low estate, looked at the sun, gathered heart, and began to ripen diligently.

But Alec was very ill, and did not see Kate for weeks.

Through his wanderings—so strangely do the thousand times overwritten grooves of the brain fool the mind and even the passions by the redawning of old traces—he talked on about Annie and their schooldays with Mr. Malison, and never mentioned Kate.

Annie went often to inquire after him, and Mrs. Forbes behaved to her with her old kindness—just a little diluted by anxiety and the possession of Kate.

When Annie thought with herself what she could do for him, she could never think of anything except saying *sangs* to him. But the time for that was long gone by. So, like many other devotions, hers found no outlet but in asking how he was.

At length, one day, he was brought down to the dining-room and laid upon the sofa. Then for the first time since his illness he saw Kate, He looked in her face pitifully and kissed her hand. She put her face down to his. The blood surged up into his cheek, and the light into his eyes, and he murmured:

"That is worth being ill for, Kate. I would be ill again for that."

She could only say *hush*, and then kiss him again, lest he should be hurt, thinking with a soundless sigh:

"I shall be forced to marry him some day."

On the Monday morning after his terrible failure, Mr. Malison felt almost too ill to go to the school. But he knew that if he gave in he would have to leave the place. And he had a good deal of that courage which enables a man to front the inevitable, and reap, against his liking, the benefits that spring from every fate steadfastly encountered. So he went, keeping a calm exterior over the shame and mortification that burned and writhed within him. He prayed the morning prayer, falteringly but fluently, and called up the Bible class. He corrected their blunders with an effort for, in truth, the hardest task he had ever had was to find fault that Monday. In short, he did everything as usual, except bring out the tawse. How could he punish failure when he had failed so shamefully in the sight of them all? And to the praise of the students of Glamerton, let it be recorded that there had never been a quieter day, one of less defiance, than that day of the master's humiliation. In the afternoon Andrew Truffey laid a splendid bunch of flowers on his desk, and the next morning it was so crowded with offerings of the same sort that he had quite a screen behind which to conceal his emotion.

Wonderful is the divine revenge! The children would wipe away the humiliation of their tyrant! His desk, the symbol of merciless law, became an altar heaped with offerings, behind which the shamed divinity bowed his head and acknowledged a power greater than that of stripes. His boys, who hated spelling and figures, hated even more the Shorter Catechism, and could hardly be brought to read the book of Leviticus with decency and hated to make bricks with straw, yet forgetting it all, they loved the man beneath whose lashes they had writhed in torture.

In his heart the master made a vow, with a new love that loosed the millstone of many offenses against the little that had for years been hanging about his neck. He vowed that he would never leave them, but would spend his days making up for the hardness of his heart and hand, vowed that he himself would be good, and so make them good, that he would henceforth be their friend and let them know it.

Blessed failure that ends in such a victory! Blessed purgatorial pulpit into which he entered full of self, and from which he came down disgusted with that paltry self as well as with its deserved defeat. The gates of its evil fortress were now undefended, for Pride had left them open in scorn. And Love, in the form of flower-bearing children, rushed into the citadel. The heart of the master was forced to yield, and the last state of the man was better than the first.

Summer flowed into autumn and there was no sign of the coming vengeance of heaven. The green grain turned pale at last before the gaze of the sun. The life within had done its best and now shrank back to the earth. Anxious farmers watched their fields and joyfully noted every shade of progress. All day the sun shone strong, and all night the moon leaned down from heaven to see how things were going on, and keep the work gently moving, till the sun should return to take it up again. Before he came, a shadowy frost would just breathe on the earth, which, although there was only death in its chill, yet furthered the goings on of life in repelling the now useless sap, and so helping the sun to dry the ripening ears. At length the new revelation of ancient life was complete, and the grain stood in living gold, and men began to put it to the sickle because the time of harvest was come.

But the feelings with which the master longed for the harvest holiday were sadly different from those of his boys. It was a delight to his students to think of having nothing to do on those glorious hot days but to gather blueberries or lie on the grass or swim in the Glamour and dry themselves in the sun ten times a day.

For the master, he only hoped to get away from the six thousand eyes of Glamerton. Not one allusion had been made in his hearing to his dismal degradation, but he knew that was only because it was too dreadful to be alluded to. The tone of additional kindness and consideration with which many addressed him only made him think of what lay behind, and refuse every invitation given him. If he could only get away from everyone's sight, his oppressed heart would begin to revive and he might gather strength to face with calmness what he would continue to face somehow, in the performance of his long-overdue duty to the boys and girls of Glamerton.

Can one ever bring up past-undone duty? Can one ever make up for wrong done? Will not heaven be an endless repentance?

It would need a book to answer the first two of these questions. To the last of them I answer, "Yes—but a glad repentance."

At length the slow hour arrived. Longing thoughts had almost obliterated the figures upon Time's dial and made it look a hopeless, undivided circle of eternity. But at length twelve o'clock on Saturday came, and the delight would have been almost unendurable to some had it not been calmed by the dreary proximity of the Sabbath lying between them and freedom. Almost the moment the *Amen* of the final prayer was out of the master's mouth, the first boys were shouting jubilantly in the open air. Truffey, who was always the last, was crutching it out after the rest when he heard the master's voice calling him back. He obeyed it with misgiving, so much had fear become a habit.

"Ask your grandfather, Andrew, if he will allow you to go down to the seaside with me for two or three weeks," said the master.

"Yes, sir," Truffey meant to say, but the attempt produced instead an unearthly screech of delight, with which he went off in a series of bounds worthy of a kangaroo, lasting all the way to his grandfather's and taking him there in half the usual time.

And the master and Truffey did go down to the sea together. The master borrowed a gig and hired a horse and driver. They all three sat in the space meant for two. To Truffey a lame leg or two was hardly to be compared with the exultant glory of that day. Was he not the master's friend from now on? And was he not riding with him in a gig—bliss supreme? Truffey was prouder than Mr. Malison could have been if he had been judged to surpass Mr. Turnbull himself in every pulpit gift. And if there be joy in the universe, what is the difference how it be divided?—whether the master be raised from the desk to the pulpit, or Truffey have a ride in a gig?

About this time Tibbie caught a bad cold and cough and for two weeks was confined to bed. Annie became her constant companion.

"I told ye I would hae the light before long," she said the first time Annie came to her.

"Hoots, Tibbie! It's only a cold," said Annie. "You mustn't be downhearted."

"Downhearted! Who dares to say I'm downhearted within sight of the New Jerusalem?"

"I beg your pardon, Tibbie. But you see, however willing you may be to go, we're none so willing to lose you."

"Ye'll be better off without me, lass. I'm not long behind Eppie Shawn."

This was the woman who had occupied the other end of the cottage who had died in the spring.

So Annie waited on Tibbie day and night. And that year, for the first time since she had come to Glamerton, the harvest began without her. But when Tibbie got a little better, Annie ran out now and then to see what progress the reapers were making.

One bright morning Tibbie, feeling better, said to her, "Noo, bairn, I'm much better today. Ye must jist run oot and play yerself. So jist run oot and dinna let me see ye afore dinnertime."

At Howglen there happened to be a field of oats not far from the house, the reaping of which was to begin that day. It was very warm, glorious with sunshine. So after a few stooks had been set up, Alec went out with his mother and Kate. Sheltered from the sun by a stook, he lay down on some sheaves and watched. He fell into a doze, not realizing that his mother and Kate had left him.

At length the sun rose till the stook could shelter him no more. Too lazy to move, Alec lay with eyes closed.

Suddenly a shadow came over him. When he looked up to find the source of the grateful relief, he could see nothing but an apron held up—hiding both the sun and the face of the helper.

"Who's there?" he asked.

"It's me—Annie Anderson," came the voice from behind the apron.

"Don't stand there, Annie," he said. "I don't want the shade. My mother will be here in a minute. I see her coming."

Annie dropped her arms and turned away in silence. If Alec could have seen her face, he would have been sorry he had refused her service. She vanished in a moment so that Mrs. Forbes and Kate never saw her. They sat down beside him so as to shelter him, and he again fell fast asleep. When he woke he found his head in Kate's lap and her parasol casting a cool green shadow over him. His mother had gone again. Having made these discoveries, he closed his eyes, and pretending to be still asleep he lay in a waking dream. But Kate soon saw that his face was awake, although his eyes were closed.

"I think it is time we went into the house, Alec," she said. "You have been asleep nearly an hour."

"Happy so long and not know it," he returned, looking up at her from where he lay.

Kate blushed a little. I think she began to realize that he was not quite a boy. But he obeyed her like a child, and they went in together.

When Annie vanished among the stooks after the rejection of her offered shadow, a throbbing pain at her heart kept her from returning to the reapers. She wandered away up the field toward a little old cottage in which some of the farm servants resided. She knew that Thomas Crann was at work there and found him busy rough-casting the outside of it with plaster.

"You're busy harling, Thomas," said Annie, for the sake of something to say.

"Ay, jist helping to make a hypocrite," answered Thomas, with a nod and a smile as he threw a trowelful of mortar against the wall.

"What do you mean by that?" asked Annie.

"If ye knew this old place as well as I do, ye wouldna need to ask that question. It should hae been pulled doon from the roof to the foundation a century ago, And here we're putting a clean face on it."

"It *looks* well enough."

"I told ye I was making a hypocrite. Not a soul wants this house to stand but the mistress doon there doesna want to waste the money. So it gets a new face and the rats stay in the walls."

Thomas went on whitening his "hypocrite" in silence for a few moments, then spoke again, "Where did Robert Bruce get that grand Bible, Annie, do ye ken?"

"That's my Bible, Thomas. Old Mr. Cowie gave it to me when he was lying close to death."

"Hmm, ay! And how came it that ye didn't take it and put it in yer chest in yer own room?"

"Mister Bruce took it and laid it in his room as soon as I brought it home."

"Did Master Cowie say anything to ye aboot anything that was in it?"

"Ay, he did. He said he put a five-pound note in it for me. But when I looked for it, I couldn't find it."

"Ay! When did ye look for it?"

"I forgot it for two or three days—maybe a week."

"Do ye remember that Sunday night that two or three of us came home with Bruce and had worship with ye?"

"Ay, well enough. It was the first time he read out of my Bible."

"Was it afore or after that when ye looked for the note?"

"It was the next day, for the sight of the Bible put it in my mind. I ought not to have thought about it on the Sabbath, but it came of itself. I didn't look till the Monday morning, before they were up. I reckon Mr. Cowie forgot to put it in after all."

"Hmm! Ay! ay! Weel, ye see, riches takes to themselves wings and flies away. And so we must not set oor hearts upon them. The worst bank a man can lay up his own money in is his own heart."

Soon Annie had forgotten her own troubles in Thomas's presence, for to her, and even in some ways to Tibbie, he was a shelter—as a river in a dry place, as a shadow of a great rock in a weary land. He was certainly not felt to be such by all whom he encountered, however. His ambition was to rouse men from the sleep of sin, to set them face to face with the terrors of Mount Sinai, to "shake them ower the mouth of the pit" till they were all choked with the fumes of the brimstone.

"How's Tibbie today?" said Thomas.

"A wee bit better," answered Annie.

"It's a great privilege, lassie, to be so much with one of the Lord's elect as ye are with Tibbie Dyster. She's some twisted sometimes, but she's a good honest woman who has the glory of God in her heart. And she's told me my duty and my sins in a manner worthy of Deborah the prophetess."

Annie did not return to the harvest field again that day. She did not want to go near Alec again. So, after lingering a while with Thomas, she wandered slowly across some fields of barley stubble through which the fresh young clover was already spreading its soft green. She then went over the Glamour by the bridge with the three arches, down the path at the other end, over the single great stone that crossed the dyer's dam, and so into Tibbie's cottage.

Had Annie been Robert Bruce's own, she would have had to mind the baby, to do part of the housework, and, being a wise child, to attend in the shop during meals. But Robert Bruce was ignorant of how little Annie knew about the investment of her money. He took her freedom of action for the result of the knowledge that she paid her way, whereas Annie followed her own impulse and never thought about what her aunt had told her about her little fortune. Had Bruce known this, there would have been no work too constant for her and no liberty too small.

Thomas did not doubt that Robert Bruce had stolen the note. But he did not see yet what he ought to do about it. The thing would be hard to prove, and the man who would steal would lie. But he bitterly regretted that such a man should have found his way into their congregation.

– Fifty –

Kate's Going

At length the oats and wheat and barley were gathered in all over the valley of the two rivers. The master returned from the seacoast, bringing Truffey, radiant with life, with him. Nothing could lengthen that shrunken limb, but in the other and the crutch together he had more than the function of the two.

The master was his idol, and the master was a happier man. The scene of his late failure had begun to fade a little from his brain. He had been loving and helping, and the love and help had turned into a great joy, whose tide washed from out of his heart the bitterness of his remembered sin. When we love truly, all the oppression of past sin will be swept away. Love is the final atonement, of which and for which the sacrifice of the atonement was made. And till this atonement is made in every man, sin holds its own, and God is not all in all.

So the earth and all that was in it did the master good. And he came back able to look the people in the face—humble still, but no longer humiliated. And when the children gathered again on a Monday morning with the sad feeling that the holidays were over, the master's prayer was different from what it used to be, and the work was not so bad as before, and school was not so hateful after all.

But the cool, bright mornings, and the frosty evenings with the pale green sky after sundown, spoke of a coming loss to Alec's heart. Kate never had shown that she loved him, so he felt a restless trouble even in her presence. Yet as he lay in the gloaming, and watched the crows flying home, they seemed to be bearing something away with them on their black wings. And as the light sank and paled on the horizon, and the stars began to condense themselves into sparks amid the sea of green, like those that fleet phosphorescent when the prow of the vessel troubles the summer sea, and then the falling stars of September shot across the darkening sky, he felt that a change was near, that for him winter was coming before its time. And the trees saw from their high watch-tower the white robe of winter already drifting up above the far horizon on the wind that followed his footsteps, and knew what that wind would be when it howled tormenting over those naked fields. So their leaves turned yellow and gray, and the frosty red of age was fixed upon them, and they fell, and lay.

And, indeed, on one of those bright mornings, the doom fell in its expected form, a letter from the Professor. He was home at last and wanted his niece to mix his toddy and scold his servants for him. Alec's heart sank within him.

Her departure was fixed in but a few days, and his summer would go with her.

The day before her departure they were walking together along one of the dirt roads leading to the hills.

"Oh, Kate!" exclaimed Alec all at once in an outburst of despair, "what *shall* I do when you are gone?"

"Oh, Alec!" rejoined Kate, "I shall see you again in November."

"Yes, you shall see me. But shall I see *you*—this very you? Oh, Kate, I feel you will be different then. You will not look at me as you do now. Oh, won't you love me, Kate? I don't deserve it. But I've read so often of beautiful women loving men who do not deserve it. Perhaps I may be worthy of it someday. But by that time you will have loved someone else!"

He turned away and walked toward home. But recovering himself instantly, he turned back and put his hand on Kate's arm. Like a child praying to its mother, he repeated:

"*Won't* you love me, Kate?—just a little?"

"I do love you dearly. You know that, Alec. Why do you always press me to say more?"

"Because I do not like the way you say it."

"You want me to speak your way, not my own, and be a hypocrite?"

"Kate, Kate! I understand you all too well."

They walked home in silence.

When the last night arrived, after it was late, he quietly walked up the stairs and knocked at her door to see her once again, and make one more appeal. Now an appeal has only to do with justice or pity. With love it is of no use. With love it is as unavailing as wisdom or gold or beauty. But no lover believes this.

There was no answer to the gentle knock of inarticulate appeal. He lost his courage and dared not knock again. And while Kate was standing with her head to one side and her dress half off, wondering if anyone had knocked, he crept away to his bed, ashamed. There was only a partition of lath and plaster between the two, neither of whom could sleep but neither of whom could have given the other any comfort.

At length the dawn came. It was the dreariest dawn Alec had ever known. Kate appeared at breakfast with the unmistakable signs of preparation about her. The breakfast was cheerless. The inevitable gig appeared at the door. Alec was not even to drive it. He could only help her into it, kiss her gloved hand on the rail, and see her vanish behind the shrubbery.

He turned in stern endurance and rushed up into the very room he had thought it impossible ever to enter again. He caught up a handkerchief she had left behind her, pressed it to his face, threw himself on her bed, and—well, he fell fast asleep.

He woke not quite so miserable as he had expected. He tried hard to make himself more miserable, but his thoughts would not obey him. They would take their own way, fly where they pleased, and alight where they would. And the meeting in November was the most attractive object in sight. So easily is hope born.

But he soon found that Grief will not come when she is called, but if you leave her alone, she will come of herself. Before the day was over the whole vacant region rushed in upon him with a ghostly sense of emptiness and desolation. He wandered about the dreary house. The flowers no longer had anything to say. The sunshine was hastening to have done with it and let the winter come as soon as it liked, for there was no more use in shining like this. Alec, though he did not have much imagination, could feel all this, for the poetic element has its share in all men. When a man is in love, what of poetry there is in him as well as what there is of any sort of good thing will rise to the surface, as the trout do in the balmy summer evenings. In love every man shows himself better than he is, though, thank God, not better than he is meant to become.

Eventually Alec found his way out, breathed the air of life of which he had been fond even before he knew Kate. The first project he undertook was to superintend the painting and laying up of his boat for the winter. It was placed across the rafters of the barn and wrapped in tarpaulins.

The light grew shorter and shorter. A few rough, rainy days stripped the trees of their foliage. Although the sun shone out again and made lovely weather, it was plain to all the senses that the autumn was drawing to a close.

All the prophetic rumours of a bad harvest had proved themselves false. Never a better harvest had been gathered. But the passion for prophecy over the whole district had not abated.

Suddenly one day appeared in the streets of Glamerton a man carrying in his hand a bundle of papers as a sample of what he had in the pack on his shoulders. He bore a burden of wrath, and began crying to whomever would listen with a loud voice:

"Yet forty days, and Glamerton shall be destroyed."

This cry he repeated at intervals of about a minute, walking slowly through every street of the town. The children followed him in staring silence, the women gazed from their doors in awe as he passed. The insanity which gleamed in his eyes and his pale, long-drawn countenance heightened the effect of the terrible prediction. His words took the town by storm.

The men smiled to each other and said that he was a madman. But as prophets have always been taken for madmen, so madmen often pass for prophets. Even Stumpin' Steenie, the town constable, had too much respect for either his prophetic claims or his lunacy, perhaps both, to take him into custody. So through the streets of Glamerton he went on his bare feet and with tattered garments, proclaiming aloud the coming destruction. He walked in the middle of the street and turned aside for nothing. The coachman of the Royal Mail Coach had to pull up his four gray horses on their haunches to keep them off the defiant prophet and leave him to pursue the straight line of his mission. The ministers warned the people on the following Sunday against false prophets, but did not say that this man was a false prophet, while with their own denunciations went on the same. The chief effects of it all were excitement and fear. There was little sign of repentance. But the spiritual physicians did not, therefore, doubt their exhibition. They only increased the dose. The prophet appeared one day. He vanished the next.

But within a few days, a still more awful prediction rose, cloudlike, in the spiritual sky. A placard was found affixed to the door of every place of worship in the town, setting forth in large letters that according to certain irrefutable calculations from "the number of man" and other such of the more definite utterances of Daniel and St. John, the day of judgment must fall without fail the next Sunday.

Glamerton was variously affected by this condensation of the vapour of prophecy into a definite prediction.

"What do ye think of it, Thomas Crann?" said Andrew Constable. "The calculation seems to be all correct. Yet somehow I canna believe in it."

"Dinna bother yer head aboot it, Andrew. There's a heep of judgments atween this and the other end. The Lord'll come when nobody's looking for him. And so we must aye be ready. But I dinna think the man that made that 'calculation' as ye call it is jist altogether infallible. For one thing, he's forgotten to make allooance fer the leap years."

"The day's already past then!" exclaimed Andrew, in a tone contrasting strongly with his previous expression of unbelief.

"Or else it's not coming so soon as the prophet thought. I'm not clear at this moment aboot that. But it's a small matter."

Andrew's face fell and he looked thoughtful.

"How do ye make that oot?" he said.

"Hoots man!" answered Thomas. "Dinna ye see that if the man was capable of making such a mistake as that, he could hardly hae been intended by Providence for an interpreter of dark sayings of old?"

Andrew burst into a laugh.

"Who would hae thought, Thomas, that ye could hae such gumption!"

And so they parted, Andrew laughing and Thomas with a curious smile.

– Fifty-One –

Rain

Toward the middle of the following week the sky grew gloomy and a thick, small, incessant rain brought the dreariest weather in the world. There was no wind, and miles and miles of mist were gathered in the air. After a day or two the heavens grew lighter but the rain fell as steadily as before, and in heavier drops. Still there was little rise in either the Glamour or the Wan Water, and the weather could not be said to be anything but seasonable.

On Saturday afternoon, weary of some poor attempts at Greek and Latin, weary of the rain, and weary with wishing to be with Kate, Alec could stay in the house no longer and went out for a walk. Along the bank of the river he wandered, through the rain above and the wet grass below. He stood for a moment gazing at the muddy Glamour which now came down bank full, and then turned and followed its course below the bridge through a wild, and now dismal country, to where the waters met.

It was getting dusk when he reached the place. With what a roar the Wan Water came down its rocks, rushing from its steeper course into the slow incline of the Glamour! A terrible country they came from—those two ocean-bound rivers—up among the hill-tops. There on the desolate peat-mosses, spongy, black, and cold, the rain was pouring into the awful holes whence generations had dug their fuel, and into the natural chasms of the earth, soaking the soil, and sending torrents rolling into the bosom of the rising river-god below. The mist hung there, darkening everything with its whiteness, ever sinking in slow fall upon the slippery peat and the heather and the gray old stones. By and by the pools would be filled, and the hidden caves, their sides would give way, the waters would rush from the one into the other, and from all down the hillsides, and the earth-sponge would be drained off.

"If this holds, we'll have a flood," said Alec to himself when he saw how the water was beginning to invade the trees on the steep banks below. The scene was in harmony with his feelings. The delight of the sweeping waters entered his soul, and filled him with joy and strength. As he took his way back through the stunted trees, each swathed in its own mist, and dripping as if it were a separate rain-cloud, and through the bushes that wetted him like pools, and through the streams that poured down the steep bank into the Glamour, he thought how different it was when he walked there with Kate, when the sun was bright, and the trees were covered with green, and the heather was in patches of blossom, and the river went clear-hearted and singing over its stony channel below. But he would rather have it thus, now that Kate was gone.

The floods of old were slower in rising, and rose to a much greater height than now. In the present day, the numerous drains provide a rapid and steady escape, so that there is no accumulation of waters, and no bursting of the walls of natural or accidental reservoirs. And I presume that from slow changes produced in the climate by cultivation, there may be a less fall of water now than there used to be, for in some parts of that country the rivers have, within the memory of middle-aged men, considerably decreased in volume.

That evening, in the schoolmaster's lodgings, little Truffey sat at the tea table triumphant. The master had been so pleased with an exercise which he had written for him that he had taken the boy home to tea with him, dried him well at his fire, and given him as much buttered toast as he could eat. Oh, how he loved his master!

"Truffey," said Mr. Malison, after a long pause, during which he had been staring into the fire, "how's your leg?"

"Quite well, thank ye, sir," answered Truffey, unconsciously putting out the foot of the wrong leg on the fender, "There wasna anything the matter with it."

"I mean the other leg, Truffey—the one that I—that I—hurt."

"Perfectly well, sir. It's not worth asking about. I wonder that ye take such pains with me, sir, when I was such a nickum."

The master could not reply. But he was more grateful for Truffey's generous forgiveness than he would have been for the richest living in Scotland. Such forgiveness gives us back ourselves—clean and happy. And for what gift can we be more grateful? He vowed all over again to do all he could for Truffey. Perhaps a sticket minister might have a hand in making a minister that would not stick.

"It's time to go home, Andrew Truffey. Put on my cloak—there. And keep out of the puddles as much as you can."

"I'll put the small foot in," said Truffey, holding up the end of his crutch as he stretched it forward to make one bound out of the door. For he delighted in showing off his agility to the master.

When Alec looked out of his window the next morning, he saw a broad yellow expanse below. The Glamour was rolling, a mighty river, through the land. A wild waste of foamy water, it swept along the fields where only recently the grain had bowed to the autumn winds. But he had seen it this high before. And all the grain was safely in the barns.

Neither he nor his mother regretted much that they could not go to church.

All night Tibbie Dyster had lain awake in her lonely cottage, listening to the quiet heavy rush of the water from which all the sweet babbling sounds and delicate music-tones had departed. The articulation of the river-god was choked in the weight and hurry of its course to the expectant sea. She was still far from well and was more convinced than ever that the Lord was going to let her see his face. Annie would have stayed with her that Saturday night, as she often did, had she not known that Mrs. Bruce would make it a pretext for giving her no change of linen for another week.

The moment Bruce entered the chapel—for no weather deprived him of his Sabbath privilege—Annie, who had been his sole companion, darted off to see Tibbie. When Bruce found that she had not followed him in, he hurried to the door only to see her halfway down the street. He returned in anger to his pew, which he was ashamed of showing thus empty to the eyes of his brethren. But there were many pews in like condition that morning.

The rain having moderated a little in the afternoon, the chapel was crowded in the evening. Mrs. Bruce was the only one of the Bruce family absent. The faces of the congregation wore an expectant look, for Mr. Turnbull always sought to *improve the occasion* by bringing collateral aid to the influences of the truth, invoking Nature herself to give effect to his persuasions.

The text he had chosen was: "But as the days of Noah were, so shall also the coming of the Son of Man be." He made no allusion to the prophetic paper which the rain was busy washing off the door of the chapel. Nor did he wish to remind the people that this was the very day foreseen by the bill-posting prophet as appointed for the coming of judgment. But when, in the middle of the sermon, a flash of lightning cracked, followed by an instant explosion of thunder and a burst of rain as if a waterspout had broken over their heads like the trampling of horses, the general start and pallor of the congregation showed that they had not forgotten the prediction.

Was this then the way in which judgment was going to be executed—a second flood about to sweep them from the earth? Although all stared at the minister as if they drank in every word of his representation of Noah's flood—with its despairing cries, floating carcasses, and lingering deaths on the mountaintops as the water crept slowly up from peak to peak—yet in reality they were much too frightened at the little flood in the valley of two rivers to care for the terrors of the great deluge of the world, in which, according to Mr. Turnbull, eighty thousand millions of the sons and daughters of men perished. Nor did they heed the practical application which he made of his subject.

When the service was over, they rushed out of the chapel.

Robert Bruce was the first to step from the threshold up to his ankles in water. The rain was falling—not in drops, but in little streams.

"The Lord preserve us!" he exclaimed. "It's risen a foot on Glamerton already. And there's sugar in the cellar! Children, run home yourselves! I can't wait for you."

"Hoots man!" cried Thomas Crann, who came behind him, "ye're so taken up with the world that ye hae no room for ordinary common sense. Ye're only standing up to the mouths of yer shoes in the hole ye undertook yerself to fill up with the cement left over after ye turned yer dry stone dyke into a byre wall that'll keep two feet more water than this oot."

Robert stepped out of the hole and held his tongue. At that moment Annie was slipping past him to run back to Tibbie. He made a pounce on her and grabbed her by the shoulder.

"No more of this, Annie!" he said. "Come home and don't be running about nobody knows where."

"Everybody knows where," returned Annie. "I'm only going to sleep with Tibbie Dyster, poor blind body!"

"Let the blind sleep with the blind, and come home with me," said Robert, abusing several texts of Scripture in a breath and pulling Annie away with him.

Heartily vexed and disappointed, Annie made no resistance. And how the rain did pour as they went home! They were all wet to the skin in a moment, except Mr. Bruce, who had an able umbrella and reasoned with himself that his Sabbath clothes were more expensive than those of the children.

By the time they reached home Annie had made up her mind what to do. Instead of going into her room, she waited on the landing, listening for the cessation of footsteps. The rain poured down on the roof with such a noise that she found it difficult to be sure. There was no use in changing her clothes only to get them wet again, and it was well for her that the evening was warm. But at length she was satisfied that her jailors were at supper, whereupon she stole out of the house as quietly as a kitten and was out of sight as quickly. Not a creature was to be seen. The gutters were all choked and the streets had become riverbeds. But through it all she dashed fearlessly to Tibbie's cottage.

"Tibbie!" she cried as she entered, "there's going to be a terrible flood."

"Let it come!" cried Tibbie. "The bit hoosie's founded upon a rock, and the rains may fall and the winds may blow, and the floods may beat against the hoosie, but it winna fall, it canna fall, for it's founded on a rock."

Perhaps Tibbie's mind was wandering a little, for when Annie arrived she found Tibbie's face flushed and her hands moving restlessly. But what with this assurance of her confidence and the pleasure of being with her again, Annie thought no more about the waters of the Glamour.

"What kept ye so long, lassie?" said Tibbie after a moment's silence, during which Annie had been arranging the peats to get some light from the fire.

She told her the whole story.

"And ye hae had no supper?"

"No. But I don't want any."

"Take off yer wet clothes then, and come to yer bed."

Annie crept into the bed beside her—not dry even then, for she was forced to retain her last garment. Tibbie was restless and kept moaning, so that neither of them could sleep. And the water kept sweeping on faster, rising higher up the rocky mound on which the cottage stood. The old woman and the young girl lay within and listened fearless.

– Fifty-Two –

The Flood

Alec too lay awake and listened to the untiring rain. Weary of the house, he had made use of the missionar kirk to get out of it, and had been one of Mr. Turnbull's congregation that night. Partly because his mind was unoccupied by any fear from without, for he only laughed at the prophecy, something in that sermon touched him deeper than anyone else in the place perhaps, awoke some old feelings of responsibility that had been slumbering for a long time.

They made him reflect upon an unquestioned article of his creed—the eternal loss and misery and torture of the soul that did not repent and believe. At the same time, what repentance and belief really meant—what he had to do first—he did not know. All he seemed to know was that he was at that moment in imminent danger of eternal damnation. And he lay thinking about this while the rain kept pouring upon the roof out of the thick night overhead, and the Glamour kept sweeping by through the darkness to the sea. He grew troubled, and when at last he fell asleep, he dreamed frightfully.

When he woke, it was a dull morning, full of mist and rain. His dreams had fled even from his memory, but had left a sense of discomfort. He rose and looked out the window. The Glamour spread out and rushed on like the torrent of a sea forsaking its old bed. Down its course swept many dark objects, which were too far away to distinguish.

He dressed and went down to its edge—not its bank, that lay far within and far beneath its torrent. The water, outspread where it ought not to be, seemed to separate him from the opposite country by an impassable gulf of space, a visible infinitude—a vague marvel of waters. Past him swept trees torn up by the roots. Down below, where he could not see, stones were rolling along the channel. On the surface, sheaves and trees went floating by. Then a cart with a drowned horse between the shafts, heaved past in the central roll of the water. Next came something he could not understand at first. It was a great water-wheel. This made him think of the mill, and he hurried off to see what the miller was doing.

Truffey went stumping through the rain and the streams to the morning school. Gladly would he have waited on the bridge, which he had to cross on his way, to look at the water instead. But the master would be there, and Truffey would not be late. When Mr. Malison arrived, Truffey was standing in the rain waiting for him. Not another student was there. The master sent him home. And Truffey went back to the bridge over the Glamour and there stood watching the awful river.

Mr. Malison sped away westward toward the Wan Water. On his way he found many groups of the inhabitants going in the same direction. The bed of the Wan Water was considerably higher than that of the Glamour here, although by a rapid descent it reached the same level a couple miles below the town. Its waters had never, to the knowledge of any of the inhabitants, risen so high as to overflow the ridge between it and the town. But now people said the Wan Water would be down upon them in the course of an hour or two, and then Glamerton would be in the heart of a torrent, for the two rivers would have merged into one. So instead of going to school, all the boys had gone to look, and the master followed them. Nor was the fear without foundation. The stream was still rising, and a foot more would overtop the ground between it and the Glamour.

But while the excited crowd of his townsmen stood in the middle of a stubble field watching the progress of the enemy at their feet, Robert Bruce was busy in his cellar preparing for its reception. He could not move his cask of sugar without help, and there was none of that to be had. In his shirt sleeves he was carrying the sugar up the cellar stairs in the coal scuttle, while Mrs. Bruce, in a condition very unfit for such efforts, went toiling behind him with the meal-bossie filled far beyond the rim. As soon as he had finished his task, he hurried off to join the watchers of the water.

James Johnstone's workshop was not far from the Glamour. When he went into it that Monday morning he found the treadles under water and realized there could be no work done that day.

"I'll jist take a stroll doon to the bridge to see the flood go by," he said to himself and, putting on his hat, he went out into the rain.

As he came near the stone bridge, he saw crippled Truffey leaning over the parapet with horror-stricken looks. The next moment he bounded to his one foot and his crutch, and gamboled across the bridge toward the other side as if he had been gifted with six legs.

When James reached the parapet he could see nothing to account for the terror and eagerness on Truffey's pale face, nor for his precipitate flight. But being shortsighted and inquisitive, he set off upriver after Truffey as fast as the dignity proper to an elderly weaver and a deacon of the missionars would permit.

As Alec came near the mill, he saw two men standing together on the verge of the brown torrent, the miller and Thomas Crann. Thomas had been up all night, wandering along the shore of the Wan Water, sorely troubled about Glamerton and its careless people. Towards morning he had found himself in the town again, and, crossing the Glamour, had wandered up the side of the water, and so come upon the sleepless miller contemplating his mill in the embrace of the torrent.

"Ye must admit it's hard, Thamas," said the miller.

"*Hard*?" retorted Thomas with indignation. "How dare ye call it hard when ye've been sticking yer own water-wheel in the midst of one of the Lord's little rivers and the Lord has spun it round and round for ye and yer forbears for a hundred years, and ye've ground yer bread and the bread of yer bairns, and now when it's the Lord's turn to make more room to send down the waters from his hills, ye grumble and complain."

"Weel, the Lord *might* hae managed without taking away my mill."

"Yer mill's not doon the water yet, Simon. It's in some extremity, I confess, but whether it's to be life or death, none kens but one. Go home, man, and go doon upon yer knees, and pray."

Alec came up and greeted the men. Before another word was uttered, their attention was attracted by a large mass floating down the river.

"What's that, Thomas?" said Alec. "I hope it won't take away the bridge."

He meant the wooden bridge a few hundred yards below them, which, inaccessible from either side, was now very little above the level of the water.

"It's the roof of some cottar's bit hoosie," answered Thomas. "What's become of them that was beneath it, the Lord only kens. The water's jist lifted the roof bodily off the hoose. There it goes—beneath the brige.—The brige's doon. It's no doon!—It's standing yet! But it canna hold much longer."

Their talk was soon turned into another channel by the appearance of Truffey, who, despite frantic efforts, made but little speed across the field to reach them, so deep did his crutch sink into the soaked earth. He had to pull it out at every step, and seemed mad in his foiled anxiety to reach them. He tried to shout, but nothing was heard beyond a crow like that of a hoarse chicken. Alec started off to meet him, but just as he reached him Truffey's crutch broke in the earth, and he fell and lay unable to speak a word. With slow and ponderous arrival, Thomas Crann came up.

"Annie Anderson!" panted out Truffey at length.

"What about *her?*" said both in alarm.

"Tibbie Dyster!" sobbed Truffey in reply.

"Here's James Johnstone!" said Thomas. "He'll tell us all aboot it."

"What's this?" he cried fiercely as James came within hearing.

"What is what?" returned the weaver eagerly.

If Thomas had been a swearing man, what a terrible oath he would have sworn in the wrath which this response of the weaver roused in his apprehensive soul. But Truffey was again trying to speak. They bent their ears to listen.

"They'll all be droont! They'll be taken away. They canna get oot!"

Thomas and Alec turned and stared at each other.

"The boat!" gasped Thomas.

Alec made no reply. That was a terrible water to look at. And the boat was small.

"Can ye guide it, Alec?" said Thomas, his voice trembling and the muscles of his face working.

Still Alec made no reply. He was afraid.

"Alec!" shouted Thomas in a voice that might have been heard across the roar of the Glamour. "Will ye let the women droon?"

The blood shot into Alec's face. He turned and ran.

"Thomas," said James Johnstone, laying a hand on the stonemason's broad chest, "hae ye considered what ye're driving the young man to?"

"Ay, weel enough, James. I would rather see my friend hanged than see him deserve hanging, or droon rather than be a coward to save himself. But dinna ye worry aboot Alec. If he doesna go, I'll go myself, and I never was in a boat in my life!"

"Come on, Thomas!" cried Alec, already across three or four ridges of the field. "I can't carry her alone."

Thomas followed as fast as he could, but before he reached the barn, he met Alec and one of the farm servants with the boat on their shoulders.

It was a short way to the water. They had her afloat in a few minutes, below the footbridge. At the edge the water was still as a pond.

Alec seized the oars and the men shoved him off.

"Pray, Alec!" shouted Thomas.

"I haven't time. Pray yourself!" shouted Alec in reply, and gave a stroke that shot him far toward the current. Before he reached it, he shifted his seat and sat facing the bow. There was little need for pulling, nor was there much fear of being overtaken by any floating mass, but there was great necessity for looking out ahead. The moment Thomas saw the boat laid hold of by the current, he turned his back to the Glamour, fell upon his knees in the grass, and cried in an agony:

"Lord, let not the curse of the widow and the childless be upon me."

Thereafter he was silent.

Johnstone and the farm lad ran down the riverside. Truffey had started for the stone bridge again, having tied up his crutch with a string. Thomas remained kneeling, with his arms stretched out as stiff as the poles of a scaffold, and the joints of his clasped fingers buried in the roots of the grass. The piers of the wooden bridge at last fell into the water with a rush, but he never heard it. The bridge floated past him bodily, but his back was towards it.

Alec did not find it so hard as he had expected to keep the boat from capsizing. But the rapidity with which the banks swept past him was frightful. The cottage lay on the other side of the Glamour, lower down, and all that he had to do for a while was to keep the bow of his boat down the stream. When he approached the cottage, he drew a little out of the centre of the current, which, confined within higher banks, was here fiercer than anywhere above where the fields allowed the river to spread out.

But completely out of the current he could not go, for the cottage lay between the channel of the river and the stream through the mill—now joined as one. He would hardly have known where to guide his tiny craft, the look of everything was so altered by the flood, except for the relation of Tibbie's cottage to the stone bridge behind it, now crowded with anxious spectators.

Alec could see as he approached that the water was already more than halfway up the door. He resolved to send his boat right through the doorway, but was doubtful whether it was wide enough to let it through. But he saw no other way of doing it, for if he could not get inside the flooding house the current would sweep him instantly past it. There was no dry ground anywhere around the place and no possible way for Annie and Tibbie to escape.

He hoped his momentum would be enough to force the door open and carry him inside. If he failed, no doubt both he and the boat would be in danger, but he would not make any further resolutions until necessity demanded it. As he drew near his mark, therefore, he resumed the seat of a rower, kept taking good aim at the door, gave a few vigorous pulls with the oars, then drew them in, bent his head forward, and prepared for the shock.

Bang went *The Bonnie Annie,* away went the door and posts, and the lintel came down on Alec's shoulders.

– Fifty-Three –

Rescue

But I will now tell how the night had passed with Tibbie and Annie.

In the middle of the night Tibbie's moaning grew gentler and less frequent, and both fell into a troubled slumber. Annie awoke at the sound of Tibbie's voice. She was talking in her sleep.

"Dinna wake him," she said, "dinna wake him, he's too tired and sleepy. Let the wind blow, lads. Do ye think he canna see when his eyes are closed? If the water meddles wi' ye, he'll soon let it ken it's in the wrong."

A pause followed. It was clear that she was in a dreamboat with Jesus in the back asleep. The sounds of the water outside had stolen through her ears and made a picture in her brain. Suddenly she cried out:

"I told ye so! I told ye so! Look at it! The waves go doon as if they were so many little pups!"

She woke with the cry—weeping.

"I thought I had the sight of my eyes," she said, sobbing, "and the Lord was blind with sleep."

"Do you hear the water?" said Annie.

"Who cares for *that* water!" she answered in a tone of contempt. "Do ye think he canna manage *it*!"

But there was a babble in the room beside them, and Annie heard it. The water was lapping at the foot of the bed.

"The water's in the house!" she cried in terror.

"Lie still, bairn," said Tibbie authoritatively. "If the water be in the hoose, there's no getting oot. It'll be doon afore the morning. Lie still."

Annie lay down and in a few minutes more she was asleep again. Tibbie slept too.

But Annie woke from a terrible dream—that a dead man was pursuing her, and had laid a cold hand upon her. The dream was gone, but the cold hand remained.

"Tibbie!" she cried. "The water's in the bed."

"What say ye, lassie?" returned Tibbie, waking up.

"The water's in the bed!"

"Weel, lie still. We canna sweep it oot."

It was pitch dark. Annie, who lay at the front, stretched her arm over the side. It sunk to the elbow. In a moment more the bed beneath her was like a full sponge. She lay in silent terror, longing for the dawn.

"I'm terrible cold," said Tibbie.

Annie tried to answer her, but the words would not leave her throat. The water rose. They were lying half-covered with it. Tibbie broke out singing. Annie had never heard her sing, and it was not very musical.

"Saviour, through the desert lead us. Without thee we can not go.—Are ye awake, lassie?"

"Ay," answered Annie.

"I'm terrible cold, and the water's up to my throat. I canna move. I'm so cold. I didna think water could be so cold."

"I'll help you to sit up a bit. You'll have dreadful rheumatism after this, Tibbie," said Annie, as she got up on her knees and proceeded to lift Tibbie's head and shoulders and draw her up in the bed.

But the task was beyond her strength. She could not move the helpless weight, and, in her despair, she let Tibbie's head fall back with a dull splash upon the pillow.

Seeing that all she could do was sit and support her, she got out of bed and waded across the floor to the fireside to find her clothes. But they were gone. Chair and all had floated away. She returned to the bed and, getting behind Tibbie, lifted her head on her knees and sat.

An awful dreary time followed. The water crept up and up. Tibbie moaned a little, and then lay silent for a long time, drawing slow and feeble breaths. Annie was almost dead with cold.

Suddenly in the midst of the darkness, Tibbie cried out,

“I see light! I see light!”

A strange sound in her throat followed, after which she was quite still. Annie’s mind began to wander. Something struck her gently on the arm and kept bobbing against her. She put out her hand to feel what it was. It was round and soft. She said to herself:

“It’s only somebody’s head that the water’s torn off,” and she put her hand under Tibbie again.

In the morning she found it was a drowned hen.

At length she saw motion rather than light. The first of the awful dawn was on the yellow flood that filled the floor. There it lay throbbing and swirling. The light grew. She strained her eyes to see Tibbie’s face. At last she saw that the water was over her mouth and that her face was like the face of her father in his coffin.

She knew that Tibbie was dead. She tried nevertheless to lift her head out of the water, but she could not. So she crept out from under her with painful effort, and stood up in the bed. The water almost reached her knees. The table was floating near the bed. She got hold of it, and, scrambling onto it, sat with her legs in the water. She went floating about for another long space, dreaming that she was having a row in *The Bonnie Annie* with Alec and Curly. In the motions of the water, she had passed close to the window where Truffey had seen her from the bridge.

Wide awake, she started from her stupor at the terrible *crash* with which the door burst open. She thought the cottage was falling, and that her hour was come to follow Tibbie down the dark water.

But in shot the sharp prow of *The Bonnie Annie* and in glided after it the stooping form of Alec Forbes. She gave one wailing cry, and forgot everything.

That cry, however, had not ceased before she was in Alec’s arms. In another moment, wrapped in his coat, she was lying in the bottom of the boat.

Alec was now as cool as any hero should be, for he was doing his duty. He looked all about for Tibbie, and at length saw her drowned in her bed.

“I wish I had been in time,” he said.

But what was to be done next? Down the river he must go, yet they would reach the lower bridge in two moments after leaving the cottage.

He would have to shoot for the middle arch, for that was the highest. But even should he escape being dashed against the bridge before he reached the arch, and even if he had time to get in a straight line for it, the risk was still a terrible one, for the water had risen to within a few feet of the peak of the arch, and the current was swift and torturous.

But when he shot *The Bonnie Annie* again through the door of the cottage, neither arch nor bridge was to be seen, and the boat went down the open river like an arrow.

– Fifty-Four –

Fall of the Bridge

Looking down the river on his way to the cottage, Alec did not know that the wooden bridge upstream had given way not long after he had entered the water. It floated down the river after him. As he turned to row into the cottage, on it came and swept past him.

The stone bridge was full of spectators, eagerly watching Alec's rescue, for Truffey, arriving back at the vantage point where he had seen Annie's danger, had spread the report of the attempt. When news of the situation of Tibbie and Annie reached the Wan Water, those who had been watching it were now hurrying toward the bridge of the Glamour.

The moment Alec disappeared into the cottage, some of the spectators caught sight of the wooden bridge coming down full tilt upon them. Already fears for the safety of the stone bridge had been talked about, for the weight of the water rushing against it was tremendous. And now that they saw this ram coming down the stream, a panic arose, with cries and shouts of terror. A general rush left the bridge empty just at the moment when the floating mass struck one of the principal piers. Had the spectators remained upon it, the bridge might have stood.

But one of the crowd was too much absorbed in watching the cottage to heed the sudden commotion around him. This was Truffey. Leaning wearily on the edge with his broken crutch at his side, he was watching anxiously through the cottage window. Even when the floating bridge struck the pier, and he must have felt the mass on which he stood tremble, he still kept staring at the cottage. Not till he felt the bridge begin to sway, I presume, had he an inkling of his danger. Then he sprang up and made for the street. Half of the bridge crumbled away behind him, and vanished in the seething yellow-brown abyss.

At this moment the first of the crowd from the Wan Water reached the foot of the bridge, among them the schoolmaster. Truffey was making desperate efforts to reach the bank. His mended crutch had given way and he was hopping wildly along. Murdoch Malison saw him, and rushed onto the falling bridge. He reached the cripple, caught him up in his strong arms, turned, and was halfway back to the street when, with a swing and a sweep and a great splash, the remaining half of the bridge reeled into the current and vanished. Murdoch Malison and Andrew Truffey left the world each in the other's arms.

Their bodies were never found.

A moment after the fall of the bridge, Robert Bruce, gazing with the rest at the triumphant torrent, saw *The Bonnie Annie* go darting past. Alec was in his shirt sleeves, facing down the river, with his oars level and ready to dip. But Bruce did not see Annie in the bottom of the boat.

"I wonder how old Margaret is," he said to his wife the moment he reached home.

But his wife could not tell him. Then he turned to his two younger children.

"Bairns," he said, "Annie Anderson's drowned. Ay, she's drowned," he continued, as they stared at him with frightened faces. "The Almighty's taken vengeance upon her for her disobedience, and for breaking Sabbath. See what you'll come to, children, if you take up with loons and don't mind what's said to you."

Mrs. Bruce cried a little. Robert would have set out at once to see Margaret Anderson, but there was no possibility of crossing the Wan Water.

Fortunately for Thomas Crann, James Johnstone, who had reached the bridge just before the alarm rose, sped to the nearest side, which was the one away from Glamerton. Having seen the boat go past with Alec still safe in it, he was able to set off with the good news for Thomas. After searching for him at the miller's and at Howglen, he found him where he had left him, still on his knees with his hands in the grass.

"Alec's safe, man!" he cried.

Thomas fell on his face and gave thanks.

There was no getting to Glamerton. So James took Thomas, emotionally exhausted, to the miller's for shelter. The miller made Thomas take a glass of whisky and get into his bed.

Down the Glamour and down the Wan Water—for the united streams went by the latter name—the terrible current bore *The Bonnie Annie*. Nowhere could Alec find a fit place to land till they came to a small village, fortunately on the same side as Howglen, into the streets of which the river was now flowing. He bent to his oars, got out of the current, and rowed up to the door of a public house. The fat, kind-hearted landlady had certainly expected no guests that day. In a few minutes Annie was in a hot bath and before an hour had passed, was asleep, breathing peacefully. Alec got his boat into the coach's house, and hiring a horse from the landlord, rode home to his mother. She had heard only a confused story, and had been getting terribly anxious about him when he made his appearance. As soon as she learned that he had rescued Annie and where he had left her, she had the horse put to the gig, and drove off to see after her neglected favourite.

From the moment the bridge fell the flood began to subside. Tibbie's cottage did not fall, and those who entered the next day found her body lying in the wet bed, its face still shining with the reflex of the light which broke upon her spirit as the windows were opened for it to pass.

"She sees noo," said Thomas Crann to James Johnstone as they walked together at her funeral. "The Lord sent that flood to wash the scales from her eyes."

Mrs. Forbes brought Annie home to Howglen as soon as she was fit to be moved.

Alec left for the city again, starting a week before the commencement of the winter session.

– Fifty-Five –

The University Again

It was on a bright frosty evening in the end of October, that Alec entered once more the streets of the great city. The stars were brilliant overhead. Below, the streets shone with their own dim stars, and men and women wove the web of their lives amongst them as they had done for centuries.

The moment he had succeeded in satisfying his landlady's inquisition, he rushed up to Mr. Cupples's room. Mr. Cupples was out. He could not call on Mr. Fraser that night. Yet all space between him and Kate growing more immeasurable the nearer he came to her, he could not rest for the feeling of distance. So he wandered out, and along the seashore till he was under the wall of the pier. The tide was low, and the wall high over his head. He followed it to the edge of the water and gazed out over the dim lead-coloured sea.

While he stood thus, he thought he heard voices in the air, and looking up, saw, far over him, on the top of the wall, two heads standing out against the clear sky, one in a bonnet, the other in a Glengarry. Why should he feel a pang in his heart? Surely there were many girls who took starlight walks on that refuge in the sea. And a Glengarry was no uncommon wear for the youths of the city. He laughed at his own weak fancies, turned his back on the pier. As he went, he glanced back towards the top of the wall, and saw the outline of the man. He was in full Highland dress. The woman he could not see, for she was on the further side of her companion. By the time he was halfway to the college, he had almost forgotten them.

It was a desolate shore along which he walked. Two miles of sand lay by the lip of the sea on his right. On his left rose irregular and changeful mounds of dry sand, upon which grew coarse grass and a few unpleasant-looking plants. From the level of the tops of these mounds stretched away a broad expanse of flat uncultivated ground, covered with thin grass. After sauntering along for half an hour, now listening to the wind that blew over the sand-hills, he reached a point whence he could descry the windows of Mr. Fraser's part of the college. There was no light in Kate's window.

She must be in the dining-room with her uncle—or—or—on the pier—with whom? He flung himself on the sand. All the old despair of the night of thunder, of the moonlight ramble, of the last walk together, revived. But Kate was indeed sitting quietly with her uncle, while he lay there on the sea-shore.

An hour later he ascended the garret-stairs, and again knocked at Mr. Cupples's door.

"Come in," came the reply in a strange, dull tone. Mr. Cupples had shouted into his empty tumbler while just about to swallow the last few drops without the usual intervention of the wine glass. Alec hesitated, but the voice came again with its usual ring, tinged with irritation, and he entered.

"Hello, bantam!" exclaimed Mr. Cupples, holding out a grimy hand that many a lady might have been pleased to possess and keep clean and white. "How's the cocks and hens?"

"Brawly," returned Alec. "Are you still acting as librarian?"

"Ay. I'm acting *as* librarian," returned Mr. Cupples dryly. "And I'm thinking that the books are beginning to know by this time what they're about, for such a thoroughly dilapidated collection of books I've never seen. Are you going to take the chemistry along with the natural philosophy?"

"Ay."

"Well, just come to me as you have done before. I'm not so good at those things as I am at the Greek, but I know more already than you'll know when you know all that you will know. And that's no flattery either to you or me."

With beating heart, Alec knocked the next day at Mr. Fraser's door and was shown into the drawing room, where Kate sat alone. The moment he saw her he knew there was a gulf between them as wide as the Glamour in a flood. She received him kindly and there was nothing in her manner or her voice which indicated the change, yet with that instinctive self-defence with which maidens are gifted, she had set up such a wall between them that he knew he could not approach her. With a miserable sense of cold exhaustion and aching disappointment, he left her. She shook hands with him warmly, was very sorry her uncle was out, and asked him whether he would not call again tomorrow. He thanked her in a voice that seemed not his own, while her voice seemed to come out of some far-off cave of the past. The cold, frosty air received him as he stepped from the door, and its breath was friendly. If the winter would only freeze him to one of its icicles. And still, that heart of his insisted on going on throbbing, although there was no reason for it to throb anymore!

He wandered through the old burgh, past its once mighty cathedral, down to the bridge with its one Gothic arch across the long-drawn Highland river, and into the wintry woods. On he wandered, seeing nothing, thinking nothing, almost feeling nothing, when he heard a voice behind him.

"Hello, bantam!" it cried and Alec did not need to turn around.

"I thought I saw you come out of Professor Fraser's," said Cupples, "and I thought a walk in the cold air would do me no harm, so I came after you."

Then changing his tone, he added,

"Alec, man, get hold of yourself. Let go of anything before you lose yourself."

"What do you mean?" asked Alec, not altogether willing to understand him.

"You know well enough what I mean. There's trouble upon you. I'm asking no questions. We'll just have a walk together."

And so he began a lengthy kind of humorous travesty of a lecture on physics. It was evident from the things he said that he not only was attempting to take Alec's mind off whatever was troubling him but also had some perception of the real condition of Alec's feelings. After walking a couple of miles into the open country, they retraced their footsteps. As they approached the college, Mr. Cupples said:

"Now, Alec, you must go home to your dinner. I'll be home before night. If you like, you can come with me to the library in the morning and I'll give you something to do."

Glad of anything to occupy his thoughts, Alec went to the library the next day. Mr. Cupples was making a catalogue and at the same time a thorough change in the arrangement of the books, and he found plenty for Alec to do. Alec soon found his own part in the work very agreeable. There was much to be done in mending old covers, mounting worn title pages, and such like. But in this department Mr. Cupples accepted very limited assistance. Books were his gold and jewels and furniture and fine clothes, and whenever Alec ventured to pick up a book destined for repair, he was conscious of two possessive eyes watching his every move.

During the few days passed in the library, he called once upon Mr. Fraser, and met with a warm reception from him. Kate gave him a kind one as before, but he had neither the satisfaction nor the pain of being alone with her.

In a few days the opening of the session began. Appearing with the rest was Patrick Beauchamp—claiming now the title and dignity of his grandfather's estate, for the old man had died. He was even more haughty than before and after classes went about everywhere in Highland costume. Beauchamp no longer attended the anatomical lectures, and when Alec observed his absence, he could not help but recall the fact that Kate could not even bear the slightest mention of that branch of study. The thought of anyone handling a corpse sent her into an immediate faint.

Had it not been for the good influences of Mr. Cupples, whether or not Alec would have continued with this aspect of his medical studies with any heartiness himself this session is more than doubtful. But the garret scholar gave him constant aid—sometimes praise, sometimes rebuke, sometimes humour—and Alec succeeded in making progress.

Fortunately for the designs of Beauchamp, during the summer Mr. Fraser had been visiting in the neighbourhood of Beauchamp's mother. Nothing was easier for one who possessed more than the ordinary power of ingratiating than to make himself agreeable to the old man. When he took his leave to return to the college, Mr. Fraser begged the young man to call upon him when he returned to the city.

Soon after the commencement of the session, a panic seized the townspeople in consequence of certain reports connected with the school of anatomy, which stood by itself in a low neighbourhood. They were to the effect that great indignities were practiced upon the remains of the subjects, and that occasionally the nearby graveyard was not safe from looting when a body happened to be needed.

Now whether Beauchamp had anything to do with what followed I cannot tell, but his innocence was doubtful at best.

Alec was occupied one evening in the medical building when he was roused by a yell outside. Looking down from the window he saw the unmistakable signs of gathering commotion of a most dubious nature. He quickly extinguished his candle and bolted down the back stairs and out a side door which was seldom used. But the moment he had let himself out and turned to go home, he heard an urchin who had peeped around a corner screech to the crowd—many of them drunk—across the yard:

"He's oot at the back door! He's oot at the back and away!"

Another yell arose, followed by the sound of trampling feet.

Alec knew his only chance lay in his heels, and he took to them faithfully. The narrow streets rang with the curses and shouts. But Alec's wind and muscles were both good, and in five minutes he was at the back entrance to his own lodging, having left his pursuers far behind.

But within ten minutes the mob was thundering at the door below. The fact that they knew where Alec lived adds to my suspicion of Beauchamp. The landlady wisely let them in, and for a few minutes they were busy searching the rooms. It was some time before Alec, from his vantage point on the roof to which he had safely retreated moments before the heavy footsteps had reached the floor of his room, saw the small mob leave the house again. When the tumult in the street had gradually died away, he crept back down the way he had come. As he passed the garret landing, to his horror he saw that Mr. Cupples's door was ripped off its hinges and lay on the floor. He entered the room and saw Mr. Cupples on his bed, holding a bloody bandage to his head. Trying to defend himself against the angry citizens, he had been shoved, had fallen against the fender, and had a bad cut as the result.

"Bantam," he said feebly, "I thought you would have your neck broken by this time. How the devil did you get out of their grasp?"

"By playing the cat on the roof," answered Alec. "I'll get the landlady."

But just as he turned to leave the room, she arrived carrying water and a fresh bandage.

“Indeed, bantam,” said Mr. Cupples, “if it hadn’t been for the gudewife here chasing them off and picking me up off the hearthstone, I would have been dead before now.”

“Not that likely, Mr. Cupples,” she said. “Now just hold your tongue and lie still. I’ll bring you a cup of tea directly.”

“Tea, gudewife! The devil can have your tea! Give me a drink from my tumbler.”

“Indeed, Mr. Cupples, you’ll have no drink at my hand.”

“Ye rigwiddie carlin!” grumbled the patient.

“If you don’t hold your tongue, I’ll go for the doctor.”

“I’ll fling him down the stairs. Here’s doctor enough!” Then he added, looking at Alec, “Give me half a glass.”

“You’ll have nothing,” interposed the landlady again. “It would be the death of you. I’ve taken everything out of here, Mr. Cupples.”

“Get out of my room!” he cried. “Leave me with Alec Forbes. He’ll give me what I need.”

“Indeed, I’ll leave no two such fools together. Come down the stairs directly, Mr. Forbes.”

Alec saw that it would be better to obey. He went back up on the sly in the course of the evening, however, but, seeing him asleep, came down again. He insisted on sitting up with him though, to which their landlady consented after repeated vows of prudence and caution. Mr. Cupples was restless and feverish during the night. Alec gave him some water. He drank it eagerly. In the morning he was better, but quite unable to get up.

Leaving him in the hands of the landlady, Alec set off for the college to do what he could in the way of preserving Mr. Cupples’s good standing at the library before any false rumours should have started regarding his absence.

The moment he was out of the room, Mr. Cupples got out of bed and crawled to the cupboard. To his mortification, he found that what his landlady had said was true and there was not a spoonful of whisky left in the house. He drained the few drops which had gathered in the sides of his tumbler, and crawled back to bed.

After the morning classes were over, Alec went to tell Mr. Fraser about his adventure and of the consequences of the librarian’s fate, he was most anxious that Mr. Cupples’s good standing not be jeopardized because of him.

"I was uneasy about you, Mr. Forbes," said the professor, "for I heard from your friend Beauchamp that you had got into a row with the blackguards, but he did not know how you had come off."

His friend Beauchamp! How did he know about it?

At that moment Kate entered and Alec forgot Beauchamp. She hesitated but advanced and held out her hand. Alec took it, but felt it tremble in his with a backward motion of reluctance.

"Will you stay and have tea with us?" asked the professor. "You so rarely come to see us now."

Alec stammered out an unintelligible excuse.

"Your friend Beauchamp will be here," continued Mr. Fraser.

"I fear Mr. Beauchamp is no friend of mine," said Alec.

"Why do you think that? He speaks very kindly of you—always."

Alec made no reply. Ugly things were vaguely showing themselves through a fog.

Kate left the room.

"You had better stay," said the old man kindly.

"I was up most of the night with Mr. Cupples," answered Alec, longing to be alone that he might think things out. "I am anxious about him."

Alec went home with such a raging jealousy in his heart that he almost forgot Mr. Cupples. Why should Kate hesitate to shake hands with him? He recalled how her hand had trembled and fluttered on his arm when he spoke of the red stain on the water, and how on another occasion she had declined to shake hands with him when he told her he had come from the dissecting room. The conviction suddenly seized him that Beauchamp had been working on her morbid sensitiveness—taking revenge by making the girl whom he worshiped shrink from him with loathing. But in the lulls of his rage and jealousy, he had some faint glimpses, perhaps for the first time, into Kate's character. Not that he was capable of thinking about it, but flashes of reality came now and then across the vapours of passion. His only comfort lay in saying over and over that Kate could not possibly be in love with his rival yet.

If he that same evening had seen Kate looking up into Beauchamp's face as she had never looked into his, with her face aglow at the sight of his Highland dress which set off to full advantage his broad shoulders and commanding height—he would have found this poor reed of comfort break in his hand and pierce his heart.

Beauchamp had quite taken her by storm, and yet not without well-laid schemes. Having discovered her admiration for poets, he made himself her pupil with regard to Byron, listening to everything she had to say as to a new revelation. At the same time he began to study Shelley and to introduce her to writings of which she had scarcely heard. She listened with breathless wonder and the feeling that now at last she had found a poet just to her mind, who could raise visions of a wilder beauty than had ever crossed the horizon of her imagination. And the fountain whence she drank the charmed water of this delight was the lips of that grand youth, all nobleness and devotion. And how wide his reading must be, seeing he knew a writer so well, of whom she had scarcely heard!

And the cunning Celt, perceiving her emotional sensitivities, used his insights against him whose rival he had become. Both to uncle and niece he had always spoken of Alec in a familiar and friendly manner. But now he began to occasionally drop a word with reference to him and break off with a laugh.

"What *do* you mean, Mr. Beauchamp?" said Kate on one of these occasions.

"I was only thinking how Forbes would enjoy some lines I found in Shelley yesterday."

"What are they?"

"Ah, I must not repeat them to you. You would turn pale and shudder again, and it would kill me to see your white face."

Whereupon Kate pressed the question no further, and an additional feeling of discomfort associated itself with the name of Alec Forbes.

– Fifty-Six –

The Coming of Womanhood

For several months Annie lay in her own little room at Howglen. Mrs. Forbes was dreadfully anxious about her, often fearing that her son's heroism had only prolonged the process of dying, that despite his efforts that awful night might yet take its toll.

At length on a morning in February, the first wave of the feebly returning flow of the life-tide visited her heart, and she opened her eyes seekingly. Through her little window, at which in summer she knew that the honeysuckle leaned in as if peeping and hearkening, she saw the country wrapt in a winding-sheet of snow, through which patches of bright green had begun to dawn, just as her life had begun to show its returning bloom above the wan waves of death.—Sickness is just a fight between life and death.

A thrill of gladness, too pleasant to be borne without tears, made her close her eyes. They throbbed and ached beneath their lids, and the hot tears ran down her cheeks. It was not gladness for this reason or for that, but the essential gladness of being that made her weep. There lay the world, white and green, and here lay she, faint and alive. And nothing was wanting to the gladness and kindness of Mrs. Forbes but the indescribable aroma of motherhood.

As the spring advanced, her strength increased till she became able to move about the house again. Nothing was said of her returning to the Bruces. What Robert Bruce's reaction might have been to the news that she was alive after all, I will not venture to speculate. But suffice it to say that they were not more desirous of having her than Mrs. Forbes was of parting with her.

If there had ever been any danger of anyone falling in love with Annie, there was much more now. For as her health returned it became evident that a change had passed upon her. She had always been a womanly child. Now she was a childlike woman. Her eyes had grown deeper and the outlines of her form more graceful. A flush as of sunrise dawned oftener over the white roses of her cheeks. She had not grown much taller, but her shape produced the impression of tallness. When Thomas Crann saw her after her illness, he held her at arm's length and gazed at her.

"Eh! lassie," he said, "ye're grown a woman! Ye'll have the bigger heart to love the Lord with. I thought he would hae taken ye away a bairn before we had seen what ye would turn oot. And sadly would I hae missed ye! And all the more that I hae lost old Tibbie. A man canna do weel without some woman or other to tell him the truth. I sadly wish I hadn't been so cantankert with her."

"I never heard her say that you were, Thomas."

"No, I dare say not. She wouldna say it. She was a kindhearted old body."

"But she didn't like to be called old," interposed Annie with a smile.

"Aweel, she's not that old now!" he answered. "Eh, lassie! it must be a fine thing to have the wisdom of age along with the light heart and strong bones of youth. I was once proud of that arm"—and he stretched out his right arm whose muscles still indicated great power—"and there was no man within ten miles of Glamerton who could lift what I could lift when I was twenty-five. But any lad in the mason trade could best me at lifting now, for I'm stiff in the back and my arm's jist red-hot sometimes with rheumatism.—Ye'll be going back to Robert Bruce before long, I'm thinking."

"I don't know. The mistress has said nothing about it. And I'm in no hurry, I can tell you that, Thomas. Ay, it's a fine thing to have thick milk for your porridge instead of sky-blue to meal and water," said Annie with another smile.

Thomas glanced at her. What could ail the lassie? She had never spoken lightly about anything before. The truth was that under the genial influences of home tenderness and early womanhood, a little spring of gentle humour had begun to flow softly through the quiet fields of Annie's childlike nature.

The mason gazed at her doubtfully. Annie saw his discomposure and took his great hand in her two little ones, looked full into his cold, gray eyes, and said, still smiling,

"Eh, Thomas, would you have a body never make fun of something when it just comes of itself?"

"We dinna hear that the Saviour himself ever so much as smiled," he said.

"Well, that would have been little wonder with all he had upon him. But I'm not sure he didn't, for all that. Folk don't always say when someone laughs. I'm thinking that if one of the bairnies that he took upon his knees had held up his wee toy horse with a broken leg, and had prayed him to work a miracle and mend the leg, he wouldn't have worked a miracle maybe, but he would have smiled or maybe laughed a bit, I dare say, and then he would have mended the leg some way or other to please the bairnie. And if it were me upon his knee, I would rather have had the mending of his own two hands, with a knife to help them maybe, than twenty miracles upon it."

Thomas gazed at her for a moment in silence. Then with a slow shake of the head, and a full-flown smile on his rugged face, he said:

"Ye're a curious cratur', Annie. I dinna rightly ken what to make o' ye sometimes. Ye're like a tiny bairn an' a grandmother both in one. But I'm thinkin' that atween the two, ye're mostly in the right. But why dinna ye join the kirk noo?"

"I never thought of such a thing. I don't even know if I'm one of the elect."

"Ye dinna ken yet?"

"No," answered Annie.

Meantime, a great pleasure dawned on Annie. James Dow came to visit her not long after this conversation with Thomas Crann. He had a long interview with Mrs. Forbes, the result of which Annie did not learn till some time later. One of Mrs. Forbes's farm servants who had been at Howglen for some years was going to leave at the next term, and she had asked Dow whether he knew of anyone to take his place. Whereupon he offered himself, and they arranged everything for his taking the position of foreman, the post he had occupied with James Anderson and was at present occupying some ten or twelve miles up the hill country.

Few things would have pleased Mrs. Forbes more, for James Dow was recognized throughout the country as the very pattern of what a foreman ought to be. One factor was his reputation for saving his employers all possible expense. Of late Mrs. Forbes had found it increasingly more difficult to meet her current expenses, for Alec's requirements at college were heavier this year. Much to her annoyance she had been compelled to delay the last half-yearly payment of Bruce's interest. She could not easily bear to recall the expression on his keen, weasel-like face when she informed him that it would be more convenient to pay the money a month hence. That month had passed, and another, before she had been able to do so. For although the home expenses upon a farm in Scotland are very small, even in the midst of plenty, money is often scarce enough.

Now, however, she hoped that with James Dow's management things would go better, and she would be able to hold her head a little higher in her own presence. So she was happy, knowing nothing of the cloud that was gathering over the far-off university, soon to sweep northward and envelop Howglen in its dusty folds.

– Fifty-Seven –

In the Library

To relieve Mr. Cupples's uneasiness about the books and catalogue, Alec offered to spend an hour or two every evening in carrying out his work in the library. This was a great relief to the librarian, and he improved more rapidly thereafter.

"Mr. Forbes," said Mr. Fraser, looking at Alec kindly one morning after his lecture, "you are a great stranger now. Won't you come and spend tomorrow evening with us? We are going to have a little party. It is my birthday, though I'm sure I don't know why an old man like me should have any birthdays. But it's not my doing. Kate found it out, and she would have a merrymaking. Myself, I think after a man is forty he should go back to thirty-nine, thirty-eight, and so on, indicating his progress toward none at all. That gives him a good sweep before he comes to two, one, and zero—at that rate I shall be thirteen tomorrow."

Whether the old man knew the real cause of Alec's gloom, I cannot tell. But with a feeling like that which makes one irritate a smarting wound or urge on an aching tooth, Alec resolved to go and have his pain in earnest.

He was the first to arrive.

Kate was in the drawing room at the piano, radiant in white—lovelier than ever. She rose and met him with some embarrassment, which she tried to cover under more than usual kindness.

"Oh, Kate!" Alec said, overpowered with her loveliness.

Kate took it for reproach and, making no reply, withdrew her hand and turned away. Alec saw as she turned that all the light had gone out of her face.

That instant Beauchamp entered, and as she turned once more to greet him, the light flashed from her face and her eyes. Beauchamp was magnificent, the rather quiet tartan of his clan being lighted up with all the silver and jewels of which the dress admits. In the hilt of his dirk, in his brooch, and for buttons, he wore a set of old family topazes, instead of the commoner cairngorm, so that as he entered he flashed golden light from the dark green cloud of his tartan.

Not observing Alec, he advanced to Kate with the confidence of an accepted lover. But some motion of her hand or glance from her eyes warned him in time. He looked around, started a little, and greeted Alec with a slight bow. He then turned to Kate and began to talk in a low tone. As he watched, the last sickly glimmer of Alec's hope died out in darkness. Beauchamp now had his revenge of mortification, and with it power enough over Kate's sensitive nature to draw her into the sphere of his flaunted triumph. Had Alec then been able to see his own face, he would have seen upon it the very sneer that he hated so much upon Beauchamp's.

Other visitors arrived, and Alec found a strange delight in behaving as if no hidden wound existed. Some music and a good deal of provincial talk followed. At length, Beauchamp urged Kate to sing, and she complied. It was a ghostly and eerie ballad from the Shetland Isles, and as Kate neared its completion her face grew pale. As the last wailing sounds of the accompaniment ceased, she gave one glance into Beauchamp's face and left the room.

Alec's heart swelled with indignant sympathy. But what could he do? The room became oppressive to him and he made his way to the door. As he opened it he could not help glancing at Beauchamp. Instead of the dismay he expected, he saw the triumph of power in the curl of his lip.

Alec flew from the house. Seeking refuge he rushed to the library, where he lay on the floor, alone with the heap of books he had that morning arranged for binding, feeling darker than the night around him.

It was a bitter hour. He had lain a long time when suddenly he started and listened. He heard the sound of an opening door, but not one of those in ordinary use. Thinking the noises those of thieves, he kept still. There was a door in a corner of the library which was never opened. It led into a part of the quadrangle buildings which had been formerly used as a students' dormitory but which had been abandoned now for many years. Alec knew this, but he did not know that there was also communication between this empty region and some of the houses and apartments of the faculty, among them Mr. Fraser's. Nor did he know that the library had been used before as a *tryst* by Beauchamp and Kate.

The door closed and the light of a lantern flashed to the ceiling.

"Why were you so unkind, Patrick?" said the voice of Kate. "You know it kills me to sing that old ballad."

"Why should you mind singing an old song your nurse taught you?"

"My nurse learned it from my mother. Oh, Patrick! What *would* my mother say if she knew I met you this way? You shouldn't ask me. You know I can refuse you nothing."

Alec could not hear his answer, and he knew why. The thought of Kate's lips there!

Of course Alec ought not to have listened. But the fact was that for the time, all consciousness of free will and capability of action had vanished from his mind. His soul was but a black gulf.

"Ah, yes, Patrick. Kisses are easy. But you hurt me terribly sometimes. And I know why. You hate my cousin, poor boy—and you want me to hate him too. I wonder if you love me as much as he does. Surely you are not jealous of him."

"Jealous of *him*! I should think not!"

"But you hate him."

"I don't hate him. He's not worth hating—the awkward clown. Although I confess some gratification in mortifying him."

"His mother has been very kind to me. I wish you would make up with him for my sake, Patrick. He may be uncouth and awkward, I don't know. But that's no reason for hating him. I love you so—though you are unkind sometimes. Patrick, don't make me do things in front of my cousin that will hurt him."

Alec knew that she pressed closer to Beauchamp, and offered him her face.

"Listen, my Kate," said Beauchamp. "I know there are things you cannot bear to hear, but you must hear this."

"No, no, not now!" answered Kate, shuddering.

"You must, Kate, and you shall," said Beauchamp. "I have tried to shield you from the knowledge of what goes on in that dissecting room in the evenings after classes are over. I once rebuked him for his unmanly behaviour, and—"

"Liar!" shouted Alec, springing into the light of their lantern.

Beauchamp's hand flew to the hilt of his dirk. Alec laughed with bitter contempt.

"Do so if you dare!" he said. "Even you, I believe, know I am no coward."

Kate stood staring and trembling. Beauchamp's presence of mind returned. He thrust his half-drawn knife back into its sheath, and spoke coldly.

"Eavesdropping?"

"Lying?" retorted Alec.

"You brute!" answered Beauchamp. "You will answer me for this!"

"When you please," returned Alec. "Meantime, you will leave this room, or I will make you."

"Go to the devil!" said Beauchamp, again laying his hand on his dirk.

"I have only to ring this bell and the watchman will be here."

"That is your regard for your cousin! You would expose her like that."

"I would expose her to anything rather than to you," said Alec. "I have held my tongue too long."

By this time Kate had slipped to the floor.

"And you will leave her lying here?"

"*You* will leave her lying here."

"That is your revenge, is it?"

"I want no revenge, even on you, Beauchamp. Now go."

"I will certainly not forget mine," said Beauchamp as he turned and left the library.

Alec could not understand the ease of his victory. But above all things, Beauchamp hated to find himself in an awkward position, which certainly would have been his case if Alec had rung the bell. Nor did he like to act on the spur of the moment. He was one who must have plans, those he would carry out remorselessly. So he went away to contemplate further revenge.

Alec found Kate moaning. He supported her head as she had done for him in that old harvest field. Before her senses had quite returned, she began to talk, and after several inarticulate attempts, her murmured words became plain.

"Never mind, dear," she said, "the boy is wild. He doesn't know what he says. Oh, Patrick, my heart is aching with love for you. You must be kind to me and not make me do what I don't like to do. And you must forgive my poor cousin, for he did not mean to tell lies. He fancies you bad because I love you so much more than him. But you know I can't help it, and I daresay he can't either."

Alec felt as if a green flame were consuming his brain. He had to get Kate home before she discovered she was not talking to her lover—and before he himself went mad! There was only one way to do it, and that lay in a bold venture. Mr. Fraser's door lay just across a corner of the quadrangle. He would carry her to her own room. The guests would be gone and it was a small household, so the chance of effecting it undiscovered was a good one.

He swooped her up, and within three minutes she was on her own bed and he was speeding out of the house as fast and quietly as he could.

Before he reached home his heart felt like a burned-out volcano.

Meantime, Mr. Cupples had been fretting over his absence, for he had come to depend very much on Alec. At last he rang the bell, knowing that Mrs. Leslie was out. He bribed the little girl who answered it, and she ran to the grocer's for him.

When Alec came home he found his friend fast asleep in bed, the room smelling strongly of toddy—the ingredients for which the girl had purchased for him—and the bottle standing on the table beside the empty tumbler. Faint in body, mind, and spirit, Alec grabbed the bottle, poured the tumbler full, and raised the drink to his lips recklessly. A cry rang from the bed, and the same instant the tumbler was struck from his hand. It flew in fragments against the grate, and the spirit rushed in a roaring flame of demoniacal wrath up the chimney.

"Damn you!" half-shrieked Mr. Cupples, still under the influence of the same spirit he had banned on its way to Alec Forbes's empty house. "Damn you, bantam! You've broken my father's tumbler. Devil take you! I've a good mind to wring your neck!"

Seeing that Mr. Cupples was only two-thirds of Alec's height, and only one-half of his thickness, the threat was rather ludicrous. Miserable as he was, Alec could not help laughing.

"You may laugh, bantam! But I want no companion in hell to cast his damnation in my teeth. If you touch that bottle again, I'll brain you and send you into the other world without that handle for Satan to catch a grip of you. And there *may* be a handle somewhere on the right side of you for some soft-hearted angel to lay a hand on and give you a lift where you don't deserve to go, you obstinate fool! After all that I have said to you—Damn you!"

Alec burst into a roar of laughter. For there was the little man standing only in his shirt, shaking a trembling fist at him, stammering with eagerness, and half-choked with excitement.

"Go to your bed, Mr. Cupples, or you'll catch your death of cold. I'll put the bottle away."

Alec seized the bottle once more.

Mr. Cupples flew at him and would have knocked the bottle on the floor had not Alec held it high above his reach.

"Toots, man! I'm going to put it away. Go to your bed and trust me."

"You give me your word you won't put it to your mouth?"

"I do," answered Alec.

Mr. Cupples relaxed before a violent fit of coughing overtook him.

Alec sat down in his easy chair and stared into the fire.

"The laddie's going to the dogs for want of being looked after," muttered Mr. Cupples. "This won't do any longer. I must be up tomorrow. It's the women! The women!"

Alec sat, still staring helplessly into the fire. The world was very black and dismal.

Then he rose to go to bed, for Mr. Cupples did not require him now. Finding him fast asleep under the blankets, Alec made him as comfortable as he could. Then he locked the closet where the whisky was, and took the key with him.

Their mutual care in this respect was comical indeed.

– Fifty-Eight –

The Library in the North

The next morning Alec saw Mr. Cupples in bed before he left. His surprise therefore was great when, entering the library after morning lectures, he found him seated in the usual place, hard at work on his catalogue. Except that he was yet thinner and paler than before, the only difference in his appearance was that his eyes were brighter and his complexion clearer.

"You here, Mr. Cupples!" he exclaimed.

"What made you lock the cupboard last night, you devil?" returned the librarian, paying no attention to Alec's expression of surprise. "But I say, bantam," he continued, not waiting for a reply, "you have done your work well—very near as well as I could have done myself."

"I'm sure, Mr. Cupples, it was the least I could do."

"You impudent cock! It was the very best you could do, or you wouldn't have come within sight of me. I may not be much at thrashing attorneys or cutting up dead corpses, but I defy you to come up to me in anything connected with books."

"Faith! Mr. Cupples, you may go further than that. After what you have done for me, if I were a general, you should lead the Forlorn Hope."

"Ay, ay. A forlorn hope's all that I'm fit for, Alec Forbes," returned Cupples sadly.

This struck Alec so near his own grief that he could not reply with even seeming cheerfulness. He said nothing. Mr. Cupples resumed.

"I have but two or three words to say to you, Alec Forbes. Can you believe in a man as well as you can in a woman?"

"I can believe in you, Mr. Cupples. That I'll swear to."

"Well, just sit down there and carry on with the books from where you left off yesterday. Then after the three o'clock lecture—what is it that you're attending this session?—we'll go down to Luckie Cumstie's and have a mouthful of dinner—she'll do her best for me—and I'll have just one tumbler of toddy, but not a devil's drop shall you have, bantam! And then we'll come back here in the evening, and I'll give you a little episode of my life.—Episode did I call it? Faith, it's my life itself, and not worth much either. You'll be the first man that ever I told it to. And you may judge my regard for you from that fact."

Alec worked away at his cataloguing and then attended the afternoon lecture. Dinner at Luckie Cumstie's followed—plain but good. And just as the evening was fading into night, they went back to the library. The two friends seated themselves on the lower steps of an open, circular oak staircase which wound up to a gallery running around the walls.

"After I had taken my degree," began Mr. Cupples, "I heard of a great library in the north—I won't say where—that needed the hand of a man that knew what he was about to put it in decent order. Don't imagine that it was a public library. No. It belonged to a great house. So I took the job, and liked the work very well, for books are the bonniest things in the world. Well, you see, I had a room to myself, besides the library and my bedroom, what a grand place it was. I didn't see anything of the family, for I had my dinner and wine and whatever I wanted brought up to me in my own room. One day as I was working away, I heard a kind of rustling. I thought it was mice, to which I've been a deadly enemy ever since they ate half of a first edition of mine of the *Fairy Queen*. But when I looked up, what should I see but a lady in a pale, pink gown, the colour of a cloud that's taking no part in the sunset, standing in front of the bookshelves at the farther end of the room. I had good eyesight and had just put the books in that part of the shelves away, and I saw her put her hand on a book that was not fit for her. I won't say what it was but it was written by some evil creature who had no respect for man or woman and whose neck should have been broken by the midwife.

"'Don't touch that book, my bonny lady!' I cried.

"She started and looked around, and I rose and went across the floor to her. And her face grew prettier and prettier the nearer I came. Her eyes went right through me and made of my life what it is and what I am. They went through every fiber of my being, twisting it up just as a spider does a fly before it sucks the life out of it.

"'Are you the librarian?' she said, soft and small.

"'That I am, ma'am,' I said. 'My name's Cupples—at your service.'

"'I was looking, Mr. Cupples,' she said, 'for some book to help me learn Gaelic. I want very much to read Gaelic.'

"'Well, ma'am,' I said, 'if it had been any of the Romance languages I might have given you some help. But you'll have to wait till you go to Edinburgh or Aberdeen, where you'll easily fall in with some student that'll be proud to instruct you and count himself more than well paid with the sight of your bonny face.'

"She turned red at that and I was afraid I had angered her. But she gave a small laugh and out the door she went. Well, that was the first time I saw her. But in a day or two there she was again. She began coming to the library nearly every day, asking me questions and wanting to see books. She seemed prettier every time, wearing long silk dresses and with diamonds for buttons. Well, to make a long story short, she came oftener and oftener and before long every time she left, I went after her—in my thoughts, I mean—all through the house. And every day she came to read with me in the afternoons and stayed till the gloaming came down and it grew dark. Man, I never saw anything like her.

"You may say I was a gowk. And you may laugh at me for crying after the moon. But better cry for the moon than not be capable of crying for the moon. And I must confess that I could have licked the very dust off the floor where her foot had been. Man, I never saw anything like her! She was just perfection itself and I was out of my wits in love with her.

"Well, one night I was working late, when my eyes were suddenly dazed with the glimmer of something white. At first I thought I had seen a ghost. But there she was, in a fluffy cloud of whiteness, with her bonny bare shoulders and arms, and just one white rose in her black hair.

"'It's so hot in the drawing room,' she said. 'And they're talking such nonsense there. There's nobody speaks to me but you, Mr. Cupples.'

"'Indeed, ma'am,' I said, 'I don't know where it's to come from tonight. For I have only one sense left, and that's almost with excess of brightness blind. Old Spenser says something like that, doesn't he, ma'am?' I added, seeing that she looked a little grave.

"But what she might have said or done, I don't know. For I swear to you, bantam, that delirium came upon me and I know nothing that happened afterward, till I came to myself at the sound of a laugh from outside the door. I knew it well enough, though it was a light, fluttering laugh. I sprang to my feet, but the place reeled round and I fell. It was the laugh that killed me, bantam. She killed me with her laugh. She had never loved me at all! And why shouldn't she laugh? And such a one as her that was no light-headed lassie but could read and understand with the best? I suppose I had gone down upon my knees to her, and then like the rest of the celestials, she took to her feathers and flew.

"But I know more than this, that for endless ages I went following her through the halls, knowing that she was behind the next door, and opening that door to an empty room, to be equally certain that she was behind the next. And so I went on and on, behind a thousand doors, always hearing the laugh, till I began to see the poor old walls of my mother's little house on the edge of the bog, and she was hanging over me, as I lay feverish, saying her prayers. How or when I had got there I don't know, but when she saw me open my eyes, she dropped upon her knees and went on praying. And I wonder that those prayers weren't listened to. I could never understand that."

"How do you know they weren't listened to?" asked Alec.

"Look at me! Do you call that listening to a prayer? Look what she got me back for. Do you call that an answer to prayers like my old mother's? Faith! I'll be forced to repent some day for her sake. But man! I would have repented long ago if I could have gotten a glimpse of the possible justice of putting a heart like mine into such a contemptible, scrimpit body as this. Man, the first thing I did when I came to myself was justify her before God for laughing at me. How could anybody help laughing at me? It wasn't her fault. But I won't let you laugh at me, bantam. I tell you that."

"Laugh at you! I would rather be a doormat to the devil!" exclaimed Alec.

"Thank you, bantam. Well, you see, once I had made up my mind about why she laughed at me, I just began following after her again like a hungry pup that stops the minute you look round at him—in my thoughts, you know—just as I had been following her all the time of my fever through the halls of heaven—of heaven as I thought them. When I grew some better and got up—would you believe it?—the kindness of the old, warped, brown, wrinkled woman that brought me forth—me, with the big heart and small body—began to console me for the laugh of that queen of white-skinned ladies. My mother thought a heap of me. But it was small honour I brought her name, with my eyes burned out for crying at the moon.—But I'll tell you the rest after we go home. I can't stand to be here in the dark. It was in the midst of books, in the dark, that I heard that laugh. The first time I let evening come down upon me in this library, all at once I heard a small snicker of a woman's laugh from somewhere. I grew fiery hot as brimstone and was out the door in an instant. And sure as death, I'll hear it again if I stay a minute longer."

They left the library and walked home. There was light in Mr. Fraser's drawing-room, and a shadow flitted across the blind. The frosty night, and the keenness of the stars, made Mr. Cupples shiver. Alec was in a feverous glow. When they reached home, Mr. Cupples set the kettle boiling for his toddy, and resumed his story.

"As soon as I was able I left my mother crying—God bless her!—and came to this town. The first thing I took to was teaching. Now that's a braw thing, when the laddies and lassies want to learn and have questions of their own to ask. But when they don't care, it's the very devil. Before long everything grew gray. I cared for nothing and nobody. My very dreams went from me, or came to torment me.

"Well, one night I came home, worn out with wrestling to get bairns to eat that had no hunger, and saw on the table a bottle of whisky a friend of mine had sent to me. I opened the bottle and drank a glass. Then another. And before long the colours began to come out again and I said to myself with pride: 'My lady can't with all her breeding and bonny skin keep me from loving her!' And I followed her about again through all the outs and ins of the story, and the past was restored to me.—That's how it appeared to me that night. Was it any wonder that the first thing I did the next night was to have another two or three glasses from the same bottle? I wanted nothing from God or Nature but just that the colour might not be taken out of my life. The devil was in it, that I couldn't stand up to my fate like a man. If my life was to be gray, I ought to have just taken up my cloak about me and gone on content. But I couldn't. I had to see things as bonny, or my strength left me. But you can't slink in at back doors that way. I was put out, and out I must stay. It wasn't long before I began to discover that it was all a delusion and a snare. When I fell asleep I would sometimes dream that, opening the doors into one of the halls of light, there she was laughing at me. And she might have gone on laughing to all eternity for anything I cared. And—ten times worse—I would sometimes come upon her crying and repenting and holding her hand out to me, and me caring no more for her than the beard of a barley stalk.

"But after a while all the whisky in Glenlivat couldn't console me.—Look at me now. You see what I am. Look at my hand, how it trembles. Look at my heart, how it's burned out. There's no living creature but yourself that I have any regard for, since my old mother died. If it weren't for books, I would almost cut my throat. Man, better lay hands on a torpedo than upon a cunning and beautiful woman, for she'll make you spin till you don't know your thumb from your big toe. And when I saw you pour out the whisky in that mad-like manner, as if you were going to have a drink of penny ale, it just drove me mad with anger."

"Well, Mr. Cupples," Alec ventured to say, "why don't you send the bottle to the devil?"

"What!" exclaimed Mr. Cupples, with a sudden reaction from the seriousness of his recent mood. "No, no. My old toddy maker won't go to the devil till we go together. Eh! We'll both have dry insides before we can get away from him, I don't doubt. That drought's an awful thing to contemplate. But speak of getting over the drink, don't think I haven't made that attempt. And why should I go to hell before my time? No, no. Once you have learned to drink, you can't do without it. For God's sake, for your mother's sake, for *any* sake, don't let a drop of the hell-broth pass your throat, or you'll be damned like me forever. It's as good as signing away your soul with your own hand and your own blood."

Mr. Cupples lifted his glass, emptied it, and, setting it down on the table with a gesture of hatred, proceeded to fill it yet again.

– Fifty-Nine –

It Comes to Blows

Several days later Alec was walking along the pier, renewing his grief by the ever-grieving sea. His was a young love, and his sorrow was interesting to him—he embalmed his pangs in the amber of his consciousness. So he crossed the links to the desolate sandy shore. There he let the sound of the waves enter the portals of his brain and fill all its hollow caves with their moaning. Wandering back to the old city, he stood at length over the keystone of the bridge, and looked down into the dark water below the Gothic arch.

Planning to go out with friends that evening, he had not gone home after classes, nor did he see Mr. Cupples all day. Expecting him but seeing nothing of him, at length Mr. Cupples left the library and went out to look for him.

Suddenly Alec heard a footstep behind him on the bridge. Looking round he saw Beauchamp, then without specific object in mind he walked up boldly to him. Beauchamp drew back.

"Beauchamp," said Alec, "you are my devil."

"Granted," said Beauchamp, coolly, but on his guard.

"What are you about with my cousin?"

"What is that to you?"

"She is my cousin."

"I don't care. She's not mine."

"If you play her false, as you have played me—by heavens!—"

"Oh, I'll be very kind to her! You needn't be afraid. I only wanted to take down your brazen impudence. You may go to her when you like."

Alec's answer was an attempted blow, which Beauchamp was prepared for and avoided. Alec pursued the attack with a burning desire to give him the punishment he deserved. But suddenly he turned sick, and, although he afterward recalled a wrestle on the bridge, the first thing he was aware of was the cold water of the river closing over him. The shock restored him. When he rose to the surface he swam down the stream, for the banks were very high near the bridge. At length he succeeded in landing, dragged himself ashore, and set out for home.

He had not gone far, however, before he grew faint and had to sit down. He discovered that his arm was bleeding and knew that Beauchamp had stabbed him. But he managed to reach home without much further difficulty. Mr. Cupples was not there. Alec got his landlady to tie up his arm. Fortunately the wound, although long and deep, ran lengthwise between the shoulder and the elbow, on the outside of the arm, and so was not serious. Washing and changing his clothes and feeling better, he went back out to keep his supper engagement.

Alec said nothing about his adventure to any of his friends. Like Scotchmen young and old, he liked to keep things in his own hands till he knew what to do with them. At first, notwithstanding his loss of blood, he felt better than he had felt for some time. But in the course of the evening he grew so tired, and his brain grew so muddy and brown, that he tried to counteract the effects of his wound with more whisky than he was accustomed to.

The moment he entered the garret several hours later, Mr Cupples, who had already consumed his nightly portion, looked at him with blue eyes, wide-opened, dismay and toddy combining to render them of uncertain vision.

"Eh, bantam! bantam!" he said, and sank back in his chair. "You've been at it in spite of me."

Mr. Cupples burst into silent tears—a phenomenon not unusual in men under the combined influences of emotion and drink.

"I want to tell you about it," said Alec.

Mr. Cupples took little notice, but Alec began his story notwithstanding, and as he went on his friend became attentive, inserting here and there an expletive to the disadvantage of Beauchamp.

When Alec had finished, Cupples spoke solemnly.

"I warned you against him, Alec. But a worse enemy than Beauchamp has gotten hold of you, I don't doubt. Do what he like, Beauchamp's dirk couldn't hurt you so much as your own hand when you lift the glass to your own mouth. You've despised my warnings. And sorrow and shame will come of it. Your mother will hate me. Go away to your bed. I can't stand the sight of you."

Alec went to bed, rebuked and distressed. But not having taken enough to hurt him much, he was unfortunately able the next morning to regard Mr. Cupples's lecture from a ludicrous point of view. And what danger was he in, he asked himself, when he drank less than most of his fellows?

Fierce as the struggle on the bridge had been, I do not think Beauchamp intended murder, for the consequences of murder would be a serious consideration to every gentleman. He came of a wild race with whom a word and a steel blow had been linked for ages. And habits transmitted become instincts. Whether Beauchamp tried to throw him from the bridge must also remain in doubt, for when the bodies of two men are locked in the wrestle of hate, their own souls do not know what they intend.

In any case, Beauchamp must have run home with the conscience of a murderer. And yet when Alec made his appearance in class, with aching head and pain from his wound, a revival of hatred was Beauchamp's first mental thought.

Although the whisky had done Alec no great immediate injury, yet its reaction made him restless all that day.

When the afternoon came, instead of going to Mr. Cupples in the library, he joined some of the same set he had been with the evening before. When he came home, instead of going upstairs to visit Mr. Cupples, he went straight to bed.

The next morning, while he was at breakfast, Mr. Cupples made his appearance in his room.

"What became of you last night, bantam?" he asked kindly, but with evident uneasiness.

"I came home tired and went to bed."

"You weren't home very early."

"I wasn't that late."

"You have been drinking again. I know by the look of your eye."

Alec had an even temper. But a headache and a sore conscience were enough to upset it. To be out of temper with oneself is to be out of temper with the universe.

"Did my mother commission you to look after me!"

Mr. Cupples turned and walked slowly away, with only the words:

"Eh! bantam! bantam! The Lord have pity on you—and me too!"

He went out at the door bowed like an old man.

I need hardly depict the fine gradations by which Alec sank after this. He was not fond of whisky. He could take it or leave it. And so he took it, and finding that there was some comfort in it, took it again, and again. The vice laid hold of him like a serpent. He had never had any conscious religion. His life had never looked up to its source. All that was good in him was good of itself, not of him.

Mr. Cupples, unseen, haunted his steps. The strong-minded, wise-headed, weak-willed little poet, wrapped in a coat of darkness, dogged the footsteps of a handsome, good-natured, sinking student friend who now withdrew all the former affection of their friendship in order that he might go the downward road unchecked. Distracted by his own guilt, Cupples drank harder than ever, but only grew more miserable over Alec. He thought of writing to Alec's mother, but with the indecision of a drunkard, could not make up his mind. He pondered over every side of the question till he was lost in a maze of incapacity.

There are facts in human life which human artists cannot touch. The great Artist can weave them into the grand whole of his Picture, but to the human eye they look too ugly and too painful. Even the man who can do the deeds dares not represent them. Mothers have to know such facts of their sons, and such facts of women like themselves.

Alec had fallen amongst a set of men who would not be satisfied till he should be as low as they—till there should be nothing left in him to remind them that they had once been better. The circle in which he began to drink had gradually contracted about him. The better sort had fallen away, and the worse had remained—chiefly older men who enjoyed making others like themselves. Encouraged by their laughter and approbation, Alec began to emulate them, and would soon have had very little to learn if things had not *taken a turn.*

– Sixty –

Rumours

Andrew Constable, with his wife and old-fashioned daughter Isie, was seated at tea in the little parlour opening from their shop when he was called out by a customer. He remained longer than was to be accounted for by the transaction of business at that time of the day. And when he returned his honest face looked troubled.

"Who was that?" asked his wife.

"Only James Johnstone, wanting a bit of flannel for his wife's coat."

"And what did he hae to say that kept ye till yer tea's not fit to drink?"

As they went on, Isie sat on her stool staring at her father and mother alternately, and watching for the result of her mother's attempt at picking the lock of her father's reticence to divulge the more serious import of the conversation. But when they sent her to bed, she knew she had no chance. Later in bed, however, the door to her room always left opened, she strained to hear the subdued conversation of her parents.

"Ay, woman," replied Andrew, "it'll be sore news to the lady over the water."

"Ye mean Mistress Forbes?"

"Indeed, I mean jist her."

"Is it her son? What's happened? Is he drowned or killed? The Lord preserve us!"

"No, it's worse than that. Ay, woman, ye know little of the wickedness of great towns—how they lie in wait at every corner, with their snares and their pits to catch the unwary youth," said Andrew, with something of the pride of superior knowledge.

He was presently pulled down from this elevation in a rather ignominious fashion by his more plain-spoken wife.

"Andrew, don't try to speak like a chapter of the Proverbs of Solomon. Say straight oot what's gotten a grip of the bonnie lad."

Therewith, Andrew proceeded to tell what he knew, but not without the continual use of heavy scriptural symbolism, mixing in grotesque fashion the imagery of St. John's Revelation with denunciations of modern city life. The little ears of Isie grew longer and longer with curious horror as the words flowed into her ears, until at length she could not disassociate the face of Alec Forbes from certain of the more graphic woodcuts in Fox's *Book of Martyrs,* three folio volumes of which lay in the adjoining room, imagining Alec's fate to be along similar lines to the saints of old.

Mrs. Constable interposed with an emphatic epithet, not admittable to the ears of this generation, as her husband continued.

"—poor deluded craters, wi'oot losing a great pairt o' what was left in him o' the eemage o' God efter the fall. When once they gae the ill-way o' drink, they're oot o' control.—But ye must hold a quiet tongue, gudewife," said Andrew at last.

"I'll warrant it's all over Glamerton afore it comes to yer ears, Andrew. But I would sorely like to ken who sent home the word o' it."

"I'm thinking it must hae been the young Bruce."

"The Lord be praised for a lie!" exclaimed Mrs. Constable. "I hae told ye before that Rob Bruce has a spite at that family for taking such a heap o' notice o' Annie Anderson. And I wouldna wonder if he has set his heart on marrying her to his own Rob and so keeping her money in the family."

"Indeed, ye may be right, gudewife. But he's a burning and shining light among the Missionars. And ye mustna speak ill o' him or he'll hae ye up afore the kirk."

"Ay, indeed he is! He's a burning shame and a stinking lamp!"

"Hoot, lass! Ye're o'er hard on him. But it's very true that if the story came frae that end o' town, there's room for rizzonable doobts."

It was long before little Isie got to sleep, what with attempting to realize the actual condition of Alec Forbes, and trying to think of the best means for his deliverance.

What rendered it probable that the rumour came from "that end of the town" was that Bruce the younger was this year a new student at Alec's college, the only other scion of Glamerton there grafted. Bruce the elder had determined that in his son he would fully restore the fortunes of the family. He was giving his son such an education as would entitle him to hold up his head with the best, and especially with that proud upstart Alec Forbes.

The recent news had also reached Thomas Crann and filled him with concern. As was his custom, he had immediately fallen on his knees before "the throne of grace" and "wrestled in prayer" with God to restore the prodigal to his mother. What would Thomas have thought if he had been told that his love, true as it was, did not come near the love and anxiety of another man who spent his evenings in drinking whisky and reading heathen poets and who never opened his Bible from one end of the year to the other? If he had been told that Cosmo Cupples had more than once, after the first tumbler of toddy but before the second, gone to his prayers for his poor Alec Forbes and begged God Almighty to do for him what he could not do, though he would die for him—if he had heard this, Thomas would have said it was a sad pity, but such prayers could not be answered, seeing that the one that prayed was himself in the bond of iniquity.

There was many a shaking of the head amongst the old women over Alec's decline, and many a word of tender pity for his poor mother floated forth on the frosty air of Glamerton. But no one ventured to go and tell her the sad tidings. The men left it to the women, and the women knew too well how the bearer of such ill news would appear. So they said to themselves she must know it just as well as they did, or if she did not, poor woman, she would know soon enough, for all the good it would do her. And that was what came of sending sons to college!

– Sixty-One –

The Supper

Some weeks later, the classmen of the *magistrands* and *tertians* met for supper at one of the popular local establishments. At an opportune moment, during the discussion of college affairs which followed over drinks, Alec felt that the moment had come which demanded public knowledge of Beauchamp's true character. He rose, therefore, and recounted how Beauchamp had sought an encounter with him by deliberate insult, had used a weapon against him though he was himself unarmed, and then thrown him from the bridge.

Beauchamp sat drinking his toddy at the head table, then glanced around at the assembly with a scornful curl on his lip.

"The accusation is false," he said. "I deny it utterly. But the real secret of the affair," he went on, "I am ashamed to say, is jealousy. Mr. Forbes knows all too well that a lady he loves prefers me to him."

Alec jumped back to his feet. "Don't bring her name into it, you brute!" he cried.

Soon a great commotion arose. It was only interrupted when a well-known voice rose clear above the confused murmur. It was Mr. Cupples standing at the end of the table. No one had seen him enter from the common room.

"I know, gentlemen," he said, "that I am not one of you and have no right to be here other than that you all know me by sight. But I am a graduate of this university, and at present your humble servant the librarian. I intrude for the sake of justice, and I ask you for a hearing."

It was accorded by general acclamation.

"Gentlemen," he resumed, "I have occupied the position of tutor to Mr. Forbes, and perhaps I can shed more light on these events that are disputed among you. Late on the afternoon in question, I had expected him in the library, and when he didn't come, I went out to look for him. I went out over the links, for he was in the habit of wandering about the seashore, but I saw no sign of man or woman along that dreary coast. I was just turning to come home again, when I came upon tracks in the wet sand. I followed them toward the links again, and before I reached the bridge I heard yelling and fighting. Before I could gather my wits I heard an awful splash in the water, then a minute later came running by with long quiet strides a young man in a kilt and all its fandangles.

"He never saw me, but I followed him all the way to the quadrangle where I saw him disappear just as the sacrist was coming out the door of the astronomical tower. 'Who was that who just ran by?' I asked him. And he said, 'It was Mr. Beauchamp.'"

By now Beauchamp's nonchalance had disappeared. His cheeks grew deathly pale. Cupples, watching him, went on.

"I saw what a damned idiot I had been to run after him. I flew back to the bridge, for by now I suspected who the other man must have been. It could be none but my own Alec Forbes, for I swear to you, gentlemen, I've seen the man Beauchamp watching and following him many a time with an evil look in his eye, as if waiting for fit opportunity to do him harm. By the time I reached the place again, Alec had pulled himself out of the water and was gone. But as I was looking about in the darkness I saw something bright and yellow glinting on the bridge, and now I beg to restore it to its rightful owner. Some of you will recognize it as a bonnie cairngorm-button. Would you pass it up the table, gentlemen, to the man who lost it on the bridge that night?"

Handing the button to the man nearest him, Mr Cupples withdrew into a corner, and leaned his back against the wall. The button made many a zigzag from side to side of the table as Beauchamp saw the yellow gleam of it coming nearer and nearer. The blood rushed into his face.

"It's a conspiracy!" he cried, leaping to his feet. His hand, following its foolish habit, fell upon the hilt of his dirk.

"Draw that dirk one inch," said the chairman rising also, "and you'll be thrown on the floor.

Beauchamp's hand dropped and he slumped back down.

"While I was still out," Mr. Cupples went on, "Alec Forbes came home with a long deep cut on the outside of his left arm between the shoulder and the elbow, and dripping wet. I have our own landlady's testimony. He told me all that happened later that same night."

Slowly the company of men rose, all eyes now on Beauchamp.

"It would seem that it is *you* who has been lying," said the chairman, "and that Mr. Forbes's charges are true."

Beauchamp was silent under the reproving stares of his classmen.

"You may go, Beauchamp," said the chairman. "You are disgraced. With attempted murder on your head, you can no longer be one of us. If we see you in the college again, the police will be notified. For the time, however, we will leave you to your own conscience."

Without a word, white as a ghost and looking at nobody, Beauchamp rose and slowly marched through the group, which now formed a double row and let him pass through them, and outside.

Beauchamp's further feelings I do not care to analyze. As he passes from that room, he passes from my history. I do not think a man with such an unfavourable start could arrive at the goal of repentance in this life. He was not seen in the city again.

– Sixty-Two –

From Bad to Worse

Meanwhile, Mr. Cupples's distress over Alec grew. His worse self continued to be uppermost in spite of what Mr. Cupples had done on his behalf. Nightly the librarian haunted his footsteps, and tried to talk to his young friend, but without avail, for Alec had grown distant. With mingled love and anger, and not a little self-reproach, he lay awake in his garret listening for the sound of Alec's late-returning footsteps trudging heavily and unsteadily up the stairs. Then, seeking to drown his own guilt over his friend, he would stretch forth his hand to his own bottle, which now rarely found its way back into the cupboard from one evening to the next.

One night, late, Mr. Cupples followed Alec through the streets. It was midnight and the youth had just been turned out of Luckie Cumstie's. But he and the friend he was with had not had enough of revelry yet. They went to another public house with worse reputation, but just as Alec was about to follow his companion inside, he was suddenly seized in the dark and pulled backwards away from the door. Recovering himself he raised his arm to strike. Before him stood a little man whose hands were in the pockets of his trowsers. The wind was blowing about the tails of his old and dirty dresscoat.

"*You,* Mr. Cupples!" he exclaimed. "I didn't expect to see you here."

"I was never across the doorsill of such a place in my life," said Mr. Cupples, "nor please God, will either you or me ever cross such a doorsill again."

"Hooly, hooly, Mr. Cupples. Speak for yourself. I'm going in right now."

"Man!" said Cupples, laying hold of Alec's coat.

"Don't stand preaching to me! I'm past that."

"Alec, you'll wish to God you hadn't when you see your mother, when you come to marry a bonnie wife."

It was true but an ill-timed argument. Alec flared up wildly.

"Wife!" he cried, "there's no wife for me. Get out of my way! Don't you see I've been drinking? And I won't be stopped."

"Drinking!" exclaimed Mr. Cupples. "Little you know about drinking. I've drunk three times as much as you. If that be any argument for me keeping out of your way, it's more argument for you to hold out of mine. I swear to God I won't stand this any longer. You come home with me from this mouth of hell!"

And with that the brave little man placed himself between Alec and the door.

But the opposition of Mr. Cupples had increased the action of the alcohol upon Alec's brain, and he blazed up in a fury. He took one step toward Mr. Cupples, who had restored his hands to his pockets and backed a few paces toward the door of the house to guard against Alec's passing him.

"Get out of my way, or I'll strike you," he said fiercely.

"I will not," answered Mr. Cupples, and the next instant he lay senseless on the stones of the court.

It was some time later when by slow degrees Mr. Cupples came to himself. He was half dead with cold and his head was aching frightfully. A pool of blood already frozen lay on the stones. He crawled on his hands and knees till he reached a wall, by which he raised and steadied himself. Feeling along this wall he got into the street, but he was so confused and benumbed that if a policeman had not come up, he would have died on someone's doorstep. The man knew him and got him home. Mr. Cupples allowed both the policeman and his landlady to suppose that his condition was the consequence of drink, and so was helped up to his garret and put to bed.

– Sixty-Three –

Evil Tidings

All night Isie Constable lay dreaming about Alec Forbes and the terrible trouble he was in at the city. If her parents would not tell Mrs. Forbes, then her duty was clear to seven-year-old Isie. But it had snowed all night and therefore it was many days before she could contrive to be about her important mission. At length she was allowed to go out and play in the garden. No sooner was she alone than she darted through the back gate and was headed across the rude temporary bridge over the Glamour on her way to Howglen.

Mrs. Forbes and Annie Anderson were sitting together when Mary put her head in at the door and told her mistress that the daughter of Mr. Constable, the clothier, wanted to see her.

"Why, she's a mere infant, Mary!" exclaimed Mrs. Forbes. "How could she have come all this way?"

"Indeed, mem. But nonetheless she's doon the stairs in the kitchen. She's a poor wee white-faced elf of a creature, but she's oldish and wise-like."

"Bring her up, Mary. Poor little thing! What can she want?"

Presently Isie entered the room, looking timidly about her.

"Well, my dear, what do you want?"

"It's aboot Alec, mem," said Isie, glancing toward Annie.

"What about him?" asked Mrs. Forbes, considerably bewildered.

"Hae ye heard nothing aboot him, mem?"

"Nothing particular. I haven't heard from him for two weeks. Speak out, Isie."

"Well, mem, I dinna rightly ken everything. But they hae taken him into a dreadful place and whether they hae left a whole inch of skin on his body I canna tell. But they hae racked him and pulled his nails off, maybe them all, and—"

"Good heavens!" exclaimed Mrs. Forbes with a most unusual inclination to break out in laughter. "What *do* you mean, child?"

"I'm telling ye it as I heard it, mem. I hope they haena burnt him yet. Ye must go and take him oot of their hands."

"Whose hands, child? Who's doing all this to him?"

"They stand aboot the corners of the streets, mem, in big cities, and they catch a hold of young lads, and they jist torment the life oot of them."

"Where did you hear all this, Isie, dear?"

"I heard my father and my mither lamenting ower him."

Annie stared in amazement at the wee blue-eyed wizened creature before her who was speaking with the decision of a minor prophet.

Mrs. Forbes rose and paced to and fro. Her spirit was troubled, however unlikely the child's tale. Yet how could she not pay some attention to the innocent little messenger of evil.

"I must go by the mail coach this afternoon," she said at length.

"Wouldn't it be better to write first?" suggested Annie.

Before Mrs. Forbes could reply, Mrs. Constable appeared at the door. She was in hot pursuit of her child, whose footsteps she had traced through the melting snow.

"Ye ill-contrived smatchit! What have ye been aboot?" she said to Isie.

"I don't see what better you could expect of your own child, Mrs. Constable, if you go spreading rumours against other people's children," reproached Mrs. Forbes.

"It's a lie, whatever she said," retorted Mrs. Constable.

"Where else could the child have heard such reports then?"

"I only telled Mistress Forbes hoo ill they were to Alec," said Isie.

Mrs. Constable turned with a subdued manner to Mrs. Forbes.

"The bairn's a curious child, mem," she said. "She's overheard her father and me speaking together."

"But what right had you to talk about my son?"

"Well, mem, that question goes rather far. What's already proclaimed from the housetops may surely be spoken of in the closets. If ye think that folk'll hold their tongue aboot yer son any more than any other body's, ye're mistaken, mem. But no one heard it from me, or my man either."

"What does it all mean, Mrs. Constable?" Mrs. Forbes asked. "I am quite ignorant. What do they say?"

"Ow, jist that he's consorting with the worst o' ill company, mem, and turning to the drink now and then."

Mrs. Forbes sank on the sofa and hid her face in her hands. Annie turned white and left the room. When Mrs. Forbes lifted her head, Mrs. Constable and her strange child had vanished.

Mrs. Forbes and Annie wept together. Then the mother sat down and wrote, begging him to deny the terrible charge, after which they both felt better. But when the return mail brought no reply day after day after day, Mrs. Forbes resolved to go to the hateful city herself.

– Sixty-Four –

A Solemn Vow

When Alec awoke in the morning, it rushed upon his mind that he had had a terrible dream. He reproached himself that even in a dream he should be capable of striking the friend who was trying to save him from disgrace. But as his headache began to yield to cold water, discomposing doubts rose upon his clearing mental horizon. They were absurd, but still they were unpleasant. It *must* be only a dream! How could he have knocked down a man twice his age and only half his size, and his friend besides? Horrible thought! Could it be true?

Haggard, he rushed out of his room toward the stairs, but was met by his landlady.

“Mr. Forbes, if you and Mr. Cupples continue on this way, I’ll be forced to give you both warning to leave. It’s a sad thing when young lads take to drink and turn reprobates overnight.”

“I don’t go to your church. You needn’t preach to me. But what’s the matter with Mr. Cupples? He hasn’t taken to drink overnight.”

“You scorner! He came home last night bleeding at the head and in the care of a policeman. He was an awful sight, honest man! They say there’s a special Providence watches over drunks and bairns. Poor man! He could hardly get up the stairs.”

“What did he say about it?” asked Alec.

“Ow, nothing. But don’t go near him, for I left him fast asleep. Go back to your own room and I’ll be back with your breakfast in ten minutes. Eh, but you would be a fine lad if only you would give up the drink.”

Alec obeyed, ashamed of himself and full of remorse. The only thing he could do was attend to Mr. Cupples's business in the library, where he worked at the catalogue till the afternoon lecture was over.

Nobody had seen Beauchamp, and the blinds of Kate's windows were drawn down.

All day Alec's heart was full of Mr. Cupples. He knew that his conduct had been as vile as it was possible for conduct to be. Because a girl could not love him, he had ceased to love his mother, had given himself up to Satan, and had returned his friend's devotion with a murderous blow. Because he could not have a bed of roses, he had thrown himself down in the pigsty. He rushed into a public house and swallowed two glasses of whisky. That done, he went straight home and ran up to Mr. Cupples's room.

Mr. Cupples was sitting in front of the fire, his hands on his knees and his head bloodstained and bound in white. He turned a ghastly face and tried to smile. Alec's heart gave way utterly, and he burst into tears.

"Eh, bantam, bantam!"

"Mr. Cupples, forgive me. I'll cut my throat if you like."

"You would do better to cut the devil's throat."

"Tell me how, and I'll do it."

"Break the whisky bottle, man. That's at the root of it. It's not you. It's the drink. And, eh! Alec, we might be right happy together after that. I would make a scholar of you."

"Well, Mr. Cupples, you have a right to demand of me what you like."

And now the dark roots of thought and feeling blossomed into the fair flower of resolution.

"Bantam," said Mr. Cupples solemnly, "I swear to God, if you'll give up the drink and the rest of your ill ways, I'll give up the drink as well. I have nothing else to give up.—But it won't be so easy," he added with a sigh, stretching his hand toward his glass.

With a sudden influx of energy, Alec reached toward the same glass. Laying hold of it as Mr. Cupples was raising it to his lips, he cried: "I swear to God likewise—and now," he added, letting go of the glass, "you dare not drink that."

Mr. Cupples threw the filled glass into the fire.

"That's my farewell libation," he said. "But, eh, it's a terrible undertaking. Bantam, I have sacrificed myself to you. Hold to your part, or I can't hold to mine."

It was indeed a terrible undertaking. I doubt whether either of them would have had courage for it had not both been under its exciting influences even then. For them the battle was yet to come.

They sat on opposite sides of the table and stared at each other. As the spirituous tide ebbed from the brain, more and more painful visions of the near future steamed up. Yet even already conscience began to sustain them. With Alec the struggle would soon be over. His nervous system would speedily recover its healthy operations. But for Cupples—from whose veins alcohol had nearly expelled the blood—delirium would surely follow.

"Now, let's have a game of cribbage," said Cupples, "to keep our thoughts from it."

They played two or three games. It was pathetic to see how Mr. Cupples's right hand, while he looked at the cards in his left, would go blindly flitting about the spot where his glass had always used to stand, and how, when he looked up unable to find it, his face shadowed over with disappointment. After those two or three games, he threw down the cards.

"It won't do, bantam. I don't like the cards tonight."

Alec's habits of study had been quite broken up of late. Even the medical lectures and the hospital classes had been neglected. But Cupples felt that if no good spirit came into the empty house, sweeping and garnishing would only incite seven to take the place of the one. So he tried to interest his pupil once again in his old studies, and by frequent changes succeeded in holding tedium at bay.

But all his efforts would have resulted in nothing had not both their hearts already been opened by one good and strong spirit—essential life and humanity. That spirit was Love, which at long last will expel whatever opposes it. While Alec felt that he must do everything to please Mr. Cupples, he, on his part, felt that all the future of the youth lay in his hands. He forgot the pangs of alcoholic desire in his fear lest Alec should not be able to endure the tedium of abstinence. And Alec's gratitude and remorse made him humble as a slave to the little, big-hearted man whom he had injured so cruelly.

"I'm tired and must go to bed, for I have a sore head," said Mr. Cupples that first night.

"That's my doing," said Alec sorrowfully.

"If this new repentance of yours and mine turns out to have anything in it, we'll both have reason to be thankful that you dented my skull. But eh me! I'm afraid I won't sleep much tonight."

"Would you like me to sit up with you?" said Alec. "I could sleep in your chair well enough."

"No, no. We both have need to say our prayers, and we couldn't do that together. Go to your own bed, and mind your vow to God and to me. And don't forget your prayers, Alec."

Neither of them forgot his prayers. Alec slept soundly—Mr. Cupples not at all.

"I think," he said, when Alec appeared in the morning, "that I won't take such a hardship upon me another night. Just open the door of my cupboard and fling the bottle into the yard. I hope it won't cut anyone's feet."

Alec ran to the cupboard and pulled out the demon.

"Now," said Mr. Cupples, "open the two doors of the window wide and fling it far."

Alec did as he was desired and the bottle fell on the stones of a little court. The clash rose to the ears of Mr. Cupples.

"Thank God," he said with a sigh.—"Alec, no man that hasn't gone through the same can tell what I have gone through this past night with that devil in the cupboard there crying, 'Come taste me! come taste me!' But I heard and did not hearken to it. And yet sometime in the night, although I'm sure I didn't sleep a wink, I thought I was fumbling away at the lock of the cupboard and couldn't get it opened. And the cupboard was a coffin set up on end and I knew that there was a corpse inside it, and yet I tried so hard to get it open. But I'm better now, and I would so like a drop of that fine beverage they call water."

Alec ran down and brought it cold from the pump.

"Now, Alec," said Mr. Cupples, "I don't doubt but that it'll be a sore day. Bring me my books over there, and I won't get out of bed till you come home. So be no longer than you can help. But eh, Alec, you must be true to me."

Alec promised, and set off with a heart lighter than it had been for months.

For a whole week Alec came home as early as possible and spent the rest of the day with Mr. Cupples. Many dreary hours passed over them both. The sufferings of Mr. Cupples and the struggle which he sustained are perhaps indescribable. But true to his vow and to his friend, he endured manfully. Still it was with a rueful-comical look and a sigh, sometimes, that he would sit down to his tea and remark,

"Eh, man! this is miserable stuff—a pagan invention altogether!"

But the tea comforted his half-scorched, half-sodden nerves, and by slow degrees they began to gather tone and strength. His appetite improved, and at the end of the week he resumed his duties in the library. He and Alec spent most of their time together and occasionally broke out laughing as the sparks of life revived.

Inquiring after Miss Fraser, Alec learned that she was ill. The maid inquired in return if he knew anything about Mr. Beauchamp.

– Sixty-Five –

End of the Session

As soon as his classes were over, Alec would go to the library to assist Mr. Cupples. On other days Mr. Cupples would linger near the medical school or hospital till Alec came out, and then they would go home together. They both depended greatly on the other.

They were hard at work one afternoon in Mr. Cupples's room—the table covered with books and papers—when a knock came to the door and the landlady ushered in Mrs. Forbes.

The two men sprang to their feet, and Mrs. Forbes stared with gratified amazement. The place was crowded with signs of intellectual labour. Not even a pack of cards was visible.

"Why didn't you answer my last letter, Alec?" she said.

It had been dropped behind some books, and he had never seen it.

"What is the meaning, then, of some reports I have heard about you?" she resumed.

Alec looked confused, grew red, and was silent.

Mr. Cupples replied for him.

"You see, mem, from the time of Adam, the human individual must learn to refuse the evil and choose the good. This doesn't come of eating butter and honey but sometimes of eating ashes and dirt. Now my pupil here, mem, your son, has eaten that dirt and made that choice. And I'll be security for him that he'll never more return to wallow in that mire. It's three weeks, mem, since a single drop of whisky has passed his mouth."

"Whisky!" exclaimed the mother. "Alec! Is it possible?"

"Mem, mem! It would better become you to fall down on your knees and thank the God that's brought him out of the fearful pit and set his feet upon the rock. If you fall to upbraiding him, you may make him clean forget his washing."

But Mrs. Forbes was proud and did not like this interference between her and her son. Had she found things as bad as she had expected, she would have been humble. Now that her fears had abated, her natural pride had returned.

"Take me to your own room, Alec," she said.

"Ay, mem. Take him with you. But caw cannie, you know, or you'll give me a devil of a job with him."

With a nod and smile to Cupples, Alec led the way.

He would have told his mother everything if she had been genial. As she was, he contented himself with a general confession that he had been behaving very badly and would have grown ten times worse but for Mr. Cupples, who was the best friend he had on earth.

"He ought to have behaved more like a gentleman to me," she said, jealousy putting her on her guard.

"Mother, you don't understand Mr. Cupples. He's a strange creature."

"I don't think he's fit company for you anyhow.—We'll change the subject, if you please."

So Alec was yet more annoyed, and the interaction between mother and son was forced and uncomfortable. As soon as she lay down to rest, Alec bounded up the stairs.

"Never mind my mother," he said. "She's a good woman, but she's vexed with me and let it out on you."

"Mind her!" answered Mr. Cupples. "She's a fine woman and she may say what she likes to me. A woman with one son is like a cow with one horn—a bit ticklish, you know."

The next day they went to call on Professor Fraser. He received them kindly, and thanked Mrs. Forbes for her attentions to his niece. But he seemed oppressed and troubled. His niece was far from well, he said—had not left her room for some weeks, and could see no one.

Mrs. Forbes associated Alec's conduct with Kate's illness, but said nothing about her suspicions. After one day more, she returned home, reassured but not satisfied by her visit. She guessed that Alec had outgrown his former relation to her and had a dim perception that her pride had prevented them from entering into a closer relation. It is their own fault when mothers lose by the *growth* of their children.

– Sixty-Six –

Failure, Tragedy, and Recovery

Meantime, it had been a dreadful shock to Annie to hear such things reported of her hero, her champion. He had been to her the centre of all that was noble and true. And yet now he had erred and had revelled in company of which she knew nothing except far-off hints of unapproachable pollution! Her idol of silver was blackened and the world became dark.

In this mood she went to the evening service at Mr. Turnbull's chapel. There she sat listlessly, looking for no help and caring for none of the hymns or prayers. At length Mr. Turnbull began to read the story of the Prodigal Son. And during the reading her distress vanished. For she took upon herself the part of the elder brother, prayed for forgiveness, and came away loving Alec Forbes more than she had ever loved him before. If God could love the Prodigal, might she not, ought she not to love him too? The deepest source of her misery, though she did not know it, had been the fading of her love toward him.

As she walked home through the dark, the story grew into another comfort. A prodigal might see the face of God, then! He was no grand monarch, but a homely father! He would receive her one day, and let her look in his face.

From that day her trouble did not return to her. Nor was there ever a feeling of repugnance mingled with her thought of Alec. For such a one as he could not help repenting, she said. He would be sure to rise and go back to his Father.

She would not have found it hard to believe even, that, come early or linger late, no swine-keeping son of the Father will be able to help repenting at last, that no God-born soul will be able to go on trying to satisfy himself with the husks that the swine eat, or to refrain from thinking of his Father's house, and wishing himself within its walls even in the meanest place, or that such a wish is prelude to the best robe and the ring and the fatted calf, when the Father would spend himself in joyous obliteration of his son's past and its misery—having got him back his very own, and better than when he went, because more humble and more loving.

When Mrs. Forbes came home, she entered into no detail and was not inclined to talk about the matter at all, probably as much from dissatisfaction with herself as with her son. But Annie's heart blossomed into a quiet delight when she learned that the facts were not so bad as the reports. Yet with the delight also came the knowledge that the evil time was drawing nigh when she would have to return to the Bruce's for the spring and summer. She would feel it more than ever, but less than if her aunt had not explained to her that she had a right to the shelter afforded her by the Bruces.

Meantime, a letter arrived from Mr. Cupples.

> DEAR MADAM,—After all the efforts of Mr. Alec, aided by my best endeavours and his diligent study, but hindered by the grief of knowing that his cousin, Miss Fraser, entertained a regard for a worthless class-fellow of his—after all our united efforts, Mr. Alec has not been able to pass more than two of his examinations. I am certain he would have done better but for the unhappiness to which I have referred, combined with the illness of Miss Fraser. In a day or two he will be returning to you in Howglen. If you can succeed, as none but mothers can, in restoring him to some composure of mind and strength of body, he will be perfectly able during the vacation to make up for lost time.
>
> "I am, dear madam, your obedient servant,
>
> C. CUPPLES.

Angry with Kate, annoyed with her son, vexed with herself, and indignant at the mediation of "that dirty, vulgar, little man," Mrs. Forbes forgot her usual restraint. She threw the letter across the table with the words, "Bad news, Annie," and left the room. But the effect produced upon Annie by the letter was very different.

Up till now she had looked up to Alec as a great, strong creature. Her faith in him had been unquestioning and unbounded. But now rejected and disgraced and his mother dissatisfied, his friend disappointed, and himself foiled in the battle of life, he had fallen upon evil days, and all the woman in Annie rose to his defence. Suddenly they had changed places. The strong youth was weak and defenceless. The gentle girl opened the heart almost of motherhood, to receive and shelter the worn bedraggled man.

A new tenderness and pity took possession of her. Indignant with Kate, angry with the professors, and ready to kiss the hand of Mr. Cupples, all the tenderness of her tender nature gathered about her fallen hero. Alec had been a bright star beyond her sphere. But now the star lay in the grass, shorn of its beams, and she took it to her bosom.

Two days passed. On the third evening in walked Alec, pale and trembling, evidently too ill to even be questioned. His breathing was short.

"If I hadn't come at once, mother," he said, "I should have been laid up there. It's pleurisy, Mr. Cupples says."

"My poor boy! You've been working too hard."

Alec laughed bitterly.

"I did work, mother, but it doesn't matter. She's dead."

"Who's dead?"

"Kate's dead. And I couldn't help it. I tried hard. And it's my fault too. I might have saved her."

He leaped up from the sofa and went pacing about the room, his face flushed and his breath coming faster and shorter. His mother got him to lie down again and asked no more questions. The doctor came and bled him at the arm, and sent him to bed.

When Annie saw him worn and ill, her heart swelled till she could hardly bear the aching of it. She would have been his slave, and yet she could do nothing. She must leave him instead. She went to her room, put on her bonnet and cloak, and was leaving the house when Mrs. Forbes caught sight of her.

"Annie, what are you doing, child! You're not going to leave me?"

"I thought you wouldn't want me here anymore, now that Alec is home."

"You silly child!"

Annie ran back to her room, hardly able to contain herself.

When Mr. Cupples and Alec had begun to place some confidence in each other's self-denial, they had dogged each other less and less through the mornings and afternoons. Finding at his Natural Philosophy examination that he had no chance, Alec had gathered his papers, left the room, and wandered out to his former refuge of misery, that long desolate stretch of barren sand between the mouths of the two rivers of the city. Here he wandered till long after the dusk had deepened into night.

A sound as of one singing came to him. He turned in the direction of it, for something in the tones reminded him of Kate. He almost believed the song was the ghostly ballad she had sung the night of her uncle's party. The singing rose and fell, and he ran toward it.

Suddenly a wild cry came from the sea where the waves were far out and ebbing from the shore. He dashed along the glimmering sands, thinking he saw something white, but there was no moon to give any certainty. As he advanced he became surer there was something in the water.

He rushed in. The water grew deeper and deeper. He plunged in and swam farther away from the shore.

Before he had reached the spot, with another cry the figure vanished, probably in one of the deep pits which abound beneath the surface along that shore. Still he kept on, diving many times, but in vain. His strength was not what it had once been, and at length he was so exhausted that when he came to himself, he was lying on his back on the dry sands. He would have rushed again into the water, but he could hardly move his limbs. He crawled part of the way back to the college.

There he inquired if Miss Fraser was in the house. The maid assured him that she was in her own room. But scarcely had he turned to leave for home when they discovered that her room was deserted and she was nowhere to be found.

The shock of this news made it impossible for him to throw off the effects of the cold and exposure and he lingered on until Mr. Cupples compelled him to go home. Not even then, however, had her body been discovered. It washed ashore a few days after his departure, and it was well he did not see it.

It soon became known that she had been out of her mind for some time. The exact cause was not known, but suspicions pointed to factors having to do with her lover. One strange fact in the case was her inexplicable aversion to water—either a prevision of her coming fate or the actual cause of it. The sea, visible from her window over the dreary flat of the links, may have fascinated her and drawn her to her death. Such cases are not unknown.

During the worst period of Alec's illness, he was wandering along that shore or swimming in those deadly waters. Sometimes he had laid hold of the drowning girl and was struggling with her to the surface. Sometimes he was drawing her in an agony from the terrible quicksand lurking in the bottom of the underwater pits.

Annie took her turn in the sick chamber, watching beside the half-conscious lad, and listening anxiously to the murmurs that broke through the veil of his dreams. The feeling with which she had received the prodigal home into her heart, spread its roots deeper and wider, and bore at length a flower of a pale-rosy flush—Annie's love revealed to herself—strong although pale, delicate although strong. It seemed to the girl she had loved him so always, only she had not thought about it. He had fought for her and endured for her at school. He had saved her life from the greedy waters of the Glamour at the risk of his own. She would be the most ungrateful of girls if she did not love him. And she did love him with a quiet intensity peculiar to her nature.

Never had she had happier hours than those in which it seemed only the stars and the angels were awake beside herself. And if while watching him at night she grew sleepy, she would kneel down and pray to God to keep her awake so that no harm should come to Alec. Then she would wonder if even the angels could do without sleep always, or whether they sometimes lie down on the warm fields of heaven between their own shadowy wings. She would wonder next if it would be safe for God to close his eyes for one minute—safe for the world, she meant. And she hoped that if ever he did close his eyes, that might not be the one moment when she could see his face. Then she would nod, and wake up with a start, flutter silently to her feet and go and peep at the slumberer. Never was woman happier than Annie was during those blessed midnights and cold grey dawns.

Sometimes in those terrible hours after midnight that belong neither to the night nor the day but almost to the primeval darkness, the terrors of the darkness would seize upon her, and she would sit trembling. But the lightest movement of the sleeper would rouse her, and a glance at the place where he lay would dispel her fears.

– Sixty-Seven –

Mr. Cupples in Glamerton

One night Annie heard a rustling among the bushes in the garden and the next moment a subdued voice began to sing a wild and wailing tune.

"I didn't know you cared about psalm-tunes, Mr. Cupples," murmured Alec from his bed.

The scratchy voice went on and he grew restless.

It was an *eerie* thing to go out, but she must stop the singing for the sake of Alec's sleep. Annie rose and slowly opened the door. The dark figure of a little man stood leaning against the house, singing gently.

"Are you Mr. Cupples?" she said.

The man started and answered, "Yes, my lass. And who are you?"

"I'm Annie Anderson. Alec's disturbed with your singing. You'll wake him up."

"I won't sing another note. How's Alec?"

"Some better. He's growing better, though slowly."

"And they trust you to look after him?"

"Ay, why not? His mother would be worn to death if she sat up with him every night."

"Well, ye're a young lass to hae such a charge."

"When did you come, Mr. Cupples?"

"Earlier this very night. But ye were all in yer beds and I dared not disturb ye. So I sat down to smoke my pipe and look at the stars, and after a while I was singing to myself. But I'll come back tomorrow."

"But do you have a bed?" asked the thoughtful Annie.

"Ay, at the hoose of a small jabbering bitter-barked creature they call King Robert the Bruce."

Annie knew that he must be occupying her room and was on the point of expressing a hope that he wouldn't be disturbed with the rats, when she saw that it would lead to new explanations and would delay her return to Alec.

"Are ye a niece, or a granddaughter of the hoose, or a hired servant, or what are ye? For ye're a wise-spoken lass and bonnie."

"I'm a servant of the house," said Annie. Then after a moment's hesitation, she added, "but not a hired one."

"Ye're worth hiring anyhow."

"Good night, Mr. Cupples," she said, holding out her hand.

"Good night—what do they call ye again? I forget names dreadful."

"Annie Anderson."

"Ay, Annie Anderson. I've surely heard that name before. Well, I winna forget *you,* whether I forget yer name or not."

Mr. Cupples had a proclivity to garrets. He could not be comfortable if any person was over his head. He could breathe, he said, when he got next to the stars. For the rats he cared nothing, and slept as if the garret were a cellar in heaven.

It had been a sore trial for him to keep his vow after Alec was gone. In his loneliness it was harder to do battle with his deep-rooted desires. He would never drink as he had before, he assured himself. But might he not have just one tumbler? That one tumbler he did not take, however. And the rewards soon began to blossom within him. The well of song returned to his lips, beauty returned to the sunsets, and the world turned green again.

Another reward was that he had money in his pocket. With this money he would go and see Alec Forbes. He had written two or three times to Mrs. Forbes asking about his young friend but received no satisfactory answer, and he had grown anxious about him. His resources were small, however, and he saved them by walking. Hence it came that he arrived in Glamerton late and weary. Entering the first shop he came to, he asked about a cheap lodging. For he said to himself that the humblest inn was no doubt beyond his means. Robert Bruce scrutinized him keenly from under his eyebrows, and debated within himself whether the applicant was respectable—that is, whether he could pay. Mr. Cupples was such an odd blend of scholar and vagrant that Bruce was slow with an answer.

"Are you deaf, man?" said Mr. Cupples, "or are you afraid to take a chance by giving a fair answer to a fair question?"

The arrow went too near the mark not to irritate Bruce.

"Go your way," he said. "We want no tramps in this town."

"Well, I am a tramp, no doubt," returned Cupples, "for I have come every step of the way on my own two feet. But I have read of several tramps that were respectable enough. If you won't *give* me anything in this shop—even information—at least will you *sell* me an ounce of tobacco?"

"I'll sell it if you can pay for it."

"There you are," said Cupples, laying the orthodox pence on the counter. "And now will you tell me where I can get a respectable, decent place to lie down in? I'll want it for a week, at any rate."

Before he finished the question, the door behind the counter opened and young Bruce entered. Mr. Cupples knew him well enough by sight from the school.

"How are you?" he said. "I know you, though I don't know your name."

"My name's Robert Bruce, Mr. Cupples."

"A fine name—Robert Bruce," he replied.

The youth turned to his father.

"This gentleman is the librarian of our college, father."

Bruce took off his hat. "I beg your pardon," he said. "I'm terribly shortsighted in the candlelight."

"I'm used to being mistaken," answered Cupples, beginning to perceive that he had gotten hold of a character. "Make no apologies, but just answer my question."

"Well, to tell you the truth, seeing you're a gentleman, we have a room ourselves. But it's a garret room, and maybe—"

"Then I'll take it, whatever it be, if you don't want too much for it."

"Well, you see, sir, your college is a great expense to humble folk like ourselves, and we have to make it up the best we can."

"No doubt. How much do you want?"

"Would you think five shillings too much?"

"Indeed, I would."

"Well, we'll say three then—for *you,* sir."

"I won't give you more than half a crown."

"Hoot, sir. That's too little."

"Well, I'll look further," said Mr. Cupples, moving toward the door.

"No, no, sir. You'll do no such thing. Do you think I would let the librarian of my son's college go out my door at this time of night? Just have your price, and welcome. You'll have your tea and sugar and pieces of cheese from me, you know."

"Of course—of course. And if you could get me some tea at once, I should be obliged to you. I have been walking some distance."

"Mother," cried Bruce through the house door, and held a momentary whispering with the partner of his throne.

"So your name's Bruce, is it?" resumed Cupples, as the shopkeeper returned to the counter.

"Robert Bruce, at your service."

"It's a grand *name*," said Cupples.

"Indeed it is, and I have a right to bear it."

"You'll be a descendant, no doubt, of the Earl of Carrick?" said Cupples, guessing at his weakness.

"Of the king, sir. Folk may think little of me, but I come of him that freed Scotland. If it hadn't been for him at Bannockburn, where would Scotland be today?"

"Almost civilized under the fine influences and cultivation and manners of the English, no doubt."

Bruce hesitated. His blue blood boiled at this insult to his great progenitor. But a half-crown would cover a greater wrong than that.

Mr. Cupples murmured to himself as he followed him up the stairs:

"Shades of Wallace and Bruce forgive me, but to see small creatures cock their noses and tails as if they had inherited the mighty deeds as well as the names of their forbears just turns my blood into the gall of bitterness—and that's the scripture for it."

After private consultation, Mr. and Mrs. Bruce came to the conclusion that it might be politic, for Rob's sake, to treat the librarian with consideration. Consequently, Mrs. Bruce invited him, after he was settled in his room, to come down to his tea in *the room*.

Descending before it was quite ready, Mr. Cupples looked about him. The only thing that attracted his attention was a handsomely bound Bible. He took it up, thinking to get some amusement from the births of the illustrious Bruces. But the only inscription he could find beyond the name of *John Cowie* was the following in pencil:

"Super Davidis Psalmum tertium vicesimum, syngrapham pecuniariam centum solidos valentem, quae, me mortuo, a Annie Anderson, mihi dilecta, sit, posui."

Then came some figures, and then the date, with the initials *J.C.*

Hence it was that Mr. Cupples thought he had heard the name of Annie Anderson before.

"It's a grand Bible," he said as Mrs. Bruce entered.

"Ay, it is. It belonged to our parish minister."

Nothing more passed, for Mr. Cupples was hungry.

After a long sleep in the morning, Mr. Cupples called on Mrs. Forbes, and was rather kindly received. But it was a great disappointment to him to find that he could not see Alec.

As he was in the country, he resolved to make the best of it and enjoy himself for a week. Every day he climbed to the top of one of the hills which enclosed the valley and was rewarded with fresh vigour and renewed life. He, too, was a prodigal returned at least into the *vestibule* of his Father's house. And the Father sent the servants out to minister to him. And Nature, the housekeeper, put the robe of health upon him, and gave him new shoes of strength and a ring, though not yet the Father's white stone. The delights of those spring days were endless to him whose own nature was budding with new life. Familiar with all the cottage ways, he would drop into any *hoosie* he came near about dinnertime, and asking for a *piece* of oatcake and a mug of milk, would make his dinner from them and leave a trifle behind in acknowledgment. But as evening began to fall he was always near Howglen that he might ask about his friend.

Mrs. Forbes gradually began to understand him better. Before the week was over, there was not a man or woman about Howglen whom he did not know, even by name. To his surprise, even his forgetfulness was fast vanishing.

On the next to last day of his intended stay, he went to the house and heard the happy news that Alec insisted on seeing him. Mrs. Forbes had at last consented, and the result was that Cupples sat up with him that night, and Mrs. Forbes and Annie both slept. In the morning he found a bed ready for him, to which he reluctantly went and slept for a couple of hours. The end of it was that he did not go back to Mr. Bruce's except to pay his bill. And he did not leave Howglen for many weeks. He struck up a surprising friendship with Thomas Crann, beginning with their mutual love for Alec Forbes, but which in time resulted in Mr. Cupples attending an occasional service with him at the missionar kirk, and sharing more than an occasional meal of oatcakes, tea, and potatoes at Thomas's house. His weeks in Glamerton, however, only served to deepen his mistrust of Robert Bruce.

One lovely morning when the sun shone into the house and the deep blue sky rose above the earth, Alec opened his eyes and suddenly became aware that life was good and the world was beautiful. Cupples propped him up with pillows and opened the window that the warm air might flow in upon him. He smiled and lay with his eyes closed, looking so happy that Cupples thought he was praying. But he was only blessed. So easily can God make a man happy!

The past had dropped from him like a wild and weary dream. He was reborn into a new and beautiful world. One of God's lyric prophets was pouring out a vocal summer of jubilant melody. The lark thought nobody was listening, but God heard in heaven, and the young prodigal heard on the earth. He would be his child from this moment on, for one bunch of the sun's rays was enough to be happy upon!

His mother entered and saw the beauty on her son's worn countenance. She saw the noble, watching love on that of his friend. And her own face filled with light as she stood silently looking at the two. Annie entered and gazed for a moment, then fled to her own room and burst into tears.

She *had* seen the face of God, and that face was Love—love like the human, only deeper, tenderer, lovelier, stronger. She could not recall what she had seen or how she had known it, but the conviction remained that she had seen his face, and that it was infinitely beautiful.

"He has been with me all the time," she thought. "He gave me my father, and sent Brownie to take care of me, and Dooie, and Thomas Crann, and Mrs. Forbes, and Alec. And he sent the cat when I prayed to him about the rats. And he's been with me—I don't know how long, and he's with me now. And I have seen his face, and I'll see his face again. And I'll try hard to be good. Eh! It's just wonderful! And God's just...nothing but God himself!"

– Sixty-Eight –

A Student Again

Annie began to perceive that it was time for her to go, partly from the fact that she was no longer wanted so much, and partly from finding in herself certain conditions of feeling which she did not know what to do with.

"Annie's coming back to you in a day or two, Mr. Bruce," said Mrs. Forbes, having called to pay some of her interest and to prepare the way for her return. "She has been with me a long time, but you know she was ill, and besides I could not bear to part with her."

"Well, mem," answered Bruce, "we'll be very happy to take her home again, as soon as you have had all the use you want of her."

He had never assumed this tone before, either to Mrs. Forbes or with regard to Annie. But she took no notice of it.

Both Mr. and Mrs. Bruce received the girl so kindly that she did not know what to make of it. Mr. Bruce especially was all sugar and butter—rancid butter, to be sure. When she went up to her old rat-haunted room, her astonishment was doubled. The holes in floor and roof had been mended, the skylight was as clean as glass a hundred years old could be, a square of carpet lay in the middle of the floor, and checked curtains adorned the bed. She concluded that these luxuries had been procured for Mr. Cupples, but could not understand how they came to be left for her.

Nor did the consideration shown her decrease after the first novelty of her return had worn off and her former discomforts had ceased. The baby had become a sweet-tempered little girl, Johnnie was at school all day, and Robert was comparatively well-behaved, though still a sulky youth. He gave himself great airs to his former companions, but to Annie he was condescending. He was a good student, and had the use of *the room* for a study.

Robert Bruce the elder had disclosed his designs for Annie to his heir, and his son had naturally declined all efforts to help his father. But he began at length to observe that Annie had grown very pretty. Then, too, he thought it would be a nice thing to fall in love with her, since, from his parents' wishes to that end, she must have some money.

Annie, however, did not suspect anything till one day she chanced to hear the elder say to the younger,

"Don't push her. Just go into the shop and get a piece of red candy-sugar and give her that next time you see her alone. The likes of her knows what that means. And if she takes it from you, you may have the run of the shop drawer. It's worthwhile, you know. Those that won't sow, won't reap."

From that moment she was on her guard.

Meantime, Alec got better and better, went out with Mr. Cupples in the gig, ate like an ogre, drank water and tea like a hippopotamus, and was rapidly recovering his former strength.

One evening over their supper Alec was for the twentieth time opposing Mr. Cupples's departure. At length the latter said:

"Alec, I'll stay with you till the next session on one condition."

"What is that, Mr. Cupples?" said Mrs. Forbes. "I shall be delighted to know it."

"You see, mem, this young rascal here made a fool of himself at the last session and didn't pass, and—"

"Let bygones be bygones, if you please, Mr. Cupples," said Mrs. Forbes pleasantly.

"Indeed no, mem. What's the use of bygones but to learn from them how to meet the bycomes? Just hear me out."

"Fire away, Mr. Cupples," said Alec.

"I will. For them that didn't pass at the end of last session, there's another examination at the beginning of the next—if they want to take it. If they don't, they have to go through the same classes over again, and take the examination at the end again—that is, if they want their degree. And that's a terrible loss of time. Now, if Alec'll set to work like a man, I'll help him all I can. By the time the session's ready to begin, he'll be up with the rest of the fleet. And I'll sit with him and blow into his sails!"

That very day Alec resumed, with Mr. Cupples again as his mentor. But the teacher would not let the student work a moment after he began to show symptoms of fatigue. This limit was moved further and further every day till at length he could work four hours. His tutor would not hear of any further extension, and declared that he would pass triumphantly.

The rest of each summer day they spent in wandering about or lying in the grass, for it was a hot and dry summer, and the grass was a very bed of heath. Then came all the pleasures of the harvest. And when the evenings grew cool, there were the books that Mr. Cupples foraged for in Glamerton—he seemed to find them by the scent.

Annie would perhaps have benefited more than either of the two men from those books, and Mr. Cupples missed her very much. He went often to see her, taking what books he could. With one or the other of these books, she would wander along the banks of the clear, brown Glamour, now reading a page or two, now seating herself on the grass beside the shadowy pools. Even her new love did not more than occasionally ruffle the flow of her inward river. She had long cherished a deeper love, which kept it very calm. Her stillness was always wandering into prayer. But never did she offer a petition that associated Alec's fate with her own, though sometimes she would find herself holding up her heart like an empty cup. She missed Tibbie Dyster dreadfully.

One day, thinking she heard Mr. Cupples walking up the stairs, she ran down with a smile on her face, which fell off it like a withered leaf when she saw that it was but Robert the student. Taking her smile as meant for himself, he approached her, demanding a kiss. An ordinary Scottish maiden of Annie's rank would have answered such a request from a man she did not like with a box on the ear, tolerably delivered. But Annie was too proud even to struggle, and submitted like a marble statue, except that she could not help wiping her lips afterward. The youth walked away more discomfited than if she had made angry protests and a successful resistance.

Annie sat down and cried. Her former condition in this house was enviable to this. That same evening, without saying a word to anyone, for there was a curious mixture of outward lawlessness with perfect inward obedience in the girl, she set out for Clippenstrae, on the opposite bank of the Wan Water.

It was a gorgeous evening. The sun was going down in purple and crimson, divided by faint bars of gold. A faint rosy mist hung its veil over the hills about the sunset. The air was soft and the light sobered with a sense of the coming twilight.

– Sixty-Nine –

Curly and Bruce

When Annie reached Clippenstrae, she found that she had been sent. Her aunt came from the inner room as she opened the door, and Annie knew at once by her face that Death was in the house. For its expression recalled the sad vision of her father's departure. Her great-uncle, the little gray-haired old cottar in the Highland bonnet, lay dying. He has had nothing to do with our story, except that once he made our Annie feel that she had a home. And to give that feeling to another is worth living for.

Auntie Meg's grief was plainly visible. She led the way into the death-room, and Annie followed. By the bedside sat an old woman with more wrinkles in her face than moons in her life. She was perfectly calm, and looked like one already half across the river, watching a friend as he passed her toward the opposite bank. The old man lay with his eyes closed. As soon as he knew that he was dying he had closed his eyes, that the dead orbs might not stare into the faces of the living. It had been a whim of his for years. He would leave the house decent when his lease was up. And the will kept pressing down the lids which it would soon have no power to lift.

"Ye're come in time," said auntie Meg, and whispered to the old woman—"my brither James's bairn."

"Ay, ye're come in time, lassie," said the great-aunt kindly, and said no more.

The dying man heard the words, opened his eyes, glanced once at Annie, and closed them again.

"Is that one of the angels come?" he asked, for his wits were gone a little way before.

"No, it's Annie Anderson, James Anderson's lass."

"I'm glad to see ye, dawtie," he said, still without opening his eyes. "I hae wanted to see more o' ye, for ye're jist such a bairn as I would hae liked to hae myself if it had pleased the Lord. Ye're a douce, God-fearing lassie, and he'll take care o' his own."

Here his mind began to wander again.

"Margaret," he said, "is my eyes closed, for I think I see angels?"

"Ay, they are."

"Weel, that's very weel. I'll hae a sleep noo."

He was silent for some time. Then he reverted to the fancy that Annie was the first of the angels come to carry away his soul, and murmured brokenly:

"Be careful hoo ye handle it, for it's weak and not too clean. I ken myself there's a spot ower the heart o' it which came of an ill word I gave a bairn for stealing from me once. But they did steal a lot that year. And there's another spot on the right hand which came o' a good bargain I made with old John Thompson ower a horse. And it would never come oot with all the soap and water. Hoots! I'm havering! It's on the hand o' my soul, where soap and water canna come. Lord, make it clean, and I'll give him it all back when I see him in thy kingdom. And I'll beg his pardon too. But I didna cheat him altogether. I only took more than I would hae given for the colt myself."

He went on thus, with wandering thoughts that in their wildest vagaries were yet tending homeward. When too soft to hear, they were yet busy with the wisest of mortal business—repentance. By degrees he fell into a slumber, and from that, about midnight, into a deeper sleep.

The next morning Annie went out. She could not feel oppressed or sorrowful at such a death, and she walked up the river to the churchyard where her father lay. The Wan Water was shallow and full of dancing talk about all the things that were deep secrets when its bosom was full. She went up a long way, and then crossing some fields, came to the churchyard. She did not know her father's grave, for no stone marked the spot where he sank in this broken earthly sea. There was no church. Even its memory had vanished. It seemed as if the churchyard had swallowed the church as the heavenly light shall one day swallow the sun and the moon, and the lake of divine fire shall swallow death and hell. She lingered a little and then set out on her slow return.

Sitting down to rest about halfway home, she sang a song which she had found in her father's old songbook. She had said it once to Alec and Curly, but they did not care much for it, and she had not thought of it again till now.

> "Ane by ane they gang awa'.
> The gatherer gathers great an' sma'.
> Ane by ane maks ane an' a'.
>
> "Aye whan ane is ta'en frae ane,
> Ane on earth is left alane,
> Twa in heaven are knit again.
>
> "Whan God's harvest is in or lang,
> Golden-heidit, ripe, an' thrang,
> Syne begins a better sang." *

She looked up and Curly was walking through the broad river to where she sat.

"I kent ye a mile off, Annie," he said.

"I'm glad to see you, Curly."

"I wonder if ye'll be as glad to see me the next time, Annie."

Then Annie perceived that Curly looked earnest and anxious.

"What do you say, Curly?"

"I hardly ken what I say, Annie. They say the truth always comes oot, but I wish it would wi'oot a body saying it."

"What can be the matter, Curly?" Annie was growing frightened. "It must be ill news or you wouldn't look like that."

"I dinna doobt it'll be worse news to them that it's news to."

"You speak in riddles, Curly."

He tried to laugh, but succeeded badly, and stood before her with downcast eyes. Annie waited in silence, and that brought it out at last.

---

* One by one they go away.
The gatherer gathers great and small.
One by one makes one and all.

Aye when one is taken from one,
One on earth is left alone,
Two in heaven are knit again.

When God's harvest is in before long,
Golden-headed, ripe, and full,
Then begins a better song.

"Annie, when we were at the school together, I would hae given ye anything. Noo I hae given ye all things, and my heart to boot in the bargain."

"Curly," said Annie, and said no more, for she felt as if her heart would break.

"I liked ye at the school, Annie. But noo there's nothing in the world but you."

Annie rose gently, came close to him, and laying a hand on his arm, said, "I'm sorry, Curly."

He half turned his back, was silent a moment, and then said in a trembling voice,

"Dinna distress yerself. We canna help it."

"But what'll you do, Curly?" asked Annie in a tone full of compassion, and with her hand still on his arm.

"God kens. I must jist wrestle through it. I'll go back to the pig-skin saddle I was working at," said Curly, with a smile at the bitterness of his fate.

"It's not that I don't like you, Curly. You know that. I would do anything for you that I could do. You have been a good friend to me."

And here Annie burst out crying.

"Dinna cry. The Lord preserve us! Dinna cry. I winna say another word aboot it. What's Curly that such a one as you should cry for *him*? Faith! It's almost as good as if ye loved me," said Curly in a voice ready to break with emotion.

"It's a sad thing that things won't go right!" said Annie at last, after many vain attempts to stop the fountain by drying the stream of her tears. "It's my fault, Curly," she added.

"Deil a bit of it!" cried Curly. "And I beg yer pardon for swearing. Yer fault! I was a fool. But maybe," he added, brightening a little, "I might hae a chance—someday, someday far away ye ken, Annie?"

"No, Curly. Don't think of it."

His face flushed red.

"That lick-the-dirt Bruce's no going to make ye marry his college brat?"

"Don't be worried that I'll marry anybody I don't like, Curly."

"Ye dinna like him, I hope to God!"

"I can't abide him."

"Weel, maybe—who kens. I dare not despair."

"Curly, Curly. I must be honest with you as you were with me. When once a body's seen one, he can't see another, you know. Who could have been at the school as I was so long, and then taken out of the water, you know, and then—?"

Annie stopped.

"If ye mean Alec Forbes—" said Curly, and stopped too. But presently went on again, "If I were to come atween Alec Forbes and you, hanging would be too good for me. But has Alec—?"

"No, not a word. But hold your tongue, Curly. Once is all with me. It's not many lasses would have told you such a thing. But I know it's right. You're the only one that has my secret. Keep it, Curly."

"Like Death himself," said Curly. "Ye *are* a braw lass."

"You mustn't think ill of me, Curly. I've told you the truth."

"Just let me kiss yer bonnie hand and I'll go content."

Wisely done or not, it was truth and tenderness that made her offer her lips instead. He turned in silence, comforted for the time, though the comfort would evaporate long before the trouble would sink.

"Curly!" cried Annie, and he came back.

"I think I see young Robert Bruce. He's come to Clippenstrae to ask after me. Don't let him come farther. He's an uncivil fellow."

"If he gets by me, he'll hae to hae feathers," said Curly and walked toward the village.

Annie followed slowly. When she saw the young men meet, she sat down.

Curly spoke first as he came up.

"A fine day, Robbie," he said.

Bruce made no reply, for relations had altered since school days. It was an unwise moment, however, to carry a high chin to Willie Macwha, who was out of temper with the whole world except Annie Anderson.

"I said it was a fine day," he repeated. "And it is the custom in this country to give an answer when ye're spoken to civily."

"I consider you uncivil."

"That's jist what the bonnie lassie sitting yonder said aboot you when she asked me not to let ye go a step nearer to her."

Curly found it at the moment particularly agreeable to quarrel. Moreover he had always disliked Bruce, and this feeling was now aggravated because Annie had complained about him.

"I have as much right to walk here as you or anyone else," said Bruce.

"And Annie Anderson has a right not to be disturbed when her uncle, honest man, is jist lying waiting for his coffin in the hoose yonder."

"I'm her cousin."

"It's a small comfort any o' yer breed ever brought her. Cousin or no, ye'll not go near her."

"I'll go where I please," said Bruce, moving to pass.

Curly moved in front of him.

"I'll see you damned!" said Bruce.

"Maybe ye may, being likely to arrive at the spot first."

Angered, Bruce moved forward again, and with an oath pushed against Curly to pass. But the sensation he instantly felt in his nose astonished him, and the blood beginning to flow cowed him at once. He put his handkerchief to his face, turned, and walked back to Glamerton. Curly followed him at a safe distance and then went to his own father's shop for a visit.

After a short greeting, very short on Curly's part, his father said, "Hoot, Willie! What's come o'er ye. Ye look as if some lass said *no* to ye."

"Some lasses' *no's* better than other lasses' *ay,* father."

"Indeed maybe, laddie," said George, adding to himself, "That must hae been Annie Anderson—it could be no other."

Had Annie been compelled to return to the garret over Robert Bruce's shop after this incident, she would not indeed have found the holes in the floor and the roof reopened, but she would have found that the carpet and the curtains were gone.

The report went through Glamerton before week's end that she and Willie Macwha were *courtin'.*

– Seventy –

Deception Revealed

The appetite for prophecy having assuaged with the passing of the flood the previous winter, the people of Glamerton had no capacity for excitement left. In consequence, the congregations began to diminish, especially those in the evening. Having ceased to feel anxiety about some impending vengeance, comparatively few chose to be chastised any longer about their sins. And others, seeing how in the flood the righteous were taken and the wicked left, felt something must be wrong with the whole affair and stayed at home. Not only had the novelty of Mr. Turnbull's style worn off, but he felt himself that he could not preach with the same fervour as before, the fact being that he had exhausted the electric region of the spiritual brain. He attempted to get up his former excitement by preaching as if he were still under its influences. But even his greatest admirers were compelled to acknowledge that Mr. Turnbull had lost much of his unction, and that except the Spirit were poured down upon them from on high, their prospects were very disheartening.

Pondering this decay of attendance, Thomas Crann concluded that there must be a contamination in the camp. If an infestation of defilement had somehow penetrated their ranks, it could be none other than the money-loving, mammon-worshiping Robert Bruce. But he did not see what could be done. Had he been guilty of any open fault, such as getting drunk, they could have gotten rid of him with comparative ease. For one solitary instance of drunkenness they had already excluded one of their best men. But who was so free from visible fault as Bruce? True, he was guilty of overreaching whenever he had the chance, and of cheating when there was no risk of being found out, but he had no open *faults.* Yet Thomas Crann knew his duty.

"James Johnstone," he said one day, "the kirk's making no progress. It's not as in the time of the apostles when the saved were added to daily."

"But that wasna *oor* kirk exactly, and it wasna Mr. Turnbull that was the head of it," returned the deacon.

"Tis all the same. The principle's the same. Tis the same gospel. Yet here's the congregation dwindling away. And I'm thinking there's an Achan in the camp—a son of Saul in the kingdom of David, a Judas among—"

"Hoots! Thomas Crann, ye're not talking aboot that poor, weak body, Rob Bruce, are ye?"

"He's not weak for the devil's work or for his own, which is one and the same. Oot he must go."

"Dinna jest, Thomas, aboot such a dangerous thing," said James, mildly happy for a lone opportunity of rebuking the granite-minded mason.

"I'm far from jesting. Ye dinna ken fervour from joking, James."

"He might take the law upon us for defaming his character, and that would be an awful thing."

"The Scripture's clear. I'm only bidin' my time till I see what's to be done."

"Ye needna burn the whole hoose to get rid of the rats. I dinna doubt ye'll get us into hot water. A body doesna need to take the skin off for the sake of cleanliness. Jist take care what ye're aboot, Thomas."

Having thus persisted in opposing Thomas to a degree he had never dared before, James took his departure, pursued by the words:

"Take care, James, that in saving the right hand, ye dinna send the whole body to hell."

"There's more virtues in the Bible than courage, Thomas," retorted James, holding the outer door open to throw the sentence in, and shutting it instantly to escape with the last word.

Abandoned to his own resources, Thomas meditated long and painfully. But all he could arrive at was the resolution to have a talk with his new friend Mr. Cupples. He might not be a Christian man, but he was honest and trustworthy, with a greater than average amount of what Thomas recognized as good sense. From his scholarship he might be able to give him some counsel. So he walked to Howglen the next day and found him with Alec in the harvest field. And Alec's reception of Thomas showed what a fine thing illness is for bringing people together.

Mr. Cupples walked aside with Thomas, and they seated themselves on two golden sheaves at the foot of a stook.

But the Cosmo Cupples who thus attracted the confidence of Thomas Crann was a very different man from the Cosmo Cupples whom first Alec Forbes went to the garret to see at his landlady's suggestion. All the flabbiness had passed from his face, and his eyes shone clearer than ever from a clear complexion. His dress was still careless, but no longer neglected, and his hand was as steady as a rifleman's.

Nor had he found it so hard to conquer his fearful habit as even he had expected. With every week passed in bitter abstinence, some new well would break from the rich soil of his intellect, and irrigate with its sweet waters the parched border land between his physical and psychical being. And when he had once again betaken himself to the forsaken pen, there was little reason to fear a relapse or doubt a final victory. A playful humanity radiated from him, the result of that powerfullest of all restoratives—*giving* of what one has to him who has not. St. Paul taught a thief to labour, that he might have to give. Love taught Mr. Cupples to deny himself that he might rescue his friend, and presently he had found his feet touching the rock. If he had not yet learned to look "straight up to heaven," his eyes wandered not unfrequently towards that spiritual horizon upon which things earthly and things heavenly meet and embrace.

To such a Cosmo Cupples, then, Thomas told the story of Annie Anderson's five-pound note. As he spoke, Cupples was tormented as with the flitting phantom of a half-forgotten dream. All at once, light flashed upon him.

"And so what am I to do?" asked Thomas as he finished his tale. "I can prove nothing. But I'm certain in my own mind, knowing the man's nature, that it was the note he took oot of the Bible."

"I'll put the proof of it into your hands, or I'm badly mistaken," said Cupples.

"You, Mr. Cupples?"

"Ay, me, Thomas Crann. But maybe you wouldn't take proof from such a sinner against such a saint."

"If ye can direct me to the purification of oor wee temple, I'll listen humbly. I only wish ye would repent and be one of us."

"I'll wait till you've gotten rid of Bruce, anyway. I care nothing for all your small separatist churches. You're all so divided from each other it's a wonder you don't pray for a darkening of the sun that you might do without the common daylight. But I do think it's a shame for such a sneak to be in the company of honest folk, as I take the most of you to be. So I'll do my best. You'll hear from me in a day or two."

Cupples had remembered the inscription on the fly-leaf of the big Bible, which, according to Thomas Crann, Mr. Cowie had given to Annie. He now went to James Dow, whose friendship he had also cultivated from being so long at Howglen.

"Did Annie ever tell you about a Bible Mr. Cowie gave her, James?"

"Ay, she did."

"Could you get hold of it?"

"Eh, I don't know. The creature has laid his own claws upon it. It's a sad pity that Annie's oot of the house or she could take it herself."

"Truly being her own, she might. But you're a kind of guardian to her, aren't you?"

"Ay. I hae made myself that in a way. But Bruce would be looked upon as the proper guardian."

"Do you have hold of the money?"

"I made him sign a lawyer's paper aboot it."

"Well, just go and demand the Bible, along with the rest of Annie's property. Thomas says she's had trouble about her chest, too, and can't get it from him. And if he makes any difficulty, just drop a hint of going to the lawyer about it. The likes of him's as afraid of a lawyer as a cat is of cold water. Get the Bible we must."

Dow was a peaceable man and did not much relish the commission. Cupples, thinking he too was a missionar, told him the story.

"Well," said Dow, "he can sit there in the congregation for all I care. Maybe they'll keep him from doing more mischief!"

"I thought you were one of them."

"No, no. But I'll hold my tongue. And I'll do what ye want."

So after his day's work, which was hard enough at this season of the year, James Dow put on his blue Sunday coat and set off to the town. He found Robert Bruce dickering with a country girl over some butter, for which he wanted to give her less than the market value. This roused his indignation and put him in a much fitter mood for an altercation.

"I won't give you more than fivepence. How are you today, Mr. Dow?—I tell you, it has the taste of turnips, or something worse."

"How can that be, Mr. Bruce, at this season of year, when there's plenty of grass for man and beast?" said the girl.

"It's not for me to say how it can be. That's not my business."

Bruce, whose very life lay in driving bargains, had a great dislike to any interruption of the process. So he turned to James Dow, hoping to get rid of him before concluding his bargain with the girl, whose butter he was determined to have even if he must pay her own price for it. But while doing business that his soul loved, he could not tolerate the presence of any third person.

"Now, Mr. Dow?" he said.

"My business'll keep," replied Dow.

"But you see we're busy tonight."

"Weel, I don't want to hurry ye. But I wonder why ye would buy bad butter to please anybody, even a bonnie lass like that."

"Some folk like the taste of turnips, though I don't like it myself," answered Bruce. "But the fact is that turnips are not a favourite in the marketplace with most folk, and that brings down the price."

"Turnips is neither here nor there," said the girl and, picking up her basket, she turned to leave the shop.

"Wait a minute, my lass," cried Bruce. "The mistress would like to see you. Just go into the house to her with your basket and see what she thinks of the butter. I may be wrong, you know."

So saying he opened the inner door and ushered the young woman into the kitchen.

"Now, Mr. Dow?" he said once more. "Is it tobacco or snuff, or what?"

"It's Annie Anderson's chest and gear."

"I'm surprised at you, James Dow. There's the lassie's room up the stairs, fit for any princess whenever she wants to come back to it. But she always was a riotous lassie."

"Ye lie, Rob Bruce!" exclaimed Dow, surprised by his own proprieties. "Dinna say such a thing to me!"

Bruce was anything but a quarrelsome man with anyone other than his inferiors. He pocketed the lie calmly.

"Don't lose your temper, Mr. Dow. It's a bad fault."

"Jist deliver the bairn's effects, or I'll go to them that will."

"Who might that be, Mr. Dow?" asked Bruce, wishing first to know how far Dow was prepared to go.

"Ye have no right whatever to keep that lassie's clothes, as if she owed ye anything for rent."

"Have *you* any right to take them away? How do I know what will come of them?"

"Weel, I'll jist be off to Mr. Gibb and we'll see what can be done there. It's well kent all over Glamerton, Mr. Bruce, in what manner ye and yer whole house hae carried yerselves to that orphan lassie. And I'll go into every shop doon the street and jist tell them where I'm going, an' why."

The thing beyond all others which Bruce dreaded was unremunerative notoriety.

"Hoots! James Dow, you don't know joking from jesting. I never was a man to oppose anything unreasonable. I just didn't want it said about us that we drove the poor lassie out of the house and then flung her things after her."

"The one ye hae done, the other ye shall not do, for I'll take them. And I'll tell ye what folk'll say if ye dinna give up the things. They'll say that ye both drove her away and kept her duds. I'll see to that—*and more besides.*"

Bruce understood that he referred to Annie's money. His object in refusing to give up her box had been to retain as long as possible a chance of persuading her to return to his house. For should she leave it completely, her friends might demand the interest in money, which at present he was obligated to pay only in food and shelter, little of either of which she required at his hands. But here was a greater danger still.

"Mother," he cried, "put up Miss Anderson's clothes in her box to go with the carrier tomorrow morning."

"I'll take them wi' me now," said Dow resolutely.

"You can't. You have no cart."

"Ye get them ready and I'll fetch a wheelbarrow," said James, leaving the shop.

He borrowed a wheelbarrow from Thomas Crann and found the box ready for him when he returned. The moment he lifted it, he was certain from the weight of the poor little property that the Bible was not there.

"Ye havena put in Mr. Cowie's Bible."

"Mother! Did you put in the Bible?" cried Bruce, for the house door was open.

"Indeed no, Father. It's better where it is," said Mrs. Bruce from the kitchen in a shrill voice.

"You see, Mr. Dow, the Bible's lain so long there, that it's become like our own. And the lassie can't want it till she has a family to have worship with. And then she'll be welcome to take it."

"Ye go up the stairs for the book, or I'll go myself."

Bruce went and fetched it, with bad enough grace, and handed it over with the last tattered remnants of his respectability into the hands of James Dow.

Mr. Cupples made a translation of the inscription and took it to Thomas Crann.

"Do you remember what Bruce read that night as you saw him take something out of the book?" he asked as he entered.

"Ay. He began with the twenty-third psalm, and went on to the next."

"Well, read that. I found it on a blank leaf of the book."

Thomas read: "*Over the twenty-third psalm of David I have laid a five-pound note for my dear Annie Anderson, after my death.*" Then lifting his eyes, he stared at Mr. Cupples, his face slowly brightening with satisfaction. Then a cloud came over his brow—for was he not rejoicing in iniquity? At least he was rejoicing in coming shame.

"How could it be that Bruce didn't see this as well as yerself, Mr. Cupples?"

"Because it was written in Latin. Since it said nothing *to* him, he never thought it could say anything *about* him."

"It's a fine thing to be a scholar, Mr. Cupples."

"Ay, sometimes. But there's one thing more I would ask you. Can you tell me the day of the month that you went home with your praying friend?"

"It was the night of a special prayer meeting for the state of Glamerton. I can find oot the date from the church books. What am I to do with it when I hae it?"

"Go to the bank the man deals with, and ask whether a note bearing the number of those figures was paid into it on the Monday following that Sunday, and who paid it. That'll tell you everything."

For various reasons Thomas was compelled to postpone the carrying out of his project. And Robert went on buying and selling and getting gain, all unaware of the pit he had dug for himself.

– Seventy-One –

The Unmasking

The autumn months wore on. Alec's studies progressed and he grew confident. In October he and Mr. Cupples returned to their old quarters in the city. Alec passed his examinations triumphantly, and he continued his studies with greater vigour than before. He made his rounds in the hospital with much greater attention and interest.

Mr. Fraser declined seeing him. The old man was in a pitiable condition, and indeed never lectured again. Alec no more frequented his old dismal haunt by the seashore for feared the cry of a sea gull or the washing of the waves on the shore would be enough to bring back the memory of the girl in white vanishing before his eyes. But the further the pain receded into the background of his memory, the more heartily he worked.

Annie's great-aunt took to her bed directly after her husband's funeral. Finding there was much to do about the place, Annie felt no hesitation about remaining with auntie Meg. She worked harder than she had ever worked before, blistered her hands, and browned her face and neck. Later, she and her aunt together reaped the little field of oats, dug up the potatoes and covered them in a pit with a blanket of earth, looked after the one cow and calf, fed the pigs and the poultry, and went with a neighbour and his cart to dig their winter store of peats. This they found too hard for them, however, and their neighbours provided the remainder of their fuel, as they had done in part for old John Peterson.

Before the winter came there was little left to be done, and Annie saw by her aunt's looks that she wanted to be rid of her. Margaret Anderson had a chronic, consuming sense of poverty, and therefore worshipped with her whole soul the idol of saving and vigilance.

Hence, as soon as Alec was gone, with the simplicity belonging to her childlike nature, Annie bid Margaret good-bye at Clippenstrae and returned to Mrs. Forbes. The repose of the winter was a contrast with the events of Annie's fall. But the rainy, foggy, frosty, snowy months passed away much as they had done before, fostering even more the growth of Mrs. Forbes's love for her semi-protégé.

One event of considerable importance in its results to the people of Howglen took place this winter among the missionars of Glamerton.

So entire was Thomas Crann's notion of discipline that it could not be satisfied merely by ridding the congregation of Robert Bruce. A full disclosure to the entire membership was necessary. But afraid of opposition, either on the part of the minister or deacons or his friend James Johnstone, he communicated his design to no one ahead of time. He knew that the higher powers, anxious to avoid scandal wherever possible, would, instead of putting the hypocrite to shame as he deserved, merely send him a civil letter, requesting him to withdraw from their communion.

Watching for a fit opportunity, he resolved to make his accusation against Robert Bruce in person at an approaching church-meeting.

The night was brilliant with frosty stars, as Thomas walked to the rendezvous. He felt the vigour of the season in his yet unsubdued limbs, and thought how the world itself would pass away before the face of him that sat on the great white throne, and how the missionars of Glamerton would have nothing to say for themselves on that day, if they did not purify themselves on this. From the faint light of the stars he passed into the dull illumination of the tallow candles, and took his place in silence at the back of the building. The church slowly gathered, and at length Mr. Turnbull appeared, supported by his deacons.

After the usual preliminary devotions, in which Robert Bruce "engaged," the business of the meeting was solemnly conducted. At length as the minister was preparing to give out a final hymn, Thomas Crann's voice arose in the dusky space. Mr. Turnbull stopped to listen, and there fell an expectant silence, for the stone-mason was both reverenced and feared. It was too dark to see more than the dim bulk of his figure, but he spoke with slow emphasis, and every word was heard.

"Brethren and office bearers of the church, it's upon discipline that I want to speak. Discipline is one of the main objects for which a church is gathered by the Spirit of God. And we must work discipline among oorselves or else the rod of the Almighty'll come doon on oor backs. But I winna hold ye from the particulars any longer. On a certain Sabbath night last year, I went into Robert Bruce's house to hae worship wi' him. When he opened the Bible, I saw him slip something oot from atween the pages and crunkle it up in his hand. Then he read the twenty-third psalm. I couldna help watching and I saw him put whatever it was in his pocket. Afterward I found oot that the book belonged to Annie Anderson, and that old Mr. Cowie had given it to her upon his deathbed and told her that he'd put a five-pound note atween the pages for her to remember him by. What say ye to that, Robert Bruce?"

"It's a lie!" cried Robert, "gotten up between yourself and that ungrateful cousin of mine, James Anderson's lass, who I've cared for like one of my own."

Bruce had been sitting trembling. But when Thomas put the question to him, believing that he had heard all that Thomas had to say and that there was no proof against him, he resolved at once to meet the accusation with a stout denial.

Thomas resumed:

"Ye hear him deny it. Weel, I hae seen the Bible myself, and there's this inscription on one o' the blank pages: 'Over the twenty-third psalm of David, I hae laid a five-pound note for my dear Annie Anderson, after my death!' Then followed the nummer of the note, which I can show them that wants to see. Noo I hae the banker's word that on the very Monday morning after that Sunday, Bruce paid into his account a five-pound note o' that very same nummer. What say ye to that, Robert Bruce?"

A silence followed. Thomas broke it himself with the words:

"Do ye not call that a breach of the eighth commandment, Robert Bruce?"

But now Robert Bruce rose. He spoke with solemnity and pathos.

"It's a sad thing that among Christians, who call themselves a chosen priesthood and a peculiar people, a member of the church should meet with such an accusation as I have at the hands of Mr. Crann. To say nothing of his not being ashamed to confess being such a hypocrite in the sight of God as to look about him on his knees in prayer, lying in wait for a man to do him hurt when he pretended to be worshiping with him before the Lord his Maker. But the worst of it is that he beguiles a young thoughtless child, who has been the cause of much discomfort in our house, to join him in the plot. It's true enough that I took the bank note from the Bible, which was a very unsuitable place to put the unrighteous mammon, and it's true that I put it into the bank the next day—"

"What made ye deny it, then?" interrupted Thomas.

"Wait a minute, Mr. Crann, and be wary of what you say. You have been listened to without interruption, and I must have fair play here whatever I get from you. I don't deny the fact. Who could deny the fact? But I deny the light of wickedness and thieving that Mr. Crann casts upon it. *I* saw that inscription and read it with my own eyes the very day the lassie brought home the book and knew as well as Mr. Crann that the money was hers. But I said to myself, 'It'll turn the lassie's head, and she'll just fling it away in crumbs on sweets and such,' for she was greedy. 'So I'll just put it into the bank with my own and account for it afterward with the rest of her money.'"

He sat down, and Mr. Turnbull rose.

"My Christian brethren," he said, "it seems to me that this is not the proper place to discuss such a question. It seems to me ill-judged of Mr. Crann to make such an accusation in public against Mr. Bruce, who, I must say, has met it with a self-restraint most creditable to him, and has answered it in a very satisfactory manner. And now the hundreth psalm."

"Hooly and fairly, sir!" exclaimed Thomas, forgetting his manners in his eagerness. "I'm no finished yet. And where would be the place to discuss such a question but before a meeting of the church? Wasna the church instituted for the sake of discipline? Such things are no to be ironed oot in a corner between you and the deacons, sir. They belong to the whole body. We're all wronged together. We are but a candle under a bushel, and not a city set on a hill. The Lord's withdrawn his presence frae us, and the cause of his displeasure is the accursed thing which the Achan in oor camp has hidden in the County Bank."

"All this is nothing to the point, Mr. Crann," said Mr. Turnbull in displeasure.

"It's very to the point," returned Thomas, equally displeased. "If Robert Bruce saw the inscription the day the lassie brought home the book, will he tell me hoo it was that he came to leave the note in the book till that Sabbath night?"

"I looked for it, but I couldn't find it, and I thought she had taken it out on her way home."

"Couldna ye find the twenty-third psalm?—But jist one thing more, Mr. Turnbull, and then I'll hold my tongue," resumed Thomas. "James Johnstone, will ye run ower to my house and fetch the Bible.—Jist hae patience till he comes back, sir, and then we'll see hoo Mr. Bruce'll read the inscription. Mr. Bruce is a scholar, and he'll read the Latin to us."

By this time James Johnstone was across the street.

"There's some foul play in this!" cried Bruce. "My enemy has to send for an outlandish speech and a heathen tongue to ensnare one of the brethren!"

Profound silence followed as all sat expectantly. Every ear was listening for the footsteps of the returning weaver. But they had to wait a full five minutes before the messenger returned, bearing the large volume of the parish clergyman in both hands in front of him.

The book was laid out on the desk before Mr. Turnbull, and Thomas called out from the back region of the chapel,

"Now, Robert Bruce, go up and find this inscription that ye ken so weel aboot and read it to the church that they may see what a scholar they hae among them."

But there was no movement nor voice.

After a pause, Mr. Turnbull spoke.

"Mr. Bruce, we're waiting for you," he said. "Do not be afraid. You shall have justice."

A dead silence followed.

Presently some of those farthest back spoke in scarcely audible voices.

"He's no here, sir. We canna see him."

"Not here!" cried Thomas.

They searched the pew where he had been sitting, and the neighbouring pews, and the whole chapel, but he was nowhere to be found.

"That would have been him, when I heard the door bang," said one to another.

And so it was. Perceiving how he had committed himself and that things were going against him, he had slipped down in the pew, crawled on all fours to the door, and in the darkness of the candlelight meeting, had got out of the place unseen.

A formal sentence of expulsion was passed upon him by a show of hands. *Expelled* was written against his name on the list of the church members.

"Thomas Crann, will you engage in prayer?" said Mr. Turnbull.

"Not tonight," answered Thomas. "I've been doing necessary but foul work and I'm not in a right spirit to pray in public. I must get home to my own prayers. I must ask the Lord to keep me from doing something myself before long that'll make it necessary for ye to dismiss me next. But if that time should come, I beseech ye not to spare me."

So after a short prayer from Mr. Turnbull, the meeting separated in a state of considerable excitement. Thomas half expected to hear of action against him for libel, but Robert knew better than to venture such a thing. Besides, there were no monetary damages that could be got out of Thomas.

When Bruce was once outside the chapel, he again assumed erect posture and walked home by circuitous ways.

"Preserve us, Robert! what's come over you?" exclaimed his wife.

"I had such a headache, I was forced to come home early," he answered. "I don't think I'll go anymore. They don't conduct things altogether to my liking. I won't trouble myself with them."

His wife looked at him, perhaps with some vague suspicion of the truth, but she said nothing, and I do not believe the matter was ever alluded to between them.

Of the two, however, perhaps Thomas Crann was the more unhappy as he went home that night. He felt nothing of the elation which commonly springs from success in a cherished project. He had been the promoter in the downfall of another man. Although the fall was a just one, and it was better for the man to be down than standing on a false pedestal, Thomas could not help feeling the reaction of a fellow human's humiliation. Now that the thing was done, and the end gained, the eternal brotherhood asserted itself, and Thomas pitied Bruce and mourned over him.

Scarcely any of the members henceforth greeted Bruce in the street or traded with him, and the modifying effect upon the weekly return was very perceptible. This was the only form in which a recognizable vengeance could have reached him. To escape from it, he had serious thoughts of leaving the place and setting up his trade in some remote village.

– Seventy-Two –

Alec's Plans

Despite his diligence and the genial companionship of Mr. Cupples, Alec occasionally found himself asking, "What is the use of all this study and labour?" Whether this thought rose from the death of Kate, or his own illness, or the reaction of his shame after his sojourn with the dark places of life, I cannot tell. The moments of such vague uneasiness were infrequent, however, and usually were dispelled by a reviving interest in his studies or a merry talk with Mr. Cupples.

What made these questionings develop into a more definite self-condemnation began with a letter he had written to his mother for money to buy better instruments and new chemical apparatus. She had replied sadly that she was unable to send it. She hinted that his education had cost more than she had expected. She told him that she was in debt to Robert Bruce for a hundred pounds and had lately been compelled to delay the payment of its interest. She informed him also that, even under James Dow's conscientious management, there seemed little hope that the farm would ever make a profit to justify the large outlay his father had made upon it.

This letter stung Alec to the heart. That his mother should be in the power of such a man as Bruce was bad enough. But that she should be exposed, for the sake of his education, to ask Bruce to put off payment—that was unendurable.

He wrote a humble letter to his mother, and worked still harder. For although he could not make a shilling while he was still in school, the future contained a great deal of hope.

Meantime, Mr. Cupples got a new hat and coat. His shirt became clean and white and it was evident to all at the college that a great change had passed upon him. These signs of improvement led to inquiries on the part of the governing staff. As a result, before three months of the session were over, he was formally installed as the permanent librarian. His first impulse on receiving the good news was to rush down to Luckie Cumstie's and have a double tumbler. But conscience was too strong for Satan, and sent him home instead to his pipe—which, it must be confessed, he smoked twice as much as before his reformation.

From the moment of his appointment, he seemed to regard the library as his own private property, or, rather, as his own family. He was grandfather to the books—at least a grandfather shows that combination of parent and servant which comes nearest to the relation he henceforth manifested towards them. Most of them he gave out graciously, some of them grudgingly, a few of them with much reluctance, but all of them with injunctions to care, and special warnings against forcing the backs, crumpling or folding the leaves, and making thumb-marks.

"Now," he would say to some first year scholar, "take the book in your hand not as if it were a turnip, but as if it were the soul of a newborn child. Remember that it has to serve many a generation after your own bones are lying bare in the ground, and you must have respect to them that come after you. So I beg you not to mangle it."

The younger students used to laugh at him. But long before they had graduated, the best of them had a profound respect for the librarian. Not a few of them went to him with their difficulties with classes, and such a general favourite was he that any story of his humour or oddity was sure to be received with a roar of laughter. Indeed, I don't doubt that within the course of a curriculum, Mr. Cupples had become the real centre of intellectual and moral life in that college.

One evening, as he and Alec were sitting together speculating on the quickest way of Alec earning some money from his schooling, their landlady entered.

"My cousin's here," she said, "Captain McTavish of the ship the *Sea-horse,* Mr. Forbes, who says that before long he'll be wanting a young doctor to go and keep the scurvy from his men while they're whale fishing. I thought of you and came up the stairs to see you. It'll be fifty pounds in your pouch, and plenty of rough ploys that the likes of you young fellows like, though I can't say I would like such things myself."

"Tell Captain McTavish that I'll go," said Alec, who did not hesitate for a moment. He rose and followed her down the stairs.

He soon returned, his eyes flashing with delight. Adventure! And fifty pounds to send to his mother!

"The captain has promised to take me, Mr. Cupples, if my testimonials are satisfactory," he said. "I think they will be. If it weren't for you, I would be lying in the gutter by now instead of walking the quarterdeck."

"Well, bantam. There's two sides to most obligations—I'm librarian!"

Alec had always been fond of anything to do with the sea and boats. This love had resulted in his building of *The Bonnie Annie.* And now he was nearly beside himself with delight. His enthusiasm continued until he heard from his mother. She had too much sense to make any opposition, but she could hardly hide her anticipation of loss and loneliness. This quelled Alec's exuberance, but could not alter his resolve. He would return in the fall of the year, bringing with him what would ease her mind of half its load.

He passed all his examinations at the end of the session.

With Alec due home for a time before his departure, Mrs. Forbes now became greatly perplexed about Annie. She could not bear the thought of turning her out this spring. She did not see where she could go, for she could not be in the same house with young Bruce.

On the other hand, she had still the same dangerous sense of worldly duty as to the prevention of a so-called unsuitable match between her son and an orphan maiden who, despite her charm and character, was of a different class altogether, the chance of which was more threatening than ever. Annie had grown very lovely, and having taken captive the affections of the mother, must put the heart of the son in dire jeopardy.

But Alec arrived two days before he was expected, and delivered his mother from her perplexity by declaring that if Annie were sent away he too would leave the house. He had seen through the maternal precautions the last time he was at home, and talking with Cupples about it, who secretly wished for no better luck than that Alec should fall in love with Annie, had his feelings strengthened as to the unkindness, if not injustice, of throwing her periodically into such a dungeon as the society of the Bruces. So Annie remained where she was, much, I must confess, to her inward content.

The youth and the maiden met every day—the youth unembarrassed, and the maiden reserved and shy, even to the satisfaction of the mother. But if Alec could have seen the loving thoughts which, like threads of heavenly gold (for all the gold of heaven is invisible), wrought themselves into the garments she made for him, I do not think he could have helped falling in love with her. But he did not see them, or hear the divine measures to which her needle flew, as she laboured to arm him against the cold of the regions to which he would be leaving.

Alec's college life had interposed a gulf between him and his previous history. As his approaching departure into places unknown and a life untried worked on his mind and spiritual condition, he felt an impulse to strengthen all the old bonds which had been stretched thin by time and absence. He must make righteous atonement for the wrong of neglect. In short, he must set his inward house in order before he went forth to the abodes of ice. Death is not a breaker but a renewer of ties. And if in view of death we gird up the loins of our minds, and unite our hearts into a whole of love, and tenderness, and atonement, and forgiveness, then Death himself cannot be that thing of forlornness and loss.

He took a day to see Curly and spent a pleasant afternoon with him, recalling the old times and the old stories and the old companions. For the youth with a downy chin has a past as ancient as that of the man with the gray beard. Curly told him the story of his encounter with young Bruce and over and over again Annie's name came up, but Curly never hinted at her secret.

The next evening he went to see Thomas Crann. Thomas received him with a cordiality amounting even to a gruff form of tenderness.

"I'm right glad to see ye," he said, "and I take it kindly of ye wi' all yer learning to come and see an ignorant man like me. But, Alec, my man, there's some things I ken better than ye ken them yet. Him that made the whales is better worth seeking than the whales themselves. Come doon upon yer knees with me and I'll pray for ye."

Yielding to the spiritual power of Thomas, whose gray-blue eyes were flashing with fervour, Alec kneeled down as he was desired, and Thomas said:

"O thou who madest the whales to play in the great waters, be round aboot this youth, and when thou seest his ship go sailing into the far north, put doon thy finger, O Lord, and strike a track afore it through the hills of ice, that it may go through in safety, even as thy chosen people went through the Red Sea. For, Lord, we want him hame again in thy good time. For he is the only son o' his mother, and she is a widow. But above all, O Lord, elect him to thy grace and lat him ken the glory o' God, even the licht o' thy coontenance. Spare him, O Lord, and give him time for repentance, if he has a chance. But if he has none, take him at once that his doom may be lighter."

Alec rose with a very serious face and went home with a mood more in tune with his mother's than the light-heartedness with which he generally tried to laugh away her apprehensions.

He even called on Robert Bruce, at his mother's request. It went terribly against his grain, but he was surprised to find him pleasant. Bruce's civility came from two sources—hope and fear. Alec was going away and might never return. That was the hope. For although Bruce had spread the report of Annie's engagement to Curly, he believed that Alec was the real obstacle to his plans. At the time he was afraid of him, believing in his cowardly mind that Alec would not stop short of brutal physical reprisals if he should offend him. Alec was now a great six-foot fellow, of whose prowess at college confused and exaggerated stories were floating about the town. Bruce was a man who could hatch and cherish plans, keeping one in reserve behind the other, and beholding their result from afar.

"Ay, ay! Mr. Forbes—so you're going away among the fish, are you? Have you any share of the take?"

"I don't think the doctor has any share," answered Alec.

"But I imagine you'll put your hand to it and help at the catching."

"Very likely."

"Well, if you come in for a barrel or two, you may count upon me to take it off your hands, at the ordinary price—to the wholesale merchant, you know—with maybe a small discount for ordering before the whale was taken."

The day drew near. He had bidden all his friends farewell. He must go just as the spring was coming. His mother would have gone to the city with him to see him on board, but he prevailed on her to say good-bye to him at home. She kept her tears till after he was gone.

Annie bade him farewell with a pale face and a smile that was sweet but not glad. She did not weep afterward. A gentle cold hand pressed her heart down, so that no blood reached her face and no water reached her eyes. She went about everything just as before, because it had to be done. But it seemed foolish to do anything. The spring might as well stay away for any good that it promised either of them.

As Mr. Cupples was taking his farewell on board, Alec said,

"You'll go and see my mother?"

"Ay, bantam, I'll do that. Now take care of yourself, and don't take any liberties with behemoth. Put a ring in its nose if you like, but keep away from its tail. He's not to be meddled with!"

So away went Alec northwards, over the blue-gray waters, surgeon of the strong ship *Sea-horse.*

– Seventy-Three –

What If...?

Two days after Alec's departure, Mr. Bruce called at Howglen to see Annie.

"How are you, Mistress Forbes? How are you, Miss Anderson? I was just coming over the river for a walk, and I thought I might as well bring the little bit of money that I owe you."

Annie's eyes opened wide. She did not know what he meant.

"It's been twelve months that you have had neither bite nor sup beneath my humble roof," he explained, "and as that was to make up for the interest, I must pay you the one seeing that you wouldn't accept the other. I have just brought you the ten pounds to put in your own pocket in the meantime."

Annie could hardly believe her ears. Could she be the rightful owner of such untold wealth? Without giving her time to say anything, Bruce went on, still holding in his hand the bunch of dirty one-pound notes.

"But I'm thinking the best way of disposing of it would be to let me put it with the rest of the principal. So I'll just take it to the bank as I go back. I cannot give you anything for it, for that would be going against the principle of compound interest, you know, but I can make it up to you in some other way, you know."

But Annie had been too much pleased at the prospect of possession to let the money go so easily.

"I have plenty of ways of spending it," she said, "without wasting it. So I'll just take it myself, and thank you, Mr. Bruce."

She rose and took the notes from Bruce's unwilling hand. He had been on the point of replacing them in his trowsers pocket when she rescued them. Discomfort was visible in his eyes and in the little tug of retraction with which he loosed his hold upon the notes. He went home mortified and poverty-stricken, but yet having gained a step toward a further end.

Annie begged Mrs. Forbes to take the money, but she would not—partly from the pride of beneficence, partly from fear of involving it in her own straits. So that Annie, having provided herself with a few necessaries, felt free to spend the rest as she would. How she longed for Tibbie Dyster! But not having her, she went to Thomas Crann who told her of a man dying of consumption, and a little money went far to make his last days comfortable.

This was the beginning of a new relation between Annie and the poor of Glamerton. And the soul of the maiden grew and blossomed into divine tenderness, for it was still more blessed to give than to receive. But she was only allowed to taste of this blessedness, for she had soon to learn that even giving itself must be given away cheerfully.

After three months Bruce called again with the quarter's interest. Before the next period he had an interview with James Dow, to whom he said that since he was now paying Annie's interest out in cash, he should not have to be exposed to the inconvenience of being called upon at any moment to pay back the principal, but should have the money secured to him for ten years. After consultation James Dow consented to a three-year loan, beyond which he would not yield. Papers to this effect were signed and one quarter's more interest was placed in Annie's willing hand.

In the middle of summer Mr. Cupples made his appearance and was warmly welcomed. He had at length completed the catalogue of the library, had got the books arranged to his satisfaction, and was brimful of enjoyment. He ran about the fields like a child, gathered bunches of white clover, made a great kite and bought an unmeasurable length of string, with which he flew it the first day the wind was worthy of the honour. He got out Alec's boat and capsized himself in the Glamour—fortunately, in shallow water, was run away with by one of the plough horses in the attempt to ride him to the water, and was laughed at and loved by everybody about Howglen. But in a fortnight he began to settle down into his more sobriety of demeanour.

Calling one day on Thomas Crann, he found him in one of his gloomy moods.

"How are you, old friend?" said Cupples.

"Auld as ye say, and no muckle further on than when I began. I sometimes think I have profited less than anybody I ken. But I would be sorry, if I was you, to die afore I had gotten a glimpse o' the face of God."

"How do you know I haven't gotten a glimpse of it?"

"Ye would be more solemn."

"Maybe so," responded Cupples seriously.

"Man, strive to get it. Give him no rest day or night till ye get it. Knock till it be opened to ye."

"Well, Thomas, you don't seem so happy yourself. Don't you think you're like one that's trying to see through a crack in the door instead of having patience till it's opened?"

But the suggestion was quite lost upon Thomas, who after a gloomy pause, went on,

"Sin's such an awful thing," he began, when the door was opened and in walked James Dow.

His entrance did not interrupt Thomas, however.

"Sin's such an awful thing! And I have sinned so often and so long that maybe he'll be forced to send me to the bottomless pit."

"Hoot, Thomas! dinna speak aboot such awful things," said Dow. "I'll warrant he's at least as kind-hearted as yersel'."

James had no reputation for piety, though much for truthfulness and honesty. Nor had he any idea how much lay in the words he had hastily uttered.

"I said he might be *forced* to send me after all."

"What, Thomas!" cried Cupples. "He *couldn't* save you? With the Son and the Spirit to help him? And your willing heart besides? Fegs! You have a greater opinion of Satan than I would had thought."

"It's not Satan. It's myself. I wadna lay more blame upon Satan's shouthers than his own. He has enough already, poor fellow!"

"So you'll be of old Robbie Burns's opinion," said Cupples, "that perhaps he might still have a chance."

"No, no, he has none. Burns was no prophet."

"But just suppose, Thomas—if the devil were to repent."

“Man!” exclaimed the stonemason, rising to his full height with slow labour after the day’s toil, “it would be cruel to make him repent. It would be too painful for him. Better to kill him. The bitterness o’ such repentance would be too terrible. It would be more than he could abide. It would break his heart altogether.—No, no, he has nae chance.”

The last sentence was spoken quickly and with attempted carelessness as he resumed his seat.

“How do you know that?” asked Cupples.

“There’s no such word in the Scripture.”

“Do you think he must tell *us* all things?”

“We hae no richt to think anything that he doesna tell us.”

“I’m not so sure of that, Thomas. Maybe sometimes he doesn’t tell us a thing just to make us think about it, and be ready for the time when he will tell us.”

Thomas was silent for a few moments. Then with a smile—rather a grim one—he said,

“Here’s a curious thing, now.—There’s neither of you convertit, and yet yer words strenthen my hert as if they cam frae the region above.”

But his countenance changed, and he added hastily,

“It’s a mark o’ indwelling sin. To the law and to the testimony.—Go away and leave me to my prayers.”

The two men obeyed. Mr. Cupples could wait. Thomas could not.

– Seventy-Four –

The Bruce

Mr. Cupples returned to work.

The weeks and months passed and the time drew nigh when the two women began watching the mail coach for the welcome letter announcing Alec's return.

At length one morning Mrs. Forbes said:

"We may look for him any day now, Annie."

She did not know with what a tender echo her words went roaming about in Annie's bosom, awaking a thousand thought-birds in the twilight land of memory, which had tucked their heads under their wings to sleep, and thereby to live.

But the days went on and Alec did not come. While they imagined the *Sea-horse* full-sailed, stretching herself homeward toward the hospitable shore, she in fact lay a frozen mass, trapped immobile in a glacier of ice. The *Sea-horse* would not return this year and the winds and snows would go whistling and raving through it in the wild waste of the north all winter long.

What had been a longing hope under the roof of Howglen began to make the heart sick. Dim anxiety passed into vague fear and finally deepened into the dull conviction that the *Sea-horse* was lost and Alec would never return. Each would find the other wistfully watching the windows. But finally the moment came when their eyes met and they burst into tears, each accepting the other's confession of hopeless grief as the seal of doom.

I will not follow them through the slow shadows of gathering fate. I will not describe the silence that closed in upon their days, nor the visions of horror that tormented them. I will not tell how they heard his voice calling to them for help from the midst of the winter storm, or how through the snowdrifts they saw him plodding wearily home. His mother forgot her debt and ceased to care what became of herself. Annie's anxiety settled into an earnest prayer that she might not rebel against the will of God.

But the anxiety of Thomas Crann was not limited to the earthly fate of the lad. It extended to his fate in the other world—all too probable, in Thomas's view, that endless fate of separation from his Maker. Terrible were his agonies in wrestling with God for the life of the lad, and terrible his fear lest his own faith should fail him if his prayers should not be heard. Alec Forbes was to Thomas Crann the representative of all the unsaved brothers and sisters of the human race, for whose sake he, like the Apostle Paul, would have gladly undergone what he dreaded for them. He went to see his mother and inquired, "How are ye, mem?" There he sat down, never opened his lips, except to offer a few commonplaces, rose and left her—a little comforted.

As she ministered to her friend, Annie's face shone—despite her full share in the sorrow—a light that came not from the sun or the stars, a suppressed, waiting light. And Mrs. Forbes felt the holy influences that proceeded both from her and from Thomas Crann.

How much easier it is to bear a trouble that comes on the heels of another than one which comes suddenly into the midst of merrymaking. Thus Mrs. Forbes scarcely felt it a trouble when she received a note from Robert Bruce informing her that, as he was on the point of leaving to another place which offered greater opportunities for the little money he possessed, he would be obliged to her to pay as soon as possible the hundred pounds she owed him, along with certain back interest specified. She wrote that it was impossible for her at present, and forgot the whole affair. Within three days she received a formal application for the debt from a new lawyer. To this she paid no attention, just wondering what would come next. After about three months a second application was made, according to a legal form. In the month of May a third arrived, with the hint from the lawyer that his client was now prepared to proceed to the extremity of foreclosure on her farm. She now felt for the first time that she must do something.

She sent for James Dow and handed him the letter.

James took it and read it slowly. Then he stared at his mistress. He read it over again. At length, with a bewildered look, he said,

"Give him the money. Ye must pay it, mem."

"But I can't."

"The Lord preserve us! What's to be done? I hae saved up aboot thirty pounds, but that wouldn't go far."

"No, no, James," returned his mistress. "I am not going to take your money to pay Mr. Bruce."

"He's an awful creature."

"Well, I must see what can be done. I'll go and consult Mr. Gibb."

James took his leave, dejected both for his mistress and himself. Going out he met Annie.

"Eh, Annie!" he said, "this is awful."

"What's the matter, Dooie?"

"That mean Bruce is threatening to turn out the mistress for a bit of money she owes him."

"He dare not!" exclaimed Annie.

"He'll dare anything but lose money. Eh, lassie, if only we hadna lent him yours!"

"I'll go to him directly. But don't tell the mistress. She wouldn't like it."

"I'll hold my tongue."

He turned and walked away, murmuring as he left, "Maybe she'll persuade the ill-faured tyke."

When Annie entered Bruce's shop, the big spider was unoccupied and ready to devour her. He therefore put on his most gracious reception.

"How are you, Miss Anderson! I'm glad to see you. Come into the house."

"No, thank you. I want to speak to you, Mr. Bruce. What's all this about Mrs. Forbes and you!"

"Great folk mustn't ride over the top of poor folk like me, Miss Anderson."

"She's a widow, Mr. Bruce"—Annie could not add, *and childless,*—"and lays no claim to be great folk. It's not a Christian way of treating her."

"Folk *must* have their own. It's mine and I must have it. There's nothing against that in the ten commandments. There's no gospel for not giving folk their own. I'm not a missionar now. I don't hold with such things. I can't turn my family into beggars just to hold up her big house. She must pay me or I'll take it."

"If you do, Mr. Bruce, you'll not have my money one minute after the time's up, and I'm sorry you have it till then."

"That's neither here nor there. You would be wanting it before that time anyhow."

Now actually Bruce had given up the notion of leaving Glamerton, for he had found that the patronage of the missionars in grocery was not essential to a certain measure of success. Neither did he have any intention of proceeding to a foreclosure auction of Mrs. Forbes's farm and possessions. He saw that would put him in a worse position with the public than any amount of quiet practice in lying and stealing. But there was every likelihood of Annie's being married someday. Then her money would be recalled, and he would be left without the capital necessary for carrying on his business upon the same enlarged scale—seeing that he now supplied many of the little country shops. It would be a grand move then, if by far-sighted generalship copying his great ancestor the king, he could get a permanent hold of some of Annie's property. Hence had come his descent upon Mrs. Forbes, and here came its success.

"You have as much of mine to yourself as will clear Mrs. Forbes," said Annie.

"Well, very well.—But you see that it's mine for two and a half more years anyway. That would only amount to losing her interest for two and a half years altogether. That won't do."

"What *will* do, then, Mr. Bruce?"

"I don't know. I want my own money."

"But you mustn't torment her, Mr. Bruce. You know that."

"Well, I'm open to anything reasonable. There's the interest for two and a half—call it three years—and what I could make on it—say eight percent—twenty-four pounds. Then there's her back interest, then there's the loss of the turnover, and then there's the loss of the money that you won't have to lend me. If you'll give me a quittance for a hundred and fifty pounds, I'll give her a receipt, though it'll be a sore loss to me."

"Anything you like," said Annie.

Bruce immediately brought out papers already drawn up by his lawyer, one of which he signed and she the other.

"You'll remember," he added, as she was leaving the shop, "that I have to pay you no interest now except on fifty pounds?"

He had paid her nothing for the last half year at least.

He would not have dared to fleece the girl thus had she had any legally constituted guardians, or had those who would gladly have interfered had the power to protect her. But he took care to word the quittance so that in the event of anything going wrong, he might yet claim his hundred pounds from Mrs. Forbes.

Annie begged Bruce not to tell Mrs. Forbes and he was ready enough to consent. He did more. He wrote to Mrs. Forbes to the effect that, upon reflection, he had resolved to drop further proceedings for the present. He said nothing about the cancellation of her note and all back interest. When she took him a half-year's interest not long thereafter, he took it in silence, justifying himself on the ground that the whole transaction was doubtful anyway, and he must therefore secure what he could.

– Seventy-Five –

The Sailor's Return

It was a dreary wintry summer for all at Howglen. Why should the ripe grain wave in the gold of the sunbeams when Alec lay frozen beneath fields of ice or sweeping about under them like broken seaweed in the waters so cold? Yet the work of the world must go on. The corn must be reaped. Things must be bought and sold. Even the mourners must eat and drink. The stains which the day had gathered must be washed from the brow of the morning, and the dust to which Alec had gone down must be swept from the chair in which he had sat.

So things did go on—of themselves, for no one cared much about them, although it was the finest harvest year that Howglen had ever borne. Annie grew paler but did not relax her efforts in the small community. She told the poor friends she had befriended that she had no money now, but most were nearly as glad to see her as before. One of them, who had never liked receiving alms from a girl in such a lowly position, loved her even better when she had nothing to give but herself.

She renewed her acquaintance with Peter Whaup, the blacksmith, through his wife who was ill. And in all eyes the maiden grew in favour. Her beauty, both inward and outward, was that of the twilight, of a morning cloudy with high clouds, or of a silvery sea. It was a spiritual beauty for the most part. And her sorrow gave a quiet grace to her demeanour, peacefully ripening it into what is loveliest in ladyhood. She always looked like one waiting—sometimes like one listening as she waited to "melodies unheard."

One night toward the end of October, James Dow was walking by the side of his cart along a lonely road across a vast moor of peat. He was headed to the nearest seaport for a load of coal. The moon was high and full. Approaching a solitary milestone in the midst of a desolate heathland, burial places of old forests, he drew near an odd-looking figure seated on it. He was about to ask him if he would like a lift when the figure rose and cried joyfully,

"Jamie Dow!"

Dow staggered back, for the voice was that of Alec Forbes. He gasped for breath. All he was capable of in the way of an utterance was to cry *whoa!* to his horse.

There stood Alec in rags, with a face thin but brown—healthy, bold, and firm. He looked ten years older standing there in the moonlight.

"The Lord preserve us!" cried Dow, and could say no more.

"He has preserved me, you see, Jamie. How's my mother?"

"She's brawly, just brawly, Mr. Alec. The Lord preserve us! She's been terrible upset aboot ye. Ye mustn't walk in on her in her bed. It would kill her."

"I have a little sense left, Jamie, but I'm awful tired. Can you turn your cart around and take me home? I'll be worth a load of coal to my mother anyway. And then you can break it to her."

Without another word, Dow turned his horse, helped Alec into the cart, covered him with his coat and some straw, and walked back along the road, half thinking himself in a dream. Alec fell fast asleep and did not wake up till the cart was standing still, about midnight, at his mother's door. He started up.

"Lie still, Mr. Alec," said Dow in a whisper. "The mistress'll be in her bed. If ye go in upon her, ye'll drive her daft."

Alec lay down again and Dow went to Mary's window on the other side to try to wake her. Just as he returned to the cart, they both heard Alec's mother's window open.

"Who's there?" she called.

"Nobody but me—James Dow," answered James. "I was halfway to Portlokie when I had a mishap on the road. Bettie put her foot on a sharp stone and fell doon and broke both her legs."

"How did she come home, man?"

"She had to come home, mem."

"On broken legs!"

“Hoot, mem—her knees. I dinna mean the bones, ye ken, mem, only the skin. But she wasna fit to go on. And so I brought her back.”

“What’s that in the cart? Is it anything dead?”

“No, mem, not a bit of it! It’s living enough. It’s a stranger lad that I gave a lift to on the road. He’s mighty tired.”

But Dow’s voice trembled, or something else revealed all to the mother’s heart. She gave a great cry. Alec sprang from the cart, rushed into the house, and was in his mother’s arms.

Annie was asleep in the next room, but she half awoke with a sense of his presence. She had heard his voice through the folds of sleep. And she thought she was lying on the rug in front of the dining room fire with Alec and his mother at the table, as on that night when he brought her in from the snow hut. As wakefulness gradually came upon her, she all at once knew that she was in her own bed and that Alec and his mother were talking in the next room.

She rose, but could hardly dress herself for trembling. When she was dressed she sat down on the edge of the bed to think.

The joy was almost torture, but it had a certain quality of the bitter in it. Ever since she had believed him dead, Alec had been so near to her. She had loved him as much as ever she would. But Life had come in suddenly, and divided those whom Death had joined. Now he was again a great way off, and she dared not speak to him whom she had cherished in her heart. Ever since her confession to Curly, she had been making fresh discoveries in her own heart. And now the tide of her love swelled so strong that she felt it would break out in an agony of joy and betray her if she just once looked into Alec’s face. Not only this. What she had done about his mother’s debt must come out sooner or later, and she could not bear the thought that he might feel under some obligation to her. These things and many more worked in the sensitive maiden, such that as soon as she heard Alec and his mother go into the dining room, she put on her bonnet and cloak, stole like a thief through the house to the back door, and let herself out into the night.

– Seventy-Six –

Away

She avoided the path and went through the hedge into a field of stubble at the back of the house, across which she made her way to the turnpike road and the new bridge over the Glamour. Often she turned back to look at the window of the room where he who was dead was alive and talking with his widowed mother. Only when trees finally rose up between her and the house did she begin to think of what she should do. She could think of nothing but to go to her aunt once more, and ask her to take her in for a few days. So she walked on through the sleeping town. Not a soul was awake and the stillness was awful. Away towards the west, the moon lay on the steep-sloping edge of a rugged cloud.

In the middle of the large square of the little gray town she stood and looked around her. All one side lay in shade, the greater part of the other three lay in moonlight. The old growth of centuries, gables and fronts—stepping out into the light, retreating into the shadow—outside stairs and dark gateways, stood up in the night warding a townful of sleepers. Not one would be awake now.

So she passed into the western road and through the trees to the bridge over the Wan Water. They stood so still in the moonlight! And the smell from the withering fields laid bare of the harvest and breathing out their damp odours, came to her mixed with the chill air from the dark hills around, already spiced with keen atoms of frost, soon to appear in spangly spikes. Beneath the bridge the river flowed maunderingly, blundering out unintelligible news of its parent bog and all the dreary places it had come through on its way to the strath of Glamerton, which nobody listened to but one glad-hearted, puzzle-brained girl, who stood looking down into it from the bridge when she ought to have been in bed and asleep.

She was not far from Clippenstrae, but she could not go there in the middle of the night, for her aunt would be frightened first, and angry next. So she wandered up the stream to the old church-forsaken churchyard, and sat on one of the tombstones. It became very cold as the morning drew on. The moon went down, the stars grew dim, the river ran with a livelier murmur, and through all the fine gradations of dawn she sat until the sun came forth rejoicing.

The long night was over. It had not been a weary one, for Annie had thoughts of her own to keep her company. Yet she was glad when the sun came. She rose and walked through the long shadows of the graves down to the river which shone in the morning light like a flowing crystal of delicate brown—and so to Clippenstrae, where she found her aunt still in her nightcap. She was standing at the door, however, shading her eyes with her hand, looking abroad as if for someone that might be crossing toward her from the east. She did not see Annie approaching from the north.

"What are you looking for, auntie?"

"Nothing. Not for you, anyway, lassie."

"Well, I'm come without being looked for. But you were looking for somebody, auntie."

"No, I was only just looking."

Even Annie did not then know that it was the soul's hunger, the vague sense of a need which nothing but the God of human faces can satisfy, that sent her money-loving, poverty-stricken, pining, grumbling old aunt out staring toward the east. It is this formless idea of something at hand that keeps men and women striving to tear from the bosom of the world the secret of their own hopes. How little they know that what they look for is in reality their God!

"What do ye want so early as this, Annie?"

"I want you to take me in for a while," answered Annie.

"For an hour or two? Oh, ay."

"For a week or two maybe?"

"Indeed no. I'll do nothing of the kind. Let them that made ye proud keep ye proud."

"I'm not so proud, auntie. What makes you say that?"

"So proud that ye wouldna take a good offer when it was in yer power. And then they turn ye oot when it suits them. I'm not going to take ye in. There's David Gordon wants a lass. Ye can jist go look for work like other folk."

"I'll go and see about it directly. How far is it, auntie?"

"Going and giving away yer money to beggars as if it were dust jist to be a grand lady! Ye're none so grand, I can tell ye. And then coming to poor folk like me to take ye in for a week or two!"

Auntie had been listening to evil tongues—so much easier to listen to than just tongues. With difficulty Annie kept back her tears. She made no defence, tried to eat the porridge her aunt set before her, and then departed. Before three hours were over she had been given the charge of the dairy and cooking at Willowcraig for the next six months of coming winter and spring. Protected from suspicion, her spirits rose all the cheerier for their temporary depression, and she soon was singing about the house.

As she did not appear at breakfast, and was absent from dinner as well, Mrs. Forbes set out with Alec to inquire after her. Not knowing where else to go first, they went to Robert Bruce. He showed more surprise than pleasure at seeing Alec, smiling with his own acridness as he said,

"I doubt you've brought home that barrel of oil you promised me, Mr. Alec? It would have cleared off a good sheave of your mother's debts."

Alec answered cheerily, although his face flushed.

"All in good time, I hope, Mr. Bruce. I'm obliged to you for your forbearance about the debt, though."

"It can't last forever, you know," rejoined Bruce, happy to be able to bite, although his poison bag was gone.

Alec made no reply.

"Have you seen Annie Anderson today, Mr. Bruce?" asked his mother.

"Indeed no, mem. She doesn't often trouble herself with our company. We're not grand enough for her."

"Hasn't she been here today?" repeated Mrs. Forbes, with discomposure in her look and tone.

"Have you lost her, mem?" rejoined Bruce. "That *is* a pity. She'll be away with that vagabond Willie Macwha, I don't doubt. He was in town last night. I saw him go by with Bobby Peterson."

They made him no reply, understanding well enough that though the one premise might be true, the conclusion must be as false as it was illogical and spiteful. They did not go to George Macwha's, but set out for Clippenstrae. When they reached the cottage, they found Meg's nose in full vigour.

"No. She's not here. Why should she be here? She has no claim on me, although it pleases ye to turn her oot—after bringing her up wi' notions that has jist ruined her wi' pride."

"Indeed, I didn't turn her out, Miss Anderson."

"Weel, ye should never hae taken her in."

There was something in her manner which made them certain she knew where Annie was, but she avoided every attempt to draw it out of her, and they departed foiled. Meg knew well enough that Annie's refuge could not long remain concealed, but she found it pleasant to annoy Mrs. Forbes.

And indeed it was not many days before Mrs. Forbes did learn where Annie was. But she was so taken up with her son that two weeks passed before that part of her nature which needed a daughter's love began again to assert itself.

Alec had to go away once more to the great city. He had certain remnants of study to gather up at the university before he could obtain his surgeon's license. The good harvest would put a little money in his mother's hands, and the sooner he was ready to practice medicine, the sooner he could relieve her of her debt.

The very day after he went, Mrs. Forbes drove to Willowcraig to see Annie. She found her clad like any other girl at the farmhouse. Annie was rather embarrassed at the sight of her friend. Mrs. Forbes could easily see, however, that there was no breach in the mutual affection of their friendship. It must be confessed, thinking of the final return of her son, that she was quite as well pleased to know that she was bound to remain where she was for some time to come.

However, she found that winter very dreary without Annie.

– Seventy-Seven –

A Meeting

Finding herself in good quarters, Annie re-engaged herself at the end of the half-year. She had spent the winter in housework, combined with the feeding of pigs and poultry and some milking of the cows. There was little hardship in her life. She had plenty of wholesome food to eat and she lay warm at night. The old farmer, who was rather overbearing with his men, was kind to her because he liked her, and when his wife scolded her she never meant anything by it.

She cherished her love for Alec, but was quite peaceful as to the future. When her work for the day was done she would go out on long, lonely walks in the countryside. And now the month of April was nearly over, and the primroses were glinting on the braes.

One evening she went out to a certain meadow which was haunted by wild flowers and singing birds. It had become one of her favourites. As she was climbing over a fence, a horseman came round the corner of the road. She saw at a glance that it was Alec, and stepped down.

Change had passed on them both since they had parted. He was a full-grown man with a settled look. She was a lovely woman, even more delicate and graceful than her childhood had promised.

As she got down from the fence, he got off his horse. Without a word on either side, their hands joined, and still they stood silent for a minute, Annie with her eyes on the ground, Alec gazing in her face, which was pale with more than its usual paleness.

"I saw Curly yesterday," said Alec at length, with what seemed to Annie a look of meaning.

Her face flushed as red as fire. Could Curly have betrayed her?

She managed to stammer out,

"Oh! Did you?"

And silence fell again.

"We never thought we would see you again, Alec," she said at length, taking up the conversation again.

"I thought so too," answered Alec, "when the great iceberg came down on us through the snowstorm and flung the ship onto the ice floe with her side crushed in.—How I used to dream about the old school days, Annie, and finding you in my hut!—And I did find you in the snow, Annie."

But a figure came round the corner—for the road made a double sweep at this point—and cried,

"Annie, come home directly. Ye're wanted."

"I will come to see you again soon, Annie," said Alec. "But I must go away for a month or two first."

Annie replied with a smile and an outstretched hand—nothing more. She could wait well enough.

How lovely the flowers in the dyke sides looked as she followed Mrs. Gordon home. But the thought that perhaps Curly had told him something was like a serpent under them. Yet somehow she had become so beautiful before she reached the house that her aunt, who was there to see her, called out,

"Losh, lassie! What hae ye been aboot? Yer face is full o' colour!"

"That's easily accounted for," said her mistress roguishly. "She was standing talking wi' a bonnie young lad on a horse. I winna hae such doings aboot my hoose, I can tell ye, lass."

Margaret Anderson flew into a passion and abused her with many words, which Annie, far from resenting, scarcely even heard. At length her aunt ceased and then departed almost without an adieu. But what did it matter?—What did any earthly thing matter if only Curly had not told him?

But all that Curly had told Alec was that Annie was not engaged to him.

So the days and nights passed, and Spring, the girl, changed into Summer, the woman, and still Alec did not come.

– Seventy-Eight –

Annie and Alec

One evening, when a wind that seemed to smell of the roses of the sunset was blowing from the west and filling her rosy heart with joy, Annie sat down to read in a rough little garden. It was of the true country order, containing the old-fashioned glories of sweet peas, larkspur, poppies, and peonies along with gooseberry and currant bushes, as well as potatoes and other vegetables. She sat with her back to a low stone wall, reading aloud the sonnet by Milton, *Lady that in the prime of earliest youth*. As she finished it, a low voice spoke, almost in her ear.

"That lady's you, Annie."

Alec was looking over the garden wall behind her.

"Eh, Alec!" she cried, startled and jumping to her feet, both shocked and delighted, "don't say that. But I wish I was a little like her."

"Well, Annie, I think you're just like her. But come out with me. I have a story to tell you. Give me your hand, and put your foot on the seat."

She was over the wall in a moment and before long they were seated under the trees of the meadow near where Annie had met him before. The brown twilight was coming on, and a warm sleepy hush pervaded earth and air, broken only by the stream below them, cantering away over its stones to join the Wan Water.

Time unmeasured by either passed without speech.

"They told me," said Alec at length, "that you and Curly had made it up."

“Alec!” exclaimed Annie, looking up in his face as if he had accused her of infidelity, but, instantly dropping her eyes, said no more.

“I would have found you before the day was over if it hadn’t been for that.”

Annie’s heart beat violently, but she said nothing. After a silence, Alec went on, “Did my mother ever tell you how the ship was lost?”

“No, Alec.”

“It was a terrible snowstorm with wind. We couldn’t see more than a few yards ahead. The sails were down but we couldn’t keep from drifting. All of a sudden a huge, ghastly thing came out of the evening to windward, bore down on us like a specter, and dashed us on a floating field of ice. The ship was thrown upon it with one side crushed in, but nobody was killed. It was an awful night, Annie, but I’m not going to tell you about it now. We made a rough sledge, and loaded it with provisions, and set out westward, and were carried westward at the same time on the ice floe till we came near land. Then we launched our boat and got to the shore of Greenland. There we set out traveling southwards. Many of our men died, do what I could to keep them alive. But I’ll tell you all about it another time if you like. What I want to tell you now is this. Every night, as sure as I lay down in the snow to sleep, I dreamed I was at home. All the old stories came back. I woke once, thinking I was carrying you through the water in the street by the school and that you were crying on my face. And when I woke up, my face was wet. I don’t doubt but that I’d been crying myself. All the old faces came around me every night, Thomas Crann and James Dow and my mother—sometimes one and sometimes another—but you were always there.

“One morning when I woke up, I was alone. I don’t rightly know how it happened. I think the men were nearly dazed with the terrible cold and the weariness of the travel, and I had slept too long and they forgot about me. And what do you think was the first thought in my head when I came to myself in the terrible white desolation of cold and ice and snow? I wanted to run straight to you and lay my head upon your shoulder. For I had been dreaming all night that I was lying in my bed at home, terribly ill, and you were going about the room like an angel, with the glimmer of white wings about you, which I reckon was the snow coming through my dream. And you would never come near me, and I couldn't speak to cry to you to come. At last, when my heart was ready to break because you wouldn't look at me, you turned with tears in your eyes, and came to the bedside and leaned over me, and—"

Here Alec's voice failed him.

"So you see it was no wonder that I wanted you when I found myself all alone in the dreadful place, the very beauty of which was deadly.

"Well, that wasn't all. I got more that day than I ever thought I'd get. Annie, I think what Thomas Crann used to say must be true. Annie, I think a person may someday get a kind of a sight of the face of God. I was so downcast when I saw myself left behind that I sat down on a rock and stared at nothing. It was awful. And it grew worse and worse till the only comfort I had was that I couldn't live long. And, with that, the thought of God came into my head, and it seemed as if I had a right to call upon him. I was so miserable.

"And there came over me a quietness, like a warm breath of spring air. I don't know what it was, but it set me upon my feet, and I started to follow the rest. Snow had fallen so I could hardly see their tracks. I never did catch up with them, and I haven't heard of them since.

"The silence at first had been fearful, but now, somehow or other—I can't explain it—the silence seemed to be God himself all about me.

"And I'll never forget him again, Annie.

"I came upon tracks, but not of our own men. They were the folk of the country. And they brought me where there was a schooner lying ready to go to Archangel. And here I am."

Was there ever a gladder heart than Annie's? She was weeping as if her life would flow away in tears. She had known that Alec would come back to God someday.

He ceased speaking, but she could not cease weeping. If she had tried to stop the tears, she would have been torn with sobs. They sat silent for a long time. At length Alec spoke again:

"Annie, I don't deserve it—but *will* you be my wife some day?"

And all the answer Annie made was to lay her head on his chest and weep on.

– Seventy-Nine –

Alec Forbes of Howglen

When Mrs. Forbes found that Alec and Annie were engaged, she discovered that she in reality had been wishing it for a long time, and that the opposing sense of duty had been worldly.

Within two years Annie and he were married and began a new chapter of their history.

Mr. Cupples came to see them every summer, and generally remained over the harvest. He never married. But he wrote a good book.

Thomas Crann and he had many long disputes, and did each other much good. Thomas grew gentler as he grew older. And he learned to hope more for other people. And then he hoped more for himself too.

The first time Curly saw Annie after the wedding, he was amazed at his own presumption in ever thinking of marrying such a lady. When about thirty, by which time he had a good business of his own, he married Isie Constable—still little, still old-fashioned, and still wise.

Margaret Anderson was taken good care of by Annie Forbes but kept herself clear of all obligation by never acknowledging any.

The farm of Howglen prospered. Alec never practiced in his profession, but he did become a first-rate farmer.

Robert Bruce had to refund Annie's money and content himself with what was owed him. He died worth a good deal of money notwithstanding, which must have been a great comfort to him at the last.

Young Robert is a clergyman, has married a rich wife, hopes to be Moderator of the Assembly someday, and never alludes to his royal ancestor.

Books and series by and inspired by GEORGE MACDONALD

This new series of MacDonald's stories culminates a forty-year attempt that began in the 1970s to acquaint new generations of readers with the works of the man C.S. Lewis called his spiritual "master." Throughout that time, it has been my prayerful life's work to make MacDonald's writings and ideas accessible and understandable to persons of all backgrounds with a complete range of literary interests. I have tried not only to expand availability of MacDonald's writings, I have attempted also to shed light on how those writings can most fruitfully be read, interpreted, and placed in the context of MacDonald's life. Listings of my own original writings, both fiction and non-fiction, are easily accessible from many sources in which, often indirectly, I try to point readers toward MacDonald. Most of the publications that bear specifically on MacDonald, as well as my new and edited editions of his books, are listed below.

M. P.

EDITIONS OF GEORGE MACDONALD'S BOOKS

Edited and published by Michael Phillips

The Bethany House Reprint Series
(18 Edited novels)—1982-1990

The Sunrise Centenary Editions of the Works of George MacDonald
(Original facsimile collector editions)—1988-1998

Edited compilations: *Discovering the Character of God, 1989*
Knowing the Heart of God, 1990
Wisdom to Live By, 1996

Young Reader Editions: *Alec Forbes and His Friend Annie, 1990*
Wee Sir Gibbie of the Highlands, 1990
At the Back of the North Wind, 1991
The Boyhood of Ranald Bannerman, 1991

Edited and annotated sermons: *Your Life in Christ,* 2005
The Truth in Jesus, 2006

The Cullen Collection of the Fiction of George MacDonald, 2018-19

BY MICHAEL PHILLIPS

George MacDonald Scotland's Beloved Storyteller, 1987
Universal Reconciliation, 1998
The Garden at the Edge of Beyond, 1998
The Commands of Jesus, 2012
Hell and Beyond, 2013
Bold Thinking Christianity, 2014
Heaven and Beyond, 2015
The Commands of the Apostles, 2015
George MacDonald and the Late Great Hell Debate, 2014
George MacDonald and the Atonement, 2014
George MacDonald's Spiritual Vision: An Introductory Overview, 2016
George MacDonald's Transformational Theology of the Christian Faith, 2017
George MacDonald A Writer's Life, 2018
George MacDonald, Cullen, and Malcolm, 2019

Available titles may be purchased at TheCullenCollection.com, from WisePathBooks.com, from FatherOfTheInklings.com, or from Amazon

Made in the USA
Monee, IL
09 December 2020

50102743R00238